AND THEN THE
END SHALL COME

BOOK THREE - THE COMING

AND THEN THE END SHALL COME

BOOK THREE

THE COMING

by Lorraine M. Cafasso

Christian Literature & Artwork
A BOLD TRUTH Publication

THE COMING

Copyright © 2020 by Lorraine M. Cafasso

ISBN 13: 978-1-949993-56-1

FIRST EDITION

BOLD TRUTH PUBLISHING
(Christian Literature & Artwork)
606 West 41st, Ste. 4
Sand Springs, Oklahoma 74063
www.BoldTruthPublishing.com
boldtruthbooks@yahoo.com

Available from Amazon.com and other retail outlets. Orders by U.S. trade bookstores and wholesalers. Quantity sales special discounts are available on quantity purchases by corporations, associations, and others. For details, contact the publisher at the address above.

Cover art & overall book design by Aaron Jones.

This book is a work of fiction. All characters in it are a work of the author's imagination.

Poem "The Sands of Time" by Marcella Burnes, used by permission.

Unless otherwise indicated, all Scriptures are taken from the KING JAMES VERSION (KJV) of the Holy Bible. Public domain.

Printed in the USA.
09 20   10 9 8 7 6 5 4 3 2 1

EPIGRAM

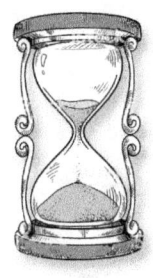

THE SANDS OF TIME

THROUGH THE SANDS OF TIME
I HEAR THE HOURGLASS CHIME.
EACH FALLING GRAIN
COMMANDS A SECOND OF LIFE'S TRAIN.

FALLING SOFTLY, GENTLY, THEN SWIRLING DOWN.
NO MORE TIME HUSHING, NOW POUNDING THE SOUND
A SECOND, A MOMENT, A TINY GRAIN OF SAND,
STACKED UPON HISTORY'S FALLEN MAN.

FROM DUST WE ARE BORN TO DUST WE RETURN,
YET TO OUR MAKER WE ALWAYS YEARN.
KNOWING IS CERTAIN,

A GLOWING OF DUST.
ETERNITIES' MYSTERY?
MAKE HEAVEN WE MUST!!!

Author: Marcella Burnes

TABLE OF CONTENTS

TABLE OF CONTENTS

TABLE OF CONTENTS

TABLE OF CONTENTS

TABLE OF CONTENTS

DEDICATION

Dedicating a book is no easy process. Even though I don't know how many people will read this dedication, it is still important to me. I am dedicating all my time and effort, all my blood, sweat and tears in writing this book, first to God, and then to Emily Radcliff.

Many will say, "Who is Emily Radcliff?" Let me tell you. Six years ago, at ten years of age, Emily moved with her mother and father, Peter and Evi, her older brother Daniel, and her younger sisters, Joy and Rebecca, from rural Claremore, Oklahoma, to rural Paraguay, South America.

Their family had been called to the mission field. The whole family was in agreement with the call and willingly left behind, houses, horses, dogs, cats and other animals. They left behind many of their belongings: clothes, toys, bikes, books, and all their friends. It was a difficult thing to do, but they were all in agreement.

There were many challenges and hardships to endure that first year. For a few months they had no home and lived in their vehicle. The heat was sweltering, even by Oklahoma standards, rising up to over 115 degrees. They all lived by faith, sometimes even for their next meal.

Being the oldest girl, Emily was a big help to Evi, who was expecting another child. She helped watch her younger sisters.

They finally found a more permanent home in the country

and began to settle in. Learning the native language of Guarani was the next big hurtle. Peter and Evi took a crash course for nine weeks, seven hours a day, but the children started to pick it up from friends they met.

As time went by they made contacts with rural Pastors and began to go out into the outlying areas, ministering to the indigenous tribes. As she grew, Emily began to take a more active part in the ministry. She began to work with the children. She brought light into their darkness. She, and her whole family had a genuine love for the people and it flowed out of them.

She was now fifteen, and a remarkable woman of God, going out and ministering at all the villages. God was using her mightily. She was running the race God had set before her. Tragically, on June 13, 2019, she was killed in a terrible car wreck while coming home from one of those villages.

Now as Christians, we know that at physical death, life is not over. God welcomed Emily for a race well run. She is now in Heaven, joining the great cloud of witnesses that are watching over the portals of Heaven and cheering us on.[1] So even after death, Emily is still fulfilling the ministry God had laid out for her. Though we miss her, we rejoice she is with her Father in Heaven.

Here on Earth, we "Raise a Hallelujah" for Emily. She is rejoicing in Heaven. We can rejoice, knowing that someday we will be there with her. We need to follow her example and run the race God has set before us.

There are no good answers as to why this happened. But we do know that God can bring good out of evil, and He did this with Emily's death. The hurt and sorrow are still there, but in its wake God has used this situation to bring salvation to many. This series was inspired by their efforts. If you would like to know more about this ministry you can contact www.uponthewaters.org.

---

[1] Hebrews 12:1

ACKNOWLEDGEMENTS

This is the third and last book of the series, And Then the End Shall Come. It has taken five years to get me here. I don't know any authors, so I have no one to compare with as far as the journey goes. Mine had highs and lows. Some of it was smooth sailing, and some of it felt as though I was stuck in a bog or sinking in quicksand.

I'd like to say that through it all I praised God continually, but I can't. I did more than my share of whining and complaining. I actually had the temerity to tell God He should find someone else to write these books, someone who had experience and knew what they were doing. Who am I that I should argue with God? I thank God for His grace. He kept the Holy Spirit after me and didn't rain down judgment upon me.

This undertaking stretched me beyond my ability, but that was the point. I was not doing it based on my ability, but on His. So my first acknowledgement has to go to the Holy Spirit, Who led me throughout the writing of this book. I sometimes strayed from the path, and He was patient, but relentless. He never let up. So now I have come to the point where I can say, "This is done. What's next?"

The next person I have to thank is Mike, my husband of fifty years. It was only forty-five years when this episode of my life started. He endured my moaning and groaning with patience and encouragement. He was with me on this whole journey. Sometimes there was smooth sailing and sometimes there were storms, but we made it to the other side.

My daughter, being an English teacher, was an additional resource. She helped me with the many grammar questions I had. She also helped me when I appeared to have writer's block. I was stuck in the mud. I knew where I wanted to go, but couldn't figure out how to get there. She suggested skipping that spot and picking up the story latter down the line, then coming back and filling in the pieces I missed. It worked.

Finally I thank my editors who have been with me for the whole ride: Cathy and Dick Ryan, Frank Rattacasa, Lore Swingle, and Elsie Hoffstatter. You helped me dot all my I's and cross all my T's.

ENDORSEMENTS

I grew up reading different tales about characters seeking swords, destroying rings and trying to save the world. I remember watching movies about lost treasure and sacred relics being stolen, then restored to their rightful place.

These stories are brought to mind when I read about the journey of Bekah and those God gathered together to seek the meaning behind the dreams they had been experiencing, and the family heirloom (a Conquistadorian gold and jeweled cross), that now had new meaning to those called on this Quest.

I read the first two books of the series with anticipation and was not disappointed. I am waiting with bated breath for the last book. The characters, their interactions and the unusual plot kept my interest. I would expect there to be a long line of people waiting to finish the series and experience the excitement of—The Coming.

Eileen Worthington
M.Ed., English teacher, 16 years

I have been a Pastor for 32 years and in knowing Lorraine Cafasso it has been a pleasure for almost forty years. Lorraine's devotion to God and His Word is sterling. She is a woman of Faith with strong Kingdom convictions based on her solid relationship with Jesus Christ.

I had the pleasure of sitting and speaking with her about her travels to Paraguay and her love for its people. She has vision and writes clearly in conveying her heart, and the heart of God for Paraguay. In addition, I've read her writings and I know her new book will inspire others to be Kingdom-minded and Kingdom Builders along with our Lord Jesus Christ.

Rev. Joseph Catanese
Retired

The urgency of the hour is evident, the sound unmistakable. It is "The Last Call". Lorraine builds upon the story of a nation, and people God is calling for His Kingdom purpose.

In a continuation of "The Call" and "The Quest", this book, "The Coming", brings an important message for today. What an amazing, God inspired trilogy this series has been.

Pastor David Knox
Grove Christian Center
Grove, Oklahoma

I have known Lorraine Cafasso through many seasons in her life. Then, at the direction of the Lord, she felt compelled to write this three volume work. This captivating, spiritual story is a platform to reveal and demonstrate spiritual reality of prayer, missions, and winning the lost.

I would encourage everyone to read these works, they are filled with very practical wisdom and powerful spiritual insight into both living in the earth and the spiritual warfare from the unseen realm that we all must come to grips with. Great job, Lorraine.

Rev. Ted Estes, D.Min.
Pastor, Lifechanger Church
Claremore, Oklahoma

CAST OF CHARACTERS
BOOK ONE - THE CALL

Akeem Farzhi – Friend from Iraq, lived with Josh's family thru college

Angie Pritchard – Bekah's lawyer Jim Pritchard's wife

Audrey Hathaway – Jim Hathaway's wife, frequented Bekah's needlework shop

Axel – Member of Manu's tribe, mentored by Daniel

Bekah Ryan – Main character – focal point of dreams

Carlos Rampone – Haydon Carlton's "handyman"

Chabuto – Manu's step-mother

Ciba – Leonardo's wife, seriously gored by wild boar

Constanzia – Edwardo's wife (a.k.a. Connie)

Daniel Albright – Joe's brother, Missionary in Northeast Paraguay

Edwardo – Young Pastor Daniel mentored in Paraguay

Emilio – Baby in basket sent downriver by mother to avoid being burnt sacrifice to evil god

Erecia – Young nursing mother who helps feed Juan

Ernesto – Wild boar hunter

Esteban Montero – Bounty hunter in Paraguay

Fuego Zangersen – Bekah's father's second wife – Bekah's

step-mother

Gabriella Zangersen – Bekah's father's first wife – Bekah's mother

Giancarlo – Member of Manu's tribe – Mentored by Daniel

Haydon Carlton – New York City jeweler

Isaac Klein – C.I.A. operative – friend of Josh's

Jean – Owner of Lobster Pot in Ogunquit, Maine

Jim Hathaway – Sergeant of Maine State Police

Jim Pritchard – Bekah's lawyer

Joe Albright – Roberta's husband – Daniel's older brother

Jose – Owner of Excelsior – arms store in Asuncion, Paraguay

Joshua Randall – Stranger from Claremore, Oklahoma and first to have dream

Juan – Manu and Noemi's newborn son

Juan – Injured wild boar hunter

Kay – Part of large prayer group in Maine

Lara – Connie's twenty-two year old sister

Leonardo – Ciba's husband – Manu's advisor

Luna – Bekah's half-sister, left behind by Fuego, so she could come to U.S. with Bekah's father

Maitie –Young man of tribe mentored by Daniel

Manu – Young Chief of the village

Mara – Riki's wife killed by wild boar

Maria – Edwardo and Connie's three year old daughter

Mario – Young man of tribe mentored by Daniel

Nana Sarah Zangersen – Bekah's late grandmother

Noemi – Manu's wife and baby Juan's mother

Paloma – Village girl sent by Manu to help Sherry with cooking, cleaning and gardening.

Paulo – Edwardo and Connie's six month old son

Penny – Sylvia's granddaughter – works at "Eye of the Needle"

Philippe – Young man Daniel mentored

Renato – Foreman of Bekah's apple orchard, close as a father, originally from Paraguay

Riki – Villager whose wife was killed by wild boar

Roberta Albright – Good friend and part-timer at Bekah's shop, Joe's wife

Sandy – Part of large prayer group in Maine

Sherry Albright – Daniel's wife, Missionary, and closest thing to a doctor for fifty miles

Shirley – Part of large prayer group in Maine

Suma – Village girl sent to help Noemi

Sylvia Jessup – Part-timer at Bekah's shop, close friend

Ted Ryan – Bekah's ex-husband

Young woman – Sent her baby down the river in a basket in response to dream from God

CAST OF CHARACTERS
BOOK TWO - THE QUEST

Alicia Hiccomb – John's wife who frequent Bekah's shop

Alma – Connie's prayer partner

Arandu – Leader of attacked village

Arasunu – Arandu's counselor

Brenda – New member of Maine prayer group

Enrico – Old man in Manu's village (a/k/a Eyo)

Hombrecito (Little Man) – Maria's puppy

Jeruti – Connie's prayer partner

John Hiccomb – Bank President of local bank in Ogunquit, Maine

Josef Muhammad – Leader of Black Death Camps in Paraguay

Kamal – Black Death member, troublemaker

Mehdi – Akeem Farzhi's friend and partner in C.I.A., with him undercover

Pearl – New member of Maine prayer group

Sol – Connie's prayer partner

Susan – New member of Maine prayer group

Tuvicha – Current old shaman of the village

Victoria – Connie's prayer partner

CAST OF CHARACTERS
BOOK THREE - THE COMING

Aravera – Leader of group of survivors from attacked village

Cipriano – Early convert, head warrior/hunter

Frank Minardi – Black Death prisoner from Hackensack New Jersey

Kauan – Renato's father, old Chiefs of conquering tribe's brother

Kauan – Son of old Chief, he and Renato are cousins, head of warriors of the village

Kent Knox – C.I.A. liaison in Washington D.C.

Luna – Bekah's stepsister, Fuego's daughter

Manolito – Haydon's man in Puerto Bahia Negra

Mbyja – Wife of Namandu, has stolen most of his power, feared by village

Miguel – Young hunter/tracker sent out to guide Renato and Ted to catch up with Questers

Namandu – Called himself the god of his village, witch doctor, perpetrator of the sacrifice of infants

Old Grandmother – Early convert, Miguel's grandmother, re-membered Renato coming to village

Osvaldo – Hunter/Tracker

Panambi (Butterfly) – 3 year old survivor from attacked village

Rob, Shane and Matt – Three of Isaac Klein's men from the

C.I.A.

Ysupi – Arandu's wife, found at burnt out village

Yvoty (flower) – Young child found with survivors at Arandu's village

SYNOPSIS
BOOK ONE - THE CALL

God calls two groups of people together as a result of a dream they all had of a remote jungle village under attack. The infant children of that village have been taken from their families and thrown into a roaring fire as a sacrifice to evil gods of the attacking tribe. Then those having the dream see Isaiah in the temple having a vision and God asking, "Who can I send?" Isaiah answers; "Send me."[2] They see that as a call to them. Through prayer they are finally guided to the country of Paraguay.

The first group is in Ogunquit, Maine and made up of:

Bekah Ryan. She owns a one hundred acre apple orchard outside of Ogunquit, Maine. She came into possession of a jewel encrusted golden crucifix that her grandmother held for her until her death. It was enclosed in a letter which revealed that her biological mother was the daughter of the Chief of the tribe where her father was a Missionary in Paraguay. Her mother had died in childbirth. Six months later her father married Fuego, the daughter of the Shaman of the village, and they moved with Bekah to the United States.

Renato is sixty-seven and was also born in Paraguay, but moved with his father to the U. S. when he was thirteen. They started working at the apple orchard. Renato was now the foreman. Bekah was a daughter of his heart, if not by blood.

Sylvia Jessup and Roberta Albright are employees of Bekah's at her needlework store, "The Eye of the Needle". Joe Albright is Ro-

---

[2] Isaiah 6:1-8

berta's husband. These three stay in Ogunquit to be a base of operations stateside. They also head up a growing prayer team.

Joshua Randall had the dream first and was directed by God to find Bekah. He is a Mission's Director at a church in Claremore, Oklahoma and part-time C.I.A. operative.

Ted Ryan is Bekah's ex-husband. He and Bekah divorced several years ago. One reason God called him was to fund the project.

The second group is in the remote jungles of northeast Paraguay.

Daniel Albright just happens to be the brother of Joe Albright and a Missionary these last four years to a remote village on a river bordering Brazil, known as the "village by the big rock".

Sherry Albright, his wife, is a nurse midwife, and the nearest thing to a doctor within twenty-five miles.

Edwardo is the young Pastor Daniel is working with at the village.

Connie is his wife. She heads up the prayer team in Paraguay, and coordinates with Sylvia and Roberta stateside.

A baby boy is saved from the sacrificial fires in a burning village and sent down river by his mother in a reed basket along with a gold and jewel encrusted crucifix, similar, but larger than the one Bekah has.

Bekah tries to get her crucifix examined and picks the wrong jeweler. Haydon Carlton is motivated by greed and immediately starts trying to obtain the crucifix using whatever means are necessary, legal or not. One of Haydon's employees, Carlos Rampone, ransacks Bekah's house looking for the crucifix, but comes up empty handed.

Prayers are prayed and decisions are made and Josh, Bekah, Renato and Ted head for Paraguay, but the shadow of Haydon Carlton follows them. He has employed Esteban Montero in Paraguay, to find them and get the crucifix, by whatever means are necessary.

During their plane ride to Puerto Bahia Negra, Josh talks to his friend from the C.I.A., Isaac Klein. Josh asks him to see if he can find out any information on Esteban Montero.

They touch down and meet Daniel and four young men of the village who are part of the small group of believers at the village. Several boats have been rented to bring back all the supplies the visitors brought with them to the village. They will spend one day in Puerto Bahia Negra and then head back to the village.

Through supernatural intervention lives are saved and more and more people turn to God. Satan is fighting with all his demonic hoards to stop this move of God; but, through prayer and faith, God's people overcome the wiles of the devil.

SYNOPSIS
BOOK TWO - THE QUEST

During the ride upriver Bekah is kidnapped and makes a miraculous escape. This is the first of many instances where God saves the day. When they reach the village they are greeted by the chief, Manu. He invites them to a celebration in their honor and questions Bekah about the crucifix and her parentage. It is revealed that Manu is not only Bekah's brother, but her twin. A strong bond forms between them and God uses Manu several times to save Bekah's life.

While at a celebration, the survivors of the attack by the evil tribe are watching from inside the jungle. They have traveled twenty-five miles through the jungle and come forward and ask to be allowed to join Manu's tribe. They offer their village treasures as an incentive to be accepted. These treasures are part of the Conquistadorian treasure captured by the natives in a rebellion over four hundred years ago. The treasure was divided up and each tribe received a share. That is where the golden crucifixes came from.

Manu offered the tribe sanctuary, Sherry saw to their injuries, and God began to heal their hearts.

Josh receives a call from Isaac telling him that there is a Black Death Camp five miles south of the village and the C.I.A. want him to investigate. They are a training camp for a radical Islamic group spreading terror all over the world. He refuses to place the village in danger, but says that he will keep his eyes open.

xvi

But God works it out. God calls an old friend from Josh's childhood, Akeem Farzhi, a C.I.A. operative working undercover in that camp. In a dream, God speaks to him and tells him to go check on the village, that evil is on the move.

Akeem sets out at night and when he gets to the village he hears his name mentioned. He comes into the room and is reunited with his old friend Josh. They are then alerted by God that Satan is on the prowl.

God has displayed Himself to the village in so many miraculous ways and the village begins turning to God in greater and greater numbers. The shaman, or witch doctor, Tuvicha, is jealous and joins with Chabuto, Manu's stepmother, another disgruntled person, to stop the move of God and call the people back to the dark gods of the past. Finally, the whole tribe is converted and Tuvicha and Chabuto, holdouts to the old gods, want revenge. They plan to take an orphaned baby and offer it in a burning sacrifice to their gods. Then they plan to go to the Black Death Camp and offer them treasure if they will attack the village.

A confrontation ensues and Chabuto is killed and the baby is saved. Through much love and prayer Tuvicha repents and he also becomes a Christian.

God had spoken to the group earlier, telling them to leave on the first night of the full moon. They were to travel at night and there would be twelve of them. They were to leave at moonrise, trusting the Holy Spirit would show them where they were to go.

A large blood moon rose as twelve followers of Jesus left the village to fulfill the Quest God had called them to.

PROLOGUE

The young boy followed his father through the dense jungle. Only the glimmer of a path in the early light of dawn was visible. The pack he was carrying on his back was heavy. After traveling for more than two hours, he was growing weary; and still, his father carried an even heavier one. The boy had two water skins hanging from his waist and a large machete tucked through his belt. It looked to be too much for him to handle, but he was strong for his size. His father was also small-framed, and his son showed no predisposition for height. The young boy was both afraid and confused; two emotions that always seemed to travel together.

Last night his father had returned with the witch doctor and his army. They were all in jubilant spirits after another victory over another enemy; everyone that is, except his father. He never appeared to take pleasure in their victory celebrations. He continued to remain subdued and withdrawn. One of his friends came over to talk to him, but he refused to listen and his friend walked away with angry words spoken.

The boy reflected upon how his father had changed in the last six months; ever since his mother had died in childbirth, and the child with her. Tears gathered in the young boy's eyes and threatened to overflow as he thought of her. He brushed them away angrily. Only babies cried, and he was on his way to becoming a man.

1

He still missed his mother. She had been a quiet woman who cared for her family. He was the only child, and his father had been so happy when she became pregnant again. His father did not know why there had not been any children after him and had counted this pregnancy as a miracle. He thanked all the gods, great and small, for their gift.

After her death the light had disappeared from his father's eyes. The boy had hoped that the latest victory would bring it back, but to no avail. His father had sent him to bed early last night. In the morning, he woke him hours before dawn with backpacks and water set out for them to travel. The boy did not know where they were going or why they were leaving. Right now he was full of questions, he was hungry, and his back hurt from carrying their supplies. He was very grateful when his father called a halt to their walk and indicated that they sit down on some large rocks on the side of the trail.

His father gave him some fruit and cold meat from last night's celebration. They ate quickly and quietly. His father then proceeded to tell him the reason for their stealthy departure. His father explained that because he was ten, he would have to begin to train to become a warrior and when he was thirteen he would begin accompanying the warriors on their battles against the neighboring villages. The father saw the light of excitement begin to grow in his son's eyes. He then began to tell his son the truth of the yearly raids against the surrounding villages. It was a well-kept secret that only the initiated warriors were told when they were heading out for their first attack on their enemies. He told of the secret rites of initiation not revealed or talked about except to those already initiated.

The father spoke first of the witch doctor who was both feared and revered by all. He told how the witch doctor went out on these forays of battle to increase his power, not only among the tribes, but in the spirit world as well. He saw the revulsion grow in his son's eyes as he began to tell of the infant sacrifice, of tearing the screaming babies from their mothers' arms and throwing them into

2

the burning inferno. He told how the warriors were promised blessings for each child they sacrificed.

The father said it had been noticed that he did not participate in the sacrifices. A curse was pronounced over him at that time. The father said he was convinced that is why his wife and newborn child died.

It was then he started to think about leaving the tribe. He was told that on their next expedition he must personally participate or he would be suitably punished, and that on the next attack, he would be taking his young son with him to be initiated in the rite of sacrifice.

There were tears in the father's eyes as he confessed that he was fifteen when he had gone on his first battle and been forced to sacrifice a baby. He told his son that he still lives with that guilt every day of his life. Through the years, he had successfully managed to evade the act of sacrifice, but just being there was causing him to despair of ever being free from guilt again.

He told his son that at night he called on the gods and asked their help. Surely there must be some gods who did not seek the death of innocent babies. He longed to escape with his son and be free of this horrible guilt. The father told his son that before the last excursion he had a dream. A new God spoke to him in that dream and told him to prepare to leave. That alone had given him hope. Tonight he was awakened again by another dream telling him to leave now with his son. In the dream he was told he would be shown the way.

The son looked up at his father with confusion in his eyes. It was almost too much for him to take in. "Where are we to go?" he asked. "How are we to get there?"

The father put his arm around his son. "I don't know," he replied. "I don't know who this new God is, but He seems very powerful. He will make a way."[3]

They continued on, walking in the direction of the river. They were people of the river, it was their lifeblood, their livelihood. Com-

---

[3] Isaiah 42:16

ing out of the jungle and into the light they saw a small dugout canoe one of the villagers had been working on. It must have broken free and floated downstream. He cut two branches into makeshift paddles. He and his son got into the canoe and began to travel downstream. The current was swift and they moved quickly, using the paddles to steer.

They traveled for many days and stopped periodically to hunt and fish. There did not appear to be anyone following them and they began to relax. They continued to thank this God for helping them and called upon Him every day for guidance. Finally, they noticed an increase in activity along the river, and observed several hunters walking on the riverbank. They knew a village must be only a short distance ahead. Storm clouds were forming overhead and thunder rumbled. As they rounded a bend with a big rock on the side of the river, they saw many canoes and small boats pulled onto shore. They turned their canoe toward the riverbank. Beaching their canoe, they noticed several men coming towards them. The boy and his father held up their hands and called out a greeting to them, and were relieved to hear words of welcome returned.

Walking forward, a large bolt of lightning streaked across the sky. It was accompanied by a deafening clap of thunder that reverberated through the trees, causing the trees to sway and the ground to shake. Another bolt followed that hit a large tree right in front of them. There was a loud bang and the tree burst into flames as it continued to sway back and forth. Suddenly it toppled to the ground trapping the young boy beneath it.

CHAPTER ONE

JUNE 23
THE VILLAGE

Renato's eyes snapped open, awakened by a loud crash of thunder. Looking out the window, he saw lightning streaking across the darkened sky. A deluge of rain began to fall outside, Renato had a flash of insight, as the dream returned to him in vivid detail. He realized that it was about him and his father. Up until this moment he had had very little recall of his life before he and his father arrived in Maine. Now, it was as though a door that had been closed to his past had been reopened and an avalanche of memories cascaded into his consciousness, flooding it with pictures of remembrances from long ago. These moments of recall were clear, and the feelings and emotions that were dredged up with them were tangible. They saturated his mind with startling information, and left him with many questions. First and foremost was why he hadn't remembered his past. Second, was why had these events been blocked from his memory. And third, why was he remembering them now?

Renato looked at his watch and realized he had only been asleep for three hours; it was 2:00 am. His thoughts immediately went to the people of the Quest he had said good-bye to only hours ago. They were on their way into the unknown, following a path God had laid out for them. He wondered if this dream had anything to do with the Quest God had called them to, and the impact it might

5

have on its outcome. It was too much of a coincidence for it to be otherwise. After years of following God, Renato did not believe in coincidences. He knew that God had a plan for his life and it was a good plan.[3] He believed that things happened for a purpose, and events took place, because God was still working out His plan of redemption.[4] But why had God chosen to reveal this to him now? With no answers forthcoming, Renato took the only other option available to him, he turned over and went back to sleep. The dark of night was not an ideal time to solve mysteries.

Hours later, when Renato awoke, he still had clear recall of his dream, and now he examined the options available to him. He decided to talk to Ted and Tuvicha and share the dream with them. He chose Ted because he wanted to keep Ted connected to the Quest. He wanted to keep him close and mentor him as a father in the faith is called to do. Ted was a very young Christian and needed continued teaching and encouragement. Involving him in this would be good for both of them.

In his later years, Renato had opportunities to be lonely. He chose to fight them. Recently, Ted had filled that void. Ted was the son he'd never had. Renato's wife had died in childbirth, forty years ago. At times, that loss still haunted him. While still in Ogunquit, Ted had admitted to being lonely. Maybe this would be a good relationship for both of them; only time would tell.

Tuvicha was a different case entirely. Up until two days ago, Tuvicha, the shaman/witch doctor, was on Satan's side, and doing everything he could to thwart the plans and purposes of God. He had fallen prey to the love of power and prestige. He had let his insecurities and jealousy open the doors to temptation, and Satan had lured him with promises of power and status. Tuvicha needed more care and attention than Ted because he had been entertaining Satan at a deeper level. He had used spells and potions to call him

---

[3] Jeremiah 29:11-13
[4] Romans 8:28

6

up, and Satan had responded to Tuvicha with his lies, deceptions, and empty promises. Tuvicha had allowed himself to be deceived. Satan was still troubling Tuvicha, trying to return with more demons than he had battled previously.[5] Renato vowed that he would not let this happen. He would take both of these men as his disciples.[6] Unlike most people, Renato realized that anyone not on God's side was on Satan's side. God calls us all to His side, He gives us all a choice—it is up to us to choose wisely.[7]

Renato decided to share this dream with Tuvicha to show him that God is involved in all the details of our lives, the past, the present and the future. We cannot change the past, but we can learn from it. The present is a constant struggle with our wants and desires. Sometimes we are willing and obedient and choose God. Other times we allow Satan to have his way in our lives. Renato was reminded of one of his favorite Scriptures: It tells us that if we sin, we have an advocate, Jesus, Who died to pay off the debt of our sins; and if we repent and ask forgiveness, He forgives our sins.[8]

Renato was sure that Tuvicha would need reinforcement in that truth[9] also. And he knew Ted needed it, because of how he had treated Bekah when they were married. He divorced her for lack of interest. His love for her had been replaced in his heart by a new love; his desire for wealth. He had been living the life of Ebenezer Scrooge. His love for money had pushed everything else, including Bekah, out of his heart.[10]

Renato had been there when Ted and Bekah married. He had known Bekah since she was a toddler. He loved her as a daughter, and she loved him with all her heart. When she was small, he held her on his knee, dried her tears when she cried, and

---

[5] Luke 11:26
[6] Matthew 28:19
[7] Deuteronomy 30:19
[8] 1 John 1:9
[9] Acts 14:22
[10] 1 Timothy 6:10

7

helped her up when she fell. If not daughter in fact, she was certainly a daughter in deed.

Renato saw that it was still early but knew that Sherry would be up starting breakfast. He had enjoyed their times of fellowship during breakfast and prayer afterwards. The group had left last night and he already missed Bekah, and all those who set out with her on the Quest. God had instructed them to travel by night and to leave when the moon was full. They set out to find the warring tribe that was taking the infants of conquered tribes and sacrificing them by fire to their evil gods.

Renato hurried because he knew Sherry would already be requiring the never-ending supply of water that had to be carried up from the river. He would get Ted to help him with the interminable task. Through the years Renato had learned that you were never too important to help with the chores. He decided he would wait to tell of his dream until most of the others were present.

Renato's thoughts wandered out over the village. He had made so many friends in such a short time since returning to Paraguay. He had grown a heart of love for the inhabitants of this village. It was as though he were one of them, and according to the dream, he had been, many years ago. It seemed almost miraculous that a language he had not used in over fifty years had come back to him with remarkable fluency. He was able to understand and communicate with everyone in *Guarani*, the language of the indigenous people of the land. He was also helpful in translating for anyone who needed that service.

Ted and Tuvicha were already in the kitchen. Ted was drinking his first cup of coffee, and Tuvicha his first cup of *terere rupa*, a traditional beverage that has been in Paraguayan culture for hundreds of years. Sherry was also drinking terere. After almost five years in Paraguay, she had developed a taste for it. She thought it was more nutritious for her than coffee, especially since she was now almost four months pregnant. She still indulged in coffee once

8

in a while, and was happy to make some for those who relished it.

Sherry was making some trays of chipa, the Paraguayan equivalent of a bagel. Paloma and Soma were also there to help with the cooking. Bekah's brother, Manu, had instructed Paloma to help Sherry with her cooking and the cleaning of her home and medical facility, because her position as 'doctor' required so much of her time. Sherry was not actually a doctor, but a nurse midwife. She was the only person for miles and miles with any kind of medical training.

Noemi had sent Soma over to help with the extra work. Noemi was the wife of Manu, the Chief. She had just been through a difficult pregnancy and miraculous birth. During delivery she had started to hemorrhage. Sherry did her very best with the limited supplies she had on hand, but she felt the presence of the spirit of death lingering nearby, waiting for his latest victim to give up the gift of life. Still, Sherry refused to give up, even when it appeared hopeless. Noemi's extremities had turned cold and were beginning to turn blue. Sherry had counted each breath with precision, expecting it to be her last, but God in His faithfulness breathed the Spirit of Life back into her. She first took one deep breath and then another. By that time the baby was crying vigorously, and Noemi had come back from the very brink of death to the land of the living. Sherry could not help thinking what a testimony that had been to those throughout the village.

This morning there was not just the usual amount of people to cook for. In addition, there were nineteen prisoners from the Black Death Camp. They were being held until someone could come to pick them up. This was going to require lots of additional work, not just for Sherry and her helpers, but for the men of the village guarding them, the men who went into the jungle or river to hunt and catch additional food, and the women had to venture into the jungle, deeper than usual, to harvest extra fruits and vegetables. It was impossible to stretch a pot of soup to feed nineteen additional mouths. They also needed to grind more corn and mandioca to make the

9

breads and chipa.

She hoped Jose was able to get in touch with Isaac Klein last night and make arrangements for these men to be picked up. Jose was the owner of Excalibur, a weapons store in Asuncion. He was also a C.I.A. contact and had arrived at the village yesterday afternoon with Akeem and Mehdi. Isaac Klein was a colleague of Josh's in the C.I.A. He had helped them on occasion during their Quest.

Akeem was a childhood friend of Josh's. His family had moved into Josh's neighborhood when Josh was in first grade. They were from Iraq. After several years their visa had expired, and Akeem's parents had to return to Iraq. Akeem was able to stay and attend school, and Josh's family took him in. Akeem had taught Josh *Arabic* and Josh had taught Akeem *English*. They both got saved during church camp in their senior year of high school, when they made a personal commitment to Christ. They attended college together and both received Master's Degrees from Oral Robert's University. After graduation, Akeem felt he needed to return to Iraq to be reunited with his family. Josh had never seen or heard from him again.

Unknown to Josh, Akeem had joined the C.I.A. after college before he returned to Iraq. There he had been working under deep cover, providing important intelligence to his contacts. Recently, he had joined a group of young rebels and had been out of touch for over a month while embedded in a Black Death training camp in the Paraguayan jungle. Mehdi, a friend from Iraq was also with him. He too was a C.I.A. operative.

As Sherry was mulling these things over in her mind, Jose walked in. He headed straight for the coffee pot and the pile of chipa on the platter. Renato and Ted verbalized what she had just been thinking. "Were you able to get in touch with Isaac Klein?" Ted asked. "Did you tell him that in addition to you, there are only two other people here with any experience shooting a gun? I'm not counting Sherry or myself. Her job here is medical. If she's not a

10

doctor in fact, she's certainly one in deed. I'm not counting myself since the only things I have ever shot at were clay pigeons."

Jose looked back at them with a huge Cheshire cat smile on his face. He laughed and said, "Isaac assured me that by no later than early tomorrow afternoon our troubles will be over. Isaac is coming down himself with seven other men. They're on a special non-commercial flight to Puerto Bahia Negra. He said to tell all of you there's no way to completely hide the cavalry when it comes to rescue you, but he will do his best to keep a low profile. They are going to impersonate several hunters going into the jungle for a shooting holiday. Maybe no one will notice. Hunters actually do come upriver on occasion. It was the best idea he could come up with on short notice. I just wonder how he is going to remove nineteen prisoners without anyone noticing. He also wants you to send four men out to watch the Black Death Camp and report any comings or goings, and to try to do this without being observed. We don't want any bloodshed or any more prisoners taken. Isaac had hoped to get here earlier, but traveling on the river at night would be foolish."

Sherry was concerned. "What kind of danger were these innocent tribesmen being subjected to?" she wondered. "I will have to talk to Leonardo. He's in charge with Manu gone." Sherry prayed all these problems would be resolved without any complications. She also wondered what Josh would think of Isaac coming down with help. She remembered this had been brought up before and Josh was adamantly against it.

Her mind started to wander to Daniel, her husband, and those traveling with him. She wondered where they were. They were probably setting up camp, eating, and then going to sleep. God had told them to sleep during the day and travel at night. He told them He would light their paths.[11]

She wondered if they would feel the necessity of posting

---
[11] Psalm 119:105

guards, or if they were confident there was no one in the area. She prayed for God to position angels around the camp to keep them safe and deflect the attacks of the enemy.[12]

At the sound of a crying baby, Sherry's thoughts returned to the kitchen, and looking up she saw Connie and Lara, her sister, carrying Juan and Emilio. Juan was Connie and Edwardo's son, and Emilio was the baby that was found floating down the river in a basket. They also discovered in the basket a large, gold, jewel encrusted crucifix, very similar to the one Bekah's Nana Sara had enclosed with her letter to Bekah. Nana Sara had instructed her lawyer that the letter be given to Bekah after her death.

It was later learned that Emilio had come from Tuvicha's village. During a raid by the warring tribe that had scourged that area of the jungle for decades, fourteen infants had been sacrificed by fire to their evil god. Sixty-two survivors of that village had walked approximately twenty-five miles through the jungle and entered Manu's village several days ago. They had all been adopted by the people of village.

Little Maria, Connie and Edwardo's daughter was skipping along with her puppy, Hombrecito, at her heels. Sherry looked again at Connie. It did Sherry's heart good to see Connie's smiling face. Her face shone with confidence. It was evident to all that her trust was totally in the Lord.[13] She looked as though God had assured her that all was well.

Ted got up and took little Paulo from Connie. He went over and sat by Lara, who was holding Emilio. Connie breathed a sigh of relief, babies can be heavy. Then she shared the reason for her smile. "I had a dream last night," she said. "I dreamt the group had traveled several miles in the dark, but God had shown them the way. I saw a light illuminating the darkness. God is surely with them and I am at peace." Everyone agreed that this was a good sign.

---

[12] Hebrews 1:14
[13] Proverbs 3:5-6

12

They hoped that God would continue to update them with additional dreams. While she was speaking Leonardo walked into the kitchen with six other men. He instructed them to carry food to the prisoners and bring them some terere to drink.

As Leonardo was grabbing some chipa and a drink, Renato stood up and began to speak. Everyone quieted down to hear what he had to say. Renato was not one to say much, so when he did speak, people paid attention. Renato started out, speaking in Guarani. Sherry, who was also fluent in Guarani, interpreted for Ted. "I also had a dream last night. I know it was a dream from God. It was rather amazing, and I don't quite know how it fits in with the Quest. I dreamed of a young boy traveling with his father. They were from the evil tribe who had been sacrificing the babies." Renato related the dream to everyone. Then he said, "At the end of the dream a deafening crash of thunder reverberated, causing even the ground to shake. It was followed by a tremendous flash of lightning. It hit an enormous tree and sent it crashing to the ground. It fell on the young boy.

"At the sound of thunder I was startled awake. I immediately knew that the young boy was me. My father had left our village to save me from having to become one of the warriors who was expected to sacrifice the babies to their gods. The dream showed us landing on the banks of a river by a large rock. It was this village we came to." Renato looked around and saw that everyone was riveted to the story.

He continued, "I now remember with clarity the subsequent events: our time living in this village, working in Asuncion, and then our move to America. I often wondered why I had no memory of my youth. While my father was alive I would question him, but he was always very secretive about our past. He would not answer and became angry when I continued to ask. Finally I just put my past behind me and was content to live the life God had brought to me. But now my life seems to have come full circle and I am waiting to see why God has brought me back to this village. What I don't understand, is why God showed this to me now, and what, if any impact it might have on the Quest. I know there must be a reason. I would like it if all of us could come together this morning to pray and see what God has to say about this." Renato sat down and waited for a response from the people.

Everyone turned and looked to Sherry. It appeared they all presumed her to be the spiritual leader of the group with Daniel, Edwardo and Josh having left the night before on the Quest. Suddenly Sherry felt overwhelmed by the challenge. Wasn't she already busy enough without taking on another burden?

Sherry heaved a sigh at what appeared to be an additional responsibility put on her, and one that would require extra time, thought and prayer. Her thoughts echoed her frustration. Didn't God see all she had to do already? Didn't He remember that she was also pregnant? Couldn't He find someone else to be the leader?

Suddenly God spoke to her in what seemed to be an audible Voice. It reverberated into her very being. "Do you question My choices? Did I not say I would not test you beyond your abilities? Haven't I always equipped those I call?[14] Where is your faith, daughter?[15] Have I not told you to trust in Me with all your heart and I will direct you in the path you should take?[16] Look around you at the people I have given you to help bear the burden. I have equipped them also. Just as Moses was encouraged to delegate his duties by his father-in-law Jethro, so I encourage you.[17] Do not be discouraged—put your faith in Me."[18]

Sherry looked up at all the people surrounding her and heard the truth in God's Word. She quickly repented of her lack of faith and her whining to God. It felt as though at least several min-

---

[14] Hebrews 13:20-22
[15] Matthew 6:30
[16] Proverbs 3:5-6
[17] Exodus 18:17-18
[18] Psalm 43:5

utes had passed while God had been speaking with her. Amazingly, the group was still waiting there for her answer. She smiled, took a deep breath, and began to delegate.

"Renato, why don't you contact everyone you feel needs to be at the prayer meeting. Set up a time before lunch. We need to know God's purpose in showing you these events. You're right; they might have an impact on the group that left last evening."

As orders were being given, Leonardo spoke up. "As you see, I have already had food sent down to the prisoners." He was happy to tell Sherry he had anticipated these issues and already had men working on filling the water barrels, and hunting parties assigned to go out morning and evening to bring in the additional food they needed. He also sent fisherman to the river and women into the forest to gather more fruits and vegetables.

Sherry felt her confidence increase as she saw people rising to the occasion and doing what needed to be done. She remembered a phrase she heard while growing up at church. "See the need, do the deed." With her confidence bolstered by God, Sherry gave into the impulse to sit down, relax, and have some breakfast herself. These people working with her were people she could trust. She felt her tension ease and went over to sit beside Renato.

Tuvicha walked over with an air of excitement. "Renato," he exclaimed, "I was there that day you and your father came to our village. I remember it clearly. In fact I was able to give you some herbal medicine which helped you. I was not yet the shaman, but his apprentice. Thankfully, your injuries were not serious. The ground was soft and the weight of the tree pushed you into it. Also, its branches bore some of its weight."

Tuvicha continued, "Renato, you immersed yourself in the tribe immediately. You were an engaging young boy who was everyone's friend. Unfortunately, your father's years of oppression in his former village appeared to warp his outlook on life. His driving force was to get both of you away, not just from his village, but from

15

Paraguay itself. He appeared to be haunted by the memories of his past, and felt the only way to escape them was to leave Paraguay.

"The Missionary who lived here then befriended both of you. He was the reason you and your father became Christians. He also taught both of you English. After making some inquiries, he discovered a man from Maine, who was originally from Paraguay. The Missionary wrote to him and asked him to sponsor you and your father. After a time, you both moved to Asuncion to gain employment and save money for the move to Maine. It took both of you over two years to raise the money you needed, but you were successful. Once you and your father left, we never heard from you again."

Renato was stunned. It seems there were still gaps in his memory. No wonder his father was so secretive, their life was a lie. Everything concerning this Quest appeared to be shrouded in secrets. What other surprises were out there?

Renato looked up and Tuvicha was standing there, patiently waiting for Renato to absorb all that had been revealed to him. The thing that impacted Renato most was his tie to the evil tribe that was sacrificing the babies. He began to think that maybe the group who left last night to go on the Quest God had called them to, might need to know this information.

Tuvicha sat down next to Renato. "My friend, I know what you are thinking. When we have our time of prayer after breakfast, we will ask God to give us clarity on these issues."

CHAPTER TWO

JUNE 23
THE JUNGLE

After they had traveled most of the night, those on the Quest were physically tired, but emotionally charged by all that they had experienced in the last two weeks. They were also anticipating the moves of God to continue with them as they traveled. Still walking in the same order they had when departing were: Philippe, Mario, Axel, Giancarlo and Maitie, the five young hunters from the village who led the way. Josh and Bekah were next. Manu followed; he wanted to stay near to Bekah, his new found sister. Daniel and Edwardo were next, and bringing up the rear were Carlos and Akeem. Carlos, who had formally been working against the Quest, had followed Bekah to Paraguay to steal the golden crucifix from her for Haydon Carlton, his employer. Akeem was an old friend of Josh's and also a C.I.A. infiltrator to the Black Death Camp that was located only five miles from their village. Nineteen members of the Black Death Camp had recently attacked the village. Through miraculous intervention, all had been captured.

They did not know for sure what the future would bring, but knew that God was involved on one side and Satan on the other. Somehow, God's plan put them in the middle. They were like pieces on a chessboard and God was making the moves. All of them were quiet, keeping their thoughts to themselves. It was not every day that a group of people set out on a Quest directed by God. The

17

last group they could think of was the Israelites setting out for the Promised Land.

The first few hours of the night were gratefully uneventful. Other than the large blood moon, whose strange light illuminated their path, there was nothing unexpected about their night. Although, the fact that they were to travel by night and sleep during the day, as God had instructed them, was rather unusual. They did not know whether it was for safety or secrecy that they traveled this way. They only knew that God said that was how they were to travel and so there was only one option open to them, obedience.

With all the excitement of the previous day, fatigue was setting in. The path they had walked along for about five hours was a known route. It was not a stressful walk, but shoulders began to droop. The moon was high and its light was infiltrating in spots along the path helping the men stay on the trail. They had seen several animals they could have killed for food, but given it was their first night and they had spare food in their packs, they left them behind. They did not want to take time to hunt and then have to clean and wrap the animals for cooking later in the day. After all, this was not a hunting expedition.

Toward morning, a bank of low lying clouds began to build and obscure the light of the moon that was now low in the still dark sky. They were all having trouble staying on the trail, if it could even be called that, and wondered if they should stop and camp where they were. They did not want to use their flashlights unless absolutely necessary.

The trail had deteriorated to nothing more than a slight separation of the ground cover at their feet. Suddenly, in the distance, they could see a light. They wondered if someone else was up ahead, hunting and camping. Manu said he was unaware of anyone out hunting. Hunting expeditions were usually brought before him to confirm. It was always good to know when armed men were in the jungle.

Josh, Daniel and Manu decided to move quietly forward to discover who or what was causing the light. At this distance, it was not apparent if it was friend or foe. It was a very bright light and they could see it clearly, but they did not see anyone in the vicinity nor hear anyone talking.

In the darkness they discovered that stealth was nearly impossible. They were all tripping over rocks and vines and plants of all sizes. They were no longer on any path, but just walking through the wild, untrammeled jungle, and without the light of the moon the dark was impenetrable. The distant light gave them a sense of direction, but it did not pierce through enough to illuminate their path. As they got closer the light grew brighter. It appeared to be a large fire. There was no one in sight, but the fire was burning brightly. There was also a significant pile of wood to feed it during the rest of the night. The rest of the group followed several yards back and caught up when the others stopped. They did not see any indication of anyone inhabiting the camp. Finally they decided by consensus, that God had prepared it.

Philippe and Maitie took it upon themselves to set several snares. They had a sack of vegetables and one of fruit they had taken with them. They also carried some chipa from yesterday. It was old, but it was still filling. They ate some, and before lying down to sleep, thanked God for His provision. They did not set a guard. They had discussed this before time and felt that God was their guardian.[19] They prayed and asked Him to position angels around the campsite to keep them safe.[20] Then they lay down on their blankets and all went to sleep.[21]

---

[19] Isaiah 58:8
[20] Hebrews 1:14
[21] Psalm 4:8

CHAPTER THREE

JUNE 23
THE JUNGLE
ANGELIC HOSTS

The heavenly guards kept watch over those God had called to fulfill His Quest. The night was dark and it was still hours before dawn. Except for the sound of insects and a few night prowling animals, all was quiet. They stood at attention, their eyes like lightning, flashing to and fro, on the lookout for any attack from their enemy, Satan. Just as they were on alert to help bring this Quest to a successful completion, Satan was on alert to sabotage it. He knew his time was drawing to a close, and he also knew what was waiting for him and his followers after the final battle took place.[22] Though Satan had been told the outcome, he still doubted God, just as he always had. He still had delusions that he would win. Despite his attempt to kill Jesus as an infant,[23] despite his attempts to test Jesus at a time of physical weakness in the desert,[24] and his apparent victory at Jesus' death on the cross,[25] he was not the victor. He was defeated because God raised Jesus from the dead.[26]

The four beings shadowing the traveling group were on alert. They had the appearance of men, but that was where the

---

[22] Revelations 20:10
[23] Matthew 2:16-18
[24] Matthew 4:1-10
[25] Mark 15:37
[26] Mark 16:6

21

similarity ended. These beings were not men of the earth, and were not created from the dust of the earth. Their bodies were not made of flesh and blood, but of light. They were beings of light. Light emanated from them wherever they went.[27] They did not sleep or grow weary. Their bodies were fed by the light of God, which penetrated all things. It even brought light into darkness. The light of God actually dispelled darkness.[28]

These beings were angels. At the moment, they were on a mission from God to protect this special group of His children. They had come in close to observe them. They knew these twelve were instrumental in fulfilling God's plan. They did not know His whole plan. They only knew their part was to protect these twelve.

Their senses were heightened to a point that was beyond human comprehension, seeing not only things of the earth, but things of the spirit. They knew that at any time their enemy Satan could be near, and any time he came in contact with God's people he brought peril. Their assignment was to keep him at bay. They could feel his skulking presence, but at the present time he was keeping his distance, waiting for a moment of weakness to attack.

Satan had also been observing these people, scrutinizing their strengths and weaknesses. He would wait, allowing their thoughts and words to snare them. All men were prone to these weaknesses. Why should these twelve be any different? He would look for the weak link and capitalize on their vulnerability.

---

[27] Acts, 12:7, Luke 2:8-9, Revelation 18:1
[28] Psalm 139:7-13

CHAPTER FOUR

JUNE 23
THE VILLAGE

After finishing breakfast, Sherry went back to check on her patients. They were part of the burned-out village to the north, and had walked twenty-five miles to reach her village. Many had been undernourished and dehydrated. Sherry originally had eighteen patients. One was a little girl about three years old, thankfully just past the age where she would have been of interest to the evil tribe. She had multiple scrapes and cuts, some of them very deep. A few were infected. She was also dehydrated and was refusing to eat or drink. Sherry was very concerned. Unless they got her eating and drinking she would not survive.

Sherry had an idea and went back to the kitchen. She asked little Maria to come with her and take Hombrecito, her puppy, into the back room to visit the little girl. Her name was Panambi, which meant butterfly in Guarani. She was a pretty little girl with large dark eyes and long black hair, just like everyone else. But there was something special about this little girl, especially to Sherry's eyes. In her short life, she had been injured, seen her parents both killed and her baby brother sacrificed to evil gods. It was quite a load for a three year old to carry.

Just as she hoped, when Maria and Hombrecito came over, the little puppy jumped up on the cot, wagging his tail and giving out kisses. After a moment's hesitation, Panambi began to smile. It was not a big smile, but it was a beginning.

Sherry had told Maria that Panambi was sick and needed to eat and drink to get better. She gave Maria some terere, the native tea, and a plate of fruit to share with Panambi. As she had hoped, after drinking the tea and eating the fruit together they were both on the floor playing with the puppy. Panambi had needed a friend. Sherry only wished everyone's injuries were healed as easily. But she would do what she could and trust God to do the rest.

As she turned to ask one of the other patients if Panambi had any other family, she heard the sound of a gun discharge, once and then again. There was no mistaking the sound. Sherry grabbed her bag and hurried down to the glade where the prisoners were being kept. That was the only place where guns would be found. There was now a crowd of people in the glade, but none of them appeared to be the prisoners.

Leonardo was already there questioning some of the men he had left in charge. Sherry spotted a body on the ground. Hurrying over, she discovered it was Ted and he had been shot. The bullet had not penetrated his skull, but had fractured it over his left temple. Sherry cleaned it and put a bandage on it. Then she had several men carry him up to the clinic. Leonardo walked with her and ex-plained what had happened. "Jose had turned to talk with one of the villagers. At that time several of the prisoners started to advance on Ted. His gun's safety was still on and he fumbled trying to release it. They took advantage of the situation and wrestled the gun from him. In the skirmish, Ted was shot and Jose was knocked out but not before he shot one of the prisoners in the leg. The other eigh-teen prisoners escaped, taking both Ted's and Jose's rifles, but the injured prisoner could not keep up with them and was left behind."

After attending to Ted, Sherry walked over to the injured man. He did not appear to be Middle Eastern so she spoke to him in English. "My name is Sherry Albright. I'm a nurse mid-wife from the United States, but I'm probably the closest thing to a doctor for forty miles. Will you let me look at your leg?"

The man gave Sherry a sour look and refused to answer her questions. "Well, we can't leave him here to bleed to death," she said to Leonardo. "Maybe when we get him up to the clinic he'll change his mind."

Suddenly Sherry stopped and looked around. "Leonardo, didn't you say Jose was knocked out? Where is he? I need to examine him also. Has anyone seen Renato?" she inquired. "I'm surprised he did not come down to investigate."

Just then Renato walked into the glade with three men walking before him at gunpoint. "I found these three hanging around. I haven't had a chance to talk to them yet. They seemed to have held back and let the others escape. They haven't said anything, but they could be Americans.

"I passed the men carrying Ted up to the clinic. Is he badly injured? Jose also ran by; he had blood running down the side of his face."

"We have three injuries," Sherry stated, "of which Ted is the most severely injured. He appears to have a fractured skull. The man sitting here appears to be American, but he refuses to talk or let me examine him. His wound is still bleeding, and I don't know if there's an exit wound. Get some men to carry him up to the clinic. We can't leave him here. Bring those three you have along too. We'll have to figure out what to do with them. Have someone find some rope and tie them up for the time being. Also, find Jose. I need to look at his head."

Two men grabbed the injured man and helped him back to the village. He did not put up much resistance. Renato herded his three and Sherry hurried on ahead. She took a moment to look back at the glade. Sherry hated this spot in the village. Not only was it the spot where Chabuto, Manu's stepmother, and Tuvicha had tried to sacrifice an infant to their evil gods, but it was the spot where sacrifices had been made for hundreds of years. They needed to

25

purge that glade and banish any evil spirit that tried to raise itself above the Name of Jesus. That place permeated evil. They must speak the Word of God, and fight back the forces of darkness that clung to it. There were still dark and dangerous things lingering in the area. Prayers needed to be prayed and blessings needed to be spoken over the glade, purging the evil and replacing it with good. She would talk with Leonardo about it the first chance she had.

She had at least one seriously injured patient. Head injuries were always tricky. She wanted everyone praying about this. Her skills only went so far. She was not a doctor, and never claimed to be one. In situations like this she called on the Heavenly Healer to take the lead. She trusted that just as He miraculously healed before, He would also do it for Ted. She would do what she knew to do and trust God to do the rest.

Sherry saw they had put Ted on one of the new cots. She asked four men to carry him over to her examination table. She sponged the blood away with some sterile water. She always had a pot of it boiling on the wood burning stove. Unfortunately, progress had not arrived at the village. There was no electricity, no running water, and the nearest town was at least a half a day away by boat. Recently, a gift of electric lights, a generator, and solar panels had been given to them. Ted was the benefactor, and now it appeared he would be the first person to benefit from their use. They had just been hooked up yesterday. Sherry asked for someone to go and start the generator so she could have some decent light.

Renato stood by Leonardo watching as the four men were tied hand and foot. Eventually, Sherry would examine the injured man whether he liked it or not. Renato was concerned that so much responsibility was being placed on her.

Leonardo was worried also. He needed some input and decided to confer with Renato. Leonardo had sent Cipriano and three hunters to monitor the Black Death Camp that morning. "My assumption is that those who escaped will head back to their camp.

26

Unfortunately, four of our men are in their path armed only with knives, machetes, and bows and arrows. They don't know these men have escaped and are coming their way. They are all good hunters, but are up against men with rifles. However, it has been observed that these men are not disciplined. There does not appear to be a leader, and they do not work together as a group. Each one follows his own way."

Renato pointed out, "They are four against fifteen; those aren't good odds. This is another time when we need some heavenly intervention."

"That's true," answered Leonardo; "also, my men have never killed another person before. I don't know what they will do if faced with that situation. I hope they hear the group of them coming and can stay hidden. Being in the jungle will give Cipriano and his men an advantage over them."

CHAPTER FIVE

JUNE 23
THE BLACK DEATH CAMP

The Black Death Camp was located five miles south of the village, and about one mile west of the river. It was composed of varying groups of twenty to thirty men brought there to train for combat. While there, they were also subjected to radical rhetoric and teaching. These men had already shown their radical intent by beheading the eight prisoners they had captured earlier. Akeem and Mehdi, C.I.A. operatives, had infiltrated the group. After escaping, they warned the village of an eminent attack, saved many lives, and helped capture the terrorists.

Cipriano and his three companions had made their way to the Black Death Camp early that morning. These men were trained hunters. As was their habit, they had walked soundlessly through the jungle.

The air was unusually warm and still. Not a leaf rustled on the myriad of trees and vines. The birds and the insects provided more than enough noise. On the way they had passed through a troop of howler monkeys high in the canopy of trees. Their cries crescendoed as the four men passed below them, sending out their warning of trespassers in the area. It was a welcome relief to pass out of their domain as they entered the camp, but it was also an advantage, knowing that they would sound the alarm if anyone else came through their area.

29

One by one the men spread out along the northern perimeter of the abandoned camp. They stayed back inside the jungle several feet to be protected from observation by anyone who might approach, or who had been left behind. There were several trails leading out from the camp. Cipriano instructed his men to stay off the trails and to maintain silence. With all that had occurred recently, he felt that vigilance was necessary. They squatted soundlessly in the brush, ignoring the bothersome insects and small animals that passed by. They used all their senses to observe the area around them.

As morning passed and the sun traveled high overhead, the howler monkeys began giving their alarm, putting them on alert. A short time later, the hunter's heightened senses picked up the sound of a large group of people approaching. Instinctively, they each drew an arrow and notched it to their bows. They were all Christians, and their hearts and minds immediately turned to God, asking for His guidance and protection.

As the group approached, it became clear that stealth was not a concern to them. They were calling and shouting to each other as they passed. It was apparent these strangers were not people of the jungle by the noise they created. All the men of the tribe were taught from childhood to walk quietly in the jungle and not to let their presence be known.

Slowly, the disorganized band of would-be terrorists started to trickle into the camp. They had no structured line-of-march, and they had no one on lookout. They straggled in singly or by twos and threes, sweating profusely.

Cipriano counted fifteen men. He knew they were the men that had been captured yesterday. They must have somehow escaped this morning. He also observed that two of them were carrying rifles. With hand signs he motioned for his men to fall back further into the jungle and stay hidden. The four hunters prayed that none of their village had been injured during the strangers' escape.

The noisy parade traveled in total disarray. Cipriano and his

30

men let them pass by. Then, while Cipriano and one of the hunters kept watch over the men in the camp, the other two hunters back-tracked along the trail to detect whether any stragglers were forth-coming. Cipriano knew there had originally been nineteen captives. Perhaps some of them had been injured in the escape. Seeing the rifles they carried caused more concern that some of the villagers may have been injured also.

After several minutes passed, the two hunters returned and reported to Cipriano that there did not appear to be any other men approaching the camp. Cipriano decided they should stay for a while, observe these men, and try to determine what they were up to.

In addition to speaking Guarani, Cipriano and Osvaldo also spoke Spanish, as well as a smattering of English. If they could get close enough without being seen, they might hear some of the escaped prisoners' plans.

After scavenging throughout the camp, the escaped prison-ers found enough food and water to satisfy themselves.

The four hunters watched and waited. In the distance they heard an approaching storm and felt the change in the atmosphere. Dark clouds began to roll in, and with a large clap of thunder that made the ground vibrate, a deluge of rain came down, soaking everyone within seconds. The four men held their positions, since they were familiar with this type of storm, but the would-be terrorists scrambled for cover inside a small building.

Cipriano decided to send one man back to their village to re-port to Leonardo what had happened and await further orders. Run-ning on a now well-traveled trail back to the village should take him about forty-five minutes. The rest of the hunters hunkered down in the rain and waited for the storm to pass.

Inside the building the fifteen men sat quarreling among themselves. Then one man rose to his feet and began to talk quiet-ly. He said they had two choices. They could try to find their way out of the jungle and admit defeat, or they could gather the weapons captured from the infidels they had beheaded and then go back to the village and kill every man, woman and child. That act would redeem them from their defeat. He was sure Josef, the leader of their movement in Paraguay, would congratulate them and make them leaders when he next came to visit the camp. As the rain began to let up, six men came out of the building and went to a small storage area. They returned with two large boxes.

The three watchers crept closer to try to hear what was transpiring. With the arrival of weapons, the voice of the man speaking had quickly escalated. The speaker was trying to motivate the men with explosive speech. It appeared to be working. From outside the building it sounded as though everyone was yelling. Then they began to fire their weapons into the air. Cipriano took no chances; he sent the other two watchers back to the village to report what was happening. He told them he would stay. If the now armed men started towards the village, he told them he would attempt to disable them one by one.

The two men left their arrows with Cipriano and he combined them with his. Now he had forty-four arrows, more than enough to stop fifteen men.

Cipriano dropped five yards back into the jungle, camouflaged by the dense growth. He hunkered down and waited, praying that God would be with him to lead and guide him. Cipriano was one the first converts in the village and his faith was strong. He recalled the story of Gideon and how he defeated an entire army with only three hundred men.[29] He only had to defeat fifteen, but in his heart he knew he could not kill them.

He needed a strategy that would allow him to incapacitate them, but still remain hidden. It would be dangerous for him. If they found he was alone, they might be able to catch him; but if he moved around and attacked from different places, they might

---

[29] Judges 7

32

think there were many people attacking them. If he could get them to panic and start running, he would be able to wound them all. Later, men from the village could come back and pick them up. He prayed again and asked God to help his aim be true and to keep him hidden from the escaped prisoners. The rain had dropped to a slow drizzle, but the wind was blowing strongly. Strong winds can cause an arrow to go astray. All Cipriano could do was trust that God would direct his arrows.

Just then the men began pouring out of the building, shouting loudly, carrying their guns and waving their machetes over their heads. As they went by him, Cipriano took aim on the last man in the line and let his arrow fly. The man dropped with a loud howl. As the other men turned back to find out what had happened, Cipriano quickly moved to another position. He fired again and another man dropped, also letting out a loud cry of pain. Panic set in and the rest of the men bolted. It was every man for himself. Now there were thirteen. He saw another man veer off the trail and took him down, telling himself not to get overconfident, and to take his time. They had five miles of jungle to travel. He was assured God was on his side, but he still needed to use all his skill and caution to successfully eliminate this threat to his village.

The rowdy group continued on through the jungle, aware that three men had been taken down. Their fear was that they would be the next to fall. Cipriano continued to follow, staying alert and looking for opportunities to decrease the number of terrorists as they continued to travel to his village.

CHAPTER SIX

JUNE 23
JUNGLE CAMP

After sleeping for about five hours, the Questers were awakened by the deafening sound of thunder and a deluge of cold rain. They were all chilled by the change in temperature, cold rain and the strong wind. They leapt up and proceeded to pack their supplies as quickly as possible. Unfortunately, there was no shelter. They did not have a tent, which was probably a good thing. The unusually high winds would have torn it to pieces. The buffeting wind was whipping up jungle debris and propelling it through the air. Large leaves and branches became projectiles, battering the group and leaving painful welts and bruises in their wake. Large bolts of lightning streaked across the storm darkened sky.

Josh called everyone together away from the group of trees they had been under, mindful of the fact that tall trees were a magnet for lightning strikes, and the sky was lit up by a series of large bolts of lightning. They huddled together seeking each other's warmth. It was useless to change into dry clothes until the storm passed. Bekah was reminded of the time in the Bible when Jesus spoke to the storm and it became calm. "Josh," Bekah called over the sound of the storm, "let's pray and take authority over this storm just as Jesus did.[31] He said we would do the things He did and even greater. He dispelled that storm,

---

[31] Mark 4:39

35

and I think we should follow his example."[32]

As the twelve gathered together, they spoke to the storm. In response to their words of faith, the four angelic guardians used their shields to deflect the attack of the enemy. One spoke to the wind, another to the rain, another to the lightning and another to the thunder. They used the Word of God and commanded the storm, "Peace, be still."

For a few moments it appeared as though the storm intensified, then the clouds began to break up and blue spread across the sky. The wind dropped to a gentle breeze and the warmth of the sun penetrated the denseness of the jungle. The storm had passed.

Josh looked at his watch. It was after 2:00 pm. There was still over four hours of daylight left. Josh called Manu over and asked, "Can you have your men check their snares, dress their kills and then search for dry wood for a small fire to cook the meal?"

Maitie checked all the snares and found all but one full. Axel cleaned the small animals and Giancarlo diligently searched for dry wood for a fire. It was not easy to find because of the torrential rain that had just passed. As he searched, he saw a rock outcropping. Underneath there was a large quantity of wood. Again, just as the previous night, the wood was already cut, stacked, and dry.

Bekah took charge of cooking. Even in the jungle she loved to cook, and she did it very well. She thought of all her friends at home she loved to feed. She thought of her garden at home and wished she had some of its produce here. Bekah had brought a pouch full of local herbs that Connie had on hand. Some root vegetables, including yams, had also been brought from the village.

Bekah lived on a one hundred acre apple orchard in Ogunquit, Maine. A few acres had been set aside for her garden. She grew everything and the garden flourished. People came from miles around to help her with it because she had established a food bank at the back of her needlework store. Most of the fresh produce was

---

[32] John 14:12

36

brought there to be distributed as needed. Many of those in need came back to help her in the garden. They wanted an opportunity to help out, just as they had been helped.

Mario carried a soup pot and she boiled water, some for the stew and some for cleanup. She would have to boil an additional pot to replenish their canteens. Bekah had found some small onions growing and browned them along with the meat which had been cut into small pieces. The pot sizzled and a wonderful aroma permeated the air, starting their digestive juices flowing. Bekah added water and covered the pot to let the stew cook.

While the stew simmered, a time of Bible study was called. Josh was impressed to teach on Jeremiah 29:11. "This Scripture tells us that God had a plan and purpose for each of our lives.[33] He told them that God had this plan before the beginning of time, and how they were born for such a time as this.[34]

"Sometimes we are called to endure hardships and make sacrifices, but God rewards those who diligently seek Him."[35] Josh also told them, "We are all part of His body, a body of believers—His Church. Someone may be the hand to gather wood, someone the eye to bring down game, someone the mouth to bring His Word to the lost and dying. Right now we are all feet, marching out to where God is leading us."[36] Josh also taught them, "The Bible talks about other gifts God gives us. If we speak, let us speak in faith. We can serve, we can teach, we can encourage others. We can give generously and we can show kindness. When everyone operates in their gift, then we work as a body, but if the ear tries to be the mouth or the nose tries to be the foot, confusion ensues."[37] Then Josh prayed for the group that God would reveal His gifts to them, and they would all see and understand what God wanted them to do.

---

[33] Jeremiah 29:11
[34] Esther 4:14
[35] Hebrews 11:6
[36] 1 Corinthians 12:15-27
[37] Romans 12:4-8

Twilight was falling and the sounds of night were emerging. The monkeys went to bed as the frogs sang them a lullaby. Wonderful smells were emanating from the cook pot and Bekah decided the stew was done. They used their cups for bowls and everyone lined up for the meal.

There were several different animals in the pot, but Bekah, being a rather adventurous eater and cook, was not bothered by the prospect. She even had two portions of the large snake that tried to squeeze the life out of baby Emilio several days ago. Thankfully Lara had been alerted by the barking of Maria's little dog, Hombrecito. She went and got Edwardo's rifle and had the courage to shoot it. Josh then had the faith to pray life back into Emilio's lifeless body.

They all joined together and said a prayer to bless the food. They also thanked God for stopping the storm before anyone was seriously injured. After enjoying the warm and tasty stew and the rest of the leftover chipa, they cleaned up and packed their gear, ready to go forward in their Quest. They again asked God to lead and guide them. They had an idea of where Arandu's village was, but none of them had ever been there before. They knew it was approximately a three day walk along the river. Arandu was the leader of the group of refugees who had been adopted by Manu's village. Arandu's village had been attacked by the large, barbarous tribe that had rampaged through the area every spring attacking villages and sacrificing their infants as a burnt offering to their gods. They were going to use his village as a launching point for the Quest. From then forward they would be in totally unknown territory.

As twilight descended, they filed out in the same order as the first night. They were still close enough to home that they had some familiarity with the area. Other than the storm, their first night and day appeared uneventful. They still had some fruit and vegetables, and Sherry had given Bekah and Josh each a large bag of some kind of jerky. Bekah had not asked what kind of meat it was, but she had tried a piece before they left and it was tasty. It was protein and so it would be nourishing and give them energy. Everyone also discovered packages of nuts and dried fruit in their packs, so they would definitely not go hungry. Setting the snare before they went to sleep worked well the previous morning so they would do it again when they stopped for the day.

After walking a few hours, they heard what sounded like a shrill scream in the distance. Everyone stopped and Bekah asked nervously, "What was that? Have any of you ever heard something like that before?" She turned and looked at Josh who just shrugged his shoulders.

Manu walked up to them and told them what all the natives already knew. 'It's a Jaguar," Manu said. "Judging from the denseness of the jungle and the high humidity, sound doesn't carry well, so he's probably no more than a mile away. We need to stay alert. He shouldn't attack a group this big, but we don't want to be surprised."

Immediately, Bekah felt fear try to rise up in her. Circumstances were again testing her faith; she was determined to pass the test. Josh did not appear concerned, but turned off the safety of his rifle, just to be ready. If they met with opposition, he would be prepared. All those who carried weapons followed his lead. Those who were native notched their arrows. If there was danger they knew God would be with them, but they would do what they could to stay ahead of trouble.

Josh encouraged everyone to pray quietly and thank God for His protection. Josh knew there were many dangers in the jungle, but he also knew God had a plan. As he prayed, a Scripture surfaced in his mind. He began to repeat it over and over. "Trust in the Lord with all your heart and lean not on your own understanding; in all your ways acknowledge Him, and He will direct your paths."[38] As faith replaced their fear, they set out again with confidence.[39]

Giancarlo led them down a path that paralleled the river.

---

[38] Proverbs 3:5-6
[39] Romans 10:17

They crossed a well-traveled trail that game used to come down to the river and drink. There, they came across a fresh kill. It was a small deer. They had probably chased the jaguar off its kill. Much of the meat was undisturbed and so Manu suggested that a portion be cut from it for the evening meal. Philippe went and chopped off several banana leaves and wrapped the meat tightly, using some rope they had brought along. Keeping alert, they moved away from the carcass and left the jaguar to finish his meal. Danger had been avoided and a meal had been provided. They all acknowledged God's hand in this and thanked Him.[40]

Because they walked in the dark, senses were continually on alert. Talk was kept to a minimum as they traversed the jungle. They were nearing the end of the jungle the young hunters were familiar with. None of them had been this way in recent months, and the jungle was not a stagnant entity; on the contrary, it was living, breathing and ever-changing. If trails were not tamed, they were overrun. Since no one came this way on a regular basis the trail was becoming more and more obscure, especially in the dark. The scream of the jaguar had been a reminder. "Stay alert!"[41]

It was easy to be lulled into a stupor. Revitalized by the break in their repetitive walk, they moved with added awareness through the night. As night lightened to dawn, the group was ready to stop. Previously, a camp had been prepared for them. This morning that was not the case. Chores were assigned, and camp was set up. Water was heated for terere and coffee. What food that was left was shared and a dinner of meat and what vegetables could be found would be cooked that morning for their evening meal. They set out snares to catch what game they could and possibly dry the meat to-morrow while they were cooking their stew. It wasn't very long before everyone was nestled down and sleeping the sleep of the weary.

Again, the four guardians kept watch. They had no trouble

---

[40] Philippians 4:19
[41] Mark 13.37

staying awake. They did not sleep: there is no night in Heaven. Everyone was surrounded with the light of the presence of God.[42]

---

[42] Revelation 22:5

CHAPTER SEVEN

JUNE 23
THE VILLAGE

After examining Ted, cleaning the gunshot wound, and giving him some antibiotics and an anti-inflammatory drug, there was not much else Sherry could do for him. She trusted God to come through with his healing.

Sherry transferred him to a cot. She raised his head to take as much pressure off the brain as she could. The problem with injuries such as this was that the injury caused the brain to swell. The next forty-eight hours would be crucial.

Noticing Lara standing in the doorway, Sherry motioned her over. "Would you help me?" Sherry asked. "Someone needs to sit with Ted and let me know if there are any changes in his condition. Let me know if he gets restless, has trouble breathing, gets feverish, or starts violently shaking; anything that appears out of the ordinary. Also, let me know if he regains consciousness."

Lara nodded gravely and brought over a chair. She and Ted had been spending more time together in the last few days and she had conflicting feelings about that. First, there was the language issue. Lara understood and could speak a little English. Ted spoke no *Guarani* or *Spanish*. Then there was the fact that he was an outsider and would probably leave when everything was over. Lastly, she did not want to be involved with anyone. She did not want a serious relationship that might lead to something permanent. Her

43

parent's marriage had been a continuous conflict. Connie, her older sister, had married young and escaped the fallout of the perpetual war between her parents. She had been left behind, not only to observe their battles, but also to experience the emotional damage of living in a continual state of turmoil.

Three years ago her parents had both died of a sickness that had claimed eight people from the village. Connie and Edwardo had taken her in. Times were better, but the scars had left her quiet and withdrawn. Ted was rocking her boat and she was not sure she wanted his attention. But she knew that Sherry needed her help, and Ted needed her help also.

With Ted's injuries attended to, Sherry looked around for Jose. She sent one of the young men from the village to find him and bring him back for her to examine. She washed her hands and asked two of the young men to bring over the injured terrorist and put him on the examining table.

Initially he resisted, but saw his actions were futile and resigned himself to the woman's attentions. Sherry looked up at him and asked, "If I untie you, will you resist? We're only trying to help you."

He looked at her and gave a slight nod of his head. "You can use your hands to brace yourself on the table so you won't lose you balance." Sherry grabbed a pair of scissors and explained that she would have to cut off the bottom of his pant leg to examine the injury.

After exposing it, Sherry was able to see that there was an entrance and exit wound. At least she would not have to go digging for the bullet. She flushed the wounds to be sure no debris was left in it. The wounds were not large and required no suturing. It must have been a low caliber rifle. She applied antibiotic salve and a bandage to both sides of the leg; then she gave him an injection to fight any infection. He still had not uttered a word. She had no time to worry further about him now. She turned him over to Renato to take care of. Then Sherry looked around to see if Jose had turned

44

up yet. She was beginning to worry that his injury might be more than it appeared.

Suddenly Sherry heard loud noises coming their way. Mehdi and Leonardo walked through the door, supporting Jose. "We found him lying on the path to the river. He's unconscious and his head is still bleeding," Mehdi reported.

Mehdi was a friend and coworker of Akeem who was now out on the Quest with the others that had set forth last night. Mehdi was also from Iraq, and a Christian, who had come to Paraguay with Akeem to infiltrate a Black Death Camp. Their assignment was to get more information about these camps to their C.I.A. contact, Jose.

Sherry ordered them to put Jose up on the examining table. She came over and sponged off the wound on his head. It appeared that someone had hit him with a heavy object, maybe the stock of a rifle. He did not seem to have a fracture, but most likely a concussion. He was going to have a bad headache for a few days. His unconsciousness was probably from running around after receiving the injury. In concurrence with that thought he began to moan and his eyes fluttered open. "What happened, where am I?" Jose questioned. "How did I get in here? The last thing I remember was running after some of the prisoners. I saw Ted go down. How is he doing?"

"Please do me a favor Jose and stay still. I'll answer all your questions when I finish taking your vital signs. You passed out and I want to see if anything else is going on beside the knock on your head."

Sherry listened to Jose's heart and lungs. She took his pulse and checked his eyes. She also had him squeeze her hands to see if there was any weakness on one side or the other. He stood up and walked across the room unassisted. Sherry was finally satisfied that other than a headache, Jose would be alright. She wished she could be as sure of that with Ted, but trusted, that in spite of the serious injury, the Great Physician was in charge.

Sherry led Jose over to a chair and sat down with him. She

45

began to explain Ted's injury to him. His face grew grave as she continued to speak. Just then, Leonardo came through the door with one of the members of the tribe who had been out guarding the Black Death Camp. He said that Cipriano had sent the rest of them back to warn them the terrorists were now armed and probably coming back to the village to exact retribution.

Jose turned to Sherry. "Give me something for this headache and then I have to go set up a defense against armed men with only three people able to use firearms. Put in a call to Heaven for us and let them know that we need some supernatural help down here." After swallowing his pills, Jose turned and walked out with Leonardo following. "Mehdi, let's go find Renato and make a plan."

CHAPTER EIGHT

JUNE 23
THE JUNGLE

Cipriano continued to follow the escaped prisoners. He stopped and prayed, asking God to continue showing him what to do. It always surprised him when the God of the universe took time to talk to him, but he knew that according to the Bible, he was a son of God, and God was personally interested in his life and in his problems.[43]

God had given him a plan, and now that they were over half-way back to the village, only seven people were still up and walking. The rest were all back along the path injured and in pain, but most importantly, not dead. Unfortunately, Doctor Sherry was going to be very busy tending to all these injuries.

His next target was in the middle of the line. He did not want to always take out the ones in the back. This would give them a pattern to expect. He varied his attack so they never knew who was next. The prisoners were all running and afraid now. They knew there had to be at least two or three attackers out in the jungle, and they were afraid to venture off the trail. Once off the path they were totally lost. They thought their best chance was to get to the camp and gather some hostages. The only problem was if there would be enough of them left to do that. Suddenly another one of them let out a howl of pain. Another shot. Now there were six left.

---

[43] 3 John 2

Their so-called leader, Ali called a halt to their advance. He spoke to the others. "We need to surrender or we will all be shot. We can't find them, but they have no trouble picking us off. I vote we lay down our weapons, walk slowly into the village, and give ourselves up. This may also give our wounded members a chance to live. The longer they lay out in the jungle, the less chance they have of survival. Either their wounds will kill them or the wild animals will."

He stopped and looked at the rest of them. Their clamor for revenge had long since passed. Now they were just dragging their weapons and trying to put one foot in front of the other. They slowly looked at each other, not wanting to be the first to give up, but fear and fatigue won out. They all dropped their weapons and sat down. Ali looked at them and said, "We can't stay here, we have to get up and get to the village." When no one moved he said impatiently, "Alright, we'll rest ten minutes and then move." He sat down and rested with the others.

Time went by and no one stirred. Adrenaline had worn off and lethargy had settled on the small group of men. They needed a stimulant to motivate them. Cipriano was glad to oblige. He notched an arrow and it fell to ground in the middle of their small circle. They all staggered to their feet and began to move out quickly down the trail toward the village. They moved faster now because they did not have heavy weapons to carry. They only had to place one foot in front of the other, but after a short distance they began to slow down. Cipriano again fired an arrow to the side of them. That was all it took. They almost ran the rest of the way. Cipriano hoped there would be guards to intercept them before they entered the village.

Several minutes later his concerns were alleviated when four men stepped out of the jungle and stopped the group. The group all raised their hands and stood still. Then Cipriano came out of the jungle behind them. After seeing that only one man had defeated all of them, they were first amazed, then angry. They were not aware of the fact that Cipriano's faith in God was what earned him the victory.

Cipriano turned the six prisoners over to the four armed villagers and went to find Leonardo to report what had happened. He hoped men would be sent out quickly to bring in the wounded. He did not want to be responsible for any of their deaths. After hearing Cipriano's report, Leonardo immediately dispatched ten men to bring in the wounded and their weapons. Even though most of the villagers did not have the skill to use the weapons, Leonardo recognized their value.

Cipriano and Leonardo immediately headed for the compound to alert Doctor Sherry that nine wounded men would be arriving shortly. They would see that everything she needed would be made available to her.

When they reached the clinic they saw that Ted was still unconscious and requiring her attention. There was also one prisoner who had been shot in the leg who still required some attention also. They looked around and did not see Dr. Sherry anywhere.

Leonardo saw Lara sitting over by Ted. He walked over and asked, "Lara, how is Ted doing? Has he regained consciousness?"

With sad eyes, Lara shook her head. "No," she answered. "Doctor Sherry says it may take a while."

"Where is Doctor Sherry?" Leonardo asked. "I thought she would be in here taking care of the wounded."

"She went to lie down," Lara said. "She told me to call her if anything changed. You need to remember that Doctor Sherry is going to have a baby and needs extra rest. She also has a lot more responsibility resting on her. Do you need for me to go wake her up? What is the matter?"

"Lara, I'm going to send someone to go get Paloma, Ciba, and Connie to help out. Send all the babies to Erecia to watch. She can find more help if she needs it. You go wake up Doctor Sherry. Tell her several wounded men will be arriving shortly.

"Cipriano, would you go alert the Ring Leaders." They were

49

five young men Manu appointed to help in time of need. We are going to need many buckets of water brought up from the river and put on to boil. We will also need lots of wood to fuel the stove."

Leonardo saw everyone moving and preparing for what seemed like an epidemic of wounded that were about to arrive. Doctor Sherry hurried into the room with Lara following. Leonardo scrutinized her appearance. She looked very tired indeed. He would have to find a way to lighten her load. He would have all these women who were coming to help her do it on a regular basis.

Sherry walked up to Leonardo. "Lara briefly told me the situation. When can I expect these men?"

Leonardo replied, "The first should show up within ten or fifteen minutes. They are strung out in the jungle between here and the Black Death Camp. Cipriano said most of them have arrows in their legs. I have already sent the Ring Leaders to see to wood and water. I sent someone to get Connie, Paloma, Noemi and Ciba as extra help for you. What else can I do?"

"See if you can get someone to bring in some food. It's late and some of us haven't eaten since breakfast. Some terere would also be helpful. Would you have someone else set up more cots? I'll also need some men to hold down the injured men so they won't make their wounds worse by thrashing around as I remove the arrows. I don't know if I have enough anesthetic to numb all their wounds."

Sherry went over and examined Ted again. There was no change, which could be good or bad. He was not any worse, but he was not any better. She went out into the kitchen, poured herself a cup of tea and grabbed a piece of chipa left from breakfast. It was hard and dry but she dunked it in her tea. Dunking always improved the flavor. Sherry had always taken a tremendous amount of teasing over the years for her dunking habit until one day, while reading the Bible, she came across the verse in John that said, "Jesus dipped the sop."[44] Now, knowing Jesus was a dunker gave her a

50

scriptural basis to stand on. Unfortunately, He did not then eat it, but gave it to the traitor. She smiled, remembering the lighthearted arguments she and Daniel had had over that. She thought about it every time she dunked. In fact, how bad could it be if they named a company after it: "Dunkin Donuts"?

She could not afford to sit; thankfully, the cup of tea and chipa lifted her up. She went over to her medical supplies and began arranging the materials she would need. She already had two big basins of sterile water waiting, and numerous bandages, scalpels, needles, thread and other assorted paraphernalia needed for these types of injuries. She hoped that some of the injuries were superficial, but could not count on that. An arrow could do considerable damage to the surrounding tissue.

Lara came walking into the room with Ciba, Connie, Paloma and Noemi. Sherry encouraged them to get some hot tea and something to eat before the patients started rolling in. Paloma hugged Sherry and said, "I knew it would be a long tiresome afternoon and I brought a fresh plate of chipa and some fruit I had cut up. Let's all go have some before the invasion. I suggested to Leonardo that we make up several trays of food and pitchers of terere and juice for everyone, even the prisoners. We'll find someone else to distribute the food. We'll be too busy helping you with the injured."

Sherry looked at her friends and thanked God for them. Given the situation, she could not have expected better helpers. They all walked into the kitchen and helped themselves to the food. The fruit was sweet and juicy and the chipa was soft and tasty. It was a wonderful pick-me-up. They sat eating for a few minutes and then joined together in prayer, asking for God's strength and guidance for all they had to do. As they finished the prayer, the first two injured men came limping in, accompanied by two guards.

Connie had worked with Sherry on several occasions and

---

44 John 13:26

had been a good helper. Sherry hoped she would be up to the task of today's session. She would keep Connie as her assistant and let the other women do what they could for the rest of the men. She instructed them to let her know if any of them were bleeding heavily or lost consciousness.

The first man had attempted to doctor himself. He had managed to pull out the arrow, but the skin had torn and there was significant bleeding. His pulse was fast and weak and his blood pressure was low. Sherry realized he had lost a considerable amount of blood. After sewing up the wound, she administered a large dose of antibiotic. She told Ciba, "Lay him down and also give him plenty of fluids and whatever he's able to eat. Make sure he's able to chew and swallow. He's very weak from the blood loss and I don't want him to choke. Do the same for everyone else unless I tell you otherwise. They probably all have similar wounds."

Sherry went and removed her soiled gloves, washed her hands, and put on a new pair. She moved to the next man and continued with her examinations. This one needed the arrow removed, but fortunately it had gone through. She had four men come over to hold him while she cut off the head of the arrow and pulled it free. Even with the arrowhead off, it was still a painful procedure, and here also was a significant amount of bleeding. She wished she had a drug to slow it down, and a supply of blood to infuse if needed, but those were useless thoughts, and so she just continued to pray.

Thinking of that brought Tuvicha to mind. Why hadn't she thought of this earlier? Tuvicha was a shaman and medicine man and had a deep knowledge of plants and their medicinal qualities. He also had done more than his share of caring for the sick and injured over the years. His help would be invaluable.

She turned to Leonardo and asked him to send for Tuvicha. Sherry did not even have to explain. Leonardo understood at once and immediately sent one of the men to bring Tuvicha to the clinic.

Tuvicha walked in following the next patient. He brought with him his large medicine bag and a mortar and pestle. As he started brewing his various potions, the room took on the different smells of his assorted herbs. Some of them were pleasant and some, slightly noxious. Once brewed, the challenge would be getting the patients to drink them. Sherry didn't worry. She knew Tuvicha to be very persuasive.

Sherry removed her gloves and washed her hands after the last patient. They all had similar wounds that incapacitated them from walking, but were generally not life-threatening. Two had lost significant amounts of blood, but though weak, were stable.

Before taking a much needed rest, she went back to check on Ted again. Lara was a still beside him, holding his hand, which in itself was good medicine. His vitals remained stable and there was no swelling at the site of his injury. That also was a miracle. With serious head injuries the brain tends to swell. That alone could cause death and Sherry had no effective way to treat that. Thankfully the Heavenly Healer appeared to be on the job, for which she was exceedingly grateful.

The prisoner with the gunshot wound was stable, no signs of bleeding or infection. Jose was also up and about. Other than the small bandage, he appeared to have no other side effects, although he did have a headache.

Ciba took Sherry's arm, led her to a chair and gave her a cup of tea. Paloma then came over with a plate of food. There was fruit, but there was also some chicken. Paloma knew that Sherry needed some meat in her diet with all the work she did. Sherry nibbled on the food and waited for the phone call from Maine. It was late in the afternoon, but she was relishing the time it left her to just relax.

She thought of the people of the village, her village. If she had not felt that way before, she certainly did now. She belonged to this village and its people were her people. She smiled at the thought of all her friends and all her new converts. Then she remembered she was supposed to have a Bible study after breakfast.

Connie saw a shadow cross Sherry's face and asked her, "What's the matter Sherry? Are you in pain? Is everything alright?"

Sherry answered in disgust, "I failed to remember the Bible study this morning. We were supposed to have it after breakfast. With so much going on I just forgot. All those new Christians are depending on me too. How will they learn if I don't teach them?"

"Don't worry," Paloma answered. "Jeruti, Sol and Victoria, Connie's prayer partners, taught the Bible study. Connie alerted them when she heard what was happening. I can tell you there were sixty-five people in attendance and they all went away with a deeper knowledge of God."

Ciba spoke up, "You need to let people help you. You can't do it all. There are several people from the village who can teach that Bible study, but it's only you who is a doctor."

Sherry remembered what God had spoken to her this morning; learn to delegate. Sherry quietly asked God to forgive her for being disobedient, and also for the sin of pride, thinking only she could do it all. Sherry smiled at her friends. "You're right. It was probably good for them to lead the Bible study. I'm sure they did a wonderful job. I'll let them do tomorrow's also. Now I am going to go and try to get a little rest. Wake me if you need me."

CHAPTER NINE

The back room at the Lobster Pot was full. It was five o'clock and people had gathered there for many reasons, food and fellowship were obvious. The other reasons were prayer and the phone call that would be placed to Paraguay.

The people gathered were the northern contingent of the Quest. They were the prayer council. They had started out as the group who had stayed behind in Ogunquit, to pray and coordinate for those who had gone to Paraguay. They were Joe and Roberta Albright and Sylvia Jessup. It seemed as though it was months ago that the first phone call had been made to Paraguay, but in reality, it had been less than three weeks.

What started out as a team of three had morphed into twenty-five or more, depending on what night of the week it was. They had groups praying continually, twenty-four hours a day in the back room of the needlework shop. What had originally been a store room had been turned into a war room. Joe looked at his watch and stood up. The room quickly quieted and Joe spoke. "As all of you know, The Questers, as we are calling them, have just finished their second day out. They were told by God to sleep during the day and travel at night. We are now going to place a call to them, and then call Sherry, who stayed in the village along with Ted, Renato and Connie. They also need our prayers, because

55

they too are in the enemy's line of fire. Everyone quiet down now; I'm going to make the call."

The room was quickly blanketed with silence. Everyone wanted to hear the news. They wanted to hear if God showed up in a tangible way again, and if so, what He had said and done. The phone rang several times and then a familiar voice answered. "Hello Josh," Joe stated. "We are all gathered together at the Lobster Pot anxiously waiting to hear any news you might have for us. But first tell us, are you all well?"

Josh's voice came over the speaker phone loud and clear. It appeared that these satellite phones were a definite asset to this Quest. "We are all doing well. Our first night out was uneventful until we were at the end of our trek. Then, up ahead we saw a fire. We cautiously approached the clearing where it was burning. It was almost as if a camp had been prepared for us. Beside the fire was a large pile of wood. It lasted the rest of the day and provided our fire for cooking our dinner that evening." Josh went on to tell other small details of their first day. Then he told of their second night and of the jaguar that provided them with their meal tonight. Then Josh asked, "Is there anything we need to know from your group up north?"

Joe responded, "We have some important news for you. Haydon Carlton was being sent over to a psychiatric facility for observation. He somehow managed to escape. The police think he had some help. At this time they have no idea of where he is or what he is planning. This is just FYI. I can't believe that he would try to leave the country and be a threat to all of you, but he's crazy. He's obsessed with Bekah and with that crucifix. Roberta and I took a trip into New York and went by his shop while we were there. It has a sign on the front door, 'Closed until Further Notice'. When we returned home we contacted Sergeant Hathaway to see if he knew that, or if he had any new information for us.

"You're not going to believe what he told us. Haydon had

a large secret room in back of his store. It was accessed through a bookcase that opened into it. In it were millions of dollars of art that he had obtained illegally. Everything was cataloged with the name of the original owner, date stolen, and value of the piece. There were over two hundred pieces in the collection, and several of them were valued at over a million dollars each. From what I understand, some of these pieces were stolen over fifty years ago. It looks like this was a family business."

Carlos spoke up then, "I've been with Haydon for over fifteen years. I knew of the collection, but had never seen it. Haydon referred to it as his inheritance. Unfortunately, I helped him obtain several of those pieces." Then Carlos turned to Bekah and confessed, "Bekah, I don't know how to apologize for having wronged you. There are no words to say to make it any easier. I was the one who broke into your house to find the jeweled crucifix. Words just don't express my regret for my actions. I don't even feel worthy to ask your forgiveness. If you want me to, I'll leave and go back to the village. I think I would be able to find it during the day."

The blood drained from Bekah's face as she took in what Carlos had just said to her. Immediately anger and bitterness flooded her mind.

At a distance, Satan smiled. These people were no different than any others. Wrong them, and their emotions rose up; they took offense. With a door now open to him, Satan next loosed resentment. These emotions were a group that fed off each other. As they settled in, he launched his favorite weapons, unforgiveness and anger. Most people were no match for these four.

Bekah raised her voice, crying out, "Carlos, how could you even have come with us knowing what you did. My house was demolished, all my belongings were destroyed. I was devastated. Nothing you say can make up for what you've done. You're right; you shouldn't be here with us. Every time I look at you I'm going to be sick over what you did to me. You took away my hopes, dreams and memories." She turned her back on him. "I don't ever want to see you again," she said through clenched teeth.

Bekah stood there fuming as these emotions did their work. She continued her rant, throwing Carlos' sin in his face over and over. "This was an easy assignment," Satan thought. The demons wielding those weapons were already preening at the thought of their reward. Then Josh and Manu came toward Bekah. She did not want to hear what they had to say. She stood there livid, thinking she had every justification to be angry. Satan's smile broadened. Justification usually won him the battle.

Josh took her arm and turned her toward him. "Bekah, you have every right to be angry, but the anger, bitterness, resentment and unforgiveness you're experiencing are an attack of Satan. They are sins and you cannot let them rule your feelings and emotions."[45]

Bekah stopped. She heard Josh agree with her. She did have every right to be angry. Then she took in the rest of his statement. Bitterness, resentment and unforgiveness were sins. The awareness of that started seeping into her mind.

Satan stood watching as his forces wavered. He sent in reinforcements. Self-pity arrived on the scene. "I can't believe this is happening to me. So much has been taken from me already. I should never have come on this Quest," Bekah moaned. Again Satan smiled, confident in his victory.

"Bekah," Josh said in a stern voice, "stop and listen to what you are saying. Remember, Satan is out there like a roaring lion, trying to make this Quest fail. We can't let him do that.[46] You need to recognize where this attack is coming from. It's alright to be angry, Jesus was angry, but He didn't allow anger to lead Him into sin.[47] You cannot let your anger turn to sin. Bitterness, anger, and resentment can fester and become a wound in your spirit. They

---

[45] Galatians 5:19-21
[46] 1 Peter 5:8

can even cause sickness in your body. Self-pity weakens you. You feel that everything that happens is someone else's fault and you take no action to fight, improve or change. But the worst thing you are feeling right now is unforgiveness. Remember that the Bible says if you don't forgive, then God can't forgive you."[48]

"Josh, can you give me some time, I need to think about all this?"

Josh knew this was an important battle and they could not afford to lose it. He told Bekah, "First let us pray for you."

Reluctantly Bekah agreed. Josh and Manu took her hands and began to pray. Manu had been praying all the time while Josh was talking to Bekah. Now he spoke what he felt the Holy Spirit would have him say. "Bekah," he said passionately, "you are my sister. We have just found each other, but I feel as close to you as if I had known you all my life. I heard you speak about being captured by Akeem, and the struggles and injuries you endured during that capture. I saw you struggle to forgive him when he first made himself known to us. Then Renato talked to you and showed you how important it is to forgive. As hard as it is, you must repent for unforgiveness and ask God to help you forgive Carlos. He is not the same man who broke into your home and destroyed it. All his past is behind him now. He is a new creation."[49]

Manu now closed his eyes and raised his voice for all to hear, those members of the Quest, those of Heaven who watched over them, and Satan and his forces, who sought to defeat them, halt the Quest, and exterminate all those involved in it. "Father in Heaven, You know all of us. You see our actions and hear our thoughts. Help us all to be pleasing to You. Help us to change where we need to change. Help us to say what You would have us say and do what You would have us do. Search every part of us

---

[47] John 2:13-17
[48] Matthew 6:14-15
[49] 2 Corinthians 5:17

so that You can show us where we need to change.[50] Help Bekah now with the sin that is harassing her. Give her the strength she needs to overcome it.[51] Thank you for everything you do for us. In Jesus' Name we pray. Amen"

The three of them stood there for a time with their heads bowed, letting the Holy Spirit minister to them. Finally Bekah raised her head and looked over at Carlos. He was sitting on a rock all by himself at the edge of the clearing. Bekah saw how alone and isolated he was and realized that she was the one who had shut him out. She had excluded him from the group by her words and actions. His sins against her had been forgiven at the cross. Her sins were still in play, giving place to the enemy and allowing a door of entry to him. She knew it was up to her to heal the breach. When unforgiveness was given a place in your life, it created a gap that grew into a chasm and swallowed you up. Bekah knew this and still she hesitated.

The heavenly protectors stood by helpless, unable to respond to the situation because of Bekah's unforgiveness. Bekah grabbed Josh's hand and cried out to him, "I know I need to forgive him, but I just can't. I don't have the strength. I'm tormented by the memory of what he did and all the chaos that ensued because of his actions."[52]

Suddenly God spoke, in a Voice so loud that it brought her to her knees. "Daughter, you bring this torment upon yourself. Unforgiveness brings torment both to the one who withholds the forgiveness, and to the one who is unforgiven. Look at the torment you have brought Carlos. I forgave him and set him free, but you have burdened him again with the results of his sin. I have forgiven the sins of the world, can you not find it in your heart to forgive this one man his sins. I gave you the ability to forgive; all

---

[50] Psalm 139:23-24
[51] Genesis 4:6-7
[52] Matthew 18:23-35

you have to do is act on it."

Bekah opened her eyes and looked around her. Nothing had changed. Josh and Manu were still next to her, the rest of the men were standing close by, and Carlos was still sitting by himself on a rock with his head in his hands.

What she could not see were the heavenly forces poised to act, and the demonic forces reveling in their victory. But God knew the heart of His daughter. He knew that in her heart, good would triumph over evil.

Bekah rose to her feet and turned toward Carlos. Suddenly the celebrating stopped and the hoard from Hell held their collective breaths. With her heart set, Bekah took her first step toward Carlos and forgiveness. Immediately, the heavenly forces attacked, and Satan and his minions fled back into the darkness.

With tears streaming down her face, Bekah walked over and laid her hand on Carlos' shoulder. He looked up, his face also awash with tears. Bekah reached for his hands and spoke words of forgiveness over Carlos. Then she completed the transaction and asked for his forgiveness.

Carlos stood up, the burden of guilt lifted by Bekah's words. Bekah stepped forward and hugged him. She said, "Now you are my brother. I will never look at you as anything else."

Carlos stood there speechless. Words would not come; only tears, but these tears had now been transformed into tears of joy. He said, "I once had a sister who was killed. I loved her with all my heart. I now see you as my sister and will do all I can to love and protect you and help in any way I can to fulfill the Quest we are on."

They both turned back to the rest of the group who stood waiting. Bekah and Carlos walked back toward them. She apologized to the group for her unforgiveness and any problem it may have caused. She asked that they finish preparing their meal and get ready to march through the night.

Suddenly they heard a loud voice say "Hey, wait a minute," and remembered Joe was still on the phone. Daniel spoke up and said, "Sorry Joe, we forgot about you. We had a little spiritual housekeeping we needed to take care of. This will help to remind us to ask God daily to search our hearts and keep sin far from us. Was there anything else you needed to share? If not, call Sherry and tell her we are fine. We will call her in the morning before we go to sleep."

Having finished one phone call they prepared for the next. Joe dialed and Renato answered. After Joe shared the news from the Questers, he inquired, "How are things going down there?" Renato gave him an abbreviated version of everything that had gone on, from the escape and recapture of the prisoners, to Ted's injury.

"Wow!" Joe exclaimed. "That's a lot happening, and a serious amount of pressure on Sherry. How is she holding up? Is she getting enough rest?"

Renato replied, "One thing this is teaching her is how to delegate. She has several helpers who have shared the load with her. The only thing now that is causing her some concern is Ted. He's been unconscious all day and I can see she is worried. We are all praying. Please keep your people praying."

"We will," Joe said. "One last thing; Daniel said tell to Sherry they are all fine and he will call in the morning."

"Will do," Renato answered. "Say good night to all."

CHAPTER TEN

JUNE 23
THE VILLAGE

Sherry knew she needed rest. She left word to call her if anything changed or if Daniel called. She knew Renato had already talked with the people from Maine, and would wake her if the need arose. She fell asleep immediately, such was her exhaustion.

The long hard day drew to a close. Everyone had been given food and drink, bandages were checked and vital signs were taken as needed. The prisoners were all in one room and tied so that no one could move around. Double watches were placed on those prisoners who were mobile.

Ted's condition remained unchanged, and Lara had not moved from his side. The night was drawing to a close with dawn just an hour or two away. Renato sat in the corner of the large room, keeping watch on all the activity going on. He had been watching Ted and Lara for the past hour and observed her tears. He got up to walk over to her, hoping to bring her some comfort. He was thankful of his ability to speak Guarani, because Lara had spoken very little English.

Renato pulled over a chair and sat down next to her. "Has Ted's condition changed at all since Doctor Sherry worked on him?"

Lara looked up with a tear-stained face, her eyes red-rimmed from crying, and just shook her head. "I don't think his God hears my prayers. I have been begging Him all day and night

63

to make Ted well and He has not answered me."

Renato took her hand. "Lara, God hears everyone's prayers, but what moves Him is faith.[53] Do you believe in God? Do you believe that Jesus is His Son and died for your sins? Have you asked Him to forgive you for them? Do you trust Him?"

More tears began to fall. "How can I trust Him when I don't even know Him?" Lara sobbed, her heart broken by grief. "I have listened to some of the Bible studies, but I was always confused. I had so many questions, and then so much happened so fast. Now Ted is badly injured. What if he dies and I never get to tell him that I care for him?"

Renato spoke softly to Lara. "Lara, would you like to pray with me? Would you like to ask my God to be your God? It says in the Bible that He gives all of us a measure of faith when we ask Him into our hearts.[54] He will give you the faith to believe in Him and then to pray for Ted. After you ask Him to be your God, He then adopts you and makes you part of His family.[55] Would you like to do that? Would you like to have the faith to pray to God, to believe that He will hear and answer your prayers, and that Ted will recover?"

Lara looked up at Renato, her eyes brimming and her face wet with tears, and nodded. She spoke with hesitation. "I've been watching all that has happened in our village. Even before all of you arrived, strange and wonderful things had been happening. Noemi came back to life after having her baby. There was so much blood and she was so still, but Doctor Sherry prayed to your God and He heard her and breathed life back into Noemi. Ciba received a terrible injury from the wild boar, and God gave Doctor Sherry the skill to sew her up. If I ask your God into my heart, will He listen to my prayer also? Will He heal Ted?"

Renato smiled and responded, "As I said, that's where faith

---

[53] Hebrews 11:6
[54] Romans 12:3
[55] Ephesians 1:5

comes in. God rewards those who persistently seek Him.[56] He responds to those who come to Him for answers, and He works things out for them when they pray according to His will.[57] Lara, will you pray with me and ask God to be your God and His Son, Jesus, to come and live in your heart?"

Lara gripped Renato's hand and replied, "I want to serve this wonderful and awesome God. I know that my old gods did not seem to do anything to help me or any of the people from my village; all we did was sacrifice to them. They certainly never healed anyone."

Renato looked into Lara's eyes. They reflected fear and hope. Renato knew that when Lara asked Jesus into her heart the fear would leave.[58] "Repeat after me," Renato said gently.

"Heavenly Father, please forgive me for all my sins. I forgive anyone who has wronged me." Renato waited for Lara to repeat the prayer. He looked up at her and observed her hesitation. He waited for her response.

Finally the silence became uncomfortable to her and she spoke out belligerently. "There are some people I don't want to forgive. They hurt me. I will ask forgiveness for my sins, but I will not forgive my mother and father. Their constant yelling and shouting at each other and at me, hurt me terribly. That is why I did not want to marry. I did not want to be put in a position where someone could do that to me.

"Theirs was an arranged marriage. Most couples from that type of marriage come to love and respect each other, but my parents never did. Their animosity grew year by year. I had to live with that every day of my life."

Renato sighed. He prayed, "Holy Spirit, help me minister to this young woman. Give me the right words to show her that her

---

[56] Hebrews 11:6
[57] Romans 8:28
[58] 1 John 4:18

unforgiveness is hurting her."

Renato sat back and looked at Lara. This was a key issue, and Satan put up one of his biggest roadblocks to foil God's plans and prevent the Holy Spirit from bringing the gift of forgiveness into her heart. As Satan screamed in his frustration, Renato spoke quietly, yet forcefully. "The Bible has many things to tell us. It is God speaking to us. The most important thing to know and believe is that God sent His only Son, Jesus, into this world to pay the price for all our sins.[59] It says that though He was not a sinner, He became sin so that we might be saved from sin.[60] He was crucified, died, and was buried. But God raised Him from the dead.[61]

"One other very important thing God asks is for us to forgive those who have wronged us.[62] He also says that if we don't forgive others, He will not forgive us.[63] Lara, do you want to be forgiven of your sins?"

He stared at her with piercing eyes. This was very important. Her salvation was hanging in the balance. As he watched, he could see the inner turmoil, the battle going on within her. But the Holy Spirit was also working in her, melting away her unforgiveness, helping her to forgive her parents. As she continued taking steps toward God, He took steps toward her.[64]

Lara began to weep, and tears streamed down her face. Renato closed his eyes and continued to pray for Lara. He could only imagine the battle going on for her soul. Satan did not let go easily. He groaned within himself, experiencing the hurt and frustration she was feeling and fighting in the spirit with all of his strength.[65] At last Lara gasped aloud, "I forgive them."

Renato watched as the Holy Spirit made a transformation

---

[59] John 3:16
[60] 2 Corinthians 5:21
[61] 1 Peter 1:21
[62] Matthew 6:12
[63] Luke 6:37
[64] James 4:8

take place. Just as a caterpillar is transformed into a butterfly, so Lara was being transformed from a sinner into a child of God. Her copious tears of sadness turned into tears of joy. Renato watched the miracle take place. What an amazing thing to witness.

Lara looked at Renato, her face shining like an angel, and said, "It is a wonderful thing. I feel like a new person."

Renato laughed, "You are. You went from a sinner to a child of God. There's no greater miracle."

Lara laughed, and then sobered. She looked over at Ted. "Can we pray for Ted now?"

Renato took her hand and laid it next to his on Ted's chest. He told Lara the Bible said that if one person can chase away one thousand enemies, then two will chase away ten thousand. She nodded and then began to pray. "My new Father, Who is God, I did not ask my old gods for anything because they were not kind, but I ask You, Who are kind, to heal Ted and make him well. Renato is here with me and we are chasing away any bad things keeping Ted from being healed. We will sit here and watch You work. Thank You."

---

[65] Romans 8:26-27

CHAPTER ELEVEN

JUNE 24

THE VILLAGE

Renato and Lara sat there watching Ted's chest rise and fall with each breath. For the first ten minutes there was no discernable difference. Then Ted groaned. They looked at each other, not knowing whether that was a good sign or not, but they trusted that God was answering their prayers.[68] Suddenly Ted put his hand up to his head and groaned again. Then he opened his eyes and stared at Renato and Lara. "Why is my head bandaged? What happened to me?" he asked with a puzzled look on his face.

Ted rolled to his side and attempted to sit up but Renato stopped him. "Don't get up yet, Ted. Let Sherry look at you first. You've been unconscious for a day."

Ted stared at Renato in confusion. "Ted, you were shot yesterday morning and had a fractured skull. Sherry treated it the best she could with the limited supplies she had available. We all prayed and trusted God to heal you. Thank God He has answered our prayers." Renato continued, "I'm going to send for Sherry. She will want to check you out before you get up and move around."

Renato turned to Lara and asked her to go wake up Sherry. "I hate to wake her," he said, "but it's almost morning and she would probably be getting up in a short time." Then he turned back to Ted. "Lara has sat by your side all day and night. She also ac-

---

[68] Isaiah 55:8-11

69

cepted Jesus as her Savior, and her first prayer was to ask God to heal you."

Before Ted could respond, Sherry hurried into the room. She stared at Ted for a moment, taking in his appearance. He was pale, but his eyes were clear. Sherry had no experience dealing with this type of injury. But, though the years, in addition to delivering babies, she had performed a few appendectomies, set a multitude of broken bones, lanced numerous boils, pulled hundreds of teeth, stitched miles of wounds, and even amputated a big toe. She helped bring life into the world, and comforted those who were departing this world, praying and encouraging them in their journey. Sometimes it was important just being there, holding a hand and speaking soft words. But dealing with Ted's injury was a whole new experience, and she had felt intimidated because of her lack of training.

Sherry first asked Ted if he was dizzy or nauseous. Then she looked at Ted's eyes to see if the pupils were equal in size and reactive to light. Finally she told him to squeeze her hands, checking his grip to judge if there was a difference between his two hands. So far he had passed all the tests. Sherry then removed the bandage on his head. There was no drainage or fresh bleeding. She was stunned to see that there was no swelling, not even a bruise. She gently palpated the area, and everything felt normal.

Sherry wondered briefly if she had made a mistake. Did Ted really have a skull fracture or only a concussion? Then she put her doubts aside. Whatever the case, the Great Healer had again taken a hand and used a gift of healing, whether His or hers did not matter. If she played a small part in Ted's recovery, it was because God was leading and guiding her.

Stepping back, Sherry asked Ted, "Sit up slowly and tell me how you feel."

Ted sat cautiously, still holding Sherry's hands. He took a breath or two and then stood, saying "It's really remarkable. With everything that Renato told me has happened, all I have is a pretty good headache, kind of like I experienced in the past with a bad hangover. Boy, am I glad those days are gone. Just give me some Tylenol and I'll be fine. I promise I'll take it easy this morning."

Sherry smiled. With Ted recovering, a huge weight had been lifted off her shoulders. She knew she shouldn't worry, but the magnitude of the current situation sometimes overwhelmed her. Before the day progressed any further she went back into her bedroom and shut the door. She knelt down at the side of the bed and began to pray. "Heavenly Father, I repent to You for letting my mind rest on the problems surrounding me instead of putting my trust in You. Help me to think on good things.[69] Help me to remember all that You have done, not just for me, but for all of us who are in this village. I know that Your grace even extends to those who have left here and are traveling in the jungle, being led by Your Holy Spirit to a place they have never been before.[70] With every problem that comes up, You always have an answer. Help me to thank You for that answer, even if I don't see it. Father, help my faith."

Immediately a Scripture came to mind. Faith comes by hearing the Word of God.[71] Sherry remembered that a morning Bible study had been started, but with everything that was happening, it had been neglected. Sherry thanked God for His forgiveness and His Word. She went back out into the clinic with new resolve.

She looked over and saw Ted propped up on two pillows, talking with Renato and Lara. The three of them were smiling broadly. Then she turned and saw Maria and Panambi sitting on the floor playing with Hombrecito, Maria's little puppy. Panambi was the only patient left in the clinic, other than the men from the Black Death Camp. Everyone who had been injured from the village that had been attacked by the warring tribe of the north had

---

[69] Philippians 4:6-8
[70] Genesis 12:1
[71] Romans 10:17

left the clinic. They had all been adopted by different families of the village. New homes would be built for them as supplies and labor became available. The people in her village were caring and generous. It would not be long before the new homes were completed and everyone was settled. Only Panambi's situation remained a question.

She walked over to examine Ted again. He was healing rapidly. There was only a scratch on his head where the bullet had hit him. Sherry smiled and thought, "Learning to trust God allowed you to see miracles."

Sherry turned to Lara and asked her if she would go and spread the word that a Bible study would be held after breakfast. Lara smiled broadly and her eyes sparkled with delight. "Oh Doctor Sherry, I am so glad to hear that. Early this morning I prayed with Renato and asked Jesus to come into my heart. Then I prayed and asked God to heal Ted, and He did!" She threw her arms around Sherry and hugged her. "Our God is so wonderful," she said with excitement in her voice and a radiant smile on her face.

Sherry smiled too. She was glad to see another person snatched from the hands of Satan and received into the loving arms of the Father. Sherry looked back over the last few weeks and marveled at all the new members of God's family. Literally, the whole village had become Christians.

Walking into the kitchen Sherry saw Paloma and her helpers Ciba, Noemi, and Connie preparing breakfast. It was a big job because not only were there the normal amount of people to feed, but now there were fifteen prisoners and several others who were participating in the Quest in one form or another. "Good morning everyone," she said as she came through the doorway. They all turned and spoke a greeting. Sitting down, Sherry poured herself some terere and grabbed a chipa.

Before she ate her breakfast, Sherry asked Connie if she would also get the word out that there would be a Bible study

72

shortly. It would be held outdoors in the meeting area to accommodate everyone. She already knew she would teach about the peace of God that, in the midst of troubles, can still rule your mind and heart.[72] Sherry went back into the clinic to check on the fifteen wounded prisoners, and anyone else needing her attention.

Turning around she saw Renato coming toward her and remembered his dream. Sherry thought that maybe she should ask Renato if he would like to share the dream with everyone at the Bible study. Dreams appeared to be playing an important role in their lives in recent days, and she didn't want to ignore this one.

Renato greeted her. "How are you doing Sherry? You look rested. Are all your patients doing well?"

"They are Renato. I had a good night's sleep and feel energized. In fact, I was so excited this morning; I thought I felt the baby move. I know it's a little early, but sometimes things can be miscalculated. I may be further along than I thought." Sherry smiled and put her hand on the small swelling that was making itself known.

Renato smiled also. With all the problems surrounding them, it was nice to have good things to look forward to. Sherry took Renato's arm as they walked to the meeting area. "Renato, I was wondering, would you be willing to share your dream with the village?"

Renato's eyes sparkled as he smiled at her. "I was just going to ask you that. Some of the village may feel left out, especially the new tribe we are adopting. This is not a secret thing, I feel everyone should know. In fact, I don't know what kind of impact it might have for those on the Quest. There may be ramifications to it we don't see. I'm wondering if I should go and catch up with them to tell them. I know I can tell them over the satellite phone, but I have this urge to go that I didn't have before. Plus I made a promise to Bekah that I would guard her with my life. I can't do that very well from here."

---

[72] Philippians 4:6-8

"I see your point. We'll talk that over later. For now, just tell about the dream. Then share anything you feel God is telling you. Try to keep it around sixty minutes. Everyone has additional work to do and we don't want to add to their burden, although I know that God can ease all our burdens. Forget the time constraint. Just say what needs saying. Everything that needs to get done will get done; it always does."

As they approached the meeting area Sherry observed that if the meeting area had walls, they would be bursting. Everyone had come for the Bible study. They were hungry to hear God's Word and understand it. These strangers, who had been with them for only a short time, brought them this wonderful gift. Every time they heard it they still hungered for more.

Instead of Doctor Sherry, they saw Renato, one of the newcomers, step forward. Most of the people felt an affinity towards him because he had been born in Paraguay. They had heard parts of his story, but they could only speculate on the whole tale. Rumor and gossip had a way of twisting the truth and they were anxious to hear what he had to say.

Sherry told Renato, "I don't think I need to introduce you. Most of the people know who you are. You can introduce yourself."

Before Renato could say anything, Tuvicha stepped forward to address the crowd. He turned to his friend and said "Renato, please let me say something before you begin."

Renato nodded, not knowing what else to do. He did not know what Tuvicha was going to say, and only hoped it would not cause confusion.

Tuvicha began, "Renato wants to tell you about a dream he had recently. As we all know dreams can be important. I believe this dream is very important. Earlier, he told several of us part of his dream. In describing it, we determined that Renato was dreaming of his past, and that he and his father came to live here, in our village, when he was around ten years old. I tell you this so you will

74

all realize that he is not just a friend, but a member of this village, part of our family."

An old man with a stick hobbled up to the front of the crowd. His name was Salvatore. He spoke in a strong voice. "Listen to me. When Renato and his father came to this village, they stayed with me and my family. His father was like a son to me. He replaced the son I had lost to sickness. Renato was like my grandson. Renato, why did you not come to me and let me welcome you home?" The old man wiped the tears from his face and searched Renato's face for answers.

Renato went forward and took the frail old man in his arms. "Grandfather," he answered, "when we came here, I did not re- member. I knew I was born in Paraguay, but I did not know where in Paraguay I had been born. When I had the dream, it showed me the story of my past. I used to question my father about our past, but he would not answer me. I determined to let the present guide my life and if God wanted me to know the past, He would show me. Well it appears He wants me to know now; He has shown me in a dream."

Renato turned back and faced the crowd. He spoke in a strong voice as he addressed them. "My father and I came from a village far to the north. It was a wicked place. It was the tribe that attacked Arandu's village."

The people drew back in shock. They knew of this village and the horrors they caused throughout the northern area. How could someone from there come to live in their village?

Renato sensed their unease and spoke up. "Please let me tell you my story." He looked around at the people surrounding him. Some he had established friendships with, others were just acquaintances. Yet even in such a short time they were important to him. "When I was a young boy, I remember playing with my friends every day. Then they stopped being my friends. My mother and father had no more friends. The village turned its back on us.

75

A short time later my mother died and it got worse. Every time the men went out to make war, on their return, my father was in more trouble. Our situation was very bad. My father was not asked by the other hunters to go out hunting for food anymore. In our village everyone shared, but now, not with us. My father went out by himself, but was not able to hunt successfully because he could not travel any distance from the village, and there was no longer any large game close by. Finally, one night my father woke me and told me we were leaving. He said that he had had a dream and this new God had told him to take me and leave our village. He was told to go south. I had many questions, but he told me to be silent and that he would answer my questions later.

"After telling me why we were leaving, we took a boat and began our trip down the river. In my dream, God showed me arriving at your village in the midst of a great storm. I was injured when a large tree was hit by lightning and fell on me. Last night we had a great storm. A loud clap of thunder awakened me and all the memories of my past flooded back into my consciousness. I woke up and remembered everything that had been shrouded in mystery.

"My father and I stayed in your village for several years, but my father was not happy. He had lost his capacity to love. There was a Christian Missionary who lived here. My father spent a significant amount of time with him and became a Christian. I did also. The Missionary found a couple in the United States who would sponsor us, but we needed to pay for our own tickets. That's when we left the village and moved to Asuncion to get jobs to earn money for passage. Normally it would have taken years, but my father worked long hours on the docks. He was able to save for our transportation to the United States.

"Growing up I realized so much happened that I didn't remember. When I had the courage to ask questions, my father would not answer me. 'The past is gone,' he would say. 'Leave it alone.' Finally, I thought to myself, I don't want to end up like him.

While we lived in Asuncion, all he did was work, come home, and then sleep. The only other thing he did was go to church on Sunday. He liked church and liked the Pastor. The Pastor taught us both English in preparation for us going to the United States. After arriving in the state of Maine I met Miss Sara, Miss Bekah's grandmother. Miss Bekah had not even been born at that time. It seems as though God has had a plan for us through all these years, and it is only now coming to pass."

The people stood there in silence, still stunned by this revelation. Then an old woman came forward. She was small and frail and one of the young men helped her. She spoke quietly to the young man. He nodded and then spoke to the crowd. "My grandmother wants you to know that she too remembers this man. When he was a young boy he would help her by gathering firewood and hauling water from the river. She was a widow and had been injured early in her life. She could not walk easily. She says he would come and check on her every day. She was very sad when he and his father left the village."

Tuvicha stepped forward again. "When Renato told some of us of this dream, I told them that I remembered that young boy. I was still apprentice to the old shaman, but he allowed me to deal with minor injuries and mix potions. After determining that Renato was not seriously injured by the tree, he allowed me to make him herbal drinks to strengthen him. I watched him grow into a fine young man before he and his father left."

That final confirmation of Renato was all the people needed. They were all so new and excited in their faith; this just appeared to be another thing that God had worked out for all of them. They didn't know what Renato was going to do, but if God's hand was on it, it had to be good. Slowly the group broke up to go about the chores of the day.

Renato walked over to Ted, Lara and Sherry. He addressed Sherry. "I want to talk to you about going after the group on the

Quest. Since having this dream, I feel strongly that I should follow them. I told Bekah I would guard her with my life, and as I said, I can't do that from here."

Before he could go on Ted spoke up. "Renato, that's just how I feel. I also promised Bekah that I would never forsake her the way I did when we were married. I think we should both go."

Sherry interrupted, "Hold on both of you. The group has been walking two nights. How will you catch up to them? How will you find them? Neither one of you is a tracker or hunter. How would you survive?"

Ted answered first. "Aren't we supposed to be listening to God, hearing His Voice, and obeying? Aren't we supposed to trust Him?"

Sherry smiled. "You're right Ted. Again I let my mind rule my thoughts instead of my spirit.[73] You would think that with all God has done here I would be quick to trust Him, but I keep falling into the trap of trying to do everything guided by my own power and intellect instead of His.

Renato encouraged Sherry. "Don't be so hard on yourself. Even Paul had trouble with those same issues. Thankfully, the Bible tells us that if we confess our sins He is faithful to forgive us and wash them away."[74]

"That's right. So I'm going to trust that you both heard from God. Now we can take steps to get you both on your way. Let's go talk to Leonardo. He will know what to do. You can't go on your own. You need a hunter and tracker to help you find the way. You will make up some time by traveling during the day. I'm sure traveling at night slows the other group down. Let's go back to the compound to look for him. Ciba is there in the kitchen helping Paloma with all the food preparation. There has been so much to do with all the added mouths to feed. Leonardo has been taking special

---

[73] Romans 12:1-2
[74] 1 John 1:9

care of her ever since she was injured by the wild boar. She has also healed miraculously and has been a big help in this present situation. Not only did God heal her body, but He seems to have invigorated their marriage."

Sure enough, when they walked into the kitchen Ciba was at the table cutting up fruit and vegetables, and Leonardo was standing behind her with his hand on her shoulder. He had such a tender expression on his face Sherry hated to interrupt, but Leonardo looked up and motioned them over.

"Renato, you did a wonderful job of sharing your story. I'm so glad the people received you. Sometimes we can all be judgmental. Have you seen Jose and Mehdi this morning? With so much happening I've lost tract of them."

"No, I haven't seen them. Are they helping to guard the prisoners?"

Leonardo replied, "No they're not. I just went back there to see how everything was going. The prisoners have all been fed and the guards have just been changed. There are five guards now. They are more than able to handle the situation."

"Do you think we should send someone to look for them," Renato asked? "After all, Jose was injured yesterday. I don't recall seeing him when I got up this morning."

"You're right. Let me send someone out to look around for them." Leonardo turned and motioned to one of the men standing nearby and sent him out to look for Mehdi and Jose.

"Leonardo," Renato began, "Ted and I need your help. Since having the dream, I feel that for some reason, God is now asking me to go on this Quest. Ted also feels the need to go. I know this seems unusual, but would you be willing to send someone to help us find the others?"

"This isn't any more unusual than everything else that has been happening around here. If you feel that God is asking this of you, I will do everything I can to help. When do you want to leave?"

Leonardo asked.

"As soon as possible," Renato answered, "but I don't want to leave you shorthanded. We need to talk to Jose and Mehdi. They would be left as the only two men who can handle a gun. I don't know how serious a situation that would be for you. These prisoners are not badly incapacitated. They may still have thoughts of trying to escape."

Just then the man Leonardo sent to look for Jose and Mehdi came back with them. Jose and Mehdi were smiling as they walked up to all of them. "I have been on the satellite phone with Isaac Klein. They have been on the river since before dawn. They will be here in less than an hour. I don't know what they are going to do with all these prisoners, but I'm glad it's not my responsibility. I hope they have some kind of plan."

Renato replied, "I do too, because we won't be here. Ted and I are going out to join the group that went out on the Quest. We both feel that for some reason, God now wants us on the Quest. We asked Leonardo if he had someone he could send with us to help. Leonardo, have you thought of someone yet?"

"Yes, I have just the person for the job, young Miguel. He is the grandson of the old woman you helped when you lived here."

Sherry broke in, "That's a wonderful choice. Daniel and I know him well. He and his grandmother were some of our first converts. Do you have someone who can take care of his grandmother? I know he wouldn't want to leave her alone."

Leonardo smiled, "That won't be a problem. She is loved by everyone. There will be many volunteers to fill that position." Leonardo again sent a man out to bring Miguel to them; then he asked the women to put together three packs with food and various supplies for Renato, Ted and Miguel.

Miguel walked in and made his way over to Leonardo. Leonardo told him the plan and asked if he would be willing to go. Miguel replied, "This is an important thing. It is not just you who needs me to do this, but God needs me. Since you will have my grandmother taken care of, I will go and tell her and put a bag together for travel. When do we leave?"

Sherry smiled. Miguel was so excited to be doing something for God. She knew he was in his teens when he first became a Christian. He still had the same enthusiasm as a new Christian. She thought, "We should all have that enthusiasm, but we let the cares of the world become a burden to us and oftentimes rob us of our joy. We could all learn a lesson from this young man."

"Miguel," Sherry said. "Don't worry about your pack; just get a few changes of clothes. Leonardo is having the women put together packs. You will leave after mid-day meal."

Jose spoke up, "Once Isaac gets here the three of you ought to be good to go. I know you have two days to make up, but God is in control of this whole project and He knows what He is doing. Maybe He will show you a shortcut."

Everyone laughed at what appeared to be a joke, but all were cognizant of the fact that God could do just that. They would follow the trail of the first group. It should be easy to follow because there were so many of them traveling together. Those facts alone would hasten their journey.

As they were finishing lunch, word came that two boats were speeding up the river. Ted and Renato stood up and called to Miguel to get his pack. They wanted to be on their way before Isaac arrived. They did not want him interfering with their plans. Sherry understood what they were doing and said a quick goodbye. "Don't worry. I'll explain to Leonardo why you left so quickly. We will be praying for all of you as you follow God's plan."

The three of them took a back path to the river to avoid the crowd awaiting the boats. They had five or six good hours of sunlight left to close the distance separating them from the first group.

CHAPTER TWELVE

JUNE 24
THE QUESTERS

Dawn was approaching. The eastern sky was brightening and the night was ending. The twelve Questers had had a quiet night. Nothing had disturbed their march. They were now in unfamiliar territory, and the only landmark they had was the river. Some wondered why God had not chosen men from the attacked village to go on this Quest, but for the most part, they trusted Him. A few of the young men raised questions, but they did not cause any discord among the group.

Everyone was tired, but certain things had to be done before they could rest. They came upon a clearing that appeared just right to make camp. There was some deadfall nearby they could gather for firewood to cook their evening meal. The young men would set out several snares that would hopefully supply the meat for their dinner. But first, before beginning any other tasks, they all knelt and thanked God for His protection, and for leading and guiding them in their Quest.

Manu assigned Maitie and Philippe to set out several snares apiece. With all the walking, their appetites had increased. They needed more than four or five small animals. Mario and Giancarlo went to get the firewood. They needed quite a bit of that also. Not only did they need it for cooking, but also for boiling water to fill their canteens and to wash their utensils. Axel was sent down to the river with the two pots to get water.

Everyone did his job quickly and cheerfully, except Axel. His job at the village had also been to carry water for Doctor Sherry, and she used a tremendous amount of it. He thought it unfair that he had to get the hard job, while everyone else had the easy ones. He did not grumble out loud, but the feeling of being put upon and treated unfairly nagged at him, especially since he was the oldest of the group of young men on the Quest. He felt that he should have been accepted into manhood and not still be treated as a child. He would find a way to show everyone that he was a man, deserving of that status. He was too old and mature to be doing these childish chores. He smiled to himself and prayed that God would show him a way to display his talents and be recognized as much better at his tasks than these other boys. He was unaware that his thoughts and feelings were obvious to the elders of the village; that immaturity was one of the reasons he had not been granted the status of a warrior/hunter.

Bekah followed a distance behind Axel to the river. She waited until he had gone back to camp before she attempted to wash some of the grime of the trail off. She daydreamed of a large tub full of hot water. She sat there and thought about it for a few minutes, then laughed at herself. "Silly girl," she said. "Learn to appreciate what you have. Be content. Paul said that whether he had lack or plenty he was content. He knew God would take care of him, and she knew God would take care of her."[75]

Sitting down and resting against a large rock, Bekah looked up into the clear blue sky and let her mind wander. Watching closely, the guardians of the Quest were on high alert. They sensed the presence of their enemy, the devil, but they did not know his plans. All they knew was that he had ventured closer and they needed to stay prepared.

Suddenly, a large snake came out of the river. It tasted the air with its tongue several times and started up the bank towards

---

[75] Philippians 4:11-13

Bekah. Unaware of its presence, Bekah tilted her head back and closed her eyes. Within moments she was asleep. The snake slithered closer still, wanting to investigate what was generating so much heat. It hunted by sensing the heat of its victim. Bekah lay very still, giving the snake no cause for alarm. She was much too big to be hunted by this snake, but if she moved, it could strike in self-defense. Though it was not venomous, given its size, its bite could be serious.

The brush rustled at the top of the bank and Manu came and stood, looking out across the river. He had a sense of unease. He contemplated how far they had come, and how much further it would be to Arandu's village. According to his calculations they might make it by tomorrow morning. He felt as though they were making good time traveling, even though they traveled at night. God did appear to be lighting their way.

Manu looked down and saw Bekah sleeping against the rock. He smiled at the thought of his newfound sister. Then his eyes were drawn to the large snake that was coiled only a few feet from her. Manu did not want to wake her, afraid that she would move and trigger an attack. He picked up several rocks and began to throw them at the snake to scare it away. He hit it with the first throw and it recoiled and crawled into the bushes that lined the river.

Quickly he went down and woke Bekah up. She smiled up at him, but then saw his distress. "What's the matter Manu?" she asked with concern. "Has something happened?"

"No," Manu answered, "but it could have. A large, dangerous snake came out of the river and was coiled close to you. If you had moved it would have struck you, and there would have been nothing any of us could have done. Bekah, you need to be extremely careful out here in the jungle. There are so many things that could hurt you."

Bekah answered, "You're right Manu. We pray every day that no weapon formed against us will be successful.[76] We pray that the angels of God will protect us and keep us from harm.[77] I believe they are on the job and doing just that. Satan may fire the arrows, but they are deflected by God's army."

"You're right Bekah. God has done amazing things, but sometimes He uses us to help. Do you remember hearing the story about how Riki tried to kill Doctor Sherry after his wife, Mara, died from the wild boar attack? He blamed her for Mara's death. I feel like God sent me back to check on her, and stop Riki from killing her, just as He sent me here to check on you and chase away that large snake."

"He certainly did Bekah. Before that I tolerated the Christians in the village. They gave me no problems, but I was not interested in learning of their God or serving Him. God used all the miracles that happened to get my attention. This miracle showed me that God really cared about me, about all of us. Looking back, I cannot imagine my life without Him. I want everyone to have an opportunity to love and serve Him. I even want the tribe that is led by the evil witch doctor to hear about the wonderful God we serve. They are serving the devil, but they don't know it."

The four guardians felt themselves recharged by the words of faith coming out of Bekah and Manu's mouth. Their eyes flashed lightning and drove off the enemy and all his demons. They had won this skirmish, but knew there would be many more conflicts before the Quest was complete.

[76] Isaiah 54:17
[77] Hebrews 1:14

CHAPTER THIRTEEN

JUNE 24

THE BLACK DEATH CAMP

Three men from the village were monitoring the Black Death Camp, watching for any activity in the area. They were told that several men came every three or four weeks to bring new people and take away selected men who had completed their training. Their leader was a man named Josef. He was from one of the Middle Eastern countries and in charge of all the training camps in South America.

The three men had come out to the Black Death Camp yesterday, after all the prisoners had been recaptured. Mehdi, who had been a C.I.A. plant, along with Akeem, had infiltrated the camp about a month ago. The three men were told that it had been about two weeks since the last visitors had come. Mehdi had told them it was probably too early for them to come back again, but better to be ready than caught unaware.

Assuming the group they were expecting would follow the river path back to the camp; they positioned themselves about fifteen feet back from it in order to not be observed by anyone coming up the river. It was unseasonably hot and the bugs were a nuisance, but they were schooled to endure hardship. They squatted on the path through most of the morning.

Before they left the village, they had been told that there would also be a group of people coming down the river heading for the village. These were friends of the American, Josh, and were sent to help protect the village from another attack by the terrorists they were expecting.

Two hours went by and the men were fighting bugs and boredom. They were eating a lunch of day-old chipa and fruit when they heard the sound of a motor. Quickly they put aside their food and picked up their weapons. They crouched down in the brush. They had a good vantage point which allowed them to see more than two hundred feet down the river. Two large boats were coming towards them at high speed. They continued past them without slowing down. They all agreed this must be the men the village was waiting for.

The three headed back to finish their lunch, but stopped short and made a sound of disgust. Sitting around what was left of their lunch was a small band of monkeys. Always opportunists, these monkeys had taken advantage of their absence and at what was left of their lunch. When the monkeys saw them, they picked up what little was left and ran up the nearest tree. The men laughed at their antics even though they realized they would not eat until evening, when they were to be relieved by the next set of watchers.

The afternoon dragged on and their relief showed up as dusk began to blanket the jungle with the sounds of the night. The volume didn't change; it was only the sounds that were different. There was a different group of insects that came out at night. Not all of them were biting bugs. Paraguay had some interesting insects. Jiggers and bullet ants were two of the most annoying. Jiggers were a type of sand flea that burrows into the skin and lays eggs. They stay in the body hatching out numerous batches of eggs that leave through the opening of the skin that the host flea initially entered. If left untreated, these infestations can cause pain, swelling, and infection. Surgical extraction is required to remove them. Natives tend to use a small, sharp object to open up the point of penetration and remove the flea and its egg sack. They were not worried too much about the bullet ants; they tended to be under the trees. They were camped in tall brush, but they wanted to avoid them at all costs because their bite was very painful.

On the other hand, the jiggers, which lived in the sand, were a nuisance everywhere. They had to constantly monitor their exposed skin, looking for infestation sites. Living in the jungle did have its drawbacks and these insects were on the top of the list.

CHAPTER FOURTEEN

JUNE 24
THE VILLAGE

Two high speed boats pulled up to the dock with four men on each boat. The first man to climb out of the boats was a tall man with curly grey hair. As the others started unloading the boats, he strode purposefully down to the group waiting at the shoreline. He introduced himself. "Buenos Dias, "he said as he greeted the group. "My name is Isaac Klein and I have come down to Paraguay with seven other men to help you handle the prisoners you have captured. I hope you will understand my Spanish. I haven't used it in a long time."

Leonardo stepped forward and answered in English, "My name is Leonardo. Manu, the Chief of the village, has placed me in charge in his absence. He has departed with Josh and eleven others. They left the night of June 22. God instructed them to travel by night. Right before you came three others left to catch up with them. They felt that they also had heard from God to set out on the Quest."

Leonardo turned to watch the seven other men exiting the boats. Like Isaac, they were wearing camouflage. They were supposed to look like a group of men going hunting, but Leonardo thought they looked out of place in the jungle. He did not see their apparel fooling anyone.

Jose spoke up, "Isaac, we have never met, but we have talk-

91

ed on several occasions. I am Jose, your contact in Asuncion. We're really glad you are here because now only Mehdi and I have the ability to handle weapons. With fifteen prisoners, we were getting nervous about them trying to overpower us and take control again"

"Well we're here to help by taking them off your hands," Isaac explained. "We just don't want to blow the cover of this operation. We would like to be able to apprehend Josef, his companions, and the other training camps, not just in the area, but in all of Paraguay. We want to sit down with you and share what we know, and also find out what you know that may help us out."

"Who just left to follow the main group," Isaac asked?

"It was Ted and Renato, with Miguel, a young man from our village guiding them. They are going to follow the trail left by the first group. There were twelve of them and their trail should be easy to follow."

Leonardo continued, "Come follow me. I will bring you up to Doctor Sherry's clinic. She has been caring for the prisoners' injuries. They have all been shot in the leg by Cipriano, one of our hunters."

Isaac questioned, "I thought you said only Jose and Mehdi were able to use fire arms."

"I did," answered Leonardo. "Cipriano shot them with arrows. He incapacitated most of them. The rest surrendered out of fear. They did not know who was shooting them. They only knew they could not catch him and he was slowly decimating their number with every arrow he shot."

Isaac whistled softly under his breath. "I'm impressed. I would like to meet this man and congratulate him for a job well done. It's unfortunate we now have to deal with all these prisoners, but, in good conscience, I cannot execute them."

"Neither could Cipriano," replied Leonardo. "There is Doctor Sherry at the top of the hill. You have her, along with Tuvicha, the old village shaman, to thank for the terrorists' health. She takes care of all of us, with her medicine and her prayers."

Isaac looked up and saw a small, blond woman standing there. She didn't look big enough or strong enough to handle all these terrorists, but sometimes looks can be deceiving. He looked forward to being introduced to her. He had a lot of questions, and he had a feeling she might have some answers, and maybe a few questions of her own.

Sherry looked down the path, watching the group approach. She immediately understood that the man talking with Leonardo had to be Isaac Klein, Josh's friend. He looked to be the person in charge.

Sherry walked forward and extended her hand. "Hi, you must be Isaac Klein. I, for one, am glad you're here. I'm Daniel's wife Sherry, and the nearest thing they have to a doctor around here. I'm a nurse midwife, but do the best that I can as the situation warrants.

"Sherry, I'm glad to finally meet some of the people I have been hearing about. Josh has told me all about the Quest you feel God has called you to. I'm actually starting to believe some of this myself. God's always been a question to me. Is He real or isn't He? Everything that has happened down here cannot all be coincidence. He appears to have had His hand on this situation and I'm glad that I'm down here to see what's going to happen in person."

"Well Isaac, don't take it personally, but I'd appreciate it if you would just take these fifteen prisoners and leave. They are all able to travel. The whole village will rest better when they are gone."

"Unfortunately Sherry, I can't comply with your wishes."

Sherry looked at Isaac, but after that statement, she didn't hear anything else he had to say. Her mind started to explode with fear and worry. What if they escape again? What if Isaac determines he can't take them all and can only take a few? What if we have trouble feeding them for an extended period of time?

These thoughts and many others clouded her mind and obscured her perspective. She was not viewing this as an opportunity

93

to serve God. Nor as an opportunity to use her faith and be a witness to an unbeliever like Isaac. She was viewing it as an opportunity to worry and be fearful.

God whispered to her, "Daughter, where is your faith? Have you mislaid it? You had it this morning. Where did it go?"

Sherry looked behind her to see who had spoken, but no one was there. She knew in her heart that God was questioning her. She again looked at Isaac. He was still talking, but she had not heard anything after his first statement. He kept talking, unaware of the inner struggle Sherry was experiencing. Sherry knew she had let doubt and fear creep back into her heart and had let the faith that had been there leak out. She immediately took steps to change that and repented for her unbelief. She said to Isaac, "What are you planning to do and how can we help you?"

"I'm not sure at the moment. We are going to have to analyze the situation. We had been thinking of walking them to a clearing about twenty miles north of here along the river. That way a helicopter could come in and pick them all up, but with most of them unable to walk any distance, that route is out. Let us get settled and then we'll look at the prisoners. Where do you want us to stay?"

Sherry turned to Leonardo and spoke to him in Spanish. "We could let Isaac stay in Bekah's room. The other seven could stay where Ted and Renato had been sleeping. We can set up a few more cots in there."

Leonardo nodded. "There are only two beds in there. We still have several cots not being used. I think there will be enough."

Isaac nodded in agreement, "That sounds perfect. Here they come with our supplies. We didn't come empty handed. We brought lots of food. Talking to Josh, I heard about your parties. Maybe we could have one. We'll even feed the prisoners. Maybe they will think more kindly of us."

Leonardo had the villagers who were carrying the supplies put them against the back wall in the clinic. They would go through

94

them later. Then he asked the new arrivals to come into the compound.

As they walked through the door Isaac saw that the room was a large kitchen. This reminded him that none of them had eaten since early morning. Isaac asked, "Is there any way we all could get something to eat now? It's been a long time since breakfast?"

Sherry saw a few trays of chipa and fruit covered on the table. That should quench their appetite. There was also terere and juice. They pulled two tables together and there was room for all. They sat and ate, relaxing for a time while getting to know each other. Later they would discuss their situation. Sherry was not sure what Isaac knew or how much she should tell him. She said a silent prayer, asking God to help her yet again. She was glad God did not seem to get tired. She wished she could say the same for herself.

CHAPTER FIFTEEN

JUNE 24
THE QUESTERS

It was after three in the afternoon and everyone was awake. The air was cool by Paraguayan standards. This was the beginning of winter and it was still in the seventies. Bekah liked walking at night because the air cooled off, but she and Josh were in the minority. Carlos and Akeem also enjoyed the cooler weather. Everyone else was native, and the night temperatures chilled them. Thankfully they had all come prepared, carrying an extra shirt or jacket. One thing everyone was glad for was the hot and nourishing soups they had been eating. Last night they had obtained a large portion of meat from a jaguar kill. Bekah was now planning another great meal, and they would probably have leftovers for breakfast.

So far there had been no shortage of food. God provided for them one way or another. Their snares had been full and this piece of meat looked mouth-watering.

Everyone went about his assigned duties without being asked. Spirits were high and the whole group was working together – or so it seemed. Axel was still annoyed at having to fetch water for the group, and each time he did it, his annoyance grew. No one seemed to notice his displeasure except for one. Satan was watching him closely, waiting for him to cross the line and give him a foot in the door. He and his minions kept their distance, but if sin reared its head, he had the means and the power to cause trouble. So far

Axel had not spoken of his displeasure or acted on it. If and when he did, Satan would be infused with fresh power and the watchers would be weakened.

The watchers were unaware of what was occurring because they could not influence people's thoughts, but the mind was Satan's playground and he did not let many opportunities pass him by.

While dinner cooked, they all gathered for a time of prayer and Bible study. Akeem asked Josh if he could share with the group about God's faithfulness. Josh was more than happy to let him speak.

Akeem told everyone the situation he was in coming over to Paraguay. "I had not felt the leading or guidance of God for a long time. I hadn't stopped believing in Him, but I had lost hope that He would ever use me or speak to me again. I was caught up with the Black Death, and imbedded in their camp by the C.I.A. My friend Mehdi and I were in constant danger of discovery. So much was happening I found myself praying again. When you run out of choices it's either put your faith in God or sink into despair. I could not allow myself to fall into despair, so I gritted my teeth and began to pray in earnest. Every night I prayed until I fell asleep. Sometimes it was coming to dawn and I was still praying, but I had no answer. Over and over I asked God to help me, to show me what I should do. Finally, one night I had a dream. God showed me in the dream to go to your village. There I heard someone say my name. God didn't speak it, but He sent someone else to speak who needed my help. That was the night we saved the baby from the fiery sacrifice."

Akeem continued. "Thank God. He answered my prayer. He worked things out so that Satan would be defeated, and the baby would be saved. I saw His hand move in all of it and it gave me hope again. God changes circumstances to conform to His will, and causes good to win the battle where evil had been triumphing.[78]

"Sometimes it appears that God is not answering our prayers. We pray and pray but nothing happens. We have to remember that God knows the beginning from the end.[79] He knows what to do to bring about a successful ending. We need to remember that God's timing isn't always our timing. But God is always faithful, even when we are not.[80] He won't allow us to be tested beyond what we are able to stand, and He always gives us a way out.[81]

"In this trial or test that we are going through now, Satan is doing all he can to cause us to fail, to doubt God. But our God is faithful. We need to remember that, and we must stay faithful to Him."

Akeem nodded to Josh, who came up and hugged his friend. "Thanks Akeem for sharing your testimony. Those are things we need to remember because we may get into some difficult circumstances during our Quest. But God is faithful. Let's all take a few minutes and pray. Let's ask God to show us what we need to do, to show us if there is any sin in our life we need to repent for, and finally, thank Him for His faithfulness."

Everyone bowed their heads and the airways of Heaven were filled with their prayers. All were cleansed from their sins and forgiven, that is all but one. Axel sat with his head down, but his heart was not contrite, it was defiant.

"God, why haven't you answered my prayers?" he whispered. "Why don't you show me things to do? I'm as good as any of the hunters in the village, but you have me with the children. You haven't been faithful to me; why should I be faithful to You?"

Suddenly, Axel heard what he was saying to himself and trembled. How could he talk to God like this? Surely something bad was going to happen to him. He decided to wait and see if there was a consequence to those ideas. Time went by and Axel thought, "Maybe God's not listening to us. Maybe we're out here on our own." The cement upholding his faith began to crumble. To build faith we listen to God's Word, we hear it in our minds, in our hearts and audibly. By contradicting God's Word, faith is eroded.

---

[78] Romans 8:28
[79] Isaiah 46:10
[80] 2 Timothy 2:13
[81] 1 Corinthians 10:13

Satan smiled broadly. Here was the opportunity he was looking for. Someone was dissatisfied. Satan thought, "I will promise him whatever he wants, if he will do what I ask." Then he chuckled to himself, "Have I ever kept a promise I made? Little does this one know that I will use him up and discard him like garbage, because that's what he will be, good for no one and nothing."

Suddenly the angelic guardians were put on alert. Evil was trying to penetrate their defenses. There was a weakness in their wall. Someone had transgressed and left the door open. Satan never missed an opportunity. He was planning an attack and they realized their defenses were weakened. They called for heavenly assistance.

Immediately a legion of angels was sent to battle the devil and his evil cohorts. As the guardians watched and waited for assistance, their defenses weakened further as Axel's word's and thoughts grew more rebellious.

CHAPTER SIXTEEN

JUNE 24
THE STRAGGLERS

After following the trail for over five hours, Miguel put up his hand and they stopped. They could see that a camp had been made here. This is where the first group had slept during the day. They still had two or three hours of light left, and after a short rest and some dry chipa and water, they set out again. Renato had asked Ted if he needed to rest, but he said "God must be energizing me. I'm not in any pain and I'm not tired." They wanted to catch up with the first group as quickly as possible.

After two more hours the shadows were lengthening and they started looking for a campsite. They found one a short time later and began gathering wood for a fire. They wanted to burn the fire through the night to ward off animals and insects. By the time the fire was lit, the temperature was already dropping.

Miguel walked a perimeter around the area, checking for any sign of danger. While walking, he saw signs of many small animals. When he got back to camp, he took out of his pack what he needed to make several snares. He hoped they would be successful; then they would have meat for breakfast. The river was nearby and they had brought a pot to boil water.

They made some hot tea to help keep them warm and ate the rest of the food in their packs. They said a short prayer thanking God for His protection and guidance; then fell asleep quickly. Unbeknownst to them, three angelic beings were at their watch posts. They circled the perimeter to keep the enemy at bay.

Each one of them slept restlessly, and after only two hours they all awoke with a start. "You won't believe the dream I just had," Ted said with an excited voice.

"Can't be any wilder than mine," Renato answered.

"Miguel," Renato called. "Ted and I had an unusual dream. Did you have one also?"

Miguel looked over at Renato and Ted. "Yes, and it was the strangest dream I have ever had. God visited me and told me some things that are going to happen so that I can prepare for them. He said we will have opposition, but He will be with us. He showed me a tall cliff with waterfalls coming over it. They were large and beautiful, but God said they were full of danger. He also said evil was stalking us, but He would protect us. He said to start out early and walk till dark; that He would protect and provide."

Renato spoke next. "I had the same dream," he said to Ted and Miguel. "How about you Ted? Was yours the same?"

"Yes. The waterfalls were like nothing I had ever seen before. They spread across the whole river, and then down cliffs on the side of the river. They had two or three tiers. The river bank had many people fishing, and there were ducks in the water and birds in the air. Didn't Sherry have a dream about being above the waterfalls and looking out below?"

Renato answered with excitement. "You're right Ted. I remember hearing about it, but I can't remember whether it had been her or Connie. That really doesn't matter. What matters is that from experience we know that God speaks to us in dreams. We need to remember as many details of this dream as possible. I also remember that the village I grew up in, the one causing all the trouble was located near a river with waterfalls, and there were caves under the falls. I wonder if this is the same place. I guess we'll find out sooner or later."

The three of them came together to pray again for God's peace, guidance and protection. Then they added wood to the fire and lay down again to sleep. They slept peacefully until dawn.

CHAPTER SEVENTEEN

JUNE 24

THE QUESTERS

Before heading off at dusk, Daniel wanted to make sure they called the village. He had not talked to Sherry since leaving two nights ago. He was missing her desperately. Also, he had a concern that she might be taking too much upon herself. These last two weeks she had not only been extremely busy, but extremely tired. He wanted to talk to her and ask if she was getting the help she needed. With the twelve Questers gone, her work load would have increased dramatically. Because of their absence, she had to shoulder a greater amount of responsibility, in addition to her medical duties.

They had just finished a time of prayer, and Bekah was cooking the meat they had stolen from the jaguar. Daniel sent the young men out to find whatever they could to add to the stew. Even though the women of the village were the gatherers, the men were taught these skills for survival in the wild. Daniel noticed that even Axel went without a complaint or a frown. He had been observing Axel since they left, and noticed that his demeanor had changed. After the phone call he was going to bring this up to Manu. He wondered if Manu had noticed, and if he thought it was troublesome.

As the stew continued to cook, they gathered around while Daniel placed the call back to the village. It rang several times before Jose answered it. "Hello, who is calling?"

"Hello my friend. Do you still recognize my voice?"

"Hello Daniel. How are you? We have not heard from you since you left and were becoming concerned. Sherry said this morning that if we did not hear from you tonight, she was going to call. This phone call will bring her some peace." Hearing a noise, Jose turned to see what it was.

Someone must have run to wake Sherry when they heard it was Daniel on the phone. She flew into the room, a large smile wreathing her face.

Jose laughed and told Daniel, "I better give the phone to Sherry before we have a tug of war over it." He handed her the phone and said, "Talk as long as you want. When you're done, I'll be in the clinic. Send someone to get me. I'm sure Isaac will want to talk to Josh, and when Josh finds out that Isaac came down with company, I'm positive he will want to talk to Isaac."

Sherry took the phone and hugged it to her chest; then she said, "Are you all right? I have missed you so very much. I had twenty things I was going to ask you, but other than 'How are you?' I can't think of one."

Daniel smiled, his love evident on his face. This was a couple who in the midst of accidents, attacks, fifteen Black Death prisoners, and numerous patients from the adopted tribe, were as caring and attentive to each other as possible. They were doing the important things to keep their marriage alive and flourishing.

Grinning, Sherry said, "I know there are important things to discuss, but I wanted to tell you I felt the baby move. He may be further along than I originally thought. We might be looking at some time in November. I know you're only gone two days, but it appears I'm actually developing a little bulge. Maybe I just didn't take the time to look. Whatever the case, he is growing."

If possible, Daniel's smile grew even bigger! "That's twice you referred to the baby as he. Do you know something I don't?"

Sherry chuckled. "Not that I'm aware of. It wasn't done purposefully. It just came out. There's no way to tell without an ultra-

106

sound, and I don't have that kind of equipment here. Besides, I don't want to know. I like the idea of being surprised. Right now the only one who knows is God, and I'm willing to leave it that way. There are so many things happening I think I should put Jose back on the phone. I will wait until everyone is done and then tell you the nineteen other things I wanted to say."

Smiling, Daniel said, "I'll talk to Jose later. Let me talk with Renato."

Sherry responded, "He can't talk with you now. That's one of the things Jose wants to tell you about."

"Is Renato alright?" Daniel asked. "Has something happened?"

"Just talk with Jose," Sherry insisted. "He will explain everything. Good-bye for now."

A few seconds ticked by and then Jose's voice came back over the telephone. "Hello again my friend. As you may have guessed, a lot has been happening here."

Jose talked about the prisoner escape. Then he told of Cipriano's bravery and the amazing recapture he performed. "Make no mistake," he said, "Cipriano is a hero, but he gives God all the glory. Unfortunately nine prisoners were injured. Thankfully, only one was serious, but Sherry treated them all. She has been very tired. We are trying to give her opportunities to rest, but it is almost impossible."

Daniel was quiet for a moment. "Thank you, Jose, for watching out for her. She tends to try to fill her plate to overflowing. She needs help delegating.

"How are Ted and Renato doing? Were they helpful in the escape and recapture?"

Jose then tells the story of the escape of the prisoners, and of Ted's injury, and his miraculous recovery. Jose again paused, waiting for a reply. Finally he asked, "Daniel, are you still there?"

"Yes, I'm just making sure that everyone knows what you are saying. Manu is translating for the young men with us. This is truly extraordinary. Is Renato there? I think we all would like to question him."

"Well, that brings me to the next issue. Renato and Ted felt like God was speaking to both of them, reminding them of their promise to protect Bekah. Also, Renato felt that there was a reason that he had this dream and felt it could have something to do with the place you are going and the people you will be meeting. Renato and Ted left this afternoon, right after lunch today to follow all of you. Miguel, one of the young hunters from the village, is their guide. I think it will only take two or three days to catch up with you. They are following your trail and they are walking during the day."

Suddenly Jose heard someone talking in the background. There was a short pause and then Josh's voice came over the phone. His voice rose in agitation. "Jose, how could you let them go? Don't you realize how dangerous this is? We don't know what is going to happen, or if any of us will even come back."

Jose answered in frustration. "I did what I could to deter them, but how can you argue with anyone who feels they have heard from God? I had lost the argument before it even started."

Josh spoke with exasperation. "I hate to lose time, but we will have to pray about this before we set out tonight and find out what God wants us to do, wait for them, slow down, or just continue on. Things appear to be getting confused, and I know God doesn't lead us into confusion. His enemy the devil does.[82] God will make everything clear to us when we pray."

"There's one more thing I have to tell you Josh."

"I hope it's good news. Did you save the best for last?"

"I don't think you are going to like this either. After Renato and Ted left, Isaac Klein arrived at the village. He drove two high speed boats up the river with seven other men and supplies. He's supposed to be on a hunting expedition with friends. I don't know

---

[82] 1 Corinthians 14:33

who he thinks he's going to fool. I don't know how he is going to get rid of these prisoners, even with the extra help. He certainly can't take them back through Puerto Bahia Negra."

"Leave it to Isaac," Josh said. "The minute I'm out of the picture, he shows up."

Suddenly the voice he had been listening to changed. "Josh, what would you have wanted me to do?" Isaac questioned. "I have fifteen would be terrorists, several of them injured, who I have to transport. Down here, no one but Jose and Mehdi were able to handle a weapon. Furthermore, at this point I don't want to leave the village totally unarmed. They may be a target for retribution. I'm really looking out for their best interest. Maybe if word gets out that we are here, people will think twice before attacking."

There was a pause, and then Josh answered. "You may be right about that. But I know our government has an interest here. They are investigating why there are so many Islamic young men coming into Paraguay, staying for several weeks, and then leaving. I'm concerned. I don't want the village to be collateral damage."

Isaac answered, "You have my word Josh. I'll make it my business to stay here until everything is settled and all of you are back, even if I have to take vacation time. They owe me several weeks as it is. Let's just take each challenge as it comes, one day at a time."

"Isaac, one thing you may not understand is that not all of us may be coming back. We have no assurance of that. All we know for sure is that God's side wins. Whether we live to see the final outcome is not guaranteed. You don't understand everything that has happened, and too much has happened to go over it with you now."

Isaac started to ask a question but Josh interrupted. He told Isaac, "Talk with Leonardo; he knows most of what has happened. Talk to Tuvicha, he is the old medicine man of the village. Talk with Arandu, he is the elder of the village that was attacked and destroyed. You might sit down and talk with Sherry. She knows everything from the beginning. You'll find out," Josh said emphatically, "that Satan is alive and well on planet earth! He is working especially hard these days because he knows his time is short. God on the other hand has a plan, a plan that was in place before time even began. We were all born for this particular time, to perform the work God has for us to do. No one else can do this.[83] It's why we are here. Knowing that is what gives us the strength and courage to go on, even when the problems seem insurmountable."

Taken aback by all that had been said, Isaac responds thoughtfully, "Josh, I don't know what to say. All of this seems so unbelievable; yet I know that you are telling me the truth as you know it. I will ask about what has been happening here. I want to find out the truth also. All these years I've been a haphazard Jew. I had a Bar Mitzvah at twelve, and haven't been back in a synagogue since then. I guess I sort of believe God was out there somewhere, but He never seems to pay any attention to me. Now that I'm down here in the jungles of Paraguay, all I've been listening to is what God has said and what God has done. Well He's got my attention, and if He wants to show me the truth—I'll listen.

"Don't worry about your people or the village," Isaac reassured him, "We'll work something out. Just stay safe, do what you have to do, and come back."

"I'll do my best. We'll be in touch tomorrow evening. The battery is running low. We'll find a spot of sunlight and charge it tomorrow while we're sleeping. It's getting dark and we need to get going," replied Josh.

"Alright, stay safe."

When the call ended, both ends of the line went dead, but the people who had been talking on them were very much alive. They also had a lot to think about. Now their training as Christians would come into play. Would they discuss things until there appeared to be no viable solution, or would they pray and put it in

---

[83] Esther 4:14

110

God's hands. Both groups realized they could not accomplish anything themselves. They could not work this out. There were spiritual forces at work and in order to come up with a solution, they needed to use spiritual intervention. They all prayed the Word of God.

Josh spoke, "No weapons formed against us shall prosper.[84] Submit to God, resist the devil and he will flee.[85] I can do all things through Christ Who strengthens me.[86] Greater is He Who is in me than he that is in the world."[87]

He used his weapons, the sword of the spirit, the Word of God, and sent them out to vanquish their enemies. They were unaware of the fact that a large group of angels was now surrounding them, and their prayers had given them the power they needed to deflect the fiery darts of the devil.[88]

---

[84] Isaiah 54:17
[85] James 4:7
[86] Philippians 4:13
[87] 1 John 4:4
[88] Ephesians 6:16

CHAPTER EIGHTEEN

JUNE 25

THE BLACK DEATH CAMP

Relief had come for the guards at the Black Death Camp in the form of three villagers and two of the new visitors Isaac had brought with him from America, Rob and Shane. The rest of the Americans had stayed back in the village to guard the prisoners, and allow the village to try to return to a normal routine. Two of the visitors were even going out with a group of hunters to track large game to feed all the extra mouths. Cipriano was in charge of the small group doing surveillance at the Black Death Camp. The new visitors were there just to observe, but they also had weapons with them in case the need arose.

It was still early. The shadows were long and dark in the dense forest, but the morning was cool. The men, who were relinquishing their watch, were chilled from their long night of surveillance. They were anxious to get home to their families and to get some rest. As they walked, they talked among themselves, wondering how the strangers would deal with the jungle and its challenges. They had been brought up dealing with the difficulties of living in the jungle, but these were city men who were unprepared for what they would consider the hardships of jungle living. The food was different, the climate was different, the animal life was different, and the insects could be a challenge, even to the locals.

It turned out that the visitors spoke Spanish, and so did the villagers. Most of the villagers also spoke some English. They should have no trouble conversing. They had brought some dried meat, fresh fruit and vegetables, and some fresh chipa that was still warm. The strangers brought bottled water, but the locals drank terere. It would have been nice to drink it hot because the air was so chilled, but they were not risking a fire, in case company was close by.

Everyone from old to young drank terere. It was comforting to drink because you shared with those around you. It was a social drink, and it was drunk from a communal cup. You formed relationships with the people you drank with. You took the time to ask about them and their families. These people knew who their neighbors were, and they would go out of their way to help them in any way they could. If there was a problem, it became their problem also. If someone had a poor hunt, food was shared. If someone was sick or injured, they were nursed back to health. There were no strangers in the village. Everyone was part of the body of the village.

Cipriano and the others settled in for a long day. The sun had risen higher into the sky. The shadows had decreased and the temperature rose enough to take the chill out of the air. Cipriano assigned the two villagers to go to the river and keep watch. He and the rest would search the camp to see if anything of importance could be found. They would all meet at the river for a midday meal.

After going through the five buildings that were there, they had collected a large amount of trash, and discovered an even larger amount of weapons and ammunition. Obviously the captives only took with them what they could comfortably carry. What they had left behind was enough to start a small war. Cipriano decided to send a runner back to the village and let Leonardo and Isaac know about the weapons and find out what they wanted done with them. He also instinctively knew they needed to be moved from the camp and hidden in the jungle in case Josef and his crew came back. It would not be good if they fell into those hands. He told the runner to have several men sent back to help move the weapons.

Rob had a pad and began counting and cataloging the cache of weapons. There were three unopened cases of AK-47's, five rocket launchers, ten cases of M-16 rifles, and enough plastic explosives to demolish a city block. Stacks of boxes, and various types of ammunitions coincided with the assorted weapons. There were far more weapons than had come down with Esteban Montero and his group. These weapons had been stockpiled for quite some time. It appeared as though they were being stored for some future attack. Just when, and where the attack was to be, remained a mystery. Rob continued to inventory the munitions. He wondered how Isaac would react to this find. As Rob was finishing, Cipriano came into the building and said they were going to the river and eat lunch together. It would be a cold meal again, but it would be tasty and filling.

After several more hours of searching the camp and surrounding area, a contingent from the village showed up with ten villagers, and two more Americans, Isaac, and Matt. Leonardo also accompanied them. When he had heard of the large quantity of weapons, he felt he should know what was happening with them so he could tell Manu the next time they phoned. They were all shown into the building where the weapons were being kept. Rob gave Isaac the list of everything that had been found.

Isaac raised his eyebrows and gave a low whistle when he saw the extent of the weapons. "It looks like they have enough stuff here to start a war. There are several other camps in a fifty mile radius from here. I wonder if they have stockpiles of weapons in those camps also." He turned to Shane. "I'm glad we brought a secure phone with us. I'm going to have to make a few phone calls about this. Deciding what to do about everything here is above my pay grade. Also, I want to know if there are Black Death Camps throughout Paraguay, or just in this area."

Isaac turned and questioned Leonardo, "Can you and your men hide these boxes in the jungle so no one will find them? Is there some way you can keep these boxes dry?"

Leonardo looked thoughtful, "We can try covering them with several layers of banana leaves. It may not keep them completely dry, but it will be a deterrent."

As Isaac was listening he took out one of the rifles and looked it over. Shocked by something he saw, he went back to the box he had taken it from and examined it more closely. Across the bottom of the box was the phrase, "Property of the United States Army".

He called Shane and Rob over to show them. "Now we have another problem. Where did they get this stuff from? Who's their supplier?"

Isaac turned back to Leonardo and explained the problem to him. "Can you and your men handle hiding these weapons?" he asked again.

Leonardo replied. "This is only half of what was here. I will show your men where we have hidden the rest of them. Can you tell me what you are going to do about the men who may be coming here and the other terrorist training camps that may be nearby? I am concerned for my village, especially those who go out into the jungle to hunt and gather food. I do not want any of them to be harmed."

Isaac answered truthfully, "I won't lie to you. This is serious. I'm going back to the village right now. Will you leave your men to work and come back with me? I have aerial maps of the surrounding jungle showing at least five other Black Death Camps in the area. Maybe you will recognize some of them and give me a general idea of how long it would take to get there."

Leonardo nodded in agreement. "Isaac, I don't know if you are a believer, but surely you can see that all of these circumstances are no coincidence. God is leading and guiding everyone for His purpose."

"Leonardo," Isaac answered, "I am basically a non-believer, but I'm a hoper. I hope there is a God and that He is in charge, but when I look at what's going on in the world, that's when I begin to doubt."

116

"I was once a doubter also," Leonardo replied with caution. He did not know this man, and so far he had only brought trouble to the village, but something inside him cried out, "Tell him of Ciba's miracle. Tell him of Noemi's miracle." Leonardo recognized the Voice of the Holy Spirit, encouraging him to speak. He whispered a quiet prayer and then said, "We have five miles to walk back to the village. Let me tell you some of the miracles that have taken place recently. They gave me irrefutable proof that there is a God and that He is in charge. I'm so glad, because His decisions are so much better than mine."

Leonardo began to tell the story of both Noemi and Ciba's miracles. He also told of baby Emilio and how God brought him back to life.

Isaac walked in stunned silence. He had heard of Jesus. He had even heard of the miracles told in the Bible, but he had never heard of them occurring to people he knew. He wondered what the full story was of what was happening down here. If there really was a God, did He actually take an interest in people's lives?

They walked the last mile without talking. Leonardo had said what he felt he should say. Now he put the matter in the Holy Spirit's hands. The Bible said that some plant the seeds, some water the seeds, and some harvest the seeds.[89] He trusted that he had planted the seed. Judging from Isaac's comments and questions, and then his silence, a battle was now being waged for his soul. Leonardo prayed fervently that Isaac would surrender to God and stand in faith with all of them. Leonardo also wondered about the other men who came with Isaac. Were they believers? Did they put their trust in the one true God? Did they see the hand of God at work here? Did they recognize the work of the devil? These questions would be answered in due time.

As they were entering the compound, Leonardo could see

---

[89] John 4:36-38

that a large group of people were gathering there. It was almost time for the phone call. He told Isaac that he would be able to talk with Josh and let him know everything they found.

People gave way as they entered. Leonardo scanned the crowd and saw Sherry talking with Jose and Mehdi. He and Isaac made their way over. "Are we ready for the phone call?" he asked. We have some things we need to discuss with Josh that are important."

Jose responded, "We were going to let Sherry talk first with Daniel. Can it wait a few minutes?"

Isaac gave a brief explanation of what they had found. Then he turned to Sherry. "I'm sorry to usurp your spot, but Josh needs to know about this right away. They all may be in more danger than they realize. There are several camps out there that may be armed just as well as this one. I won't tell them to come back; I know that's not possible. I know they believe that God sent them. Maybe I'm starting to believe that too, but I want them forewarned. Also, the men that set out yesterday will have no idea what they may be up against. Maybe Josh might consider waiting a day or two for them to catch up. They will be moving quicker than the first group because there are fewer of them and they are also following that group's trail and traveling during the day."

Sherry answered quickly. "You're right Isaac. Personal feelings can wait. The success of the Quest is more important."

She addressed Jose, "Let Isaac call. He can ask to talk with Josh first. Thankfully we have a speaker phone and everyone can listen and give their input."

The call was placed and Sherry handed Isaac the phone. "Hello," Daniel's voice answered. "Hello Daniel, this is Isaac. I know you were expecting Sherry to be talking, but I need to talk to Josh, and to all of you, and let you know of new circumstances that have arisen."

Daniel responded, "No problem. You're on speaker phone. Go ahead, we're all listening."

118

Isaac proceeded to relate the incidences that occurred that day. He told them of the weapons they found in the Black Death Camp, and his concern for the Questers. Having done more extensive aerial searches before leaving the U.S., they were certain there were more Black Death Camps in the area, and were unsure if they had access to the amount of weapons found in this camp. He stressed the amount of weapons found and they all wondered what the planned purpose was for them. Isaac also suggested that because of the situation, they wait for Ted, Renato and Miguel. He expected Josh to balk at that suggestion, and was surprised when he agreed.

"You're right about waiting for Renato, Ted and Miguel. That has been on my mind since I found out they had left to follow us. With Renato being older and Ted having been injured, I'm not sure how long it will take them to get here. I think waiting one day, until tomorrow night, should give them adequate time. If they don't show by then, they might have gone a different way. We'll let you know when they show up.

"Isaac, are you going to call Washington about the small armory you found? What do you think the likelihood is of all these camps having the same type of weapon supply?"

"Josh, I'm concerned that they do. I haven't mentioned it yet, but the boxes these weapons came in are stamped 'Property of the Unites States Army'. It's possible their supplier may have an unending supply. I'm going to call Washington and have them check into this. We'll know more when we find out who these weapons came from."

"One more thing Isaac, before I give the phone to Daniel, do you think you can call in some favors and find out what's going on with the search for Haydon Carlton? He's the man who's responsible for the break-in at Bekah's home. He's convinced Bekah knows the whereabouts of a hoard of treasure left by the ancient Guarani people back when the Spanish enslaved them in the 1600's, and made them work in the mines. He escaped from custody about a week ago while being transferred to a psychiatric facility for testing. He has the motivation and the means to get down here if he wanted. That would just be one more issue that needs handling."

"I remember you telling me about him, Josh. Dealing with someone who has gone off the deep end is hazardous because you never know what they are capable of. They're unpredictable. I've got a few people who owe me. I'll see what I can find out. All of you have a good night's rest, but watch your back."

Isaac gave the phone to Sherry and everyone moved away to give her some privacy. Daniel's voice came over the phone and Sherry turned off the speaker. She took the phone and went into her bedroom. Ten minutes later she came out of her bedroom with tears in her eyes. She swiped at them as she put the phone down.

Sherry said, "Josh didn't tell you Bekah almost got bit by a large snake, but Manu saved her. He seems to have a habit of doing that. Isaac, you may not be aware of this, but this was not the first time Manu saved Bekah's life. He also helped to free her from the rocks on the jetty when a tree hit the jetty and trapped her. God appears to be sending him to the right places at the right time. It's comforting to know that Manu is being used by God to care for those around him."

CHAPTER NINETEEN

JUNE 25
THE STRAGGLERS

It had been a long day and everyone was tired, but something was driving them to go on. It wasn't fear, it was a compulsion. They were all in agreement that they should walk until the light gave out. Judging from the shadows, it would not be more than an hour or two. No one spoke. They concentrated on putting one foot in front of the other. Whether they were in prayer or deep thought wasn't known, but the silence was almost audible.

They continued on for another mile or two and suddenly Miguel's head came up and he stopped. "I smell smoke," he said.

Renato and Ted sniffed the air but didn't smell anything. They decided to go on for a short way, testing the air as they went. After going over a short rise they stopped. Not only did they smell smoke, they saw smoke.

They picked up their pace and heard voices. Recognizing several of them, they raised their voices and shouted a greeting. Silence descended. Then they heard a loud whoop and several bodies started pouring down the trail. They grinned at each other. No one wanted to admit concern, but a huge weight was removed from everyone's shoulders. Moving forward, they embraced their friends.

Josh went forward and hugged all three of them. "Thank God you arrived safely. You are an answer to our prayers. We found out you were coming yesterday, but we weren't concerned until today. Isaac called and told us they found that the Black Death Camp was supplied with enough firepower to start a small war, and that was just at the camp near the village. They also determined that the weapons were the property of the U.S. Army. In addition, they know of several camps in the area, and are concerned that they may have assembled an arsenal similar to this one."

Ted spoke up, "We have no news from the village, but assume everyone is well. We traveled till dark last night and started at dawn this morning. We traveled at a good pace most of the day, but by late afternoon, instead of slowing down we increased our stride. We all felt an urgency to move quickly. We don't think we were followed, but we can't be sure. I'm just glad my injury didn't slow us down. All I had was a slight headache, and it wasn't a problem."

Renato spoke next. "I'm so glad we finally got here. Did anyone tell you why we felt we had to come?"

"Yes," Josh replied. "They said you and Ted both felt you had given Bekah a promise to protect her. You felt that staying behind had broken that promise. They also said Renato had an extraordinary dream."

Renato cut in, "That's right. I did have a remarkable dream. I'll tell all of you about it after we eat something and get a drink. Where is the campsite?" Renato, Ted, and Miguel followed everyone back to the campsite. There were more than enough rocks for everyone to sit on. Renato took off his pack and groaned when he sat down. "I didn't realize how tired I was. We seemed to have been fueled with supernatural adrenalin, but now my gauge is reading empty, and I need to fill my tank."

Someone passed him a drink of terere. He drank it with relish. Then he realized everyone had been eating and drinking. It must be mealtime.

Daniel said, "This is usually the time we set out on our journey. Tonight we will take a break. Then, we will stay the day tomorrow and hear all the news and make additional plans. It will also give us time to pray together. We will head out again tomorrow night."

Renato felt someone looking at him. He looked up and there stood Bekah with the sweetest smile on her face. "I missed you," she said. "In fact, I missed everyone, especially Sherry. How are all her patients? Tell me, how is the little girl Panambi? She was so sweet. Is she doing better?"

Renato reached out and drew her into a hug. He planted a soft kiss on her forehead and replied, "I missed you also, and yes, everyone is doing well. Maria, Hombrecito, and Panambi have become great friends.

"After having my dream, I immediately felt there was a connection to the dream and the Quest. I also felt it was wrong that I did not go with you. I had promised to protect you with my life, and I could not do that being separated from you."

Ted spoke up quickly. "I felt the same way. I had promised to do my best to keep you safe during this Quest. I felt that staying at the village was breaking my promise. Renato and I prayed together and felt that God was sending us. Miguel came as our guide."

Josh walked over and rested his hand on Ted's shoulder. "I was very upset when I found out you both were following after us. Now that you're here, I feel that the group is complete. Why it seemed you had to stay behind is a mystery. Maybe it was to help with the prisoners. Maybe it was a test of obedience. I don't know if we ever will find out, but I'm glad you're here and it feels right. We'll take time tonight to pray and ask God to speak to us. We want to be sure we are doing His will."

Miguel walked over to join with the other young men that were there. They all knew each other well. They had played together when they were young, and hunted together as they got older. Miguel was anxious to hear their observations. Everyone had a point of view and he was eager to hear them all.

The newcomers were given a bowl of stew and some cornbread. They had just about run out of their supply of chipa, and what was left was so hard, the only way to eat it was to dip it in your stew and let it soak. Bekah carried cornmeal in her pack and made a large batch of cornbread in the morning and at night. They carried any leftovers to sustain them during their nightly march. Several extra snares were set out. There were more mouths to feed and they would be eating some additional meals since they were staying in camp an extra day.

Bekah thought she would ask one of the young men to go with her tomorrow into the jungle to look for roots, fruit and vegetables to supplement the meat they would be eating. Maybe she would ask that young man Axel. He seemed rather quiet lately. She didn't think she would need an interpreter. Everyone spoke at least a smattering of English.

After the meal was finished, each person came together for a Bible reading and a time of prayer. After praying Josh said, "I want to ask all of you a question. Has God shown any of you why we are walking in the jungle to the village instead of taking a boat? We could have taken Daniel's boat and one of the large motorized canoes and made much better time. We could have packed more food and equipment. It would have been a lot easier."

Josh looked over the group to see if anyone had an answer. "Well I'll tell you what I think. I've been praying about this and the Scripture that comes to mind is when the Holy Spirit led Jesus in the desert to be tempted by the devil.[90] I think some of us are going to have our own personal temptations, tests or trials to go through. The Bible says to watch and pray to avoid temptation."[91]

"That's true," Daniel said. "Didn't the Bible also say that God would not allow us to be tempted more than we could bear? He said He would also show us a way out, a way of escape so we don't fail.[92]

"God is so faithful. He allows us to be tested to strengthen us, not to cause failure. He wants us to succeed. Satan wants us to

---

[90] Matthew 4:1-11
[91] Matthew 26:41

124

fail. We all need to remember the Holy Spirit lives inside us and will speak to us in some way to show us what to do. We just need to pay attention, and keep our hearts right."

Daniel turned to Bekah and asked, "Bekah, would you sing 'Great is Thy Faithfulness'? It doesn't hurt to be reminded of that on a daily basis. Manu, do you think you need to interpret?"

"No, I don't think so. We all had some English before Bekah arrived, but talking to all of you and listening to you every day has increased our understanding. If they don't understand all the words, they will certainly understand the spirit of the song."

As Bekah raised her voice and began to sing, the guardians from Heaven listened with wonder at the sound of praise going up before the throne of God.[93] They knew God's Word. They heard it continually. They also heard praise continually. They watched these people as Bekah sang. Their minds and hearts were filled with the knowledge of God and what He had done for them. Their trust in Him was exemplified in this song of praise. It demonstrated their love and obedience to God and rose to His throne as a sweet smelling aroma.

Unfortunately, there was discontent in the group; and Bekah was not the only one to notice Axel's withdrawal. Satan was ever on alert to take advantage of a weak link. He would stay vigilant. He needed to find a way to cause trouble. Discontent, discord, and division, lead to strife, and strife threw open the door to let in the hordes of Hell.

Human nature being what it was, discontent never stays stagnant; it festers and grows. It was like a virus that infected one cell. The body's immune system was able to take care of it, but if left untreated, it would spread. Our spirits had an immune system that needed to be fed. Prayer, praise, and hearing God's Word were the medicine that was needed to combat a spiritual infection.

Satan was aware of these facts and was doing everything

---

[92] 1 Corinthians 10:13
[93] Ephesians 5:2

125

he could to isolate Axel so that he could bombard him with other feelings and emotions that would cause him to falter. The angels kept their eyes riveted on Axel, watching him carefully to be sure he did not cross over the line. The Questers did not need sin in the camp. Sin had grave consequences, and wherever it turned up, there was always collateral damage.

Satan rubbed his hands together in anticipation. He always loved a good fight, and it appeared that he would have an advantage if he was able to continue his influence over Axel.

CHAPTER TWENTY

JUNE 25
THE VILLAGE
THE DEMON HORDES

Satan called his demon hordes to him. He was in the fight of his life and wanted all the offensive forces he could garner. He knew the Word of God, he knew of all the Scriptures that prophesied his defeat, but given the punishment that he was condemned to, he had no recourse but to fight on.

He looked around as the crowd gathered. He had a very large army, and they were all eager and willing to fight. They curried his favor, and winning this battle would guarantee them substantial rewards. They were all highly motivated, and knew that Satan had rewards for those who were successful in their assignments, but the punishment for failure was beyond imagination. God motivated with love, Satan motivated with fear. With the help of sinful man, he felt confident he had enough power to defeat the Quest and spoil the plans of God.

There was already dissatisfaction amongst the Questers. Given man's track record of sin and unfaithfulness, he felt some measure of confidence. Eternity hung in the balance, and Satan wanted to tip the scales as much in his favor as possible. Success dangled out there; just like it had when he had deceived Adam and Eve into doubting God and eating the forbidden fruit in the garden. He thought he had won then, but God always had a plan. He couldn't see everyone's future as God could, and that was a hindrance. But he knew people, and their weaknesses. He could only lie to people and manipulated them in their vulnerability. He wanted to believe his success was still possible.

The place he had picked to hold this gathering was very special to him. It had a long history of demonic activity. In fact, it was already inhabited by legions of demons. It had been used as a place of sacrifice for thousands of years, both human and animal. He was slightly nervous about the small group of Christians who called this part of the Paraguayan jungle their home, but he felt that given the size of his army, their impact would be trivial. He had a long history of underestimating the people of God. He would be sure to assign extra workers to the fight. He did not want to go down for the count.

While all this was going on, Sherry had uneasiness build up inside her. It was as though her spirit was sounding a warning. "What would I be uneasy about," she thought? Then she laughed. Her whole life was in turmoil. What wouldn't she be uneasy about?

Sherry went through her mind of potential problems: the Black Death Camp, and everything it involved, the Questers, the other Black Death Camps, the evil village, feeding the extra fifteen prisoners and the extra eight C.I.A. agents, and lastly that she was approximately four months pregnant with hers and Daniel's first child.

She examined each one of these topics to see if they were the cause of her unease, and felt confident they were not. She prayed quietly, asking God to show her what the source was of this uneasiness. "Am I forgetting something?" she asked herself.

She went over her to do list: work on digging the well, set up solar panels to generate electricity, check on Mara's children and make sure they were being well cared for. Mara had been a woman of the village. She and Ciba, Leonardo's wife, had gone into the jungle searching for roots and fruit. They had both been attacked by a large and vicious wild boar. Unfortunately, Mara died of her injuries.

128

She was already dead by the time they got her back to the village.

Her Husband Riki was very angry that Sherry had not saved Mara and placed a curse on her. He later attempted to kill her, but Manu intervened and Riki was killed instead. Mara's children were given to Chabuto, Manu's step-mother to care for. Subsequently, Chabuto, along with Tuvicha, the witch doctor had taken the youngest child to sacrifice by fire to their god. They had felt their power weakening and hoped this sacrifice would strengthen them. They were stopped by Josh, Akeem, Manu and several men from the village. Chabuto fell into the fire and died. A fight then took place between the forces of darkness and God's people for the soul of Tuvicha. God's people won. Unfortunately, the glade had never been cleansed of its evil.

That was it. Thinking on that prompted her to remember that all offerings to the old gods were made in the glade. Sherry had felt it necessary to cleanse the glade of evil spirits, but with everything happening around her, she had not followed through with that thought. She asked for forgiveness in not immediately taking care of that situation. She purposed to ask Leonardo to take a walk down there after lunch with her. It was less than a half mile from the village.

She found Leonardo, or he found her. He came into the kitchen and took a piece of chipa and poured some terere from a pitcher. He sat down at the kitchen table and asked, "What's going on? Do you have time to take a break?"

"Yes," Sherry stated. "I'll take time because I need to talk to you. Do you remember when we talked about the glade, and how it needed to be cleansed from the evil that had been perpetrated there?"

Leonardo interrupted, "I do remember that, and that's what I was just coming to talk with you about it. God reminded me of it this morning. What do you think could be the matter? You don't think the evil has come back, do you?"

Sherry answered, "There was terrible evil done in that glade.

129

It was a place of sacrifice to Satan. The people who made the sacrifices may not have called his name Satan, but if you are not worshipping and sacrificing to God, Satan is the only other alternative. He has gone by many names over the years, but eventually, they will all have to bow to the Name of Jesus.

"As Christians, we don't sacrifice people or animals. We don't even sacrifice things we have grown or things we have made. God asks that we sacrifice ourselves to him, not in a physical sense, but spiritually.[94] Just as Jesus said, "Not my will, but Thy will be done."[95] God also asks that we present our bodies as a living sacrifice. He doesn't want us to kill ourselves, but the Bible says that we do that by renewing our mind. In doing that, we take on His thoughts and attributes, and our lives become an expression of Who He is. We become a better witness to people because we look more like Him.[96]

Sherry looked at Leonardo and asked him if he understood. He nodded and replied, "Yes, it's easy to understand. We let the evil spirits in and now they think that place is theirs. We must make them leave so they don't bother us again. When we think and act like Jesus, Satan has no strength to fight us."

Amazed at his acuity, Sherry nodded, "That's exactly right. Not only that, but after they leave we need to dedicate this place to God. Maybe this is where we should hold our church services, since the gathering place is getting so crowded. That would surely make Satan angry and please God very much."

She suggested that after lunch they take four or five other strong believers and some oil and anoint the glade and pray over it. Leonardo agreed and said he would come back with the people and the oil.

It was mid-afternoon when Leonardo showed up with Meh-

---

[94] Romans 12:1
[95] Matthew 26:39
[96] 2 Corinthians 3:18

di, Connie, Sol, Victoria, and Alma. Sherry and Connie carried their Bibles and Leonardo carried the anointing oil.

Sherry said, "Before we leave, we need a plan. We need to gather some Scriptures that will address the issue. Maybe we need to get more people praying. This may be more of an issue than we anticipated. Sol, will you go out into the meeting area and see who is there. Ask if they will pray. Then, go over and see if Noemi is home and ask her to find some people to pray also.

"Now let's think of some Scriptures we can use to combat the enemy and all his demons." They opened their Bibles and looked up several Scriptures. "Be strong in the Lord and in the power of His might. Put on the whole armor of God to be able to stand against the strategies of the devil, for we don't fight against flesh and blood but against all the powers and princes of the dark and evil world."[97] "Greater is He in you than he who is in the world."[98] "In this world you will have tribulation. Be of good cheer, I have overcome the world."[99] They overcame evil by the blood of the Lamb and the word of their testimony, and were not afraid to give up their lives."[100]

"This will give us some ammunition if there is resistance. Also, we need to send out angels to go before us and all around us to fight the enemy and deflect the weapons he launches against us. Let's sing some hymns while we go."

They started singing Amazing Grace in Guarani. Almost everyone could sing it. Mehdi recognized the melody and sang it in English. They followed with "How Great Thou Art", and "Great is Thy Faithfulness". They were approaching the glade as they finished. As they continued forward, they noticed the glade looked different. "Has anyone been down here since the prisoner's escape?" Sherry asked. "Do any of you smell that terrible odor? It smells as if

---

[97] Ephesians 6:10-17
[98] 1 John 4:4
[99] John 16:33
[100] Revelation 12:11

something has died and rotted."

They all stopped before they entered the glade and assessed the area. "Look at the trees," Sherry said. "They are all dying. Their leaves are turning brown. Did you notice how many vines are growing in them and across the ground? It's as if the ground was suffocating."

"My goodness," Alma called out, "the ground is swarming with insects. Several species I recognize as poisonous."

"Remember," Sherry encouraged them all, "God gave us the power to walk on serpents and scorpions, and all the powers of the enemy, and not be harmed."[101] Sherry examined everyone to be sure they were all still walking in faith. They prepared to go forward when they also heard singing. Stopping, they turned and witnessed an unusual sight. It appeared as though the whole village were following them, singing hymns of praise to God. Sherry smiled, thinking how much it would please God to see His people coming together, and walking in faith to go out and fighting the enemy. She wondered if He had the same smile when David picked the small stone from his pouch to fight Goliath.[102]

They all stopped when they came together. "What are all of you doing here?" Sherry questioned. Even Tuvicha was with the group and she didn't know if that was a good idea. Until recently, he had been a member of the devil's army, and had been infested with a host of demons. Though set free, Sherry had never been in a situation like this, and she was unsure how strong the demons were and if they could reinfest him. Then a Scripture came to her. "He whom the Son sets free is free indeed."[103] "I didn't want you to have to battle Satan so early in your walk of faith," she said to Tuvicha. "I see that I was wrong. Sometimes, we tend to have greater faith as new believers than as experienced Christians. Let's all join hands and lift our voices as we come against Satan and his evil hordes.

---

[101] Luke 10:19
[102] 1 Samuel 17:42-51

132

When Jesus sent out His disciples, they came back rejoicing, saying, "Even the devils obey us when we use Your Name."[104]

Sherry turned back to the glade. As they entered there appeared to be movement all around them, but they could not see what was happening. Darkness had encompassed them. In faith, they forged forward and Sherry encouraged, "Let's keep saying our Scriptures. Then let's sing our hymns. The Bible says God inhabits the praises of His people.[105] If He inhabits our praise, then He's right here with us. It also says that, "If God be for us, who can be against us?"[106] We have already won this battle.

Everyone stood in the middle of the glade, singing and pronouncing the Word of God. Other than the smell, and the darkness, their natural senses did not detect any noise or motion around them now. Sherry prayed, "Lord, show us the battle. Show us there are more with You than with Satan. Show us his defeat. Let these new believers build their faith by seeing the Word of God in action."[107]

They stood there in silence, each one grabbing another's hand so as to be joined in unity. Slowly, the light appeared to emanate from the darkness of the glade, and it shone brighter and brighter. They saw thousands of strange, dark forms writhing on the ground. Then they saw other forms, that looked like beings of light, swirling through the air. These forms were clothed in white, and a bright light appeared to emanate from them. They were uncountable. They gave the impression of warriors, but no weapons could be seen, yet the demons acted as though they were under their control.

The leader of these beings came forward and stood before them. His voice boomed across the glade. "We have defeated the demon hordes. Now you need to dedicate this place to the Lord, God Almighty. Cut down the totem and burn it completely. Walk

---

[103] John 8:36
[104] Luke 10:17
[105] Psalm 22:3
[106] Romans 8:31
[107] 2 Kings 6:15-17

133

through every inch of the glade and speak the blessings of God over it. Then anoint all the remaining trees with oil. Invite the birds and insects, and animals to come back and repopulate this place."

He turned to the defeated demons and spoke in power and might, "Return to the depths from where you have come. Tell your leader, the deceiver, that his time is close."

Suddenly the sky was bright and birds were singing. Everyone looked at each other in amazement. Then the bright entity, who had fought for them, turned back to the villagers and spoke. "Remember your adversary, the devil, is like a roaring lion seeking whom he may devour.[108] Be strong, be wise, and be courageous."[109] While everyone was staring in awe of what they had just seen and heard, they were suddenly alone. The glade was as before, slightly overgrown, but no sign of demonic activity.

Sherry spoke to Leonardo as they walked back to the village. "Can you take care of the totem and anointing the trees and anything else you can put oil on? Perhaps you can just sprinkle some all over the floor of the glade. We want to be sure nothing finds an opportunity that would open the door to their return. We're told in the Bible that when the demons leave we must replace them with God or many more will come back than were there originally."[110]

Leonardo gave a whoop of victory. "It's nice to win a battle; especially when the enemy was the only one to suffer injuries. I will send for two axes to cut down the totem. Many people brought oil. They are already about the work of reclaiming the land for God."

Sherry and Leonardo walked back up to the village. They were still in awe of all that had transpired. Sherry said. "We're going to have a lot to tell the Questers when they call; those in Ogunquit also. Maybe we can look into how to do a conference call and talk with them both at the same time. Sherry felt energized as she went

---

[108] 1 Peter 5:8
[109] Joshua 10:24-25
[110] Luke 11:24-26

back to the compound. She felt an urgency to talk to the Black Death prisoners and share the love of God with them, share His Word with them, and tell them of some of the miracles that had been occurring recently. Surely some of them would listen. She smiled. She truly had a captive audience.

She knew for a fact that they all spoke English. Mehdi had told her that it was spoken fluently in the camp. Sherry wanted somebody with her in this undertaking, someone to pray while she was speaking. Someone to pray with before she even went in to where the prisoners were being held.

As Sherry walked into the kitchen, Tuvicha walked in right behind her. "Was that not a wonderful thing we got to participate in this afternoon? I was glad to get rid of all those demons, and send them back to where they belong. It is hard for me to believe that many of them used to live inside me. I was such a terrible person." Tuvicha hung his head in shame.

"Tuvicha, don't let the enemy lie to you. You have no reason to be ashamed. You repented and asked Jesus to be your Savior. You gave Him your heart. Remember you are a new creation. God doesn't look at your past. He sees you as you are now, and has a plan for your future.

"Right now I need someone to help me. I want to go to the prisoners and share some of the Gospel with them, and some of the miracles that have occurred. Would you come and pray while I am speaking to them?"

"I would love to come and pray for you," Tuvicha replied. "I am still so amazed that the God of the heavens and the earth would take time to listen to my prayers. But I know He does, because He answers me. I hear Him inside me. He speaks to me and I tell Him how much I love Him and want to serve Him. This gives me another opportunity to serve Him."

Sherry smiled and took his arm and they walked into the compound together. When they walked into the back room where the prisoners were being kept, the whole place was in an uproar. Mehdi, Ernesto, and Osvaldo were guarding the prisoners, but at the moment, it did not appear that any guarding was necessary. All the prisoners were lying on the floor and appeared to be asleep. The three guards had a look of surprise and awe on their faces.

Sherry and Tuvicha hurried over. "What happened here?" Sherry asked.

The three looked at each other, expecting the other to speak. Finally Ernesto spoke up. We were standing here watching the prisoners. They were pretty quiet, not giving us any trouble. Suddenly, a man clothed in white, with brightness all around him appeared, and began to speak.

"He spoke directly to the prisoners. He said, "Those whom I love I rebuke and discipline to show them their faults and teach them, so be eager and repent,[111] change your ways and seek God and His will for your life. Behold, I stand at the door knocking. If you hear My Voice and open the door, I will come in and have fellowship with you and restore you. I will then dwell in you and you in Me."

Then He disappeared and the men all fell down. "Could that have been Jesus?" Ernesto asked.

Sherry and Tuvicha stood there unable to answer. Then the men on the ground started stirring. One by one they sat up and looked around. Then one of them who was brave enough to ask, questioned, "Who was that man? Did you hear what He said?"

"Yes," Ernesto answered. "We believe that was Jesus, and He was giving all of you an opportunity to turn from the life you have been living and give your life to Him. I can't believe how special you all are that He made a personal trip to speak to you. In the Bible, there is a story of the Good Shepherd, who leaves the ninety-nine sheep to go search for the one who was lost.[112] I believe that is what happened here. Please don't miss this oppor-

---

[111] Hebrews 12:7-9

tunity. Surely you can see that something supernatural happened. Is there any other way to explain it?"

The prisoners sat there and talked quietly amongst themselves, then one spoke for all. "None of us are Arabs here. Most of us know the story of Jesus. Some of us have even attended church in the past, but became disillusioned. God just didn't seem alive anymore, but this was certainly alive and exciting. We think you are right and that it was Jesus. We want to repent and give our lives to Him. Can He even begin to forgive us for everything we have done? We took part in the beheading of the ten men we captured. It's like we are different people than we were before we got involved with the Black Death."

"You were different. You served Satan by doing what you did. Now, by submitting to God, Satan is thwarted and you are God's. The Bible says that when we become God's, our bodies are the dwelling place of the Holy Spirit, Whom we received from God. It says we don't belong to ourselves anymore, or to Satan, but we were bought with the price of the blood of Jesus and so we should honor God in our body and in our life."[113]

The men still looked hesitant, and one asked, "Will you all please pray with us and tell us what we can do to make up for the terrible things we have done?"

"There's nothing you can do. Jesus already paid for your sins by dying on the cross. The Bible says if you confess your sins He is faithful and just to forgive them and cleanse you from all sinfulness," Sherry answered. "You can either stand or kneel, or stay where you are. It's not the position of your body, but of your heart that counts."

Everyone decided to kneel and they all prayed. After praying, the men jumped up and began shaking hands with each other. Then they looked over at their jailers and said, "What do we do now?"

Sherry said, "It's not my decision to make. You must realize

---

[112] Luke 15:3-7
[113] 1 Corinthians 6:19-20

we might be a little concerned that this was an act, and that you are not all born again. Please be patient with us. I will find Isaac and let him come and talk with you. It will be his decision to make, not mine. Please wait here."

Isaac was thrilled to hear what Sherry had to say when she found him. But then, just like her, caution asserted itself. "Let's get the leaders of the village together with the prisoners and have a time of prayer. God is the only One that can answer these questions." He sent Ernesto to gather Leonardo, Jose, Mehdi, Connie, and Cipriano together.

Sherry called out to Ernesto. When you get everyone assembled, I'd like you to stay also. You have been a Christian longer than some of the rest of them. We need your insight too."

Ernesto bowed his head in humility, awed to be given such an honor. He hurried about, and everyone was there with the prisoners and waiting for him and Cipriano. "All present," he said.

The prisoners were all standing in a group, a look of expectation on their faces. They had just seen Jesus and trusted He would make everything right.

A man from the group of prisoners stepped forward. My name is Frank Minardi. I come from Hackensack, a town in northeastern New Jersey. I've been with this group for about six months. There are three men from Paraguay in the group. The rest of us are from America. We've been talking among ourselves and wonder if there is a terrible job that no one wants, that we could do under supervision. We understand your predicament. Until recently, we were your enemies."

Ernesto smiled. "I could suggest a few. Several outhouses need replacing. New holes need to be dug and old holes filled in. The trench for the waterline needs to be dug, and until it is running, the never ending supply of water needs to be brought up from the river. We have people who could supervise you."

Cipriano spoke up, 'This is all well and good. It may be a

138

great idea, but what does God have to say about it? It appears He has an interest in these men. Let's ask Him what we should do."

Sherry answered, "Cipriano, you always manage to bring us back to God. Thank you. He's right. We all need to sit or kneel or stand and ask God for wisdom in how to handle this situation. He told us if we lack wisdom, we should ask for it, and He would give it to us liberally.[114]

"Frank, other than the prayer to get saved; have any of you men ever prayed before?"

Frank looked at Sherry and answered, "I don't know about the others, but as for me, not in a very long time. When I was a kid I prayed the 'Now I lay me down to sleep' prayer, and I was an altar boy. Does that count?"

A soft smile broke out over Sherry's face. A picture just came to her mind of sitting and praying with her child before bedtime. It suffused her with warmth, and with love for this yet to be born child. She brought herself back to the present circumstances and answered. "Well it's better than nothing at all. I want to encourage all of you men to just talk to God. He knows what's in your heart already, but He likes for you to communicate with Him. Just the way a wife appreciates hearing her husband say he loves her. She already knows it, but it warms her heart to hear it. Wouldn't you want to warm God's heart? Ask for His help, He likes that too."

"Cipriano, since this is your idea, will you lead us in prayer?"

He nodded, and bowed his head. Others around the room followed his example. "Father of the universe, we are so privileged to be considered children of God. You give us strength when we are weak, hope when we are in despair and wisdom when we ask for it. We ask now God for that wisdom. Speak to us. Show us how to handle this situation with the prisoners. We want to trust them, but we also want to be sure. We need discernment. Thank you Lord,

---

[114] James 1:5

139

not only for hearing our prayers, but also for answering them."

The group stayed there and prayed quietly for several minutes. Then they heard someone coming in the compound calling for Leonardo. He looked up and quickly left so as not to cause interruption. A few minutes later he came back into the room and said, "I think I have an answer."

Everyone waited anxiously for him to explain. "That was Miguel's grandmother. She has taken in a family of four from Arandu's tribe, and with the added usage, her outhouse is filled to the brim. She needs a new one immediately. Didn't I hear someone volunteer for that duty? It appears as though God has answered our prayers. There will still be supervision, but we will not keep you bound."

They were in agreement, and the prisoners were immediately set free. There was no one occupying the rooms in the hospital, so cots would be setup for them there. The village had a store of clothes they would draw from to clothe themselves, and food would be provided. Cipriano apologetically stated that they would still post a guard at night indefinitely.

The former prisoners shouted for joy. They were free of ropes that bound them physically, and they were free of the satanic ropes that had bound them spiritually.

Sherry was elated. This was another thing she would tell Daniel about when she spoke to him next.

CHAPTER TWENTY-ONE

JUNE 25
OGUNQUIT, MAINE

It was in the black, silence of the night a Voice called, "Sylvia," and repeated again, "Sylvia". Sylvia's eyes sprang open, and she immediately sat up in her bed. All drowsiness left her as she listened intently. The house was quiet except for the muffled sound of Penny's soft snore, coming from the adjacent bedroom. She lay back down and started to settle into her soft pillow when she once more heard the call.

There was no mistaking it, someone was calling her name. Then she remembered in the Bible when God called to the young boy Samuel. Samuel did not recognize God's Voice, but the priest Eli told him to say, "Speak, Lord for Your servant is listening."[115]

At that moment Sylvia realized that God was speaking to her. She immediately called out, "Lord, I'm listening; what do You want me to do?"

Sylvia listened and waited. She wondered if she had in fact dreamed the Voice. After all, she had been awakened from a sound sleep. Then the Voice spoke again. "Get up, get dressed, and go immediately down into the garden. Don't turn on any lights. There will be a man in the garden waiting for you. Go with him."

Stunned, Sylvia stood for a minute and then replied, "Yes Lord." She hesitated at Penny's door, unsure whether or not to

---

[115] 1 Samuel 3:9

141

wake her, but God had said immediately, and so she went on down the stairs. Going through the house she reached the back door without mishap. She had lived in this house almost fifty years and could have navigated it blindfolded.

The moon was up, and through the window in the door, she could see the shape of a man standing at the corner of the garden. Sylvia opened the door and the man turned towards her. The moon was only starting to wane and its light illuminated his face. She caught her breath in recognition. It was Haydon Carlton.

Immediately doubt tried to overtake her. She had been sure it had been God's Voice she had heard, but in the wake of these circumstances, her faith began to falter. Satan again smiled. These smiles were a contradiction to his character. He was unaccustomed to smiling, but lately he had detected what he thought were chinks in God's plan. He saw what he recognized as flaws and he was always the opportunist, ready to take advantage.

As was her habit, when she was faced with a dangerous situation, or one she could not control, Sylvia called out to the One Who held her in the palm of His hand.[116] She spoke His Words in her mind and renewed her faith with His promises.[117] She knew no matter who she was with, where she was, or what happened to her, God would never leave her or forsake her.[118] All these thoughts flashed through her mind in a moment, but it was enough. Sylvia smiled. It transformed her into a woman of faith. Satan observed and it and it turned his smile into a grimace.

Haydon Carlton pulled a gun from his pocket and began to walk toward Sylvia. She could see the gun as he got closer to her. "You won't need the gun. God woke me up and told me to go with you."

Startled by what she said, he faltered slightly. Even non-

---

[116] Isaiah 49:15-17
[117] Romans 12:1-2
[118] Deuteronomy 31:6

believers take at least some notice when someone says 'God told me.' But Haydon had a hard heart, and the only faith he had was in himself. All his life he had had no one to depend on but himself, and, according to his thinking, he had done a good job. This bunch of do-gooders was not going to put him off his game. He was a winner, and until encountering this group, he always got what he wanted.

He grabbed Sylvia's arm and started toward the road where a dark sedan was parked. "Get in the car, and don't try anything. Remember, I still have this gun and I won't hesitate to use it, on you or anyone else who gets in my way."

Sylvia was glad he didn't think to search her. She had picked up her cell phone that had been on the kitchen counter charging. She didn't know how much of a charge it had in it, or if she was even going to get a chance to use it, but its weight felt comforting. She just hoped no one called her and alerted him to its presence.

As they started down the road, Sylvia turned to look back at the house. Penny's light was on. Had she seen or heard what had happened? Had God awakened Penny and given her a task? These were questions she had no answers for. She would just have to keep reminding herself that God had a plan and it was a good one. If Penny was part of that plan, she would have to trust God that Penny was in the palm of His hand also.

Sylvia prayed quietly as they drove. She didn't pray for herself, but for Penny. Penny was only nineteen and a young Christian, but she had been with the Quest from the beginning. In fact, she and Sylvia had been kidnapped by Haydon Carlton once already. He threatened Penny's life unless Sylvia called Bekah in Paraguay. He was insistent on talking with her. Circumstances turned against him and they were rescued. Haydon was arrested, but had somehow managed to escape. Now she was dealing with him again, but just as then, God was with her and His presence comforted her.

143

Penny continued staring as the dark sedan pulled away. She sat there for a moment, her thoughts in complete disarray. She knew the next few minutes could mean the difference between success and failure for the Quest and life and death for Nana Sylvia.

Her first memories of summer were here at the house in Ogunquit, Maine with Nana. Papa had been gone a long time. She only had a few memories of sitting on his lap. It was Nana who had always prayed with her, and when she was twelve she accepted Jesus as her Lord and Savior. It was Nana who bought her first Bible and took her to church. It was Nana who planted the Word of God in her. Now it was time to see if all that work was going to produce fruit.

Penny had watched Nana pray so many times for God's help. He always seemed to answer her. Nana talked to God all day long. Sometime she was jealous that God got more attention than she did. She smiled at that thought now, because Nana's actions had had such a powerful effect on her life. She was also becoming a woman of prayer.

Penny took the time now to pray and ask for God's guidance. She did not want to rush into things as she would have done in the past. She might be a scatterbrain at times, but she was moving past that into a fine, young woman of faith. She waited patiently to get God's guidance on what to do next.[119]

Five minutes went by and then ten. Suddenly the ringing of her phone shattered the deep silence that had encompassed her room. Penny quickly answered it. "Hello, this is Penny."

"Well hello there, pretty as a penny, this is Haydon Carlton speaking and I have your grandmother with me."

"I know," Penny answered. "I saw her get in the car with you."

"Well aren't you the little snoop. I hope you didn't make any

---

[119] Isaiah 40:31

144

phone calls yet, because I would hate to hurt her."

Penny's skin crawled as she listened to him speak. "No, I haven't called anyone, except God. I've been praying ever since you both left. He hasn't answered me yet, but I know He hears my prayers.[120] The Bible says He does."[121]

Penny took a breath and continued. "But I know I'm supposed to tell you that there definitely is a God and it is not too late for you to serve Him and not Satan. Because when you don't serve God, you serve His adversary Satan. Now, just looking at your life and what you have done since I found out about you, it doesn't appear that you are serving God. However, if you are sorry for your sins and repent, God will forgive you and give you a new life in Christ Jesus."[122, 123]

"That's hilarious," Haydon said, laughing uproariously. "Do you think I've gotten where I have today by serving anyone but myself? If you look at my worth, I seem to have done pretty well on my own, wouldn't you say? Why would I want to share, or return what I have taken? You must think I am very foolish."

Penny started to point out the flaws in his statement. "How's that been working for you? Let's see, right now you are fugitive from the law. All your treasure has been confiscated, and you're trying to run away with a hostage. That doesn't sound very successful to me."

Haydon cursed vehemently. "You just shut your mouth and listen or you'll never see your grandmother again, at least not alive," he laughed. "She's not such a bad old lady, and I'd hate to have to hurt her, but I will if I need to, and you'd better remember that. It's not her I want, it's Bekah, and this old lady is going to help me find her if she ever wants to see you again."

---

[120] Psalm 34:17
[121] James 5:16
[122] 1 John 1:9
[123] 2 Corinthians 5:17

"Well this is what you better remember," Penny replied with conviction, "God is the one I listen to. He tells me to call for help or not. It's not your decision; it's up to Him. You don't scare me and you don't scare Nana either. Our trust is in God. He has a plan, and all things work together to bring His good plan to pass."[124]

Haydon sat there in shock, astounded that this wisp of a girl was arguing with him. Then he realized the line was dead. He was stupefied. She had hung up on him. Who did she think she was? She couldn't talk to him this way. He looked over at Sylvia with a grimace, "You heard what I told her. You better behave yourself. I'll take care of her when the time comes. We're on our way to Paraguay to finish my business with Miss Bekah Ryan, and no one is going to find us, or stop us."

Haydon continued on his way north. His collection may be lost to him, but he had picked up large amounts of cash he had stashed in several hiding places. He had many such places all over the world. He was a man of power and means and he was going to exert that power and use those means to get what he wanted. He was also going to punish those people who had thwarted his plans. He had a plane waiting across the border in Canada to take them to Paraguay. By tomorrow afternoon they would be in Puerto Bahia Negra with ten men he had hired to accompany them into the jungle. The men had also made the arrangements for two boats, supplies for at least ten days, along with a large quantity of weapons and ammunition.

Haydon was taking control of the situation. He was tired of being humiliated. There would be no more mistakes. Anyone who got in his way would live to regret it, or maybe die regretting it. Haydon smiled as he drove basking in the good opinion he had of himself. He had no idea of the hornet's nest he was stirring up. Little did he realize that angelic beings were with them; sent to foil

---

[124] Romans 8:28

146

the works of the enemy and assist Sylvia. They waited for her to speak and she waited for direction from God.[125]

The car sped away into the darkness, but Sylvia was not concerned. She had heard the Voice of God and obeyed. Now it was up to God to fulfill His plan. Sylvia sat and prayed quietly. She determined she would not speak until God gave her something to say.

---

[125] Proverbs 3:5-6

CHAPTER TWENTY-TWO

JUNE 26
OGUNQUIT, MAINE

It was very early in the morning when Penny put the phone down and got back into bed. She did not want to do anything until she had prayed. If she had learned anything from Nana Sylvia over the years, it was that taking action before praying is a sure way to guarantee disaster. She also knew it was not just Nana Sylvia's life in jeopardy, but everyone who was connected to the Quest.

Penny immediately fell into a deep sleep and dreamed. Several hours later she awoke filled with excitement. She had a momentary setback when she remembered she could not share her dream with Nana Sylvia. The uncertainty and fear of the happenings of last night tried to rob her of her faith and her motivation. Penny knew where those thoughts came from, Satan, the liar. God brought Scriptures to mind that would drive out fear[126] and remind her of His protection. She remembered that no weapon formed against her would prosper.[127]

After taking time to pray, Penny called Joe and Roberta, members of the Quest who had stayed behind to coordinate communication, establish a prayer army, and also deal with any other issues that might come up. She looked at the clock and was amazed it was so late. She began to second guess herself. "Why hadn't I called last night? Why did I sleep so late? They could be

---

[126] 2 Timothy 1:7
[127] Isaiah 54:17

in Paraguay already. Nana could already be dead."

These thoughts buzzed around in her head like a swarm of angry bees. She started to succumb to their onslaught when she answered the phone. "Good morning Penny," said a jovial voice. Immediately, Penny marshalled her thoughts. "Joe, something has happened." Penny proceeded to tell him the events of the previous night.

"Wow," Joe said. "I didn't see that coming." Agitated, he questioned, "Why didn't you call me right away?"

Penny explained, "I was going to. That was my first reaction. Then I remembered, pray first, respond after prayer. Nana has been teaching me that all my life. I didn't want to fail the test. Anyway, Haydon called me, and I think I startled him. I told him I saw him take my grandmother. Then I said that I was praying for him, and God was giving him another opportunity to make a choice, but the time was growing short. He needed to make up his mind whether to serve God, or the devil."[128]

"You're right, Penny," Joe agreed. "God hasn't said to stop, so let's all pray for him. Jesus died for him too.[129] As long as there's life, there's hope. We all need to be reminded of that. Now, I think we should call in all our prayer support and bring them up to date on what has taken place. I'll call Jean to see if it's alright to meet there at ten thirty, this morning. Then I'll start the ball rolling to notify the prayer team.

"We also need to call Sergeant Hathaway and report Sylvia's kidnapping. We'll ask him to meet us at the Lobster Pot at ten o'clock. I'm sure he will want to question you. I think we should fill him in on everything that is going on. Then he can decide what action he needs to take. I'm pretty sure if Haydon and Sylvia haven't left the country by now, they will shortly. I don't know how much preparation Haydon has put in his plan, but he seems to be mov-

---

[128] Deuteronomy 30:19
[129] John 3:16

150

ing quickly. Was there anything else God showed you?"

"Yes, but I'll share it when everyone is together. Let's start the prayer chain and inform everyone to meet at the Lobster Pot at ten thirty." They ended the call and Penny went to shower and get dressed.

Penny did some of her best praying in the shower. Today was no exception. God showed her the dream again with more clarity. He also gave her understanding to some of it. Penny wished they didn't have to operate by faith. Sometimes it seemed as though God expected more of her than she thought she was able, but He knew her from top to bottom and inside out. He knew what she was capable of better than she did.[130]

Joe and his wife Roberta were long-time friends of Bekah's. Roberta, along with Sylvia, was also employed at Bekah's needle-work shop. They, along with over twenty-five others, showed up at the Lobster Pot each evening. Jean, the owner, had been provid-ing them with the back room free of charge. She even provided coffee and cookies; sometimes she even stayed for prayer.

Sergeant Jim Hathaway showed up at ten on the dot. Ro-berta, Joe and Penny sat down with him and told him everything that had happened from the beginning, from the first dream to Sylvia's abduction.

He sat there quietly through the telling, trying to absorb all the happenings, and the ramifications of what it all meant. Jim considered himself a Christian. He had been raised attending church, but he had never seen or heard anything like the story he had just been told. It sounded more like the plot of one of those suspense novels he liked to read.

When they were through with the story, he just sat there for a moment. "Don't rush into judgment," he had always been told, and he still followed that advice. He looked at Joe, Roberta and Penny and said, "That's one astounding story. My first thought

---

[130] Psalm 139:1-6

would be to say you are all crazy except for three things. First, after the break-in I did a little checking up on Joshua Randall. Did you know he was carrying a gun the night of the break-in?"

"No, not at that time," Joe answered. He told us the next morning. Also, that he sometimes worked for the C.I.A. Josh has a friend in the Washington office he works with from time to time."

Sergeant Hathaway continued, "I have a friend who works at the State Department. He was able to verify that Josh did in fact work for the C.I.A.

"Second, I called the church in Claremore, Oklahoma that he said he worked for and they confirmed he was on their staff, but had taken a leave of absence.

"Third, Sylvia is missing. She and my mom were best friends. I've known her all my life and there was never a more honest and devout person than Sylvia Jessup."

Sergeant Hathaway looked at the three of them and asked, "Do any of you have a clue as to where Haydon Carlton might have taken her?"

"Yes," they all said.

Joe answered, "Penny, you talked with him. Did he say anything definitive?"

"Not today, but he took Nana Sylvia and me prisoner once before and he did it to find Bekah. He thinks she has found a treasure in Paraguay and he wants it. I think he's taking Nana to Paraguay to find Bekah and recover the so-called treasure. Unfortunately, I think he has gone off the deep end and there's no guessing what he might do next. We are all meeting here to pray. God has been leading and guiding us in this endeavor. He hasn't led us this far to stop now. Stay and pray with us. You will see that God is still working today."

Just then Audrey Hathaway, Jim's wife walked in. She stopped in surprise as she saw her husband standing there. "What are you doing here, Jim?" she asked.

"I could ask you the same question. I'm here on official business," Jim stated. "A kidnapping has been reported and I came to question and investigate."

Jim took in Audrey's appearance. She was casually dressed, but carried her Bible and a pad. "My guess is you're here for the prayer meeting. Well I was just invited to stay, and since you're here, I think I will."

Joe led Audrey and Jim to seats and then turned to look over the crowd that was assembling. It was starting to resemble a church service, it had grown so large. There were now almost forty people in attendance.

Prayer had not slacked off as time went on, as sometimes happens; but increased. God had a veritable army of people who were assigned to pray on this problem and they were more than able to meet the challenge. Their solution to the challenge was, "Let's see what God can do."

With everything that had happened so far on this Quest, they knew God was more than capable of coming up with a solution to any circumstance the enemy tried to put before them. In fact they knew God already had the answer. He knew the solution before the problem even existed.[131]

They spent the first fifteen minutes praying. Then someone got up and read a Scripture. It said that whenever God's Word is spoken in faith it accomplished the task it was sent to do.[132] Several other people got up and also read Scriptures. Then Joe got up and told everyone that Sylvia had been taken by Haydon Carlton.

Momentarily it got noisy as everyone expressed their outrage and disbelief at this change in circumstances. Joe held up his hands for quiet. "Everyone remember, from the beginning, God's been in control. Let's not forget to keep it that way. Nothing we can think of on our own would be better than what He already

---

[131] Isaiah 46:9-10
[132] Isaiah 55:11

has planned."

Joe turned to Penny, "Penny, please tell everyone what happened."

Penny gathered her thoughts. Sometimes it was like chasing leaves in the wind, but this time God was helping her stay focused.[133] "I woke up some time during the night. I'm not sure what woke me. Maybe I heard Nana Sylvia go out the back door. I got up and looked out the window into the garden. I saw a man standing there and Nana Sylvia was walking towards him. They talked; then he took her arm and helped her into the car parked on the road. Then they drove off. I recognized the man. I saw his face in the street lamp. It was Haydon Carlton."

A murmur went through the prayer group. Penny continued, "About ten minutes later he called me. We had quite a conversation. I think he's going to Puerto Bahia Negra to find Bekah. He has been trying to intimidate Bekah ever since she refused to sell him her crucifix. He knows she's in Paraguay. He's fixated on capturing her and gaining a treasure of enormous proportions. He thinks she knows where to find it.

"After talking with him, I prayed again. I felt that I should get some sleep and then call in the morning to tell everyone. While I was sleeping, God gave me a dream. I don't understand all of it, but I know it's from Him, and it's meant to lead and guide us."

Penny focused her eyes on the group and began to relate the dream to everyone. "I don't understand the whole dream. In some of the dream, the meaning is obvious; other parts not clear to me at all. But one of you may see something I do not. Wait until the end to ask me questions. I don't want to lose my train of thought."

Praying was a good way to begin, Penny thought, so she prayed, "My Father in Heaven, You are so great my mind can't even begin to imagine. God, we are praying for Your Kingdom to

---

[133] 2 Corinthians 10:5

154

flourish on Earth as it does in Heaven. We want to do Your will in order to facilitate that. We thank You for all You have provided for us: our families and friends, our homes, our jobs. We thank You that even the food we eat You provided. I ask that if there is any sin in our lives, You show it to us so that we can repent of it. We also forgive anyone who has sinned against us. Don't allow us to stray into temptation, but lead us away from it. Deliver us from any evil that is trying to attack us, and in all this we give You all the honor and all the glory, and all the praise forever and ever. Amen.[134]

"I know that God is always with me, but I like to keep reminding myself. I had this dream after Nana Sylvia was taken by Haydon Carlton. As I said, I believe he's bringing her to Paraguay, trying to use her to get to Bekah. I don't know what's going to happen, but I trust that God has everything under control. Worrying won't change a thing, so we should let God work it out.[135] After talking with Haydon, I went back to sleep. I felt God tell me to contact Joe in the morning. When I woke up this morning I remembered the strange dream I had and I knew it was from God. I'm going to share it with all of you the best I can. It was a very disturbing dream, and I would be afraid, if I gave in to fear. So right now, can we all take authority over the spirit of fear?[136] The Greater One lives in us and leads and guides us."[137]

Penny faltered. "I have to admit to you I don't understand this dream. Maybe when the time comes we will learn all that we need to know. I dreamed I was in the jungle with the group going out to find the tribe causing all the trouble. God showed me all the people there. I didn't see their faces, but just knew they were there. God also showed me that one of them was entertaining Satan with his thoughts, just as Judas did before he betrayed Jesus.

---

[134] Matthew 6:9-13
[135] Matthew 6:34
[136] 2 Timothy 1:7
[137] 1 John 4:4

Also, that same young man gave the impression of sitting apart from the group. There also looked like a shadow of some sort was around him. I don't know the exact meaning of that, but it didn't appear to be good. We must pray for him and all of them that they remain faithful. I don't know whether we should warn the Questers about this or let God deal with it. God showed me all this as if I was there, but they could not see me and I could not speak to them.

"The Questers are heading north and will reach Arandu's village tomorrow. There are more of them now. Renato, Ted, and a young man from the village are with them. Everyone looked fine. No one had any injuries, but I saw a few strange things. Renato had what appeared to be a black tattoo under his arm. It looked luminescent. I don't know if anyone else saw it. Nobody paid any attention to it; it was as if it wasn't there. Everyone else acted normally.

"When they get to Arandu's village, they are going to see the charred remains of the village, and the remains of the large fire that was used to sacrifice the babies. They are going to stay there one day and pray, asking God how they should proceed. You see, they don't have all the details of what they are to do either."

Penny hesitated and then said, "I believe some time went by. Maybe they were traveling north toward the blind tribe. I call them the blind tribe because Satan has blinded their eyes, and lied to them. Unfortunately, they do not know the truth. That is one of the reasons God sent us all on this Quest. It was to bring them the truth so that the truth would set them free.[138]

"I don't know how to describe the rest of the dream. I saw a large and mighty waterfall. The water crashed and cascaded down into what looked like a lake, or maybe a very large river. Behind the waterfall there were many large caves. Inside these caves was all manner of wealth: gold, jewels, artifacts like Bekah's cross. There were swords, and pieces of armor, helmets, shields, and chainmail, all jewel encrusted. Maybe this is the treasure Hay-

---

[138] John 8:32

don Carlton is searching for.

"There was also a very large village set on the west side of the falls. It consisted of upwards of two hundred buildings. There were at least fifty or sixty canoes and some larger boats set on the side of the river. Many people were fishing in the lake and along the shore. There was a very large cultivated area west of the village with what looked like a variety of different kinds of crops. It even looked as if there was an area of some kind of fruit trees. It appeared this village had been there for a long time.

"As I looked, I saw very few men. There were mostly elderly women and children. It also appeared there were guards set at intervals around the village, but they were the only men I saw with weapons. While I was observing this I felt like a spy. Maybe that's what I was doing, spying so I could warn our people what to expect. Of course, I don't know when what I saw took place. It could be what was happening today or next week. Maybe they were out to attack another village. I hope not. There may have been some other things in the dream, but this is all I remember. I'm sure if I forgot anything important God will remind me. If God shows me anything else, I'll tell you right away. I just ask everyone to please keep my Nana in your prayers."

The room was quiet for a moment. Then everyone began to talk, asking questions and making comments. Joe had to stand up and ask everyone to be quiet for a moment. "Roberta, please take notes of the questions and comments so we will be able to go over them later and see if any other light is shed on the subject."

Joe then turned to Audrey and asked her to introduce her husband. Audrey stood and reached for Jim's hand. Pulling him to her side she said, "Some of you may know him, but for those of you who don't, this is my husband, Sergeant Jim Hathaway. He's here to pray, and also to follow up on the kidnapping of Sylvia Jessup. Hopefully, he will be able to keep us informed of any information they discover."

Joe said, "We'll make our phone call tonight and tell everyone down there what has transpired up here. Let's meet back here at seven."

CHAPTER TWENTY-THREE

JUNE 26

THE BLACK DEATH CAMP

Isaac thought about the twenty-six boxes of assorted weapons that had been removed from the terrorist training camp to several spots in the jungle. Tracks had been covered and only the native men who placed the weapons there would be able to find them. We could use a few of their tricks of camouflage, he thought. Even though these were illiterate men who had not had the benefit of any formal education, they were knowledgeable in things they needed to know to survive in the jungle.

Isaac and his men had arrived two days ago and he was unsure his life would ever be the same. Everywhere he went and everyone he talked with, they all had the same story. Jesus had come into their lives and changed them. They all wanted to tell him about all the miracles that had taken place in the last few weeks. Normally, he would chalk this up to exaggeration, or even paranoia, but these people had been through some extraordinary situations. There was a ring of truth and sincerity about them that argued that point. Not only that, but everyone wanted to pray for him. He didn't know whether to laugh or convert.

He had not darkened the door of a synagogue for almost thirty years. To him the Bible was a book of fables that he did not have time to read, or to listen to stories of Daniel in the lion's den or David killing Goliath with a sling shot. Isaac thought that if there really was a God, He would have more believable stories than these fairytales.

Isaac walked back to the village with Leonardo. He was looking forward to a meal and then turning in for the night. It had been non-stop action since they had arrived, and he was bone weary. He had been on many missions where he was in foreign countries among the native peoples, but this mission was different. First, they were dealing with an extremely dangerous group of people. The Black Death was a scourge, not just to them, but to the entire planet. Yet, here he was in the backwater country of Paraguay, where the Black Death had established what appeared to be a strong foothold.

Then he had a coworker, Josh Randall, who seemed to have fallen off the deep end. He was claiming that God had talked to several people in a dream, and was guiding them through the jungle to a radical tribe who sacrificed babies, in a fire no less, to their god. In addition, the whole village appears to have succumbed to this paranoia. Everyone he had come in contact with had a story they wanted to tell him about how God had changed their lives. Well he was very happy with his life just the way it was. He wasn't comfortable with everyone's religious zeal. He just wanted them to leave him alone.

Thankfully, almost everyone had returned to their homes for their last meal of the day. After he ate, that's what he intended to do. He had the room that had been Bekah's. Thankfully, he had privacy. He walked slowly back to the compound, trying to stop all the confusing thoughts that were boomeranging around in his mind. He just wanted to lie down and sleep.

Looking up he saw Sherry in the doorway, almost as if she were waiting for him. He grimaced, but trudged on, hoping he could get by her with minimal conversation. "Isaac," Sherry called out. "I'm just making myself a pot of tea. Daniel gets me this wonderful blend every now and again from a friend. It's so soothing, espe-

160

cially after a hectic day. Would you like a cup? I might even be able to find some kind of cake to go with it."

All Isaac heard was 'cup of tea', and his head came up and his pace quickened. He loved tea. In fact, he had several connections who brought him exotic blends when they came into town. He decided one cup of tea would be worth having to endure yet another conversation.

Isaac smiled at Sherry, "You have no idea how enticing that invitation is. Lead the way."

They walked into the large kitchen and thankfully, it was empty. He could hear the teapot whistling a piercing call. Sherry quickly went over and took it off the stove. She had the teapot warming. She dumped its contents into a bucket, and then filled it with the freshly boiled water. Then she measured the tea, put it in the pot and put on its lid. Immediately a sensation of peace pervaded the atmosphere as the aroma of the tea infiltrated every corner of the room. Isaac closed his eyes and smiled.

He had tasted many different and unusual teas, but he did not recognize the aroma of this one. Sherry let it steep for a few minutes while she cut two pieces of cake. Bringing them to the table, she sat down and poured the tea. "How do you take yours? I don't have milk, but I have wonderful honey."

Isaac smiled a genuine smile. "That would be perfect." They sat in companionable silence as they finished their tea and cake. Sherry made a move to gather the dishes and put them in the sink. Isaac stopped her. "Relax," he said. "Let me get that."

Isaac came back to sit with Sherry, all thoughts of sleeping had vanished from his mind. Here was someone he could talk to. He knew she was educated and was not likely to be subject to superstitions and fantasies. He knew that Josh was also educated, but Isaac believed that the woman, Bekah, had muddled his thinking with her story. He was not aware that Josh was the first person to have the dream from God.

161

He sat down across from Sherry and questioned her, a confused look on his face. "Sherry, what is happening down here? I'm hearing all kinds of confusing stories and don't know what to believe. Will you tell me the truth, without any embellishments, about what you think happened and what the ramifications are for all of this?"

Sherry smiled a sad smile. "I can try, but unless you are a believer, all that has happened will seem like a fairytale."

Isaac put his face in his hands and stayed that way. While Sherry waited, she prayed quietly under her breath. Finally Isaac looked up. "I've never been a believer in much of anything except myself. I worked hard to get where I am and I don't think God, or His divine plan had anything to do with it. If God does actually work in our lives, why is this world in such a mess?"

Sherry closed her eyes and said a quiet prayer. "God, help me explain the Gospel to this man. It appears he sincerely wants to know the truth. Your Word says that when we know the truth we will be free.[139] Help his eyes to see and his ears to hear what You are doing and saying today.

"I'm going to start at the beginning," Sherry explained. "Stop me any time you have a question. How much of the Bible are you familiar with?"

He answered hesitantly, "I had to study the first five books for my Bar Mitzvah. That was over thirty years ago. I was married to a Christian woman twenty years ago. I went to church with her once or twice, but it was not for me. In fact, her zealous faith drove a wedge between us. I blamed God for the demise of our marriage. It was easier for me to blame Him than to blame myself. I know she believed in prayer, and she even prayed for me after our divorce. Her name is Margaret. I called her Peg. As far as I know, she never remarried and neither did I."

Sherry smiled when she heard Isaac describe his marriage.

---

[139] John 8:32

162

It appeared there were still some feelings there under the surface.

Isaac paused to gather his thoughts and then continued. "I've never been one for religion. I only believe in what I can see. God is too much of a myth. I can't see Him or touch Him. I tried praying a few times, but He never answered my prayers. Up till now I've gotten along pretty well without Him. If He is real, He hasn't seemed to bother with me and I don't bother with Him."

Sherry questioned, "Did you ever think that your being here might be an answer to Peg's prayer? Maybe God preserved you and brought you here for a purpose. God has somehow brought us all here and woven us into His tapestry. He used Rahab the harlot to help the Israelites attack Jericho. She was not a Jew, but she helped them escape and God counted her a believer.[140] Maybe your help is needed and God is calling you to His side.

"I believe there are only two masters in this world, God and Satan. You have to make a choice. God calls us all to choose whom we will serve.[141] You know that something is happening down here, and you are even questioning if it could be God. Look at all the people down here who have taken a leap of faith. The Bible says that all of creation is waiting in eager expectation for the sons of God to be manifest.[142] I propose to you, that is what is happening here. God is showing Himself strong on our behalf and we are standing up for Him."

Isaac looked at Sherry in disbelief. "How can you believe all this? You tell me about some bad or evil people. You tell me a story about a village being attacked and babies being sacrificed by throwing them into a fire. Do you have anything to back up this story? Do you have one shred of evidence that any of this is true and not just coincidence? Maybe these people who you say were healed would have gotten better without God's help. Maybe the so-called dead

---

[140] James 2:24-26
[141] Deuteronomy 30:19
[142] Romans 8:19-22

163

baby would have recovered on his own. Maybe the medication you gave to Noemi kicked in at just the right time and her heart strengthened. I'm sure there's a logical explanation for all this."

Sherry hung her head. She felt a tear slide down her cheek. Then she said, "Over sixty people from the village that was attacked are living here. They had fourteen babies burned in a sacrificial fire. They can tell you how real it was. That, along with everything else that has happened, should be enough to convince you." She put her head in her hands and continued to pray quietly, not wanting to say too much.

Then she thought she heard weeping and slowly raised her head. There sat Isaac with his face awash in tears, shoulders shaking with gut wrenching sobs. He looked up at Sherry and sobbed, "Who am I kidding? As much as I want to chalk this up to wild imaginations and coincidence, when you reach the bottom line, your gut betrays you with what's happening. You realize you cannot deny the truth any longer. There is nothing else it could be but God. Too many strange and unexplained happenings can only be explained by a supernatural occurrence taking place. Thankfully, I still have enough faith to believe that good things come from God."[143]

Sherry smiled a hopeful smile. "If you have enough faith to believe what I've told you, then you have enough faith to get saved. Why fight God? You can't win. Nobody ever has. Like they say, 'It's His way or the highway;' and in this instance, the highway is the road to Hell and damnation."

If anything, Isaac looked even worse. "I don't know if I can believe all the things you do. Remember, I'm a Jew. It's part of my genetic makeup. Based on what you have told me and what I have observed, there should be enough evidence to convince me, but something about all this keeps me questioning."

Sherry sighed. "I don't know exactly where you can cross

---

[143] James 1:17

the line with skepticism, but I feel you are on the edge. It's like you are hearing the still small Voice of God, but you want the lightning and thunder.[144] God sometimes speaks in a whisper that only your heart can hear. Isaac, you have come to a crossroad. Do you acknowledge that you were wrong in your beliefs? Do you acknowledge that you are a sinner and need a Savior, and that God sent Jesus, His only Son, into the world to die for our sins, and reconnect us with the God of the universe? Now, as unbelievable as that may seem, Jesus is seated at the right hand of the Father praying for us. I can tell you that God is as real to me as you are. He leads me and guides me. He picks me up when I fall. He comforts me when I am down. I love Him and serve Him with all of my might."

Isaac cried out, "I want to believe, but I don't know how! I want to have your faith, your peace, and your comfort. How do I do it?"

Sherry's eyes sparkled. "The Bible says anyone who calls on the Name of the Lord shall be saved.[145] Call out to Jesus. He will hear you and save you. God knows your heart. He will know if you are sincere or not."

Isaac took a breath. He did not know what to say or how to say it. Finally he shouted, "Jesus, if You are real, come and save me." He sat there with his eyes closed, waiting for an answer. Finally, he opened his eyes and said, "Well either He's not real, or He doesn't want me."

Sherry sat and watched, her heart crying out to God to answer this man's plea. Suddenly Isaac's expression began to change. A look of wonder came over his face and he jumped to his feet and started shouting. "He heard me! He heard me! I can't believe He answered me. He talked to me!"

Sherry was smiling now. "Tell me, what did He say?" It was so exhilarating to see someone excited about the wonder of God.

Isaac shouted, "He said, 'I am real'. He whispered it, He

---

[144] 1 Kings 19:11-13
[145] Romans 10:12-13

shouted it. I don't know which. All I know is I heard Him. He's real, He's real, and He cares about me."

Isaac suddenly stopped shouting and sat down heavily. "How do I thank God? How do I make up for all the terrible things I've done? Sherry, I've even killed people."

"Isaac, when you get saved, Jesus' blood washes all your sins away. Big ones, small ones, it makes no difference to God. It's as if you never did them."[146]

But what about the people I've killed. What is the penalty for that? God punished Cain for killing Abel. What punishment will he give me?"

"Even if it were a cold-blooded murder like Cain's was, God will forgive you, if you repent and turn from your sin. Killings that may have taken place during war are another matter entirely. You are allowed to defend yourself and your country. All that matters is that when you come to God you start off with a clean slate. Remember I told you, it's as if you never sinned. God is not like us. He doesn't have an ax to grind or a grudge to carry. One thing He does require is that we forgive others just as He forgave us. If we don't forgive others, He can't forgive us."[147]

"That's it?" Isaac questioned. "That's all I have to do is forgive people?"

"Well no," Sherry answered, "but forgiveness is not as easy as it sounds."

"But what should I do?"

Sherry thought for a moment and then replied, "The Bible says that we live on the earth, but Heaven is our home. While on the earth we are part of the army of God. We have to learn how to fight. God has even given us armor to wear while fighting the battle.[148] We have Bible study here every morning after breakfast. I

---

[146] Isaiah 43:25
[147] Matthew 6:15
[148] Ephesians 6:10-17

166

suggest that you make that a part of your day. We also have times of prayer. If you can't come, pray on your own. Prayer is nothing more than talking to God. You did it today and He answered you. Before you go to sleep have another talk with God. Maybe He will speak to you in dreams. That's what started this whole thing. We all had a dream.

"Come on, it's almost time to eat. After that we may get a call from Maine, or maybe from the Questers. We usually hear from one group or both. Maybe you'll get to tell Josh you got saved. Won't he be surprised?"

"You have no idea," said Isaac. "Josh gave up on me a long time ago."

CHAPTER TWENTY-FOUR

JUNE 26

THE QUESTERS

The day had passed quietly. They had visited with each other, rested, and a few of the young men had even gone out hunting. They would eat well tonight. Bekah had asked Axel if he would help her look for some fruit and roots in the jungle, but he made an excuse and so she asked Manu if he would go. They came back loaded with good things to eat.

While Bekah was preparing for the evening meal, Manu remembered he wanted to take some time to talk with Axel. Looking for him, he saw him sitting off by himself. He walked over and sat down. He was concerned that something was bothering this young man and he did not want there to be any opportunity for the enemy to find an open door by someone having taken offense.

"Axel, I see you off by yourself all day. What is the matter? What's troubling you? Has someone said or done something to offend you?"

"Now he asks," Axel thought with resentment. He looked up, shielding his anger, not wanting to express his feelings openly. Unfortunately, when feelings of anger and resentment are hidden, they bloom into a garden of iniquity. "I'm fine," he lied. "I spent the afternoon praying," he lied again.

Manu sat there for several minutes trying to talk with Axel, trying to draw him out further, but he continued to say that he was fine and just wanted some quiet time praying. Manu could not fault him for that, but he had a feeling that Axel was not being truthful. He would discuss this later with Daniel. Daniel knew Axel well. Maybe he would have some insight into this situation. Hopefully it was just his imagination and everything was well. He said a quick prayer, asking the Holy Spirit to bring anything that was hidden to light so that it could be dealt with.

Meanwhile Philippe, Maitie, Giancarlo and Mario had cleaned the game they had brought back from their hunt and Bekah was working her magic on it. They had even killed a small deer and were cutting it up to smoke it through the night. The smoked meat would provide them with some non-perishable food in case they were not able to hunt. They laughed and joked over their chore, not noticing Axel sitting apart and staring at them with malevolent eyes.

No one seemed to be watching him. No one took notice of his anger, but he was wrong. Satan had noticed, and was wringing his hands in gleeful anticipation. He remembered dealing with a situation similar to this one in the past. People don't change. He would entice this one with delusions just as he had done to Judas long ago. Again, there would be a traitor in their midst and he would bring the Quest to a grinding halt. He had just the bait to snare him. Let him stew in his own juices for a while. He was in no hurry. He wanted to make sure this fish had taken the bait before he set the hook.

Renato was also sitting apart on the opposite side of the camp, but Satan could find no stronghold in him. Renato was watching the others and praying for each of them, one by one. He was praying for the five young men, soon to cross into adulthood and take on the challenges and responsibilities that position entailed. Then he noticed that there were only four young men. Axel was missing from the group. As he looked around, he spotted Axel on the other side of the camp with a frown on his face. What was his problem, he wondered? Suddenly a Scripture came to mind. It

170

was the one where God was speaking to Cain and telling him that sin was crouching at his door and that he must resist it. In his mind Renato saw Axel with the same downcast face that Cain had.[149]

Renato turned his prayers toward Axel. First and foremost, he did not want this young man to lose his soul to Satan. He did not want Axel to be lost just like Judas had been lost when he betrayed Jesus. Second, unity was important when you are fighting any enemy, but fighting Satan brought things to a different level. They all needed to be certain they had no sin in their lives so they could be sure God's protection was around them.

What Renato saw in Axel at this time disturbed him. Actually it scared him because he knew that one sin could bring defeat upon them. He remembered one man's sin caused Joshua to lose the battle at Ai.[150] He did not want anyone's sin to cause them to fail at the Quest God had given them. He continued in prayer until the meal was served. He prayed not just for Axel, but for every member of the group.

Renato got up and walked over to where Axel was sitting. He stood there until Axel acknowledged his presence. Finally he looked up and Renato said, "You looked lonely over here all by yourself. Would it be alright if I sat down with you?"

Axel didn't answer the question but lied saying, "I'm not lonely, I like being alone. You don't have to come over to keep me company."

What he said bordered on rudeness, but the way he said it tipped the scale. Renato appeared to take no notice of the rebuff. He continued to talk, and sat down without Axel's invitation.

Axel now directed his anger at Renato. He stood up and demanded, "Why are you bothering me old man? You're not even a member of our village. Nothing you say could be of any importance to me. Why don't you just get up and leave me alone."

[149] Genesis 4:6-9
[150] Joshua 7:11-12

Renato was startled at his disrespect. Even dealing with strangers, everyone was taught from a young age to be polite. This was a sure sign something was wrong with Axel. Renato chose to ignore the disrespectful attitude. He spoke quietly to Axel. "I'm sorry to disturb you, but I needed someone to pray with me and you were the only one not busy at the moment."

As Renato watched, Axel seemed startled. Then he shook his head, lowered his voice, and questioned Renato, "What did you ask me?"

Renato smiled at Axel. "I needed someone to pray with me. Do you have the time?"

Satan watched as his potential collaborator sat back down with Renato and they began to pray together. But he was not concerned. He had made a rather large inroad. There were definitely some chinks in the armor. He would continue coming back to this one and break him down. He was already distancing himself from the group. Satan would watch him as a lion does his prey, looking for points of weakness so he would have an advantage.[151] Satan would have to find ways to interfere with Renato's efforts to befriend Axel.

The prayer time was ended even before it started. Daniel called everyone over. He was going to make the phone call to the village now, even though it was a little early. He was interested to find out what they had done today. Things were happening so quickly it was hard to keep track. As they all sat around, waiting for someone to answer, Axel began to back away. But he bumped into someone. He turned around in surprise and saw it was Renato again.

"Don't you want to hear what's going on? Stay and listen."

"No, I can't," Axel made an excuse. "I need to go down to the river and get more water. I'll find out later."

Renato asked quietly, "Can't that wait until later?"

Axel raised his voice again. "I told you I need to get water.

---

[151] 1 Peter 5:8

That's the job they gave me. I guess they thought it was the only thing I was smart enough to do," he said with bitterness. "The other four hunted; I got the water."

Renato backed off, "Maybe we can pray another time; when you are not so busy, I would enjoy talking with you."

"Sure," grumbled Axel, as he walked off muttering to himself. He looked back at Renato and said to himself, "He is probably only interested in all the jewels we're going to find. And if we do I want my fair share of them. None of it should go to these interlopers."

Axel focused his mind on the treasure. He had not seen the jeweled crucifix, but he had heard talk of it, and he knew about the village's treasure. Greed suddenly reared its head in the garden of his heart. There were more weeds there than before. Love, joy, peace, patience, kindness, goodness, faithfulness, gentleness, and self-control were being strangled by anger, bitterness, greed, quarreling, jealousy, and selfishness.[152] Axel's mind was being overtaken by sin, and it was turning the garden of his heart into a field of weeds, and thorns.

All the way down to the river Axel continued to murmur and complain. He looked around, careful that no one was paying any attention to him. But he was wrong. Satan was again smiling and patting himself on the back. "This is going to be easy," he said, "like taking candy from a baby."

Axel continued to grumble, spilling water on the way up with careless disregard. In his mind, these people were no longer friends. Thoughts came to his mind. They did not value him. They did not even like him. They certainly didn't appreciate all he did for them. He began to scheme what he could do to get even with them, to get retribution for all that had been done to him. The love for his friends had been exchanged for bitterness, anger, jealousy, envy, and hatred. All the attributes that defined him as a Christian

---

[152] Galatians 5:19-23

had been replaced. Even his appearance looked different. He was no longer the smiling, helpful young man they were familiar with; now he wore a scowl on his face and a look of anger in his eyes.

Satan's smile grew even broader. This was working out better than he had hoped. Men were so easy to fool. Most times they wanted to believe his lies. It made his job easier. Instead of being open and honest with each other, they held things in and let thoughts and emotions run away with them. He would let this man's thoughts run wild and see where they took him.[153]

When Axel came back in the camp, he went back to his seat on the side of the clearing. He would listen to what was being said. Maybe there would be something he could use to his advantage.

He had already distanced himself to the extent that it was them against him. Fellowship had been broken and now he was alone.

---

[153] Romans 12:2

CHAPTER TWENTY-FIVE

JUNE 26
THE VILLAGE

Silence fell over the assembled group as they waited for the telephone to ring. The crowd was smaller to some extent. There were fewer villagers. Many had to hunt and cook for their families, and also had various jobs about the village. Their places were partially taken by Isaac and the seven men he brought with him.

Isaac was almost unrecognizable from the dour man who had landed only two days ago. He was coming down the path with his arm around Leonardo and his face was wreathed in a smile. He was anxious to talk to Josh and tell him what had happened to him, what he had experienced. They went and sat down next to Sherry. She was also smiling, anxious to talk with Daniel. Other than his frequent trips to Puerto Bahia Negra for supplies, they had been separated very little in the last four years. As she sat there with anticipation, the weight of responsibility fell away, leaving her looking like a teenage girl with no worries, instead of a mature young woman sharing the care of the village with Leonardo.

The phone rang. Leonardo was sitting next to it, but he gave it to Isaac to answer. "Hello," he said in an excited voice.

Josh answered, "Isaac, is that you?"

"Yeah, it's me, and you won't believe what's happened."

"Is everything alright?" Josh asked with a voice of concern.

"Everything is wonderful! I got saved! Can you believe it?"

There was a stunned silence on the other end of the telephone, and then, shaking his head, Josh answered, "Nothing is impossible with God, but this is truly remarkable. All these years I've witnessed to you and it fell on deaf ears. What happened?"

"Well, I'm a little surprised myself. I couldn't help noticing some of the amazing things that have happened down here. It can't help but get your attention. Then I spent time with Leonardo and he told me firsthand what happened to his wife Ciba, Noemi, and little Emilio. After that I spent over an hour with Sherry over a cup of tea. I think the tea relaxed me enough to listen. Sherry shared from her heart and from the Bible and my heart was changed. Now I'm a different person than I was before."

"Isaac, that's really great, and we'll have to talk when we get back together, but right now let me tell you what's happened here. Renato, Ted and Miguel got here last night. They made great time and all is well with them. It actually feels as though they should have come to begin with. I don't understand what happened, but it all appears to have worked out. Now we need to know what's happening down there. Have you found out any more information? Have you talked to the captives? Are they being cooperative?"

"You're not going to believe this Josh, but they all got saved. It seems Jesus came to visit them. He spoke to them. Sherry and Leonardo saw them all on the ground when they went to check on them, as if they had passed out. Then they all woke up and started questioning, "Was that really Jesus we saw?" They had lots of questions. They even expressed remorse for the beheading of Esteban Montero's men. They wanted to know if God could forgive them for doing that. They all prayed and want to become working members of the village. They even volunteered to dig some new outhouses. We explained that we believed them, but for the time being they would be under light guard. They thanked us. Unfortunately they knew nothing of the inner workings of the Black Death.

But they did say that some of the supervisors were due back in about two weeks.

"We also found out several other things, some from searching the camp, the buildings, and the aerial surveillance of the area," Isaac answered. "We discovered several boxes of assorted weapons including rocket launchers, AK-47's and several boxes of M-16's. The added surprise is that the boxes are labeled 'Property of the U. S. Army'. Let me tell you it was a shock to see that. I'm making some phone calls tomorrow to Washington to make sure they know. Also, there are several Black Death Camps in a fifty mile radius from the village. I wonder if any of the villagers have ever come upon those camps. Maybe you can ask some of those young hunters you have there with you. Will you question your young men? I'll ask Leonardo to question the men here who go out to hunt. I don't want you to be surprised by running into some of them."

"Thanks. I don't want to run into them either," Josh agreed. "Now that you're down here, who's your liaison back in Washington?"

"They put Kent Knox in that spot. I'm supposed to call him every morning around nine. I'm surprised he hasn't called me already. I've missed two days. I'll call him tomorrow morning. He's the one you need to be calling if you have any information for him or need some information from him. Now tell me, what is going on in your camp? Is everyone well?"

"Yes," Josh replied. "We will be heading out in two hours, after our evening meal. I'm glad Renato, Ted and Miguel are here. For some reason, it just seems right. I think the rest did all of us some good. We will be refreshed starting out tonight; I hope. We may even reach Arandu's village tomorrow if we make good time."

"Did Leonardo want to say anything to Manu? Has there been any trouble in the camp?"

"No, he heard your question. He just said to say we are all praying for you. That includes me," said Isaac, "and that's a first. Sherry is standing here and she is waiting rather impatiently to speak with Daniel."

"Say no more." Phones changed hands and both Daniel and Sherry spoke into the phone with voices filled with emotion. Everyone moved away and gave them privacy to talk. Sherry wanted to tell Daniel how much she missed him. She wanted to tell him how much she realized she depended on him. She wanted to tell him how much she needed him, but she couldn't. First she had to tell everyone about the prisoners, and then about what happened at the glade. She spoke for almost fifteen minutes, and then paused. "Does anyone have any questions?"

Josh asked, "Did you find out who the prisoners are and where they are from?"

"Just barely; three are from Paraguay, the others are American. Their leader is a guy named Frank Minardi from Hackensack, New Jersey. We're going to put them to work under supervision. They volunteered. We're not being foolish, we prayed. We're going to keep a watchful eye on all of them.

Sherry then told the story of what happened at the glade. You won't believe it, but things are already looking better down there. It was so exciting to see that our heavenly protectors were able to put the enemy to flight."

She didn't want Daniel to get upset and feel bad because he wasn't here with her. She knew he had responsibilities to God and to the members of the Quest that he was traveling with. They had to put God and His Quest first. God would provide for them what was needed.[154] He would be their comfort, when comfort was needed.[155] Sherry kept her voice cheerful, telling Daniel all the interesting things that had happened during the day. She hoped she was successful in hiding her feelings.

Daniel on the other hand told Sherry at least three times in their conversation how much he missed her. He knew she missed

---

[154] Matthew 6:26
[155] John 14:16-17

him, but he let her think she was fooling him. It was important to her that he think she was strong. It was important to him that she knew how much he missed her. They both said good-bye with smiles on their faces.

CHAPTER TWENTY-SIX

JUNE 26

THE QUESTERS

Bekah looked at the group and allowed herself a satisfied smile. With all the meat the hunters had brought in and all the fruit and vegetables she and Manu had found, dinner had been a hit. Everyone had a full belly, and there was enough for breakfast tomorrow.

The sun was hovering on the horizon, appearing to rest on a skyline of trees. As it began to scatter its color through them, the colors of the gloaming mesmerized her senses. The greens of the jungle were transformed. A different hue of color altered the environment they inhabited. A hush fell over the jungle. The sounds of daylight were diminishing as the creatures of the light were taking their rest and the creatures of night were slowly awakening. They emerged from their dens and hiding places to go off into the night and continue with their never-ending search for sustenance. There was a short pause between day and night. If you weren't paying attention, you missed the changing of the guard.

Again God's hand took up His palette of colors. His hand was especially present in the dawn and the gloaming. The colors of dawn were recognizable: pink, orange, gray, gold, peach, lavender, different shades of blue, and there were hundreds more colors she had no name for. The colors of the gloaming were related, but different. There was an intensity to them that affected Bekah in some intangible way. Dawn's colors changed and developed over thirty or forty minutes. The colors of the gloaming did not change and develop. They were there, then, they were gone. Just a few short minutes were allowed for this special time, and if you failed to take notice of it, it was lost to you.

As the light faded, Bekah said a prayer of thanks to God for the beauty of His creation. She looked around and everyone was packing his gear. They were actually getting a late start; it must be at least eight o'clock. The phone call from the village took longer than usual.

Suddenly, the phone rang again. Bekah happened to be standing next to the phone and answered it.

"Hello," a voice answered.

Bekah was quick to recognize Joe's voice and pick up the tension in it. Bekah immediately went into worry mode, wondering what prompted this phone call from Maine. "What's the matter? Is something wrong?"

"Yes, I'm sorry to say there is. Sylvia has been taken by Haydon Carlton."

Bekah heard his answer. There was a long moment of silence as Joe waited for Bekah's response. She did not have the ability to give an immediate answer. Time appeared to stand still; then reality rushed back like a wave crashing over her, onto the shore. A sob rose up into Bekah's mouth. "No," she cried. "How did this happen?" Then, before Joe could answer, she realized everyone needed to hear this, and she put the phone on speaker.

"Joe, I've just put the phone on speaker. Would you repeat to everyone what you just told me, and everything else you know about the situation?"

Joe said, "I'm going to let you have it firsthand. Penny was involved with this. She saw Haydon Carlton take Sylvia. He even called her several minutes after they left. I'll let her tell you."

"Hi Bekah; please forgive me. I'm so sorry I couldn't save Nana Sylvia. She woke me up when I heard her go down the stairs. Then I heard the back door open. I looked out the window and he was standing there in the garden. She went right to him, almost as if she knew he was there. He took her arm and brought her over to his car. As she was getting into the car she looked up at my window. I could see her face. She did not look afraid at all, but determined."

Penny started to cry, "I feel as though I've failed; but I prayed right away. Nana always tried to teach me not to act impulsively, but to wait to see what God was doing in the situation. It was only a few minutes later that Haydon Carlton called. He sounded so smug, as if he had the winning hand. He doesn't know that in the end God wins, and if by that time he's not on God's side, he loses. I almost feel sorry for him. I think we should put Haydon on our prayer list, not only so everyone will be safe from him, but also, so that he will be saved and snatched from the devil's hands."

Bekah began to speak and you could hear her anger. Her voice rose and made a harsh sound. She began to speak harshly concerning Haydon Carlton. Then it stopped. Everyone looked at her with expectation. Those on the other end of the line silently wondered what was happening.

Bekah was listening to the Voice of the Holy Spirit. He was urging her not to speak in anger and frustration, but to speak as God would. He reminded her that God sent His Son to die for Haydon also.

She remembered what Penny had just said and revised her comments. She thanked the Holy Spirit for helping to keep her from judgment and condemnation. Finally she spoke. "I think you're right Penny, we do all need to pray for Haydon now." Bekah turned to the others, "Just as Penny said, Haydon is being used as a pawn by Satan and being moved from space to space to serve Satan's will. Maybe Sylvia will have a chance to witness to him.

183

Let's pray for people to cross his path and present the Gospel of faith, love and hope to him.[156]

"Remember the Bible says that our battle is not with flesh and blood.[157] It's a supernatural battle and God has given us supernatural armor and weapons. We can't fight this like we would a regular battle. We can't give Satan a black eye by punching him, but we can take up the Word of God which the Bible calls the Sword of the Spirit and push him back with that."[158]

"I wonder what damage Haydon can do if he makes it to Puerto Bahia Negra," Joe speculated. "The village already has to keep a watch out for Josef and the Black Death. Now they are going to have to watch out for Haydon and his companions also. Have you talked with Leonardo, Jose or Isaac?" Bekah questioned. "Are they aware of these circumstances?"

"No, we have not called them yet," Joe responded. "Do you want us to call?"

"We talked to them earlier, maybe you should call. This way they will be getting the information first hand. Tell them to call us if anything comes up that we need to know. Otherwise, we will call them tomorrow night before we head off. We should reach the remains of Arandu's village by dawn."

"Wait," cried Penny. I remembered something I didn't tell you. I had a very unusual dream, and several things happened in it that pertain to the Quest, or at least I think they do. In the dream I saw a very large village by a lake, but there were mostly women, children and old people with just a few guards. Also, I saw a small group of people camping in the jungle. Bekah, I saw you. You were the only woman there. I couldn't see anyone else's faces. I saw everyone moving about, but one person seemed to separate himself from the group. He also had a dark shadow about him.

---

[156] Matthew 9:37-38
[157] 2 Corinthians 10:5-6
[158] Ephesians 6:12-18

God showed me that this person was entertaining Satan with his thoughts just as Judas did right before he betrayed Jesus. Please pray about this. I don't know why God showed this to me and not to one of you. I'm sure you would have known what to do."

"Thank you for the warning," Josh said. "Every day we commission angels to surround us and keep us safe. So far they have done a very good job, and I expect them to keep up the good work."

"Well, we will continue to pray for you twenty-four hours a day," Joe said. "We are waging a mighty battle here and Satan is bound to be hindered in his efforts. Right now we will say Goodnight, and God bless and keep you."

Josh turned to the others after the call was ended. He took care not to look at Axel and betray his concern. He would talk with Manu and Renato the first chance he could get. Right now, prayer was needed.

Josh spoke to the group. "This was an unsettling phone call. We've all just heard some disturbing news about Sylvia being taken by Haydon Carlton. That in itself calls for a time of prayer. The rest of the dream about a traitor like Judas also needs prayer and repentance. It's good for all of us to repent on a regular basis. The enemy tries to trip us up in many ways through each day. Sometimes we entertain the thoughts he plants in our minds. We think on them and allow them to take root. Let's all look at the garden of our minds and see if anything is growing there that would not be pleasing to God. If there is, we can repent and pull it out, and replace it with a prayer of thanksgiving."

They knelt and took the time to examine their hearts and minds, asking God to show them if they had sinned. All took time to pray and repent, all that is except Axel. He knelt, but his mind was far from prayer. He thought, "How did she find out? Who told her? She wasn't even here. She's just making up stories to look important. All these people just want to be important. They all want to be rich. I can't stand to be around any of them."

Satan just kept on smiling. This was too easy. He didn't even have to work at it. People were so predictable.

CHAPTER TWENTY-SEVEN

JUNE 27
THE SURVIVORS

It was almost dawn when the Questers started looking for Arandu's village. It had been a long, uneasy night. The fact, that there might be a traitor among them weighed heavily on their hearts. No one wanted to think it was him, or look accusingly at anyone else.

They had seen signs of trails in the area and were currently following one, hoping it would take them to the village. They had traveled slower than usual, trying to watch for anything that was out of the ordinary. Although, what was ordinary about walking through the jungle at night. They trusted that their angels were still surrounding them and deflecting all the fiery darts the enemy launched in their direction. Right before the sun broke the horizon, they started smelling whiffs of smoke. They were surprised there was still something burning. It had been several days since the attack and it had also rained several times.

They slowed down, suspecting the village was just around a bend in the trail. What they saw when they reached it left them speechless. Most of the homes had been burned, but there were several that appeared to have been patched up. There was a central fire that twelve people were sitting around, eight men, three women, and one child. Five of the men were uninjured. The rest had injuries rang-ing from moderate to severe, except for a little girl of about four years old. But she was dirty from head to foot and appeared very lethargic. She did not even react to their appearance. Her long, thick, black hair was full of snarls, leaves, and twigs. Her clothes were torn and ragged. All of them were thin and disheveled. The group appeared to be cooking breakfast. Most of the men rose when the Questers came into the village and picked up their weapons. Manu immediately put his hands up as a sign of greeting. He told them who they were and where they came from. He told them that all the survivors from their village had been adopted by his village and that he was the Chief.

Manu asked for permission to enter the village. When it was given, everyone came forward and they were invited to sit around the fire. There did not appear to be much food, but the rules of hospitality were observed. Bekah noticed that as visitors, they were asked to eat first. Most of the people looked as though they hadn't had enough to eat for quite a while. Thankfully, Bekah knew they had a generous supply of food left over from the previous night. Manu got that out and asked Bekah to help prepare and share it.

The survivor's eyes brightened when they saw the food. Hunger had been a constant companion since the attack. All their supplies of food had been carried off by the attackers and they had been left to die. The few men healthy enough to hunt could not risk taking an extended trip to hunt large game because of the injuries of those left. The small game had disappeared from around the village a long time ago, so snares were not successful close to their village. Savory smells started to permeate the air and everyone watched the pot with hungry anticipation.

The small girl came over and took Bekah's hand. She brushed her face with it and then looked up at Bekah with large dark eyes and spoke. Bekah quickly looked for Renato or Manu to interpret for her. Renato was standing next to her and saw her dilemma. He listened silently and then said something to the little girl. Renato turned to Bekah with a sad smile on his face and told

Bekah what the little girl had said.

"She said her name is Yvoty, which means flower, and she wants to be your flower. Her parents, brothers and sisters are dead and she said nobody wants her."

Bekah felt tears fall from her eyes as she listened to Renato's translation of the little girl's story. Such a beautiful little girl, and she had had such a hard life already. Bekah took the little girl's hand and squeezed it and gave her a hug. She looked over at Manu. "Is there something we can we do for Yvoty, and not just her but the rest of these people? Why can't we send out our young men to hunt? They could bring in a large quantity of food. That would help tremendously."

Manu answered Bekah, "Given their situation and lack of resources. We can send out the hunters, and between the five of them, they should bring in plenty of food which should last awhile. You and I can go out to look for fruit and roots in the jungle. Josh and Akeem can gather firewood. Carlos can keep the fire going, and Daniel and Ted can carry water. Edwardo, will you scout the perimeter? Let me know if you see anything unusual. Renato, do you think you would be able to talk to the people and find out if they can travel? Maybe we can get them started for our village tomorrow. We'll have to see how badly they are injured."

Renato answered, "I think that's a great plan. I'll start talking with them right after we finish eating. That way they will get comfortable with us."

As the group dispersed, Renato observed there was not a speck of food left over from breakfast, and everyone had eaten his fill. Renato sat down and explained to the group of people left around the fire what was going on. They did not show any interest. They did not appear to even be paying attention. Renato could see that they had lost hope and desire. When so much has been taken from someone, it crushes their spirit.[159]

---

[159] Proverbs 15:13

Renato continued talking to them. He told them his story. He told them about the Quest and what had happened thus far. Then he shared with them about his God. "I believe my God is the One true God. He's still leading and guiding us. He led us here to help you, and to tell you the truth about Him. Our God is a loving God. He loved us so much He sent His only Son Jesus to die as a sacrifice for our sins.[160] He was dead for three days and nights and then God raised Him up from the dead.[161] Has your god ever raised anyone from the dead? Your god appears to be a god of death, but our God is a God of life.[162] In fact Jesus says He is the way, the truth, and the life. He doesn't ask for sacrifices from you. When you accept God's sacrifice of His Son Jesus and what that sacrifice did for you, He adopts you into His family and you become His child. Has your god ever sacrificed anything for you? No, all he ever wants is more sacrifices from you. Has your god ever loved and cared for you? Does he listen when you ask for his help? I know he does not."

"God cares about all of us," Renato continued. "When we first came to Paraguay, we were on our way to Manu's village and Miss Bekah was kidnapped by evil men. We all prayed and God provided a way for her to escape. Does you god answer your prayers?" Renato paused and thought, "I'll let them think about that and answer that question themselves."

"Would you like to be part of the family of God? If you do, Jesus will come when the Spirit of God breathes His life into you, and live in your heart. The Spirit of God will help you do what is good and pleases God, and to not sin. Sin is being disobedient to God's will, and separates us from Him. If we do sin, God has made a way for us to come back. If we are truly sorry, we can go to Him and ask forgiveness for our sins and He will forgive us.[163]

"You can serve Him here on the earth, and when you die,

---

[160] John 3:16
[161] Acts 2:23-24
[162] John 14:6
[163] 1 John 1:9

you get to live with Him forever in Heaven.[164] If you choose not to serve God, Who blesses you, there is a place where the evil one, Satan, who torments you, will be sent to, and when you die, you too will also be sent there to be tormented with him forever."

The group of people looked at Renato blankly and said not a word. Finally a voice inside Renato said, "The enemy is at work here and you must defeat him." Renato responded with a start. Then he recalled the Scripture that told him to be strong in the Lord and His power and might. He couldn't fight this battle with earthly weapons. It said our problem was not with flesh and blood, but we are fighting against powers, principalities, rulers of this dark world, and spiritual forces of evil in the heavens.[165]

"The Scriptures go on to instruct you to put on God's armor. If you're fighting a spirit, you need spiritual weapons." He spoke as he put on the armor. "I buckle the belt of truth around me and the breastplate of righteousness. On my feet I put the readiness of the Gospel of peace. I take up the shield of faith which can extinguish all the fiery darts of the enemy. I put on the helmet of salvation and lift the Sword of the Spirit which is the Word of God. Along with these weapons I will pray whatever and however the Spirit shows me."[166]

Having said all this, Renato began to circle the group of people saying, "I come against you Satan in the mighty Name of Jesus."[167] Then he began to notice that with the exception of the four hunters and the little girl, all were seriously injured. Some were burned, some looked as if they had been beaten, and a few even appeared to have been stabbed. He was surprised no one had seen these injuries. He realized even their eyes had been blinded. Renato remembered that Jesus said He only did what He saw the Father doing.[168] He remembered Jesus said to lay hands on the

---

[164] John 14:2
[165] Ephesians 6:10-12
[166] Ephesians 6:13-18
[167] John 14:13-14
[168] John 5:19-21

sick and they will recover. Renato immediately went to each that were injured and prayed for them to be healed in Jesus' Name. He immediately saw infections disappear, wounds close up, and swelling and bruising vanish.[169]

With faith in the mighty Name of Jesus, Renato then commanded the demons to leave these people.[170] The group slowly began to stir. They looked at each other and then at him in confusion. "Who are you?" they asked. "What did you do to us? I thought I was going to die of my injuries, but they are going away as we speak." One woman who looked as though her arm had been broken stood up. The look of pain and discomfort left her and she began to carefully move it around.

Those with injuries began to get up and walk around. The rest just stood there in confusion.

Renato asked, "Do you remember what I said to you?"

"Yes," they all said, nodding their heads.

One of the women said, "I thought it was in a dream. Your God seems too good to be true."

"The things that I told you are marvelous and they are true. God cares for all of you so much that He not only sent His Son to die for you, but also He sent us here to bring you His message of hope and love. I can also tell you that all your fellow villagers who traveled to our village have renounced their old gods and accepted Jesus as their Savior and my God is now their God."

He turned to Yvoty and told her, "There is a little girl living in our village who came from here. Her name is Panambi. Did you know her?"

Yvoty eyes brightened and her face lit up with joy. "She was my best friend."

"When all of you travel to my village you will see her. Now that you are all healed of your injuries, you can travel. It might take

---

[169] Mark 16:18
[170] Luke 10:17

192

you three or four days since you're traveling with a child and some of you are elderly. We will provide you with food and God will guide you. But first you must answer my question. Do you want to accept Jesus, Who died for your sins as your Savior? If you do, will you let me pray for you?"

Everyone agreed.

"Before I pray, would you tell your old gods that you will not serve them anymore?"

They looked at each other, a little hesitant. This was a big step. One spoke up, "We are afraid our old gods will try to harm us further. Can your God protect us?"

"Yes He can. He tells us that those who believe can call on angels and tell them to go out and protect people from our enemy, Satan. They have kept us safe on our trip. Even though Bekah was kidnapped, God made a way for her escape. He will do that for you also."

Again they looked at each other and nodded their agreement. Renato had them all repeat a prayer. He smiled when he noticed that even little Yvoty was praying. He remembered that in the Bible Jesus said not to stop the little children from coming to him.[171]

Renato was walking over to talk with Josh and tell him what had transpired when one of the older women approached him. "My name is Ysupi. When the attack came I was able to run into the forest, but one of their warriors saw me. He ran after me and hit me with his club. It broke my leg. He laughed, kicked me, and left me to die. Our hunters found me when they came back from their hunt and carried me into the village. Those who were dead we buried, and those of us left didn't know for sure who was still alive and where they went."

Renato listened with interest and then responded, "I'm happy to tell you that the people from your village traveled through the

_____
[171] Matthew 19:14

193

jungle to our village. Some were seriously injured and died along the way, but sixty-two arrived. Many were injured and our doctor helped them. She also prayed for them. I'm happy to say all sixty-two survived."

Ysupi looked at Renato and her tears traveled down her wrinkled cheeks. "Do you know if one of them was named Arandu? He was my husband of thirty-four years. All my children and grand-children are dead. He would be my last hope. Can your God bring him back to me?"

"I am happy to say that I saw Arandu three days ago. It seems God doesn't have to bring him here, we are sending you to him. He is at our village. He had a broken arm, but it is healing quickly. To-morrow you will start back to our village. You will see him soon."

Ysupi's eyes continued to flow with rivers of tears, but they were now transformed into tears of joy. Renato smiled at her and squeezed her shoulder. She grabbed his hand and drew it to her cheek. Renato was overcome with emotion at the gratitude of this woman. He told her, "Somehow our God worked this out. The Bible, God's Word, says that God works out all things for good to those who love and serve Him.[172] It probably didn't seem a good thing when you were chased and had your leg broken. It didn't seem good to still be here with no food and no help. But if you had left and wandered around the jungle, we might never have found you and you would have still been without hope. Now, not only is Arandu alive and well, but you have been healed by the one true God, Jesus lives in your heart, and the Holy Spirit leads and guides you. What a wonderful outcome to a terrible tragedy."

Ysupi gave Renato's hand another squeeze and then hurried off to tell her companions that Arandu was alive and well, back in their village, and that there were sixty-two other survivors there also.

---

[172] Romans 8:28

CHAPTER TWENTY-EIGHT

JUNE 27
THE QUESTERS

Renato looked at his watch and saw that more than two hours had gone by. Two of their young men had come back carrying a deer. Axel said, "Mario and I came back with the deer I killed. The rest are staying out to see if they can get another." Axel looked very pleased with himself and Renato was glad to see a smile on his face.

All the appointed tasks were accomplished and everyone came and sat around the fire drinking some fresh terere. The rest of the hunters had come in with some game birds and two small wild boars. They would dress and smoke the meat so it would last for many days. There was meat for them to take on their journey and meat for the survivors to take on their way to the village. The only issue was who to send back with the twelve.

The obvious choice would be one of the five young hunters; however, God doesn't always choose the obvious.[173] It would have to be someone who spoke the language, for the survivors spoke some Spanish, but no English. That left the five hunters, plus Miguel, Manu, Renato, and Edwardo. They needed the five hunters. That left Manu, Edwardo, Miguel and Renato. Because of Renato's dream, he needed to continue on with the Quest. It appeared the choice was between Manu and Edwardo and Miguel. Finally

---

[173] 1 Samuel 16:5-13

Carlos, the newest Christian of the bunch, spoke up and suggested, "Don't you think we should spend some time praying before we make this kind of decision?"

Everyone stopped talking and looked at him. Then they all sheepishly admitted that they had forgotten whose Quest this was. Everyone agreed that prayer should be their first consideration. Without another word, they bowed their heads and began to pray fervently. When they were through praying, Manu stood up and asked everyone to be quiet. He then told them he felt that God had asked him to make the decision since he was the Chief of the village. Manu said, "I think that two people need to lead these survivors back to our village, Edwardo and Miguel." Edwardo's head immediately came up, but he did not argue. "You're right Manu. I thought I was mistaken when I heard God say I should go back, but you hearing it, is confirmation from God."[174]

Manu explained that he felt two were needed. None of the survivors were strong enough to hunt or defend the group from danger. One of them always needed to stay with them while the other hunted or scouted ahead. Manu looked around. "Is there any disagreement?" he asked. Everyone was quiet. Manu continued, "I also feel that the rest of us should leave tonight. We may not get as far as usual, but I feel that we need to keep going.

"Edwardo, you can stay for another day if you need to. Let them rest. Also, travel during the day. Hopefully, you will be heading away from danger, not towards it."

Suddenly the telephone rang. As Josh picked it up he put it on speaker. An unfamiliar voice answered his hello. "Hello Josh, this is Kent Knox speaking. I don't know if you remember me, but we met about five years ago on a briefing you did on terrorist activity in the Amazon region. You had just submitted a paper on the subject and it was very well received. In hindsight, we can see that

---

[174] 2 Corinthians 13:1

you were right about a great many things. Paraguay, then a small and insignificant country in South America has turned into a terrorist hot bed just as you had foreseen."

Josh smiled, "Sometimes I hate being right. I had no intensions of being here now, or any other time. That paper was a hypothesis."

"Well, hypothesis or not, you're stuck smack dab in the middle of it. Other than the one camp, have you seen any signs of other training camps?"

"No," Josh answered decisively, "and we haven't been looking for any either. We have our hands full doing what we're doing."

"Unfortunately," Kent responded with sympathy in his voice, "we have gotten some clearer satellite pictures and have discovered several more, and two of them are in your area. One is fifteen miles north of you, just above a waterfall. It's a large camp, about twice the size of the one you found. The other is about fifteen miles east of you in the Brazilian jungle.

"The one north of you appears to house about seventy-five members of the Black Death Camp. The one east of you houses about one hundred fifty members. As far as we can see, they do not appear to be paying any attention to the locals. It's unusual that the one east of you is inland. So far, all of their camps have been on or near the river, and this is the only one on the east side of the river. It appears that because neither of them can access the river, the one north of you has built a helipad. The one east of you has a small runway that can accommodate a two engine plane. These allow them to bring in and take out people and also to bring in and take out munitions, and other supplies. It seems everyone departs from Puerto Bahia Negra, which would take about two hours. There must be a cell operating near there, but so far we have not been able to find it."

Josh put his head in his hands. He finally looked up and said, "I know you're not telling me all this to keep us safe. What's the bottom line?"

197

"I can't divulge my source because we are not on a secure line, but you need to get your people out of there quickly. You may be safe in the southern village, but even that's not certain."

Kent paused, trying to give Josh a chance to take this all in. "I'm sorry to have to tell you this, but Washington has instructed me to let you know it's time to punch in. You are now back on the clock."

"Listen Kent, there are twenty-seven people out here, me included. Twelve of these were people we just found in a burned out village: eight men, three women and one small child. We are sending them back to our village to the south when they are able to travel. One of our gun bearers, and a young hunter from our village, will go with them for protection. That leaves me with five men and one woman with weapons experience; one of them has only shot clay pigeons, and the woman, only target practice. Now, you're asking me to set out to spy on these terrorist camps. Are you crazy?"

"Josh, I appreciate your problem, but what's more important, the needs of the few or the needs of the many?"

"There is no way I am abandoning these people. That's not even taking into consideration the fact that all of us believe that we are here because God called us and we are on a mission for Him. I'm sorry, but my commitment to Him is greater than my commitment to our government. Thirteen of us are heading out at dusk for the tribe whose village is at the base of the waterfall. We will all pray this afternoon, asking God's guidance. If anything changes, we will call you."

"Josh, I'm sorry you feel that way. I understand Akeem Farsi is with you. Let me speak to him."

Akeem came forward, a stony frown on his face. "I'm here. What do you want?"

"Akeem, I want you to take command of the group. You are in charge now. Take your five men with weapons experience and follow the river to the waterfall. Try to skirt the village and climb to the top of the falls. Do a reconnaissance of the Black Death Camp.

198

Try not to make them aware of your presence. I know this will be a challenge, but we have no one else in the area that can gather the information we need."

Akeem smiled a wry smile. "Kent, you don't understand. I don't take orders from you, I take orders from God. We all do, and He has called us from diverse places to go on this Quest for Him. We don't even know the whole picture, but our faith in Him keeps us going. I can say we are heading in the direction you asked for. Lucky for you, that's the direction God wants us to go. As for taking command, God put Josh in charge, and until He says otherwise, that's how it will stay. That's all we have to say for now. Call us tomorrow morning and we'll let you know how far we traveled."

After shutting off the service, they put the phone on to charge; then they all sat down together in a circle. Josh and Akeem stood in the center of the circle. Akeem spoke first. "I may have taken liberties when I said that Josh was in charge. I know that Daniel has been here a long time and also had the dream. I know that Manu is Chief of the village, and he had the dream too, but I also know that God put Josh in charge. Are we all in agreement about that? Until He says different, that's how it's going to stay.""

Everyone either nodded or vocalized a yes. "Good," said Akeem. "Now I can sit down."

Josh stood there alone, surrounded by the members of the Quest. "Before we do anything else, let's take a time of prayer, to renew our commitment to the Quest God called us to, and to listen to any further direction He may give us. I don't know how much trouble I may be in by refusing to carry out those orders I received, but we are in God's hands and He will direct us.

"I'm going to read Psalm 139. It has a great deal to say about our situation. I think it will comfort us and give us encouragement.

> 1 O LORD, You have examined my heart
> and know everything about me.

2 You know when I sit down or stand up.

   You know my thoughts even when I'm far away.

3 You see me when I travel

   and when I rest at home.

   You know everything I do.

4 You know what I am going to say

   even before I say it, LORD.

5 You go before me and follow me.

   You place Your hand of blessing on my head.

6 Such knowledge is too wonderful for me,

   too great for me to understand!

7 I can never escape from Your Spirit!

   I can never get away from Your presence!

8 If I go up to Heaven, You are there;

   if I go down to the grave, You are there.

9 If I ride the wings of the morning,

   if I dwell by the farthest oceans,

10 even there Your hand will guide me,

   and Your strength will support me.

11 I could ask the darkness to hide me

   and the light around me to become night—

12 but even in darkness I cannot hide from You.

To You the night shines as bright as day.

   Darkness and light are the same to You.

13 You made all the delicate, inner parts of my body

   and knit me together in my mother's womb.

14 Thank You for making me so wonderfully complex!

   Your workmanship is marvelous—how well I know it.

15 You watched me as I was being formed in utter seclusion,

   as I was woven together in the dark of the womb.

16 You saw me before I was born.

   Every day of my life was recorded in Your Book.

Every moment was laid out

before a single day had passed.

17 How precious are Your thoughts about me, O God.
  They cannot be numbered!

18 I can't even count them;
  they outnumber the grains of sand!

And when I wake up,
  You are still with me!

19 O God, if only You would destroy the wicked!
  Get out of my life, you murderers!

20 They blaspheme You;
  Your enemies misuse Your Name.

21 O LORD, shouldn't I hate those who hate You?
  Shouldn't I despise those who oppose You?

22 Yes, I hate them with total hatred,
  for Your enemies are my enemies.

23 Search me, O God, and know my heart;
  test me and know my anxious thoughts.

24 Point out anything in me that offends You,
  and lead me along the path of everlasting life.[175]

When Josh finished reading he stood there quietly, letting the Holy Spirit minister to them. "God is aware of our every action, our every thought. He knew what we would think or do even before we were born. We can't hide from Him. We can't hide our thoughts from Him. David was in a battle with extreme enemies just like we are. David hated God's enemies, and we do too. But God also asks us to love those who come against us, and pray for them."

He repeated verses twenty-three and twenty-four of Psalm 139. Then he said, "Let's all ask God to look inside us, examine every thought, and remove any that offend Him. As David, the writer of that Psalm said, we want Him to lead us along the path of everlasting life. Everyone take some time and ask God to show us how

---
[175] Psalm 139, New Living Translation,

to proceed. We just need to get quiet before Him and listen. God always wants to speak to us. Our problem is we don't always listen. Sometimes we don't want to hear what He has to say."

Everyone nodded his understanding. Josh continued, "One thing I feel that we should do is have a time of repentance. We have been so busy trying to do what God has asked us to do that we have stopped spending time with Him. Let's spend some time examining ourselves; then we can confess our sins and repent. We can either confess them quietly to God, or we can confess them one to another. The Bible says that when we do that, we will be healed. I don't know about all of you, but my body is sore, my spirit is failing, and my mind is in turmoil."[176]

Josh looked from face to face as he paused. On some he saw understanding, on some he saw confusion, and on one he saw a dark cloud. He again felt an urgency in his spirit to talk with Manu and Renato. This was important, and should not be put off any longer.

Edwardo went over to where the survivors were sitting and explained what they were doing. He explained that when they repented, their hearts were free to talk to God, because they were not burdened with the guilt of their sins. Then they were more able to hear Him when He answered. They all agreed that this was a good thing and wanted to participate.

Everyone spread out in the clearing and found his spot. Some knelt, some sat, and others stood with heads bowed. The murmuring of many voices was heard, some in great distress. The small group of survivors was all talking amongst themselves. Finally, Aravera, who appeared to be the leader, walked over to Edwardo and questioned him. "We have never prayed like this before and don't know if we are doing it right. We are trying to talk with God, but all we seem to be able to do is groan. Is something the matter?"

Edwardo looked perplexed, and then understanding came

---

[176] James 5:16

to him. He turned to the group of them and answered, "The Bible has a lot to say about prayer. Jesus even demonstrated how to pray. But it also told us what to do when we want to pray, but don't know how. It says the Holy Spirit, God's Spirit that lives inside us, makes groanings. Those groanings pray the will of God.[177] Can you trust Him to do that?"

Everyone nodded eagerly. They were all anxious to find out more about this new God they were serving. Never had their old gods given them any indication that they heard their prayers or cared about them. They were eager to serve this new God. They gave their hearts to Him fully.

Edwardo told them how Jesus' disciple, His close followers, asked Him to teach them how to pray. Jesus told them to pray to the Father, Who is in Heaven. Next He told them to praise Him and pray that His Kingdom of truth, love, and light come and be established here on Earth as it was in Heaven. He prayed that God's will also be established on Earth. He told them Jesus wants them to ask and rely on God for all their needs every day. Jesus said we need to pray for God to forgive us our sins as we forgive those who have sinned against us. God tells us that if we don't forgive, He can't forgive us. Then He finished by praying that they not be led into temptation, but delivered from evil.

Edwardo pause before going on to see if everyone understood. Then he asked if anyone had any questions. At first no one said anything. Then the little girl, Yvoty, spoke. "What's God's Name? What should I call Him?"

Edwardo smiled. "He wants you to call Him Father, because He says in His Word, the Bible, that He had adopted us into His family and that we are now His sons and daughters."[178]

"Wow," murmured Yvoty in awe. "You mean God is my Father now, because my father was killed."

---

[177] Romans 8:26
[178] 2 Corinthians 6:18

203

"Yes," Edwardo declared. "He will be your Father and love you as His daughter. No one could love you better."

"But what about my mother, who will be my mother," she asked?

Edwardo paused before answering, because he did not want to give the child the wrong answer. "God will provide a mother for you. You must be patient."

Yvoty smiled, but her voice wavered with emotion. "I will pray for God to hurry. I want my mother to hold me. Sometimes I am so lonely."

Edwardo sat Yvoty on his lap and hugged her. "Oh, to have the faith and innocence of a child," he thought. He sat there, quietly holding her and then a thought came to him. "Miguel," he called. "Can you come over here please?"

Miguel walked over and smiled at Yvoty. He sat down next to Edwardo and she immediately climbed over into his lap and gave him a big hug. Edwardo thought, "This is going to be easy."

"Miguel, Yvoty told me that she is sad and lonely because she has no family, no one to love her and take care of her. Would you be willing to be her family here on Earth? I already explained to her that God is her heavenly Father, but she needs some family down here."

Yvoty's face immediately brightened at the prospect of Miguel being her family. Then the smile started to fade as no response was forthcoming.

Stunned by the question, Miguel hesitated to answer. He had just been watching Yvoty play and her interaction with the people. He had been thinking about his future and whether he would ever have a child as sweet and loveable as she was. Now it appeared God had heard his thoughts and provided an immediate answer.

Worried by his hesitation, Edwardo questioned God. "Did I make a mistake? Did I not hear Your Voice telling me to ask Miguel to adopt Yvoty?"

Miguel looked up and became aware of Edwardo and Yvoty looking at him expectantly. Her smile was beginning to fade and tears were gathering in her eyes. He realized he must have been standing there silent, while they were waiting for his answer.

He smiled, and hugged her tightly to himself. "Sorry if I seemed to hesitate," he explained, "but I had just been praying and thinking about my future. I asked God if I could have a child as wonderful as Yvoty. Apparently, God's answer was yes, and I didn't even have to wait. I can't think of anything better than being part of your family, Yvoty. Even though I am not married yet, some day there will be a mother. For right now, I will be your father. Is that alright with you?"

Overcome with happiness, Yvoty stood up and shouted to the people nearby. "I have a family! I have a family! Miguel wants to be my father. God gave me to him." She hugged Miguel, and then started jumping up and down with excitement.

All the people smiled and laughed with her. They were hungry for laughter and God had provided it. They all felt the joy of the Lord bubble up within themselves. It healed their hearts and minds and spirits.[179] This new God was surely a miracle worker. Look what He has already done for us, they thought. He sent people to help us and bring us hope. He fed us. He healed us. He is going to take us through the jungle to a new home, and now He makes a home for one of our orphans. He must indeed be a very good God.

Being a Pastor, Edwardo already thought of these people as part of his flock. He smiled as he watched people whose lives had been ravaged by the enemy laugh and shout and clap their hands with the joy of the Lord.[180]   Having lost so much, they were grateful for everything the Lord had given them.

Then he encouraged the people to pray, and just rest in

---

[179] Proverbs:17:22
[180] Isaiah 55:11-13

God's peace. Edwardo taught the people that praying is just talking to God and that it can be done at any time. "God likes us to talk to Him," he said. "How do you get to know anyone without talking to them? God is always waiting to hear from you. He doesn't want you to be a stranger with Him, but a friend."The grace of God continued to smile on the people through the afternoon. People went about their chores with a prayer on their lips.

It was almost time to prepare the evening meal and still everyone in the camp was praying, and all in agreement, save one, Axel. He had not acknowledged the sin God had pointed out to him, nor asked for forgiveness, yet God decided to give him another chance.

There was stillness in the jungle. The birds stopped singing, the insects stopped their drone, and the monkeys stopped their clamor. Then a whisper of a breeze began to blow through the jungle, gaining volume and velocity. They heard a rumble, but were astounded because everything was still. The trees remained still. The insects still flew and the birds still soared, but the rumble gained intensity. What was happening? Then a resounding Voice spoke out of the maelstrom.

Only the Questers heard the thundering Voice of God. Their hearts quaked at the sound of it. The survivors were puzzled by what they saw. They did not hear the sound of God's correction and chastisement. "You have allowed yourselves to become distracted from My Word. Let those returning take the food you are now preparing. I will feed you with My Word, and provide sustenance for your bodies. As you direct your steps along the path I have laid out for you, I will illuminate it further.[181] Go north along the river. Do not worry about ambush. Do not try to hide. My Word is in you and it will be your weapon against the enemy. I relish your time of repentance, but there is one among you whose heart is double-minded.[182] Keep your eyes open and beware of the enemy's cunning. Keep

[181] Proverbs
[182] Psalm 37:23

your hearts pure and your mind on Me. I am the way, the truth, and the life."[183]

As the Voice of God withdrew, the sounds of the jungle were evident again. Everyone was stunned at what God had said. The survivors were especially shaken, because they had never experienced the presence of God. They knew something had taken place, but could not comprehend what had occurred. They had only just come to know Him, but fear left them as God also sent the Holy Spirit to minister peace and comfort to them all. The Questers all repented for their careless disregard of God's instructions, and determined to stay completely in His will.

Unfortunately, there was one among them whose heart was not steadfast. He had been lured by the promises of the enemy. His pride and greed had allowed him to become deceived, just as Eve, in the garden had been deceived. She disregarded God's Word and listened to the voice of Satan.[184]

Renato watched Axel, whose face wore a frown. Renato was reminded of Cain before he murdered his brother Abel. God spoke to Cain and asked him why he was so downcast. God told Cain if you do what is right you will be rewarded, but if you don't, sin is lying at your doorstep waiting to capture you, but you must overcome it.[185] Renato prayed that Axel would not go the way of Cain, but would repent and follow God, the true source of success and happiness.

Josh was also watching Axel. He noticed the dark cloud surrounding Axel appeared to be getting darker. He did not want to lose anyone to the enemy. He needed to make time to talk with Manu and Renato. It was a priority.

---

[183] John 14:6
[184] Genesis 3:1-6
[185] Genesis 4:6-7

207

CHAPTER TWENTY-NINE

JUNE 27
THE QUESTERS

All of the Questers began packing their gear. There were only three or four more hours of daylight, but they felt God wanted them to leave immediately. They would travel till dark, eat whatever food was available, then have another time of prayer before starting out for their night walk.

While everyone was packing, Josh took Renato and Manu aside to talk with them about Axel, and what God had showed him. "I saw a dark cloud, first on Axel's face, and when God spoke, it spread to his shoulders. I am concerned that Axel has become resentful of the jobs given to him. He also appears to be envious of the other young men. Manu, have you talked to him? Do you know of a reason he would act this way?"

"Josh, I have known Axel since he was a child. He has always wanted more than he had, and especially, he wanted to be important. If someone caught a big fish, he claimed to have caught a bigger one. If they made a bow, his was better. He was never satisfied. He always claimed to be the best, whether it was true or not. I held back accepting him into manhood, hoping that more time would have helped his maturity, but it seems to have had an opposite effect. He has become bitter and resentful, feeling he's too good to be asked to get water or collect firewood. I'm afraid Satan has noticed and is tempting him with promises of recognition and rewards; promises he never seems to keep."

Renato added, "I tried to talk with him before. He was almost rude to me. He was not interested in talking with me or listening to anything I had to say. I am concerned for him. Let's all keep our eyes open and pray for him while we're traveling." They all agreed and went back to packing for their departure. Within half an hour they said good-bye to all the survivors and Edwardo and Miguel.

It was a bittersweet parting. Edwardo was excited to see Connie, Maria, Emilio, and Paulo, but he was saddened not to be able to complete the Quest. He understood that God had a plan. God hadn't changed His plan. This was all part of it, and everyone needed to accept the changes with a good attitude. Then all of those continuing the Quest gathered around Edwardo and Miguel, laid hands on them, and prayed for a safe journey for them and all of the survivors. They dispatched angels to go with them to quench the fiery darts of the enemy.[186]

The Questers picked up their packs and headed out in the order they had been following since they left the village, with the five young hunters in the lead. Everyone looked back and waved to Edwardo, Miguel and the survivors; then they put one foot in front of the other and marched out with a new and greater commitment.

There was a clear path along the river and they followed it. There was little talk. Most kept to their own thoughts and prayed quietly as they walked, but the young hunters were on edge. Something was not right among them. There was an uneasiness plaguing them that had not been there previously. Finally Mario addressed the issue. "We all heard God and what He said. One of us is double-minded. What did He mean by that, and who is it?"

Finally Axel said, "You're talking like it's one of us. It could just as easily be one of the others. You heard them talking about that guy Carlos. It's probably him, or maybe it's Bekah. She's al-

---

[186] Hebrews 1:14

ways seems to have problems forgiving people. We don't want her unforgiveness to give us a problem."

Again, the forces of darkness were on alert. The demons of gossip and a critical spirit attacked, bringing with them doubt and unbelief. Axel grumbled and went on in anger. "So many decisions are being made and we get no input in the process. Why don't we vote when there is a decision to make? That would be fair. Surely God wants everything to be fair."

All the young hunters were stunned by the ferocity of Axel's words. They looked back and forth at each other in confusion. What was Axel saying? Finally Mario spoke up. "Axel, what are you saying? Why are you criticizing Bekah and Carlos? They both repented openly of their sins and God forgave them. We have no right to judge them. Also, God doesn't ask for a vote. He tells us what to do and we do it."

Axel raised his voice. "Well you can all think what you like, but I told you how I feel. I don't want to talk about it anymore." Axel increased his pace and left the others behind. He wanted to be alone and sort out all his feelings. "Why was everyone always picking on me?" he asked himself in frustration. "It's not my fault they don't think of these things. I'm just trying to show them the truth. Why won't they listen to me?"

Self-pity joined the party, accompanied by low self-esteem. Satan was again smiling. He had caused dissention in the ranks. He was winning the battle. He remembered another battle he fought. There was dissention there also. Judas carried the money bag and felt very important. He was jealous of Peter, James and John, who always seemed to have Jesus' attention. With the proper persuasion, he betrayed Jesus. With the proper persuasion, this one would also turn on his companions.

The Questers continued on, unaware that a major battle was being fought and life and death hung in the balance. The angelic forces were still on guard, but words of doubt had been spoken which hindered their power. Unrepentant sin had also been spoken, which weakened them further. Those in leadership needed to pay attention and take authority over the situation.

The four young men watched Axel outdistance them. They were unsure what to do. Finally Mario said, "We all need to repent for even listening to what Axel was saying. Then we need to take authority over this situation and ask the Holy Spirit to intervene." They all agreed and prayed as they walked. Then Mario said, "I will go and catch up to Axel. I will talk to him. We used to be close, like brothers. Maybe he will listen to me." Mario jogged ahead.

After several minutes, Mario saw Axel as he was going around a bend in the river. He called out to him, running to catch up. As Mario rounded the bend, he saw Axel standing there, and a dark cloud appeared to be surrounding him. He called out, "Axel, what are you doing?"

"I'm doing what I want to do. I'm tired of taking everyone else's orders. Just go back and leave me alone." Axel turned and started up the trail again. Mario grabbed him by his arm and swung him around. Anger and malice were shining in Axel's eyes. Axel was taller, older, and stronger than Mario. In addition, Satan, and all his hoards from Hell were lending strength to Axel. With a quick movement, he drew his machete and slashed at Mario, catching him in the neck. Immediately blood started spurting from the wound. With a look of shock, Mario fell to the ground.

As soon as he saw what he had done, Axel let his machete fall. He dropped next to Mario, trying to staunch the flow of blood. Mario lay in an ever widening pool of crimson. He tried to speak, but the light of life was fading and speech was impossible. Axel knelt next to him with tears running down his face. "What have I done?" he cried.

God sighed, a sigh of grief and Satan howled in fiendish delight.

Axel quickly got up and wiped the blood from his machete.

He looked down at Mario's lifeless body and stood for a moment in shock. Chaos flooded his mind as the magnitude of his actions began to sink in. His breath came in gasps as he continued to watch Mario's blood soak into the ground.

"Murderer, killer, traitor," reverberated in his mind as he stood there. Then he heard the others coming up the hill. He sprinted down the hill and turned into the dense jungle. "You can't let them find you," his mind thundered. "Get away quickly before they catch you and kill you. Mario was their friend; they won't let his death go unavenged."

Fear and confusion pushed him into panic. He turned into the dense jungle and crashed through the undergrowth. He battled through it, trying to leave a minimal trail. Fear kept pushing him, and adrenalin gave him strength. Unfortunately, it was short lived. He had traveled less than a mile into the jungle, but he hoped that was enough. His breathing came in tortuous gasps and his body was awash with sweat. He was covered in scrapes and scratches, but it was his heart that had received the worst injury.

As his breathing slowed, he listened for sounds of being followed, but everything was quiet. Even the sounds of the jungle were unaccustomedly absent. It felt as though the jungle was bereft of life and he was marooned, sentenced to a life of solitude as punishment for taking the life of his friend.

Axel was unaware of the battle being fought around him for his soul. Anger, despair, and self-pity, were dancing around him, making so much noise, they drowned out sorrow, grief, and repentance. Satan could feel victory in his grasp. Not only were his minions at work here, but the rest of the Questers were succumbing to the same attack.

Axel tried to bring his thoughts under control, but to no avail. He stood there with his chest heaving and Satan continued to lie to him. "You have done the unforgiveable. God will not pardon this sin. It is too great. You cannot go back to your people. You are an outcast now, just like Cain after he killed his brother Abel."

The Holy Spirit spoke to him, but he did not pay attention to His Voice. Scriptures tried to rise up in his spirit, but instead of listening, he called out in anger. "Why did this have to happen to me? Why didn't Mario let go of me? If he hadn't grabbed me this never would have happened."

The Holy Spirit was saddened. Instead of repentance Axel was trying to shift the blame somewhere else. Again, the Holy Spirit told Axel, "If you will just repent and confess your sins, God is ready and willing to forgive you and cleanse you from all your sins.[187]

Axel hardened his heart. Instead of coming closer to God and asking for forgiveness, he moved further away. He took his machete and began to cut his way through the jungle. "Where would he go?" he wondered. He could not live alone in the jungle; it was not safe. A bizarre thought crossed his mind. "Go to the tribe to the north. They are evil. They will take you in."

Satan smiled as his thoughts took root in Axel's mind. He was encouraged by the present circumstances. All was not lost. He still had a chance to defeat God's plan. He would take advantage of Axel's guilt and the rest of the Questers despair and discouragement. They were two of his foremost weapons and he would use them to benefit his cause.

---

[187] 1 John 1:9

214

CHAPTER THIRTY

JUNE 27

PUERTO BAHIA NEGRA

During the flight from Canada to Puerto Bahia Negra, Haydon Carlton had been busy. He had several names given to him by men who lived on the shadier side of life. He required the help of some associates in Paraguay who needed to be men who asked no questions, and followed orders without question. They needed to be men who were comfortable walking on the wrong side of the law, and be able to bring a large assortment of weapons and ammunition with them. Haydon had not wanted to try bringing weapons into the country. He also wanted an explosive expert. He was covering all his bases.

Haydon knew lovely Bekah was after a treasure, a very large treasure, and he wanted her to do all the work. She had a rabble of people with her and he hoped they were capable of finding and digging this treasure up for him. When he confronted them and asked for the booty, he would have his wild card, Sylvia Jessup, one of Bekah's best friends. She was his ace in the hole. If they were unable to excavate the treasure, he would move in with his army, his arsenal, and his explosive expert. Then he would leave the rabble behind and he and his companions would carry out the treasure. If Bekah and her cohorts happened to make it out of the jungle, good for them. He would be well on his way to anonymity, with a treasure equivalent to Midas' in his possession.

215

He smiled to himself. He felt like a Robin Hood, robbing from the rich and giving to the poor. Haydon laughed. He was already rich, and now he would be richer. Let the poor take care of themselves if they were able. His only concern was for himself.

He looked over at Sylvia Jessup. She was finally asleep. He had listened to her prattle for hours as she spouted off about God sending Bekah and her friends on a Quest to reach a group of people who had never heard the Gospel before. She actually seemed to believe this fairytale, but he was too smart to fall for all that nonsense. If he believed in any god, it was himself. He smiled at a humorous thought. It would really be impressive if everyone bowed down and worshipped him.

Sylvia was becoming more of a problem than he wanted to deal with himself. Haydon was almost tempted to just kill her and be done with her, but she still might be an asset if they could get her to where they were going. Since she was an old lady, she would need help if they had to travel in the jungle. He needed a strong, young woman to help her, and also buy her some suitable clothes for the journey. He had the name of a person to look for. Her name was Luna. From the information he had gathered, she was a woman in her thirties who had been around and knew the score. He would pay her five thousand dollars to accompany them. That was probably more money than she'd seen in her lifetime. Things were looking good. He decided to take a short nap before landing.

The change in cabin pressure awakened Hayden, and for a moment he was disoriented. That had happened to him several times recently. An instant of concern surfaced, but he immediately submerged it into his subconscious. He had no time or patience for worries. He would not allow anyone or anything to distract him from his objective.

The wheels touched the runway and the plane slowed to a bumpy stop. Haydon looked out the window and a motley crew was there to greet him, eight middle aged men and one very beautiful

216

woman. The men were what he had expected, but the woman was a diamond in the rough. She was tall for a native, five foot eight or nine inches. She had typical dark eyes, and olive skin, but her long, wavy hair was her crowning glory. She spoke to one of the men; it almost appeared that she was in charge.

When the doors to the small jet opened, Haydon descended the steps and a tall man of forty or so came forward, and the beautiful woman was right behind him. He introduced himself. "My name is Manolito and these are my men. We agreed to $100,000 up front, and two pieces of treasure, our pick, and three more your pick after the job is done. We will stay with you until all the treasure is recovered and all the loose ends are dealt with. If the treasure is half what you described, our cut is small to what you will be taking home."

"You are right, but I am still taking all the risk, and spending all the money right now. I have a $100,000 cashier's check you can deposit right now as a show of good faith."

Luna elbowed Manolito out of the way and spoke impatiently. "I'm Luna and you are lucky to have me with you. I will not only help with the old woman, but I will keep evil from befalling you in the jungle. When you go after the treasure of the gods, you make them angry. I will make the proper sacrifices to keep you safe."

Haydon shuddered. After listening to Sylvia rant about her God for hours, now he had another woman ranting about her gods. It was too much. "I don't believe in your gods. They have no power over me. I'm not paying for any sacrifices. If you want to sacrifice something, find your own."

Luna lowered her eyes and spoke solemnly. "Have it your way. I will not be responsible for you or your men. When the gods come for payment, don't look for my help."

"Fine by me," Haydon spat back. "I don't believe in gods, not yours or any others. I've made my way in the world without them, and I'm not going to sacrifice to them now."

"That's fine, but I want my money now also, $5,000 as

agreed." Haydon then handed Luna a cashier's check.

As Haydon walked the short distance into town and entered the store to pay for the two boats and the gear he had ordered, he turned back to the crowd at the jet. All the men were gathered around Luna and as he watched, he saw money changing hands. They were paying her. He wondered what for and how much. Later, as Carlton walked back to the jet he saw that the old lady was still sleeping. "Let her sleep," he thought. That worked for him; one less issue to deal with now.

Luna grew up enmeshed in witchcraft. Her grandfather baptized her in the dark arts, and as time went by she excelled in her strength, understanding, and practice of them. She had no self-control over her desires and used the dark arts to fulfill her cravings. People of her village finally recognized the evil in her and were going to punish her, but she escaped into the jungle, only to show up in Puerto Bahia Negra. She made her living selling her black arts to whoever was willing to pay the price. These local men knew her and were paying her for her protection.

No one was aware that Luna was Bekah's stepsister. After Bekah and Manu's mother died in childbirth, Luna's mother, Fuego enticed Bekah's father to marry her and bring her to the states. She took advantage of Bekah's father's sorrow at his wife's death. She also used the dark arts she was raised in to turn him to her desires. Fuego even sold her daughter Luna to her grandfather, the tribe's witch doctor, to raise money for their plane tickets.

Sylvia stared at Carlton through slitted eyes and watched him turn away. "Let him think I'm still asleep," she thought. "It allows me time to pray and hear from God."

She prayed that all the fiery darts the enemy was wielding would be quenched,[188] and that angels would surround all those involved in the Quest, not just in Paraguay, but back in the United States also.

---

[188] Ephesians 6:16

After praying for over an hour, she stilled her voice and mind to listen. Sylvia was not just speaking but listening to what God answered.

As her mind quieted, her breathing slowed and she slept. In her dream, God took her to a high cliff deep in the jungle. Over the cliffs, cascades of water were falling, a sight of beauty, marvelous to behold. They fell as ribbons of water, some narrow and some wide, some tumbled tier upon tier. She had been to Niagara Falls, and its beauty and magnitude paled in comparison to the falls of her dream.

Suddenly, Haydon kicked Sylvia's seat and jarred her awake. She smiled up at him and he backed up in confusion. "What was with this old lady?" he wondered. "Doesn't she know I could have her killed with one word? All her fear has probably put her over the edge." he thought.

He went back out and called Luna over. "Go take a look at the prisoner, then go and purchase whatever you need for her and yourself for ten days in the jungle.

Luna went into the plane and introduced herself to Sylvia. She thought it would be easier to try to get off on the right foot.

Sylvia was still sitting in her seat when a woman of striking beauty walked down the aisle towards her. Then God spoke in a still small Voice and said, "This woman is destined to play a part in this Quest. Pray for her; speak My Word to her and over her. Do not grow weary in it." Momentarily, a smile faded from Sylvia's, face to be replaced by a look of determination.

Walking down the aisle, Luna paused and then spoke. "My name is Luna and I will be taking care of you while you are in Paraguay. Will you please stand up so I can see your size? I am going to purchase clothes and supplies for us during our time in the jungle."

Sylvia's face radiated a genuine smile. "My name is Sylvia and I'm from Ogunquit, Maine. You are a very beautiful, young woman. I hope we can be friends."

Luna was taken aback by that response. Didn't this woman

219

know she was a prisoner? Being friends was the last thing she had in mind.

As Luna left to shop, a guard was placed at the jet's exit ramp. He did not try to come on board, and Sylvia did not try to leave.

As the afternoon waned, Luna returned with her purchases and everyone went down to the dock. Except for these last purchases, everything had been preloaded that afternoon. Haydon, Manolito, and three of his men were on one boat. Four men, Luna, and Sylvia were on the other boat.

It was late afternoon when they departed. Once the sky grew dark, they would tie up to shore, but Haydon wanted to get as much distance between them and the city as possible. There were always nosey eyes looking for information they might sell to interested parties, or just troublemakers, profiting from someone else's weaknesses. He wanted to be away from this place.

After two hours they tied up. A four hour watch was set and a quick meal was eaten. By that time everyone was tired and they all turned in except the watch. Tomorrow was going to be a big day.

During the night God spoke to Sylvia in another dream. She was in a native village by the large and beautiful waterfall. It was not a peaceful village, but one filled with turmoil. Most of the inhabitants appeared to be rioting. The men had spears in their hands and the women were shouting and arguing. At the center of everything was a woman tied to what looked like a totem pole that had been placed in the middle of the village. A short distance away, on a small hill, stood the rest of the Questers. Sylvia jumped and woke herself up. She recognized Bekah, who was tied to the pole, and Josh, Ted and Renato. She assumed the others were the people from Paraguay who were also part of the Quest. What she couldn't see was that there was a legion of angels standing by, waiting for the word to be given.

Sylvia didn't know how far into the future this was, but felt an urgency in her heart to pray fervently. She prayed protection over all God's people in Paraguay. She didn't know the extent of the Christian population, but she knew that Christians everywhere needed prayer in these perilous times.

The news she watched this morning as she sat waiting in the plane had shown an organized strike by the Russians in the Middle East, that poor piece of real estate that was the cradle of all Christianity. In a swift and unsuspected move, they had fired on Hezbollah strongholds in the West Bank. They also bombed the suspected nuclear sites in Iran, suspected chemical weapons plants in Syria, and all known Black Death strongholds. The Russian President was being hailed as the greatest peacemaker since Sadat and Gandhi. The people of the world were referring to him as the leader they had all been praying for. Israel also voiced its gratitude for his raids on their enemies. What they didn't know was that this charismatic leader's actions and rise to power was a sign of the beginning of the end.

Sylvia tried to recall all the end time Scriptures she knew. This was an area of the Bible she wished she had studied in greater depth. She knew there would be wars and rumors of wars. That was already occurring. The sun would darken and the moon would turn red. There had been several eclipses and blood moons in the last few years, and numerous earthquakes. It had also been prophesied that Israel would be attacked and a new charismatic leader would rise up and take control of the world. Israel had been under attack since becoming a nation in 1948, and it appeared that these attacks were still happening. All the news organizations of the world heralded the rise in prominence of one of our world leaders. He was being touted as a new savior of the world.[189]

What any of these things had to do with Paraguay and their Quest she did not know. She fervently wished she had a Bible with her in order to study these events.

---

[189] Matthew 24:4-14

221

CHAPTER THIRTY-ONE

JUNE 27
THE QUESTERS

Philippe was the first of the group to come upon Mario's body. He let out a loud wail and ran toward him. The body lay across the trail on the ground, surrounded by a large pool of blood. His eyes were staring, wide open. His face bore an exaggerated grimace.

All of the Questers experienced a stirring in the air, as though people were milling around them. What they could not see were the forces of darkness, and the legion of angels waiting to battle with them. Axel's sin had opened the door for these demons. The angels were waiting for the words of faith to release them to go forth into action.

Everyone gathered around the fallen member of the Quest. Josh was the first to realize they must take a stand and declare the Word of God, the Sword of the Spirit, to combat the enemy and his forces.[190] "In the Name of Jesus, I declare that greater is He that is in me than he that is in the world."[191]

The forces of darkness wavered as the Word of God was spoken. Into the battle went the legion of angels, their flaming swords drawn and their strength renewed. "Not by might, not by power, but by Your Spirit,"[192] Josh shouted. The others took up their swords

---

[190] Ephesians 6:17
[191] 1 John 4:4
[192] Zechariah 4:6

and began quoting Scriptures of conquest. "If one can put a thousand to flight, two can put ten thousand to flight."[193] Another sword swung, "Be bold, be strong, for the Lord your God is with you."[194]

Over and over they wielded their swords and the forces of darkness turned to flee. Satan was standing there, another defeat added to the tally, but he could not give up. He had no other choice and would fight until the end. The specter of that was looming, and the end was drawing closer and closer as each day passed.

Satan and his hoards withdrew to a safe distance and then turned to watch the Questers react to the death of Mario. Maybe one of them would say or do something to give them another opening. He had not run out of tricks yet, not by a long shot.

God sat on His throne observing what was happening. The blood of righteous Mario cried out to him from the ground, just as the blood of righteous Abel had cried out to Him as he died at the hands of his brother Cain.[195] God received Mario into Glory and now he sat with that great cloud of witnesses[196] watching one of the battles of the ages taking place on Earth in the tiny country of Paraguay. Monumental things were happening in the world and the calendar of Heaven was moving forward.

Daniel, who had been mentoring Mario for some time, grieved over the young man. He felt the loss as he would a younger brother. Mario's friends Philippe, Giancarlo, and Maitie were confused and upset. "How could this happen," they asked? "How could Axel do this? He was our friend. He was a Christian. Christians don't murder other Christians."

Josh replied, sympathy filling his voice, "Unfortunately, they do. Many wars have been fought in the Name of God against other Christians. The enemy starts a whispering campaign just like he did with Eve. He sows seeds of doubt and deception. Then he tells

---

[193] Deuteronomy 32:30-31
[194] Joshua 1:7-9
[195] Genesis 4:10
[196] Hebrews 12:1

224

you what you want to hear. 'Did God really say?'[197] Satan asked Eve. Don't you know if you eat the fruit you will be like Him?'"[198] Josh concluded by saying, "We all noticed Axel was acting differently. He was downcast, angry and rude.[199] Satan found an opening and took advantage. Remember, the Bible says Satan is like a roaring lion looking for someone to devour.[200] Axel became a loner. He kept apart from the fellowship of the group. Satan picked him off like a lion does to a solitary animal. We must all be wise to his tactics and learn from this."

Daniel spoke to the young men, "Maitie, you come with me to the river to get water to clean Mario for burial. Giancarlo and Philippe take your machetes and start clearing a place to dig a grave. The rest of you look for stones to pile upon it."

It was two hours past dark when they were finished. They were all hot and dirty, but felt they needed to go on. There was no apparent sign of where Axel had gone, and none of them felt the urge to go after him. Maybe he would come back repentant. They could only hope and pray.

They didn't cover the mileage they had hoped for, only six or seven miles. As dawn broke, they stumbled into a clearing. They dropped their gear and headed to the river to wash off the sweat and grime of the previous evening. Without any preparation of food, setting of traps, or boiling of water, the Questers unrolled their bedding and dropped, asleep almost immediately.

There were now ten angels keeping watch, one for each of them. The enemy was still circling, but keeping his distance. Not one of the foul hoards would penetrate their defenses this day. The Questers needed a time of rest, peace and restoration. The light of the Word of God continued shining despite how things appeared.

---

[197] Genesis 3:1
[198] Genesis 3:5
[199] Genesis 4:6-8
[200] 1 Peter 5:8

CHAPTER THIRTY-TWO

JUNE 28
THE RIVER

The sun was well up in the sky and the only one stirring was Sylvia. She had been up for almost two hours and spent the time wisely in prayer. So many things were happening and she was certainly glad God was in charge and not her. It was amazing, that in the midst of all these criminals, she was at peace. She knew God had a purpose for her here, and he would show her what was required of her. She was thankful that a woman her age could still be used by God.

The men got up slowly and went to the back of the boat to relieve themselves. Luna hopped over the side of the boat and walked into the jungle. She came out a few minutes later and ambled back to Sylvia. "Well, old woman, you need to take care of yourself and get back into the boat before we have to send someone out after you. Don't even think of escaping, because there is nowhere to go."

While Sylvia was ashore, someone started getting breakfast ready. Sylvia could smell bacon cooking when she got back in the boat. She went back and sat by Luna, who was brushing out her long and shiny hair. "You have such beautiful hair," she said to Luna.

After turning and making a face at Sylvia, Luna replied, "Don't try to be my friend. I was hired to watch you, and see that you don't escape. Other than that, I care nothing for you."

Sylvia was startled by such a belligerent response. "I'm not going to try to escape. You're right, where would I go? But tell me this; is it wrong to be nice to one another? I was telling the truth about your hair. It's lovely. I care about everyone here. I spent the morning praying for all of you, that God would keep you safe and lead and guide you."

"Well I for one don't want you praying to your God for me. I have my own gods and they are all I need. My gods and I take care of the boys, and we don't need any help from you or your gods."

"I don't have many gods Luna, only one. He is the one true God, and He's all I need."

Luna retorted, "Well if He's all you need, He's not doing a very good job. You got yourself kidnapped and ended up here?"

"I wasn't kidnapped, God asked me to come. God called my name and woke me up, and I saw Haydon in my garden. It was dark, but I saw his face. God told me to go with him, and here I am."

"Well aren't you Miss High and Mighty, God talks to you. It must be difficult conversing with the rest of us down here."

"Luna, God cares for everyday people. He cares for everyone so much that He sent His only Son to be a sacrifice and die for their sins, even yours and mine. God watched His only Son Jesus, die on a cross so we could be free. After three days God raised Him from the dead. Then Jesus spent forty more days teaching and encouraging those who believed in Him and telling them that He would see them again in Heaven, where He was going to be with His Father, God. Then God did as He promised, and brought Jesus back up to Heaven."

Luna spat, "I've heard all the stories about your God. What has He done for me and my people? Nothing! Where was He when I needed Him, when I was growing up? My grandfather abused me. Did God hear me crying? No! Did He care? No! When I cried for help, He was silent, but my gods came to my rescue. They gave me help. They taught me strange and powerful things. I don't need your God!"

"Well I need Him," Sylvia replied, "and I will continue to pray for everyone. There will come a day when your gods let you down, abandon you. Just remember to call on the Name of Jesus and He will save you."

Luna spat, and walked off with a huff, but Sylvia got back to prayer. She determined that every free moment would be spent in prayer, even for those who appeared to be a lost cause.

After they were on the river for several hours Luna came back to sit by Sylvia. "Do you need to go ashore again? I will ask them to stop the boat."

"Thank you. I wondered when we would be stopping again."

"I'll go first and then you can go. Just be careful. If there's a problem, call for help."

Sylvia was helped ashore, and walked ten feet into the jungle, enough to ensure privacy. Getting back on the boat she observed that Luna was still sitting near where she had sat at the back of the boat. Encouraged, Sylvia gave her a big smile and asked, "How is your day going?"

Luna just gave Sylvia a dirty look and walked to the front of the boat.

Word came back they would be stopping for the night early. They were several miles south of a village they were seeking. Haydon was certain it was the one Bekah was at and wanted to sneak in and surprise them. He had no idea that guards had been set along the river to alert the village if any strangers were approaching. His plan was to go in through the jungle with guns blazing, and shoot anyone who gave resistance. Manolito had tried to tell him that though this was a good plan, there might be a better way.

Haydon looked down at Manolito and told him, "You keep your ideas to yourself. You were hired to follow orders, not give them."

Manolito struggled with his temper. This man was a brag-gart and a liar and everyone already knew that. Manolito had no problem taking orders from someone he respected, someone who knew what they were talking about, but this man was a fool. Let him lead the way through the jungle. Let him fall into the bogs. He would keep quiet and let this man bury himself.

CHAPTER THIRTY-THREE

JUNE 28
THE QUESTERS

Everyone woke with a start as the sound of the phone roused them from a deep and dreamless sleep. As he answered the phone, Josh looked at his watch and realized it was almost noon. The sky was dark and he could hear rumbles of thunder in the distance. He answered with a groggy, "Hello," and awaited a reply.

Kent Knox spoke from the other end of the line, "Well hello to you. You sound terrible. Is everything alright?"

"Just a little tired," Josh answered. "I don't know if we told you but we travel by night. We've only had about four hours of sleep and we traveled a long time yesterday." Josh was not about to tell Kent anything that had happened. He didn't know if he should tell anyone yet. They all needed to pray and process what had taken place.

"Sorry to bother you," Kent answered. "I don't know if you can get the news down there in the jungle, but in case you haven't heard, Russia attacked all Hezbollah strongholds in the Middle East. They also attacked all known Black Death strongholds there, as well as Iran's suspected nuclear sites and Syria's suspected chemical weapons sites. The whole planet is in an uproar. Many are heralding the Russian President as a modern day savior of the world. Even North Korea is singing his praises. Maybe because they're concerned they might be next. The only countries that appeared to be a little standoffish are Israel and the U.S. I, myself,

231

don't see how he can go from enemy, to savior of most of the free world, overnight. I smell a rat.

"Another concern is that he may go further afield and look outside the Middle-East for more targets. Unfortunately for you, Paraguay may be in his crosshairs. If we know about the Black Death Camps down there, they probably know also."

Josh's mind was whirling with the ramifications of the information he had just been given, but also, with the grief of what had occurred yesterday. His mind cried out, "Father, how much more stress can we deal with?"

A thought rose up in his mind, "Don't speak of the situations until you have had time to pray."

Josh refocused on what Kent was saying and then asked, "Have you talked with Isaac about this? What does he have to say? Are you aware that the weapons they found at the Black Death Camp were labeled 'Property of the U.S. Army'? Also, I still haven't had any information given to me about the prisoners. Has anyone interrogated them? There are nineteen of them. Did anyone tell you that at the time of escape, Renato found three of the prisoners who appeared to hang back, almost as if they wanted to be caught? These are things that could shed light on some of the questions we have."

Kent replied, "I haven't had a chance to talk with Isaac yet. With so much happening around the world, he dropped down on my priority list until I saw the memo about the Black Death Camps and talked with you yesterday. I will talk with Isaac next and see what he has found out. I'm sure we'll have interminable talks and meetings up here and decide nothing. Maybe these attacks by Russia will goad someone to take action. Anything you want to add before I hang up?"

Josh thought of a million questions, but chose to heed the Word he had heard and do nothing until they had prayed. "No, not now," he answered. "Call us back later when we have had a chance to pray, and assimilate all that has happened." Josh was talking not just about the attacks, but also about the murder of Mario by Axel. He hesitated calling it murder, but what else could it be. He would seek God's wisdom on this and so many other matters that seem to be swirling around them. He felt as though they had stumbled into a hornet's nest, and the angry hornets were buzzing on all sides, stinging them with their weapons.

As Kent hung up, Josh looked around at the group. What he saw brought despair to his heart. He could not see God's plan in what had happened. He knew all things worked together for good to those who love God and are called according to His purpose,[201] but he had trouble finding a purpose for what had happened yesterday. Then he asked himself, "What is God's purpose?" The answer helped to renew his mind to God's way of thinking.

"We mustn't think like the world thinks," Josh said to the others. "The world would tell us we've failed. We might as well turn back. But we can't think like the world. We need to be transformed, be changed by renewing our minds. In doing this, we can prove what is the good, acceptable, and perfect, will of God."[202]

Josh shared his insight with the group. "It wasn't God's will that Axel kill Mario. His will is that we all go forth in His power and might to bring the Gospel to the northern tribe. We need to realize that Satan is doing everything in his power to stop us. Somehow Axel started listening to Satan instead of the Voice of the Holy Spirit and this tragedy occurred.

"God is still with us. His purpose has not changed. We all need to stay focused. After seeing how Axel had been distancing himself from the group, Satan took advantage of the situation, and like a roaring lion, picked him off.[203] From now on before we start our trek and before we go to sleep, we need to pray God's bless-

---

[201] Romans 8:28
[202] Romans 12:2
[203] 1 Peter 5:8

233

ing and protection on us, and question anything we see that might cause a rift in our relationships. We cannot afford to give the enemy a foothold. Also, I'm asking Bekah if after our prayers she will sing 'Great is Thy Faithfulness.' It will reinforce the fact that even when we are not faithful—God is always faithful."[204]

"One last thing we need to pray for is Axel. He is out in the jungle all alone. We need to pray and bind the enemy from harassing him, and that he repent and ask God's forgiveness. We also need to make sure that we forgive him."

They all stood and joined hands, all feeling that the touch on one another would bind them closer together. They all prayed fervently, and then Bekah lifted her voice and it rose up before the throne of God.

God smiled at His children and sent the Comforter, the peace giver, His Holy Spirit, to strengthen their hearts and minds. He affirmed each one in their own hearts, and lifted their spirits. By their words, they had driven back the forces of darkness. He gave them rest, and they all lay down and continued their sleep in peace.

---

[204] 2 Timothy 2:13

CHAPTER THIRTY-FOUR

JUNE 28

THE VILLAGE

True to his word, Kent called the village next and Sherry picked up the phone on its first ring. "Hello," she said in a bright, perky voice, hoping that it might be Daniel calling. But it was a voice she didn't recognize.

"Hello," he said. This is Kent Knox. I'm calling from Washington and I'd like to speak to Isaac Klein."

"I'm sorry. I can't get him right now. Are you his contact at the C.I.A.," Sherry asked?

"Well, yes I am," Kent answered in a puzzled voice. He wondered what Isaac could be doing that he couldn't come to the phone.

Sherry proceeded to solve that mystery. "Isaac has spent all morning interviewing the captives from the Black Death Camp, trying to get any information out of them that might be helpful. He ought to be done soon. Do you want me to have him call you back?"

"No," Kent answered in an irritated voice. "Let me talk with Jose or Mehdi."

"Sorry, they're both helping. I don't think they should be too much longer. I just brought them a drink and it looked as if they only had two or three left. Do you want to leave a message?"

"Who was this woman," Kent thought with annoyance. "Did she think she was their private secretary?" He was also concerned with how much she knew about what was happening.

235

"They were down to the three stragglers, the ones who hung back when the fifteen others escaped," Sherry replied.

Failing to keep the irritation out of his voice Kent asked, "Who are you, and how do you know everything that is happening?"

Sherry's voice lost a little of its brightness, and she spoke with a sharp edge. "Listen, I don't need your attitude. We have enough going on down here without somebody else butting in. I'll leave a message for Isaac and he can call you back when it suits him."

As Sherry went to hang up she heard Kent shout, "Wait a minute. I'm sorry. I'm truly sorry. So much is happening and I don't want to lose control of the situation. I let my stress take control of the circumstances."

"Well I accept your apology and I forgive you. We have our share of stress down here. We've got nineteen members of the Black Death here in the village we have to guard. In addition to that, we also have to feed them, and that's with five of our hunters gone on God's Quest. But God helps us. He tells us not to worry, that He will take care of us.[205] So far, what hunters and fishermen we have are bringing in record catches, and no one has gone hungry.

"Let me ask you Kent, are you a Christian?"

"Now wait a minute. I didn't call you to get preached at. I believe in God, but my beliefs are my personal business. How would you like it if someone asked you what you believed?"

"I'd be excited to tell them. Can I tell you, Kent?"

"Thanks, I appreciate your openness, but maybe another time. Please have Isaac call me when he's through."

"I will," Sherry replied. Then she shouted, "Wait a minute, don't hang up; here they come. Hold on and I'll tell him you are on the phone."

Sherry put her hand over the phone and said to Isaac, "Kent Knox wants to speak with you. Find out if he's a Christian," Sherry whispered.

---

[205] 1 Peter 5:6-7

"Hey buddy, how's it going up there in civilization? Are you wearing a suit and tie, because I'm sure not."

Kent laughed. "What are you wearing, shorts and a t-shirt? All kidding aside, we have big problems that you are probably not aware of."

As Mehdi, Jose and Leonardo came into the room, Isaac put the phone on speaker. There were several other people listening in the room, but there were no secrets anymore. Everyone had a right to know what was happening. He'd deal with the repercussions of that decision later.

Kent started explaining to them all that had taken place around the world yesterday, and then said he feared they might be in the crosshairs also. Their Paraguay mission was probably not as secret as everyone thought. These days there were very few secrets. Everyone knew everyone else's business.

When he finished telling of the worldwide happenings, he got down to local business. "What have you found out from the prisoners, especially the three who hung back? How many of them appear to be Americans? Did that make any difference in their co-operation?"

"Let me take these questions one at a time," Isaac replied. "We didn't get any information from the sixteen, but the three who hung back gave us an interesting story. They are not American or from the Middle East. They are Paraguayans. They were unhappy with their life and their jobs. They felt they were being held back because they were Guarani, Paraguay's indigenous tribe. In this country, they are looked down upon as second class citizens. They had heard rumors of an uprising that was going to take place and that those in authority would be removed.

"They foolishly signed up. They had no family to leave behind. They were in the right place at the right time to get picked up for this new army that was forming. They enjoyed the fighting and the shooting, and they ignored the zealous rhetoric, but when the group rebelled and cut off the heads of their prisoners, they knew they were in trouble. They want asylum."

Kent laughed. "I'll bet they do. Do you believe their story? It could just be a con. How do we know they are who they say they are?"

Isaac had laughed also; then he got serious. "One thing that separates them is they speak Guarani, the indigenous language of the country. They pretty much joined this for a lark. They were all in low paying jobs and thought they had nothing to lose. They heard someone talking about the initial meeting at a bar and thought they would go and see what it was about. They were recruited and brought to the Black Death Camp, but the killings showed them they had made a big mistake. They actually gave us quite a bit of good information.

"We already knew of the two bigger Black Death Camps up near the area Josh and his group are headed for. What we didn't know is what they found up there. Rumor is that they found uranium up on top of a waterfall. They are bringing in explosives to open a shaft. They are also going to extend the runway up there to be able to carry in and out larger freight shipments. Two of them were actually transferred up there for four weeks to help build housing. They said they were using indigenous villagers as a slave work force. Did you know that back in the 1600's, the Spanish used the indigenous people as slaves to mine for gold, silver, and precious gems?"

"No, I was not aware of that," Kent said.

"Josh told me after years of bondage the slaves rebelled, killed all their oppressors, took all the treasure that had been held there and hid it. Bits and pieces of it have turned up over the years, but never the mother lode. In fact, Bekah, the woman who is out on the Quest with Josh and the others, is being hunted by a man, Haydon Carlton, who thinks Bekah knows where the treasure is." Isaac continued to relate to Kent the rest of the story, from beginning to end. He talked for over twenty minutes and Kent didn't interrupt once. Then he paused, concerned that maybe Kent hung up.

"Kent, are you still there," Isaac questioned?

"Yes, I'm here. I just don't know what to say about all this. Several people have the same dream, a baby is found floating down the river with a large gold encrusted crucifix in the basket with him. People are killed, babies are sacrificed, a baby raised from the dead, and the list goes on. I'm stunned by it all. It's almost unbelievable. Have you verified all this, Isaac?"

Isaac began to laugh, "I not only verified it; I held the baby who had been killed, squeezed to death, by a large snake. Seeing everyone down here, and how God has His hand in all this, I could not help myself, I became a Christian."

"What?" Kent raised his voice in astonishment, "You were an atheistic Jew. How did this happen? Were you brainwashed?"

"I don't know if I would call it that. I just saw and heard of so many things happening that I started paying attention. All the things that went on couldn't have been by accident or coincidence

"Unfortunately, now we have a total of nineteen prisoners, almost half of them wounded, that we have to get out of here. Do you have any suggestions for that?" Isaac waited for a response but the phone was silent. "Kent, are you still there?"

"I am," he replied, "but I'm having trouble buying all this. I had heard Josh had a strange arrangement with our office and his church. I figured he'd gone a little off the deep end. But you, you've been nothing but a straight arrow. No question marks that I know of. How can you throw that all away? Are you going to do anything to jeopardize your job? I have it from a very reliable source, that the next area promotion will be yours. You don't want to risk that promotion by getting involved in all that religious stuff that's going on down there; do you?"

"You know Kent, someone either believes in God or he doesn't. If he does, he will want to obey Him, do what God is asking him to do. If he doesn't, he will do whatever he wants to do, whatever

239

he thinks is to his benefit.[206] I've changed from the second category to the first. My priority now is to obey God. I believe all the people who came down from the States, have willingly put their lives in jeopardy. All of the people in this village, through no fault of their own, have been put in harm's way. They already escaped two attacks from armed and dangerous men under miraculous circumstances.

"Maybe you have to be here and see it to believe, or maybe you can hear it from someone you know and trust, who has never lied to you or misled you. Maybe God has to hit you on the side of the head with a 2 x 4. Whatever it takes, I hope it happens, and when it does I hope you call and tell me."

Kent cleared his throat and spoke hoarsely. "No one has ever spoken to me like this before. I need some time to digest what you said. Let's see if we can get back to business. Can you tell me how many able-bodied prisoners you have who can walk to the burned out village where Josh has just left? Maybe we could walk them there and fly them out."

"That's not going to work," replied Isaac. "It's a two or three day trek, with eight prisoners. We'd have to send four or five men to guard them. That would leave us short-handed here, especially if Joseph brings more people to the Black Death Camp. Then there would be an almost certain chance that they would come and attack. They would also have better leadership than the previous attacks."

"How have they been acting since they were brought here, Are they angry, radical, have they made any attempts to escape?" Kent asked.

"No," Isaac answered. "They seem perfectly happy to stay here and eat our food. It's like they're being waited on hand and foot."

"Maybe that's the problem," Kent responded. "Perhaps you need to get them to work for their upkeep. Have them go set snares and search for food. Let them go fishing. Tell them if they don't work

---

[206] Judges 21:25

240

and produce, they don't eat. It might motivate them, especially if they go hungry for a day or two. I'm not saying starve them, but make it worth their while. Doesn't the Bible even say something like 'if you don't work, you don't eat?"[207]

Isaac laughed, "You just might have come up with a good idea. I'll talk with Leonardo and see if we can come up with a plan. See if you can work out something on your end to help us out down here. Give me a call back when you have some good news."

"That may be some time. I talked with Josh right before I called you. I woke them up. He said they are walking at night and sleeping during the day. I don't understand that. They have weapons. What are they afraid of?"

"It's got nothing to do with fear. God told them to walk at night and sleep during the day. That's what they've been doing."

"That doesn't make sense," Kent replied. "They would make so much better time walking during the day."

"You're right. But if you feel that God has told you to do something, wouldn't you do it?"

"Well God hasn't ever spoken to me. Maybe I'm not one of the privileged few."

"Maybe you're not," Isaac said, "do you want to be?"

"Don't you start in on me. That woman was also checking out my religious background; too much is happening right now for me to worry about whether God talks to me or not.

"It may take some time for things to settle down, if they ever do, but I'll pray for you. Let me know if anything else comes up. Hopefully we'll talk soon."

---

[207] 2 Thessalonians 3:10-12

CHAPTER THIRTY-FIVE

JUNE 28
THE SURVIVORS

Edwardo and Miguel sat with the twelve survivors of the burned out village. Edwardo looked them over, evaluating them for travel. Just one day of rest and a few good meals and they looked like different people. They sat up straighter; they talked and laughed with each other. The specter of death and destruction no longer lingered upon them. They had been set free. Now the Spirit of God lived in them and helped them resist the attacks of the devil.

Seeing the change in their countenance, and their added energy, he felt confident to ask them, "After our mid-day meal, I would like to head back to my village if you all feel you are able to travel. Are you up to the challenge?"

Everyone, including little Yvoty, voiced their agreement. They were anxious to leave this place of death and destruction. The fond memories they had had of this place had been burned up with everything else.

Each one had a small parcel they carried with any possession they may have salvaged. Edwardo carried the food that was left from the hunt of yesterday. It should be enough to last them until they reached his village. It only needed to be supplemented with some fruit and vegetables and roots they could gather as they traveled. Edwardo carried his rifle, hoping that the only thing he would have to use it for was food.

In their eagerness, they were already putting out the fire and preparing to leave this place behind them. Before they set out, they prayed God's protection, and that the Holy Spirit would lead and guide them. Edwardo commissioned angels to go before and behind, and to the left and right to protect them from all the fiery darts of the enemy. He looked back and saw Miguel holding Yvoty's hand. He was confident Miguel would watch her to be sure she could keep up. If she tired, he could carry her for a while. She was a spunky little girl and she looked over at him and smiled. Edwardo set out, and Miguel and Yvoty brought up the rear.

Edwardo followed the same trail the Questers had taken when they came from his village. He was determined to walk until dark. They would make good use of the daylight, walking as long as everyone was able.

After about an hour walking at a steady pace he glanced back and saw Yvoty holding on to Miguel's hand. It made him smile to see the joy in both their faces. It also made him long to be re-united with his own family. Edwardo continued on for another hour then held up his hand and everyone stopped. Turning around he asked, "Do we need to stop and take a rest?" He observed that the five young hunters who had not been in the village during the attack were still fresh, as well as Miguel. The rest were dragging. Edwardo told them to sit down, and have something to eat and drink. He realized that he would have to slow down the pace in order to accommodate the elderly and the injured.

One of the young hunters had taken the initiative to walk around the perimeter. He came back with a large bunch of ripe bananas. They tasted good and were a wonderful source of energy. God was so good in providing for all their needs.

After a short time of rest and a drink of the ever present terere, they all rose and began the walk again. This time, to Yvoty's delight, Miguel swung her up to ride on his shoulders. She sat there with a huge grin on her face, calling out to all the other travelers.

Miguel also walked with Ysupi, the oldest, giving her his arm to lean on. They all walked on; traveling slower, but making better progress. From her vantage point, Yvoty had a great view. From time to time she would get down and walk along the group, humming and singing as she passed. Her song and her smile encouraged everyone following. Edwardo was hoping they would be able to walk at least ten more miles today. That put his village within reach in two days. He prayed they would be able to keep up the pace.

Edwardo enjoyed listening to little Yvoty. She reminded him of his own daughter Maria. Since God showed up and the village had turned to Him, Maria had also changed dramatically. Where, before she had been quiet and withdrawn, now she was confident and outgoing. She was a chatterbox.

He was concerned that after Eyo had been killed by a wild boar, protecting her, that she would withdraw again. But she determined that God needed her help. Maria said she felt that He had too much to do, and that was why Eyo was killed. She told Edwardo that she was going to pray to God every day, and remind Him of all the people that needed His help so He would not forget. Maria told Edwardo God told her that was a good idea, and He would take care of it.

He wasn't sure she actually heard the Voice of God, but Edwardo thought, if he were God, that might be the kind of answer He would give a little child. God seemed to have a special relationship with children. Jesus even corrected His disciples, and told them to allow the children to come to Him."[208]

Thinking of Maria brought Connie to his mind, and his eyes filled. What was going to happen to everyone? Something was going to happen, he knew that for sure, and he knew it would be soon. He just didn't know how much collateral damage there would be, and what would need to be dealt with.

---

[208] Matthew 19:12-14

245

Since he was a junior member of the Quest age wise, Edwardo sometimes felt that he was passed over when input was asked for. He had had an opportunity or two to be offended, and if he dwelt on that offense, it could easily lead to sin. Cain was offended because Abel's sacrifice was received and his was not. He brooded over it and God questioned him. "Cain," God said, "sin lies at your doorstep; don't give in to it. If you do what is right you will be rewarded."[209]

Edwardo was well aware of his feelings and emotions. He knew that sin started in his mind and then moved to his heart. If not dealt with, he would fall sway to Satan and his evil works. But Edwardo had a remedy that he practiced every morning. He prayed to God His Word, that he found while reading his Bible.

"Our Father in Heaven, I ask you to search every part of me. I don't want to hide anything from You. You know my heart and my thoughts. If there is any evil or wickedness in me reveal it to me so I may repent and ask Your forgiveness. Lead me and guide me so that I may serve You all the days of my life."[210]

It was such a comfort and brought peace to his heart to know that he stood before God blameless.[211] He wondered what had happened to Axel. How did he let the enemy into his mind and heart? He prayed for Axel, that he would recognize his sins and ask for forgiveness.

Edwardo's mind returned to his village and all the people living there. They were his people, and were friends, one and all. The village was small enough to know everyone. They were like a large, extended family. In addition, there were almost thirty additional mouths to feed, some C.I.A., some Black Death captives. What would become of all these people? How were the natives of his village coping with such an influx of people? Most of them

---

[209] Genesis 4:3-7
[210] Psalm 139:23-24
[211] 1 John 1:9

were a burden; they could not hunt or fish. They could not comb the jungle looking for good things to eat.

It was a worry to him, and he knew God's Word said not to worry, but to seek to please Him and do His will and all their needs would be taken care of. God even said not to worry about tomorrow. Today had enough difficulties.[212] Worry was a hard sin to avoid. It kept coming back. Through past experience, Edwardo recognized that he would have to repeatedly repent and put worry far from him again and again. He would use God's Word, the Sword of the Spirit, to bring his mind into submission again.

The day drew to a close. Days were growing shorter, and nights much cooler. He had plenty of food, but the people had little to combat the cold. He would send out the young men to gather a large quantity of firewood to cook with, and for a hot drink. Then they would build up the fire, and add to it as needed through the night to keep everyone warm. He would have the women put some meat and vegetables together to make a warm and nourishing stew.

He looked over and saw Miguel holding Yvoty on his lap, singing her a song. What a strong young man he had become. After the meal there was not much talking. It had been a long day and everyone was tired. But God had given them all strength and they had covered around ten miles. They sat around the fire, but instead of lying down, they asked to hear more about God. Edwardo smiled. How it must warm God's heart to hear their eagerness to learn of Him, despite their weariness.

He told them the story of Moses and how God had led the people of Israel out of Egypt and into the wilderness to wander around for forty years because of their unbelief. He had done many mighty miracles for them and they still doubted Him. He had provided for them during those forty years. Their shoes and clothing did not wear out. He provided food and drink for them and kept

---

[212] Matthew 6:25-34

247

them safe. "He provided for them because He loved them," Edwardo said. "He is doing the same thing for all of you. Now I will pray that God sends His angels around our camp to keep us safe from any harm, whether from animals or from our enemy the devil."

Everyone lay down, and the blessed sleep of peace washed over them.

CHAPTER THIRTY-SIX

JUNE 28
THE QUESTERS

A well-aimed kick in the ribs woke Josh and the rest of the Questers. They were surrounded by a tribal people who looked very fierce and war-like. The first thing Josh did was look for Bekah. He spotted her on the side being held by two of the attackers. Her hair and clothes were drenched, as though it had rained. She must have been down by the river and got knocked into the water. He glanced at everyone else and no one seemed worse for the wear.

There were about thirty warriors surrounding them and all were armed with spears, knives, and machetes. They gathered up all their belongings, their weapons, and even the satellite phone. Nothing was left behind. Everyone was pushed or shoved to get them moving. They learned quickly that there would be no talking. Breaking the rule brought a poke in the ribs with a spear; not enough to incapacitate, but enough to bleed liberally and ensure that you were quiet.

They were marched north until dusk. Then they were herded together and made to sit. All this time Bekah had been kept separately. Surprisingly, they took her aside so she was able to take care of bodily functions in private. She was thankful for small blessings.

Bekah wondered where their protection had been. They had commissioned angels every night to go before them, and surround them as they slept during the day. The enemy had made a few attempts on them, but he had been thwarted. Could this be part of God's plan? She prayed, as she knew everyone else must be doing, for God's protection. None of them knew God's complete plan. They just knew they were to seek out the large tribe that was causing all the trouble. God had His way of doing things, and it was far superior to anything they could come up with. God had spoken, and so it would be, of that she was certain.[213] Now it appeared that that large tribe had found them.

Two of the enemy warriors approached her and grabbed her by the arms. Bekah didn't try to struggle. She knew it would be fruitless, and she wanted to maintain her dignity before these men and not show fear.

They brought her over to the man in charge. He motioned her to sit. He then had someone bring fruit and a drink for her. Bekah motioned to her companions and he shook his head no. She then shook her head no, angering him. He motioned to someone and they brought the others food and drink.

Bekah wondered what this man wanted from her that he would acquiesce to her wishes. She put that away for later consideration. She didn't know how strong an influence she had over him, but she did not want to wear it out.

She thanked him, and offered a blessing over the food. Then she ate. As always, the fruit down here tasted like nothing she had ever tasted before. Even the fruits and vegetables she was familiar with tasted better when grown down here. She wondered if the virgin soil had something to do with it. She would save that thought for later also. She had this man sitting before her to think about.

"God," she prayed, "what would You have me say or do?" Nothing seemed to be happening. She knew God was running the show, but He appeared to have taken a timeout. Bekah remembered a Scripture that talked about waiting on the Lord. Someone

---

[213] Isaiah 55:8-11

had put the Scripture to music. Even though no one would understand, Bekah began to sing. Between her voice, which sounded like it came from Heaven, and the words, which ultimately did, she prayed it would touch everyone who heard it.

"But they that wait upon the LORD shall renew their strength; they shall mount up with wings as eagles; they shall run, and not be weary; and they shall walk, and not faint. Help me Lord, help me Lord to wait."[214] This became her prayer. She hoped the rest of the prisoners would take note and agree with it.

She opened her eyes when she was done and saw that the camp had come to a standstill. No one moved. Then the one in charge became angry, and started shouting at her. Renato shouted from across the camp in Guarani, "She does not understand. She does not speak Guarani, but I do and can translate for you."

The men guarding the prisoners looked to the leader for direction. He nodded his approval and they brought Renato over. Renato nodded to the leader and then to Bekah. "May I sit?" he asked. The leader nodded, and then began to question Renato.

"Who is this woman and what kind of power does she have? Did she place a curse on us? What did she sing?"

Renato smiled to himself. God was still with them. He must have encouraged Bekah to sing. It had the desired effect. Other than the leader of the tribe, his men were much more peaceful.

"She is a woman whom God speaks to. Maybe God will speak to you through her."

Renato expected the leader to be eager to have her speak to God for him, but instead he got very angry and began shouting. Renato was roughly returned to the group of prisoners and Bekah was hauled away somewhere out of sight. Bekah sang on and off through the night, and the leader finally brought Maitie, one of the young hunters out. He told Renato to tell Bekah if she was not quiet,

---

[214] Isaiah 40:31

this man would be beaten until she was.

Bekah sent back word that she would stop. Not because of what he threatened, but because her voice was tired. Renato told the leader, "She said if you had trouble sleeping, she would sing you to sleep."

With what sounded like a growl, the leader got up and grabbed Maitie. He dragged him over to where Bekah was being watched. He threw Maitie onto the ground and began to kick him unmercifully. After about ten kicks Maitie lay still and Bekah was crying. The leader turned to Renato and said in a vicious voice, "Tell her if she disobeys, someone else will be made an example of."

Bekah asked, "If he is alive, may I tend his wounds?"

The leader spit at her and said, "If he lives, he lives. If he dies, he dies. He is of no consequence. Through him you learned a valuable lesson. Don't cross me."

Bekah sat up through the night, quietly praying for God to heal Maitie. She prayed that God would be with them and keep them safe. Lastly, she prayed for faith and courage. She had never in her life imagined being in a situation such as this, and had never seen anyone hurt intentionally. Bekah prayed the Holy Spirit, the Comforter, would come and minister to all of them.

CHAPTER THIRTY-SEVEN

JUNE 29
THE JUNGLE

Haydon Carlton sat at the bow of the boat with a look of consternation on his face. He was surrounded by Manolito and his seven men. They held their guns on him. Manolito spoke with concern, "Mr. Carlton, I tried to talk to you yesterday about your plan for approaching the village. You said you wanted to go through the jungle and rush the village when we get there. I tried to tell you that rushing through the jungle was dangerous, but you wouldn't listen. Now you have no choice."

Haydon Carlton scowled at him. "Who do you think you are? I'm in charge of this operation," he said belligerently. I'm the one paying you. You owe me your loyalty." As he was saying that he was thinking, "Just wait till I get hold of a weapon. I'll show you who's boss. I'll make an example out of one of you, and it won't be pretty."

"If you will just be quiet and listen, I'll tell you why your plan is all wrong." Haydon was quiet. Manolito was unsure if he was listening or not. Trying to talk to him was like trying to talk to a rock.

"The problem with the jungle is that we are unfamiliar with it, and the natives from the village are. They know where the dangerous animals are, where the bogs and quicksand are, and where the biting and stinging insects are. They can lead us into those areas and let the jungle win the fight for them, or we can stumble upon them ourselves. Either way, we would never be seen again.

"What we need to do is see which way the wind is blowing

and start a fire that will run right into the village. It's not so dry that it will become a wildfire, but enough to send all the villagers to their homes to grab what they can and escape to the river. They have boats they can take to ferry people to the other side of the river. One thing they will want to take is their village treasure; every village has one. That alone might be worth your trip."

At the sound of the word treasure, Haydon started paying attention. Maybe this guide was not as dumb as he appeared. "It sounds as though you have put some thought into this. Is here anything else you have thought of?"

"Once we set the fire, we need to take our boats north and hide just south of the village until we see them starting to head across the river. Then we drive up in our boats with our weapons ready and stop them. We then take their treasure. Then, if you still want that woman, we will take a prisoner or two and force them to tell us where she is."

"I like it," said Haydon greedily. "Does every village have a treasure?" he questioned. "How many more villages are there along the river?"

"There are at least two. One is around twenty miles upriver. There is another much larger one. It is about forty miles upriver by a waterfall. They are said to be a very barbaric tribe. They believe in human sacrifices. No one goes looking for them. They have a witch doctor who calls on his gods to guide them. No one has ever succeeded in stopping them."

Haydon thought about this tribe and reserved judgment until after they had taken care of this nearby tribe. "Have the men start four fires across the jungle. It hasn't rained in a few days, so they should burn."

He looked up as large plumes of white smoke began to rise up into the sky. He could hear the fire crackle as it began to take hold. "All right, everyone in the boats. Manolito, break out the weapons. Every man should have an AK 47, a rifle, and a hand-

254

gun. Be sure and take sufficient ammunition. If they put up a fight, we'll need it."

Sylvia had been sitting in the back of the boat listening to all these plans. She began to protest when they started the fire and Haydon told Luna to tie her up and keep her quiet. "He can't do this. They're a poor, defenseless village. They probably don't have any weapons."

Haydon heard Sylvia talking to Luna, "All the better for us," he shouted back to them. "We can cut them down without worrying about return fire."

Luna spoke softly to Sylvia. "That is the village I am from. Though they drove me away, I do not want to see them cut down by these men. Can you not ask your God to protect them?"

Sylvia whispered, reassuring Luna, "God has told us many things in His Book. One thing He said was if we ask His guidance He will answer us.[215] He also said if we only have faith the size of a small seed, we can move mountains.[216] Let's pray quietly and ask for God's help."

Horrified, Luna responded, "I cannot pray to your God. My gods will be angry with me."

"Well then, pray to your gods. Do they answer your prayers?"

"No, only my curses; and I have to make sacrifices for them."

Sylvia reassured Luna, "My God made His own sacrifice. He sent His Son Jesus to die for our sins. Then He raised Him from the dead. Have your gods ever done anything like that for you?"

Luna shook her head, "No."

"You only have to believe, be sorry for your sins, and turn from your gods, which are no gods at all, but devils. Then, if you ask, Jesus will come and live in your heart. He will give you a new heart. Then you will no longer want to sin. Will you pray with me? God wants to answer your prayers."

---

[215] Jeremiah 42:2-6
[216] Matthew 17:20

Luna looked up at Sylvia with fear in her eyes. "My gods will be angry at me. They will bring harm to me. They told me if I ever left them something terrible would happen to me."

"Remember what I said. My God answers my prayers. I can pray for angels, God's warriors, to protect us.[217] If we are doing God's work, troubles may come, but God will help us in our times of trouble.[218] Don't be afraid, I'm here with you and so is God. He says He will never leave you or reject you.[219] Won't you pray and ask God's help in your life? Won't you ask Jesus to live in you, instead of serving your evil gods?"

Luna was quietly crying. She grabbed Sylvia's hand and said, "If you pray with me, I will believe. I will serve your God."

Sylvia smiled a soft and gentle smile. She reached for Luna's hand and began to pray. "Our Father in Heaven, You are greatly to be praised. I know that You are smiling at Luna, waiting to hear her prayer. Luna, repeat this prayer. Dear Jesus, I believe God sent You, His Son, to die for my sins. I believe that God raised You from the dead. I ask You to come live in me and be my God. I reject my false gods. I ask You to forgive all my sins. Please help me to love and serve You. Amen"

As Luna repeated these words a transformation took place in her, not only spiritually, but her physical appearance also began to change. The lines of hardness, bitterness, and anger left, and her face softened with the love of God shining from it. She was truly transformed.[220]

Now Luna asked, "Can we pray for the people of the village?"

"Yes we can, with confidence, knowing that God hears our prayer, and if we pray according to His will, it will be done.[221]

"Our Father in Heaven, Luna and I come to You in Jesus'

---

[217] Hebrews 1:13-14
[218] John 16:33
[219] Hebrews 13:5
[220] 2 Corinthians 5:17
[221] John 15:16

Name asking You to protect the people of the village that these men are threatening. I don't know how You will do it, but Your Word says that with You, all things are possible.[222] I thank You for answering our prayers. Amen."

Luna smiled at Sylvia. The two of them sat in the back of the boat, quietly holding hands. Haydon turned to the two of them and shouted, "Get out of the boat. We don't need you anymore. We'll get all we need from this village, and either Bekah will be there, or they will know where she is. One way or another, we will find her."

Luna turned to Sylvia in alarm. "What are we going to do? They are abandoning us."

"It doesn't matter," Sylvia replied with assurance. "Remember, I told you God would never abandon you. Let's just trust Him and see what happens."

They watched the boats disappear as they started up river. They looked over at the jungle and saw a smoldering trail where the fire had already burned a large swath from the surrounding area. They were both unaware that the Black Death Camp was only a mile ahead, and the fire was already approaching it. Those men in the boats were in for a big surprise.

Suddenly, there was a large explosion, followed quickly by several more. There were also other minor explosions of varying magnitudes. If they had been closer, they would have felt the shock of the concussions. Now they wondered what had happened. They knew the village was about five miles away, and that explosion was closer than that, so they were not concerned for the village on that account. But they did not know what was ahead and had a concern about traveling in that direction.

Both Luna and Sylvia hurried north on a small trail that skirted the river. It was probably an animal trail and they both hoped they would not meet any. They knew God was with them and that

---

[222] Matthew 19:26

gave them comfort in the midst of all the turmoil around them. They looked up and saw the smoke from the fires, but they also saw large black clouds of smoke that spread out in every direction.

"It must have been a large blast," Sylvia said. "There was a camp south of the village and inland. It was an Islamic terrorist training camp. They are not there now, but that might have been a weapons stash."

"What's going to happen," Luna asked? "Why isn't God doing anything? You said He would take care of us."

"And He is," Sylvia replied. "Are you hurt? Are you lost? Are you hungry? God is seeing to your needs just as He promised. We need to remember that God has a plan, and we are part of it. Maybe there's a reason we are out here walking now. We need to trust Him."

"I suppose you are right," Luna said. "I've never trusted my gods before. It was always hard to do."

Sylvia smiled. "Sometimes our God has ways of giving us more faith. Every time we see prayer answered our faith grows. Yours is growing now, just knowing that God is keeping you safe."

They had walked about an hour and came across the smoldering remains of the Black Death Camp. They did not stop to look. Some of the brush in the area was still burning, and they could see the main fire as it worked its way north. They had a concern for the people of the village. What were the people doing? Did they know someone was coming to attack them? Did they have enough weapons, and people trained to use them? What would happen when Haydon Carlton found out Bekah was no longer there?

All these questions ran through their mind as they walked. They had to fight the ever present fear of the future. What would happen? Yet God told them in so many ways not to worry about tomorrow; deal with today, tomorrow had enough problems of its own.[223]

They continued on, Sylvia praying out loud, enabling Luna

---

[223] Matthew 6:34

258

to hear the Word of God as she prayed. They had walked another hour when they looked up and were surprised to see two men standing in front of them. They motioned them to stop.

Luna spoke to them in Guarani, telling them that they were friends, that Sylvia was a friend of the people from America. She had been kidnapped by another American. He was trying to capture someone named Bekah, and he had two boats full of armed men heading for the village.

The men appeared to be surprised by what she was saying, but not concerned. "What did you say," asked Sylvia? What do they want? Where are they from?"

One of the men spoke up and startled them because he spoke in English. "We are from the village by the big rock. We have been watching these men since yesterday. We know what they want. Miss Bekah is not here. She and her companions left several days ago. We are ready for these criminals. They will not escape. Come with us. We will take you to the village. Most likely they have already been captured."

As they walked along they suddenly heard the sound of machine guns being fired. The two men spoke quietly to each other and then one took off running. "Don't worry; we are less than an hour away from the village. He went ahead because he is better with weapons than I am, but I am more than able to keep you both safe. Also, you have to be aware that God, Himself, is on our side, and that there is a heavenly host of angels fighting for us. We are more than conquerors, more than overcomers.[224] The enemy may think he has us at a disadvantage, but if God is for us, who can be against us.[225] We tend to look at things with our natural eye, but there are things happening in the spiritual realm that are unseen to us. War is being waged, battles are taking place, and our God has never lost one."[226]

---

[224] Romans 8:36-39
[225] Romans 8:31-32

After walking a distance, Sylvia asked, "How much farther to the village? There's no more gunfire, do you think the fighting is over?"

"It should take ten or fifteen minutes to get there. I don't know what is happening, but I know we can trust God. Try to be at peace as we finish our march."

---

[226] 2 Kings 6:17

CHAPTER THIRTY-EIGHT

JUNE 29
THE VILLAGE

The village had been sending out scouts ever since the capture of the Black Death Camp terrorists. Last night they noticed the light of a campfire about a mile south of the camp. Upon checking they saw nine men and two women. One of the men and one of the women were white. All of the men appeared to be well armed. Word was sent back to the village and it was determined that this was probably Haydon Carlton and Sylvia Jessup, Bekah's friend who had been kidnapped. Knowing they were coming gave the village an advantage. Having several men from the C.I.A. to fight alongside them was another advantage.

Manolito again had suggested to Haydon that a reconnaissance party be sent to scout out the area to see exactly where they were in relation to the village, and see where they would become visible to the residents of the villager. These things would show them when to have their guns raised, ready for battle.

Unfortunately for them, poor leadership and arrogance on the part of Haydon Carlton doomed their assault. He would not take advice from anyone. When they rounded the curve in the river, they were met with three large boats from the village. Everyone in the boats was armed and ready with high powered weapons. The first thing that was fired was a grenade launcher, aimed at Haydon's boats. Both boats immediately began to sink. All the men were

261

wounded in the gunfight that followed; some were seriously wounded, and the rest of the wounds were superficial. All their weapons had been dropped and were lying in the bottom of the boats. Only Haydon Carlton retained his out of pure stubbornness, though he didn't have the strength to use it.

Isaac and his men were quick to come up alongside the boats and remove the passengers and weapons before the boats sank completely. Haydon was the last to be removed. He sat there cradling his gun, a pathetic figure, rocking himself and crying, "I've lost my treasure, I've lost my treasure." It appeared he might also have lost some of his mind. They were not going to take any chances with him. They tied him up and put him in the back of their boat.

Cleanup was taking place. The rest of the men had been captured and were being tied. The battle was over, and God's side won. That was cause for celebration. The only loose ends were the two boats that had sunk in the middle of the river. That would require extra manpower to move them. That would be relegated to another day, once the enemy was out of the way. The second loose end fell to Sherry, who would have to examine and treat nine injured men. Now they only had to find out what happened to Sylvia; they prayed she was safe. They would interrogate Haydon Carlton and see if he would give them some answers. The Black Death and the barbarous northern tribe still needed to be dealt with, but they were grateful. They had no problem with one victory at a time. They also saw that the smoke from the fire was diminishing as it crossed over the swamp. They praised God for His intervention and gave Him all the glory.

Just as everything was finishing up, Sylvia and Luna walked into the village along with their guide. He brought them to the compound, which right now was the center of activity.

Luna was extremely nervous because the last time she had been in the village they had wanted to punish her for witchcraft. Would they believe Sylvia when she told them she had asked Jesus to forgive her sins, told her gods to leave, and asked their God to be her God?

Sylvia saw Satan begin to torment Luna and she squeezed her arm, reassuring her. "It's going to be alright," she said. "God says that greater is He that is in you than he that is in the world.[227] The greater One lives in you. You need to remember you are part of God's family now and these people are your brothers and sisters in Christ. Just as you forgive those who have hurt you in the past, they will forgive you."

Sylvia looked up and saw a blond haired young woman standing at the gate of the compound. Knowing there couldn't be very many blond haired young women in the village, she assumed this was Sherry Albright, Daniel's wife. Sherry watched the two women approach.

Sylvia introduced herself. "Hello, you must be Sherry Albright. I'm Sylvia Jessup from Ogunquit and this is my friend Luna. I'm part of the Quest. I'm sure you heard that God woke me up and told me to go with Haydon Carlton. He abandoned me and Luna back at their camp when they left earlier. As we started walking toward your village, I told Luna of God's love for her, and that He would forgive her sins. She just accepted Jesus as her Savior.

Luna didn't know what to say or how to respond to Sherry's questioning eyes. "I just rejected all my false gods who Sylvia told me are devils. I don't want them back, but I don't know if they will stay away. I was never afraid of them before, but I am now. Will you let me stay here? I promise I will do anything I am asked to do; just please, don't send me away."

Sherry questioned, "Why wouldn't we let you stay? You're more than welcome. We can certainly find room for two more people. I'm sure there are many families that would be more than happy to take you both in."

---

[227] 1 John 4:4

263

"You don't know me," Luna said. I was the daughter of Fuego, a witch who live here many years ago. I was a witch also, but now I am a Christian." She looked at Sylvia for confirmation. "Miss Sylvia has taught me of God's love and forgiveness. Do God's people really forgive? Will the people of this village forgive me? I do not want to go back to my old life, but if the people who live here will not accept me, I will have no one, and nowhere to go. Will you and Miss Sylvia pray for me that I find favor in the eyes of the people? I will work very hard to not be a burden to the village."

Sherry put her arm around the young woman and assured her that people were very forgiving. "Forgiveness is very important to God. His Word says that if you don't forgive, He can't forgive you."

Sherry turned to Sylvia. "We have all been praying for you. Penny told everyone about Haydon Carlton taking you. She also told us that she told him God was offering him a time of repentance. It doesn't look like he took advantage of it. In fact, it looks as though his mind has been affected more than the injuries to his body. We'll talk more about this later; I need to see to all these injuries."

Sherry no longer had to work by herself. She had several women who knew what was needed and followed through. One woman saw to boiling water. Another went to get lights set up and the autoclave working. A third saw that wounds were clean, and a fourth put pressure bandages where they were needed to stop the bleeding. She may not be a doctor, and they might not be nurses, but they worked well together as a team.

It was more than two hours before Sherry finished. Her last patient was Haydon Carlton. His physical injuries were minor, but his mind appeared to be severely disturbed. She asked Leonardo to be sure extra guards were assigned to him and that he was restrained. She didn't know if his problem was mental or spiritual, but either way, he was dangerous.

The sun was setting and the cooking fires were lit. There were several enticing aromas wafting through the air. Sherry walked into the kitchen and Paloma and Noemi were setting out plates of meat, vegetables, fruit and bread. Sherry's stomach felt as though it were singing the "Halleluiah Chorus". It was all she could do to wait and pray, but she did, gratefully.

"Where are Sylvia and Luna?" she asked. "Have they eaten yet? Have they been given someplace to sleep?"

Noemi answered, "They are over at the meeting area. They are resting and eating. Several people are making them feel welcome. Connie said she would keep them. She knows Sylvia from the prayer group in Maine. They will pray with her prayer group tomorrow, but tonight they will rest. Tomorrow they will also teach Luna about prayer, faith, and fighting the devil. It will be a busy day for her."

Sherry sighed. That was one more thing taken care of. The last she could think of was the call to Maine. They had not called in a day or two and she felt very guilty. It was hard to keep up with everything. Also she wanted to ask if they had been in touch with the Questers. She had tried to call twice today and they had not answered. It had been two days since they last talked.

Sherry asked Paloma if she would gather the people for the call. Isaac and his men would want to be part of that, also Jose, Mehdi, and Leonardo. She walked slowly over to the table with a plate of food in one hand and the satellite phone in the other.

She had time to finish her meal before everyone was present. Then she placed the call to Maine. It was picked up on the first ring. They appeared to be a little anxious also. Joe answered, and it was good to hear his voice. "How are all of you doing up there?" Sherry asked. Do you want to go first, or should we?"

"Not much is happening up here," Joe replied, "Other than the news about Russia, which is pretty amazing. Have you heard about that? Do you think it will in any way interfere with the Quest?"

"So much has been happening down here we haven't had time to dwell on that particular problem. I'll give you the good news first," Sherry answered. "We have Sylvia here, safe and sound. The Holy Spirit helped us win a gun battle with Haydon Carlton and eight armed men.

"When Jose showed up several days ago he brought a small arsenal with him. We surprised them with grenade launchers. Their two boats are still sunk in the river. We'll retrieve them tomorrow. Three of them had severe wounds, the rest were superficial. Haydon Carlton appears to have lost touch with reality. He just babbles about his treasure. I think his mind is gone.

"Sylvia also showed up with a new friend, Luna, Fuego's daughter. During the trip up river, and walking to the village through the jungle, Luna gave her heart to the Lord. God is full of surprises. She is sitting with some of the women over at the meeting area. Then she and Sylvia will stay with Connie. I think they will help each other."

Then Joe responded, "God is so good. He always has everything under control, even when we can't see it.

"That brings me to the other news," Sherry said with a sigh. "I hope it's not bad, but I am worried. We haven't heard from the Questers since early yesterday. We've tried to call them twice, but no one answered. Maybe the phone is broke. I hope that's all it is."

Joe asked, "Who talked to them last?"

"It was Kent Knox from Washington. Isaac knows him. That was yesterday morning."

"Well we haven't spoken to them since then. Let's both keep trying. Maybe their battery went dead, maybe the phone got wet, or maybe it broke. There could be any number of factors why we haven't heard from them. Not all of them are bad. We need to remember angels are protecting them, the Holy Spirit is leading and guiding them, and it is God's plan they are following. We know there may be casualties, but we need to remember that all things work together for good to those who are called by God for His purposes.[228]

---

[228] Romans 8:28

"Remember," Sherry reminded him, "Penny had a dream and it showed them captured. If they are, we know it's part of God's plan. We just need to remember that He's working it out for good. We need to trust Him.

"As far as what is happening with Russia; all over the world the new President is being touted as a savior, just what everyone has been praying for. I know he's not my Savior, and I know the Scriptures concerning the end times, how a new world leader will rise up and people will turn to him instead of God. We know there will be times of trouble. Jesus said that in this world we would have trouble, but to be of good cheer because He has overcome the world."[229]

Sherry replied, "I'm glad we have that hope. I think of that Scripture when I start to worry. I know I'm selfish wanting Daniel here with me, but I have a little baby inside me who is going to want a father."

Joe replied with emotion in his voice, "Sherry, we are all praying here. Teams pray twenty-four hours a day. We pray God's Word, we resist the devil and he is fleeing.[230] This reminds me of war. You are all on the battle front; we are at home, lifting all of you up in prayer. Don't get weary; know that when the time comes, God will infuse you with the power you need to overcome the enemy."[231]

Joe offered up a fervent prayer, "We up here pray for each and every one of you down there to be infused with the Holy Spirit. We pray He give you peace and rest. We pray God's blessings and protection on all of you. Sleep well."

Sherry was moved to tears. "Thank you Joe. We will rest well and be ready to start tomorrow built up in faith and power by the Holy Spirit."

---

[229] John 16:33
[230] James 4:7
[231] Galatians 6:9

267

CHAPTER THIRTY-NINE

JUNE 29
THE SURVIORS

After a good night's rest, Edwardo wanted to make good time today. If they pushed really hard, they might make it to the village tonight. They made good time yesterday, traveling on an already worn trail, and traveling by day. They also had food in their packs they could eat on the way. Again, Edwardo started out in the lead. This time he had Yvoty on his shoulder. He sent Miguel out ahead of the group to scout the trail and make sure there were no surprises. He encouraged them all to pick any fruit they might see. It would add some flavor to the dried meat they had in their packs.

They made their first rest stop after two hours of walking. Everyone said they still felt good and wanted to go on, but Edwardo thought it better to take a short rest. Yvoty grabbed his hand and asked, "Edwardo, who are those big men who are walking all around us? They are not from our village, I do not recognize them."

"Where are they? What do they look like?"

"Well," Yvoty answered, "they are very big men, they are dressed funny, and they have big white wings."

Everyone smiled thinking that Yvoty was making up a story. Edwardo knew differently. "How many of them are there," he asked?

"There are many," she responded, "more than I can count."

"Are they before us or behind us?"

"They are all around."

"Can you talk to them," Edwardo asked?

"I don't know, but they have been talking to me."

"What did they say?"

"They said to be sure to keep following the river. They said not to be afraid because God had sent them to guard us and lead us to safety. They also said their way is quicker and if we follow them we will get to your village before dark."

The people listened in awe. They now realized this was not a childish fable, but indeed, some kind of messengers from God who were out there helping them. It gave them all comfort, knowing that God was protecting them.

They all prayed, thanking God for His protection and told Yvoty to let them know if the angels said anything else.

While getting ready to continue their walk, Edwardo bent down and gave Yvoty a big hug. "You must be very special that the angels show themselves to you and talk to you," he said.

"I asked them why they didn't show themselves to the older people. They said it was because they would not believe it."

This brought Edwardo up short. Surely they didn't mean him also. He repented anyway. It was always better to stay penitent than to ignore sin in your life. "I believe," he prayed. "Help me overcome my unbelief."[232] When he finished praying, he got everyone organized and they set off at a good pace. They were encouraged and invigorated by what Yvoty had told them.

Twilight was starting to permeate the jungle. The birds went to sleep and the bats now flew from tree to tree. Everyone's steps were starting to drag. It had been a long day, yet Edwardo knew they were close. "Only a little farther," he promised them. He saw signs of the village all around him. Trails were especially more in use. He saw signs of hunting and foraging. "Come on, don't give up, it's just over that hill."

---

[232] Mark 9:24

As they topped the hill, less than half a mile away, the lights of the village spread out before them. A soft breeze brought the smell of roasting meat. Their faces lit up and their steps quickened.

As they got closer, Yvoty was so excited she could not sit still on Miguel's shoulders any longer. He put her down and she ran ahead shouting, "We're here, we're here!" People started congregating to see what was happening. Then they recognized Edwardo and Miguel and a call went out through the village.

Someone went to alert Connie and old grandmother. Jubilation spread throughout the village. As the group continued walking along a path, crowds started following. With so much uproar happening, and all the concern for the Questers, it was nice to have an excuse for a party.

Connie walked down with Sherry, Maria, Panambi and Hombrecito to see what all the commotion was about. From the top of the hill she saw a group of strangers coming toward them. Then she recognized Edwardo and Miguel and broke into a run. Maria also recognized her father and joined the race. When Edwardo started for Connie, Panambi saw Yvoty and she began to run toward her. People were cheering and shouting, ecstatic over a wonderful turn of events. Finally Ysupi came out of the crowd, her eyes searching for Arandu.

Arandu stood next to his friend Tuvicha, watching the crowd grow. He finally recognized some of the people from his village, but his eyes continued to search. There she stood, next to a tree, looking right at him. Ysupi had tears streaming down her face as she made her way to him. Arandu put his arms around her and kissed the top of her head. They held each other close, both faces filled with joy, and covered in tears. Those from their village clapping and cheering with delight as another seeming miracle manifested in their lives.

"Husband," Ysupi said, "I had already buried you in my heart. This is resurrection day. This new God we have come to serve is surely the most powerful in all the world. He brought you back to me. Just thanking Him doesn't seem to be enough, but it is all we can do, and we will do it gladly every day."

"I am staying with Tuvicha, who was the witch doctor for the tribe. He now serves the one true God. We have many discussions about Him at night. There is room for us there until we can get our own shelter. He will be so happy to finally meet you. I talk about you all the time."

Panambi and Yvoty also had a reunion, jumping up and down, laughing and giggling as little girls do all over the world when they are celebrating. Maria came over with Hombrecito, and joined in the celebration. The villagers looked on and smiled. It was yet another miracle that such young children should survive the trauma and hardships of the attack and journey and still be alive. Surely God is pleased with the outcome of these events.

Finally Miguel's searching gaze found his grandmother. He walked over to her and surrounded her with his arms. "I have returned," he said. "God is so faithful. He sent angels to guide us safely home. Are you well Grandmother?"

"I am always well when I see that you have returned safely. God promised me that I would see you enter manhood, and so you have. We may not have had the ceremony and celebration, but I see that you have reached maturity. Now I can rest these weary bones and go on to my reward. I have waited a long time to see the face of God. He talks to me and I talk to Him. I even feel His presence in the dark of night, but I have never seen His face. I know now I will see it soon."

Miguel knew not to argue with her when she spoke of her God. He knew her thoughts and she knew His. Miguel was sad at the thought of her death, but he also knew that she suffered every day with pain in all her joints. Yet she always had a smile for everyone. No one had to question whether she was a Christian. He remembered going to say "good night" to her and she was praying in her sleep. It seemed she was in constant touch with God. He prayed his life would exemplify that same kind of devotion.

Miguel gave her his arm as they walked to what appeared to be a spontaneous feast. Room was made so that she could sit on a chair, and just as in childhood, he sat at her feet. It was a good homecoming.

Miguel called Yvoty over to meet his grandmother. "Yvoty, this is my grandmother. Now she will be your grandmother. She will love you as her own."

Yvoty stood in awe of the old woman sitting on the chair. "Grandmother, I know you. I dreamed of you after the bad men came and burned the village and killed all my family. You told me not to be afraid. You said I would be part of your family, since I had none of my own."

Everyone listened in wonder of what the little girl had shared, but old grandmother reached over and picked Yvoty up onto her lap. "You're right my sweet one. What is your name?"

"My name is Yvoty Grandmother. I am so glad to see you."

The young child and the old woman hugged each other and Old Grandmother rocked her as she held her in her arms. The people looked on in approval.

Peace once more permeated the village. Emotions settled. People started to head to their shelters. Tomorrow was another day.

CHAPTER FORTY

JUNE 29
CAPTURED IN NORTHERN VILLAGE

The ten remaining Questers were all together in a small thatched hut. It was not big enough to be called a house. There was only one room. There were no tables or chairs. The dirt floor was covered by mats. Three walls were decorated with murals depicting what appeared to be their gods. The fourth wall showed what looked to be a priest or witch doctor standing before a tall statue almost double his height. It gave the impression of being carved in stone, and was surrounded by a raging fire.

They stood there gazing at it with horror, well aware of this village's form of sacrifice. Now they saw an actual depiction of it.

Finally, they tore their eyes off the mural and looked at each other. Last night they were given minimal care, and very little food or water. This morning they were taken to the river singly, by one of the natives. They were given some kind of soap and told to wash. No words were spoken, but the message was clear. They were given clean clothes to wear, very beautiful clothes, also beautiful golden, gem encrusted jewelry. It was the same type of jewelry as Bekah's cross. Her cross had been taken from her when they had first been captured. The natives were very interested in it.

Several trays of food and drinks had been brought into the hut. Whatever their captors were planning, at least they would be well fed.

275

There had been the sound of drums all day. They had awakened with them early in the morning. Now, it sounded as if they were growing in intensity.

They looked at each other, dressed in their finery. Then all their eyes turned to Bekah, who had just been escorted into the hut. She had also been dressed in regal clothing. Of all of them, she appeared the most regal. Her clothes were exquisite. They appeared to be made of some kind of animal skin, with golden and silver beading as decoration.

Before anyone said a word, they joined hands and knelt in prayer. They had learned through this journey, that when fear and confusion tried to invade, prayer, and the Word of God were the only weapons that could shut out the adversary. His were the weapons of fear, and confusion. God's Word brought peace and comfort to those who opened their minds and hearts to Him. He even told you what to think to bring peace to you mind and spirit.[233] Satan on the other hand tried to bombard the mind with fear, doubt, discouragement, failure, self-pity, despair, and hopelessness. He has a long list of weapons, but God is more than able to overcome him if we seek Him first and not succumb to the wiles of the devil.

Everyone prayed quietly, then, Josh spoke out. "Oh God, the only God, I thank you for hearing our prayers. You know the situation surrounding us, so we put our trust in You. Your Word says that all things work for good to those who love and serve You, and are called according to Your purpose.[234] We kneel here before You, trusting that You are working out Your plan. We will not walk in fear because we have complete trust in You. Thank You, that You are with us always."

As his voice fell silent, Josh felt a stirring. Everyone opened his eyes. Within the circle, a small light began to grow to what had the appearance of a small pillar of fire. Then as the light grew, the

---

[233] Philippians 4:6-9
[234] Romans 8:28

sound grew, until it sounded like a raging forest fire. Smoke appeared and filled the room, but it didn't smell like smoke. It seemed to infiltrate them; every cell of their body was now on fire. They were filled with the presence of God. They all breathed deeply, inhaling that presence into their being. Along with it came exhilaration. They no longer had a care, fear, or doubt. They were anxious to see what would happen, what God would do.

In the past God had been called on to send down fire from Heaven to burn up the sacrifice.[235] He had sent manna from Heaven to feed the Israelites in their journey to the Promised Land.[236] He sent fire and brimstone to destroy Sodom and Gomorrah.[237] If He did all this, Satan was no match for Him. They stood up as one and shouted to the Lord with a voice of triumph.[238]

Upon hearing the noise, several men came running in with spears. They looked around and saw everyone with their hands raised. Bekah suddenly began to sing "Amazing Grace". As always, when Bekah sang, peace permeated the atmosphere. Everyone on the Quest spoke English well enough that the message of the song came through to them. Even the men who came in to check on them lowered their spears in uncertainty. Seeing the results, she sang it again and Manu translated into Guarani.

The men began to back out of the hut in fear and confusion; that is all but one. Looking closer, they realized it was Axel. Everyone was stunned. They had never expected to see Axel again, least of all here.

"I cannot stay, but I wanted to tell you I am sorry. I wish I could go back in time, but I can't. I can't ask God to forgive me, my sin is too great. I can tell you that tonight, after moon rise they are planning to sacrifice Bekah in the fire. The witch doctor and his wife

---

[235] 1 Kings 18:22-40
[236] Exodus 16:1-34
[237] Genesis 19:24-25
[238] Psalm 47:1

believe she will bring great power and strength to the village. He has been concerned that his power has been slipping away, and that the god he serves is also losing power. If you can convince him that our God is more powerful than his god, maybe he will listen to you. His goal is to rule all the tribes in the area. I'll help in any way I can, but I must leave now."

The color drained from Bekah's face when she heard these words, and the spirit of fear, which had done its best to stay close at hand, attacked with a vengeance. Everyone was aware of its attack and took up their swords of faith, knowing that this village of people and their witch doctor were not their enemy. They were fighting against evil spirits in the heavens. They took up the Sword of the Spirit, which is the Word of God, and wielded it against their enemy, the devil. As they spoke words of faith, a battle ensued between God's angels and the forces of darkness.[239]

They fought not only against the spirit of fear, but against every force of darkness that reared its head up to attack. Josh called to Ted and Renato to come over and lay hands on Bekah. As they stood and prayed for her, a special gift of faith rose up in her and fear fled from the room. Bekah rose up and spoke in a loud voice that thundered out into the surrounding area. "I will not let the sacrifices you have endured be in vain; for out of it will come redemption for the lost. Do not be troubled or afraid. I have not left you comfortless.[240] The 'end of the age' is approaching; therefore, speak the Word and make disciples until you hear the sound of the trumpet." [241]

The Voice continued, "I will give you a tongue to speak their language, and ears to hear and discern it. You will understand everything that is being said and they will understand everything you say."

At the sound of the commotion, more warriors came running

---

[239] Ephesians 6:10:16
[240] John 14:27
[241] Matthew 28:19-20

278

into the building. They expected to see a physical battle occurring, but all they saw were the ten prisoners standing in a circle around Bekah and holding hands. Then the witch doctor entered and all those of the village gave way to him. None wanted to be the object of his wrath.

Bekah stepped forward and stood tall. She spoke, and her words were like a fire that cut through the darkness. She spoke under the anointing of God, and everyone understood her in his own language.[242]

"I am not afraid of you or your god. You may be able to kill my body, but my soul and spirit will live with my God forever.[243] However, I believe my God is able to keep me from harm. He once saved three children from being burned up in a furnace. If He can save them, He can save me.[244]

The witch doctor was astounded. He thought he had put this woman in her place last night, but it appeared he was wrong. No one dared to talk to him in such a manner. Who was this woman and what gave her this courage? "Why are you here? Where do you come from?"

Bekah understood him perfectly and answered, "I come from a faraway land; so far it would take many months to walk there. We were sent here by our God. He spoke to several of us in a dream. He showed us how you and your warriors attacked a nearby village and took their infants to sacrifice to your god. A young woman of the village prayed and asked God to save her son. God told her to prepare a way to send him down the river. When you attacked, she ran to the river where she had hidden a basket and sent him and a golden crucifix in the water. Two days later he landed in the reeds near the village by the big rock."

The witch doctor was dumbfounded. This woman must

---

[242] Acts 2:7-8
[243] Luke 12:4-5
[244] Daniel 3:19-30

have strong magic to know all this. He coveted her power. Their last attack on a nearby village had given them fourteen infants, almost a record, but instead of strengthening his power, he felt it drain even more. He desperately needed the power this woman appeared to possess; sacrificing one so full of power would solve all his problems. First, he would steal the power from her. Second, he would remove any competition that might weaken his influence over his people.

He took a closer look at this woman and felt desire stir in him. He took a moment to reassess the situation and then spoke. "Whose woman is this? Who speaks for her?"

Renato looked at Josh, and Josh nodded to him. "I do," Renato replied. I am her father."

"I am Namandu, the god of this village. I have been endued with power by Tupa, the supreme god." Namandu was extremely tall for a native. He was several inches taller than Josh. He also appeared darker than the other natives. His hair was long and black like everyone else's, but his eyes were black, not brown. He was dressed as everyone else was, except he wore a heavy gold chain with a large ruby medallion surrounded by gold. He looked to be about sixty years old. He had a deep voice that reverberated throughout the room. As he stared at her, she looked him right in the eyes. She was not intimidated by him at all. She had courage and beauty. He felt his desire grow.

At the same time, there were other eyes watching from the door of the hut. A woman, named Mbyja, tall and haughty, stood there and observed the interaction. She spit on the ground and uttered a curse, then whirled around and went back to her dwelling. "I will take care of this situation," she said to herself. "I have hidden the extent of my powers from him until now. I will rob the remaining power he has, and I will be god of this village, and no one will stand in my way."

Renato stepped forward with Josh right behind him on one

280

side and Ted on the other. They were all stepping forth to protect Bekah, just as they had promised. Namandu nodded to Renato, "Step forth and say what is on your mind."

"My name is Renato and Miss Bekah is my daughter, not by blood, but by love. I could not love her more if she was the daughter of my blood, but she is the daughter of my heart. Her mother was a member of the village on the river by the big rock, but her father was white. I was born in Paraguay. In fact, I was born in this village. My father and I left here around sixty years ago."

Namandu was speechless for a moment. Then he questioned, "What was your father's name?"

Renato answered, "His name was Kauan."

"Raise your shirt," Namandu demanded.

Renato thought to refuse, but decided to pick his battles, and this demand was not one to cause a conflict. He stepped back from Bekah and removed his shirt. Though small in stature, Renato's body was thick with muscle. He had spent his entire life working in the apple orchard, pruning or cutting down trees, cleaning away debris, picking up and carrying crates of apples. It was demanding manual labor, and kept his body physically fit.

Namandu walked toward Renato and turned him to see his back. Just below the shoulder blade and to the left, almost under the armpit, was what appeared to be a small mole in the shape of a crescent moon. Namandu stood there looking at it for a moment, then he questioned Renato, "Do you know of the mark you have on the left side of your back?"

Surprised, Renato answered, "I know that it is there. As far as I know, I was born with it. Why do you question it? Does it have some significance?"

While Namandu and Renato talked, warriors were filling the room preparing for action. No one dared to question the witch doctor. He considered himself a god, and he wielded power as a god would. He was quick to anger, and punishment was meted out

281

swiftly and harshly. They now were all prepared to carry out his commands.

The warriors were again surprised. Namandu answered Renato with quiet respect. "I must tell you that the mark is not one you were born with. You were tattooed at birth. It is the mark of the High Chief."

There was a murmur among the warriors in the room. Namandu quickly turned and glared at them and silence descended. He returned his attention to Renato. "Since you consider her your daughter, I will spare her from the fire if you will give her to me as a wife. I sense the power in her and desire to join with her and partake of that power."

"Do you defer to me as Chief?" Renato asked. "Is there no Chief in the village? Do women choose their own husbands or are all marriages arranged for them? Also, Miss Bekah has very high standing in the tribe. It was discovered that Manu, the Chief and Bekah are brother and sister, but not only brother and sister, but twins."

Namandu hissed with excitement and surprise. Being the sister to the Chief of a village carried its own power, but being his twin carried additional power. This was an unusual situation that had presented itself to him. He needed to consult his gods on the best way to take advantage of it.

"Instead of a sacrifice tonight, we will have a celebration and welcome you back to the village, and all those with you. Animals will be killed and food will be cooked. Tonight we celebrate. Miss Bekah will sit with me and my wives during the celebration and tell me of her power. I can feel the intensity of it just by standing next to her. She must tell me of her gods so that I can know them and partake of their power."

Bekah had stood quietly as she listened to this conversation, experiencing the peace and comfort of the Holy Spirit. Now she spoke up. "My God is the supreme God, higher than all other

282

gods. He only shares His power with those who serve Him, and only Him. All my friends who travel with me also serve this God. He calls all people to serve Him and He rewards those who diligently seek Him."[245]

Bekah paused, considering what to say next. "I will sit with you and your wives. I will tell you of my God, who is above every god. I cannot see my God, but I know He is always with me. He says in His Book that He wrote for everyone who serves Him that He will never leave us or abandon us.[246] We can talk to Him any time of day or night and He will listen to us. He loved us so much He sent His only Son, Jesus, as a sacrifice to die for us, to pay for our sins, and not just our sins, but the sins of the whole world. Then He raised Him from the dead and brought Him back up to Heaven to rule with Him at His right hand.

"I will tell you and your villagers more of my God tonight at the celebration. I pray that He will speak to you and you will listen to what He has to say." Having said all that, Bekah turned and walked back to Renato, Josh and Ted.

Again, the warriors in the room readied their weapons. No one dared to turn their back on the witch doctor. He had established a protocol year ago when he came into power, and had it rigorously maintained. The punishment for breaking it was death. In fact, the protocol for just about any transgression was death. There was no grace or mercy in this village.

Many years ago the Chief and the witch doctor ruled over the tribe together. The Chief had been the counterbalance to the cruelty of the witch doctor. His restraint helped to curb the witch doctor's excesses. They were often at odds with each other, but respected each other's position in the tribe. Twenty years ago a woman was found wandering in the jungle. She was young and very beautiful. The witch doctor took her for his wife. Her name was Mbyja.

---

[245] Hebrews 11:6
[246] Hebrews 13:5

Less than a year after her arrival, the Chief became sick and died, and Namandu took full control, with Mbyja assisting, using her particular skills on any who opposed.

There had been some opposition when no Chief was picked to replace the one who had died. But as opponents started dying off, opposition diminished and finally ceased. Now Mbyja stood just outside the hut the prisoners were being held in and listened to what was being said. She would make sure that these interlopers would suffer the fate of all those who interfered with her plans.

Mbyja had seen the look Namandu had given Bekah. She was familiar with his wandering eyes. He had taken several younger wives over the years, but they had all fallen prey to some accident or sickness and died. Again, nothing could be proven, but all suspected. None was brave enough to bring an accusation.

Satan watched as his plan unfolded. His best student stood before him. She had mastered all the spells. She knew all the sacrifices that needed to be made, all the words that needed to be spoken, and within her lived a legion of his best demons, fighting to be sent out to battle. He was more than prepared for this attack. His enemy was weak and afraid. He could feel victory within his grasp. He was not concerned about Bekah and what she might say tonight. He had found the weak spots in her armor, fear and unforgiveness. He had plenty of ammunition in that area.

Namandu turned to leave and passed Mbyja at the doorway. "Ask her to come with you now. She will be more pliable without her friends around to encourage her. Tell her you have someone you want her to meet. I will be waiting for her."

Namandu agreed, and turned back to get Bekah. He seemed to approve everything Mbyja suggested. She always made it feel as though it was his idea. Sometimes he thought to question her, but in the end he always did as she wished. She enticed him with promises and he fell victim to her power. Namandu thought he held the power of the gods. Yet, over the years Mbyja had drained him of it little by little until what he had left was negligible. He was starting to feel an emptiness inside him, the absence of power. He tried to compensate for it by making additional sacrifices, but year by year the supply dwindled, and the power diminished. During the last two years he had started sacrificing malcontents from his own village. For a time, he felt renewed, and it kept the people obedient to his commands.

Namandu turned around and walked back into the hut. He signaled to two of the warriors still in the building. Walking up to Bekah he said, "I would like for you to come with me now to meet my wife. I know she would like to meet you. I will take you to my house. She will be waiting there." He turned to the rest of the prisoners and addressed them. "All of you are free to wander around the village, talk with people, and ask questions. We will all meet back together tonight at the celebration. But first I want to know how you speak and understand our language? When we first captured you, you did not have that ability, and now you do."

Bekah answered, "My God has given me a gift that He speaks of in His Book. People can understand me and I can understand them. I have experienced this before. I don't know if this will continue, or if it will stop, but for now I thank Him and give Him all the glory."

He took Bekah's arm and tried to steer her out the door, but Renato, Josh and Ted blocked his path. He stopped and raised his hand. "I will only tell you once, get out of my way. If you do not, Bekah will go back to being the sacrifice instead of the bride."

Renato, Josh and Ted looked at Bekah. They saw not fear, but determination. The Holy Spirit was with her. He would guide her and comfort her. They would not react to this situation. They would wait until God showed them what to do. They moved aside and let Namandu and Bekah pass.

After Namandu left, the warriors that were in the hut started to talk with Renato about the tattoo on his back. They all knew what

285

it meant and were in awe of the fact that there was someone of the royal line left; for it was indeed a royal line. It could be traced back thousands of years, back when the Chiefs were appointed by the gods. They wanted to know if he had power also, like his daughter and the witch doctor.

They also told of another who had power in the village, the witch doctor's wife. They talked of her quietly, and kept watch, for they were more afraid of her than the witch doctor. They revealed that it was the dark arts which she commanded that had killed the Chief, and anyone else that opposed her. They wanted to know if Renato came to set them free.

Renato thought this was the perfect time to tell them of someone Who had come to set them free. He said that Jesus, the Son of God came to bring them the truth, and the truth would make them free. Renato told them in a strong and powerful voice, "It is this Jesus, the Son of my God, Who can set you free."[247]

Renato told them of the sacrifice God made because He loved them. He sent His Son, Jesus, to die for our sins.[248] He told of the resurrection, and finally His ascension into Heaven. He also told them Jesus would be coming back very soon for those who believed in Him and served Him.

The warriors all stood there stunned. They had never heard of a god sacrificing his son to die for them. What a strange thing that was. They were always commanded to sacrifice babies to their gods. None of those gods ever did anything to show their love. They spoke together quietly and then told Renato they wanted to serve His God.

Renato himself was surprised that these men were so eager to serve God. Then he realized that the Holy Spirit had to have been working in their hearts before they had come to the village. All the prayers that had been going forth from them, the village, and

---

[247] John 8:31-32
[248] John 3:16

the prayer group in Maine, were breaking the hard ground of their hearts, making them ready to believe the Word when it was presented. God was working in ways they could not immediately see, but it bolstered their faith to know that He was with them.

Renato prayed for them to receive Jesus as their Lord and Savior, and they asked Him to forgive their sins. When the prayer was over, they wanted to know if Renato would be willing to be the Chief. They asked if he was protected from the curses of Mbyja. Her magic was very powerful. Could their God protect him? Would He protect them?

Renato told them, "God said in His Word that we could tread on serpents and scorpions and they wouldn't hurt us.[249] Our God is the God of the entire world, what we can see, and what we can't. He even said that He gives us power over the enemy. Jesus said He came to destroy the works of the evil one, who we call the devil or Satan."[250]

So Renato prayed God would protect them, and also help them to fight the enemy. Then Renato sang 'Amazing Grace' for them again in Guarani. Again, the Holy Spirit brought His peace and comfort to them all. They turned to each other in amazement and then bowed down before Renato in reverence and awe. Renato quickly raised them up and said, "I am not a god, I am just one of our God's children, as you are now too. Only He deserves your worship."[251] Renato began to praise the Lord in Guarani and they all followed his example.

The rest of the Questers just stood and watched. They also thanked God for His love and grace and mercy. If it weren't for God being with them, none of the remnant from the burnt out village would have been saved, none of their own village would be have been saved, and none of these men in the hut with them would now

---

[249] Luke 10:19
[250] 1 John 3:8
[251] Acts 10:25-26

be saved. Satan was being defeated one step at a time.

Then they went out among the people. The warriors scattered, telling all their friends and family that the great and mighty God had visited them in the hut. The prisoners knew Him, and told them that He loved them and wanted to be their God. They shared in awe that this God does not demand sacrifices, but loved us so much He sacrificed His Son, Jesus to die for our sins and set us free. They explained to them that they could pray and ask forgiveness and ask Him into their hearts and He would come and set them free.

It was as if a great light had come into the darkness.[252] It was as if they had been blind and now they could see the truth.[253] The Wind of the Holy Spirit was blowing through the village, and the people were experiencing His grace.

---

[252] 2 Corinthians 4:6
[253] 2 Corinthians 4:4

CHAPTER FORTY-ONE

JUNE 29
NORTHERN VILLAGE

Not realizing that the Gospel of Jesus Christ was now spreading through the village like wildfire, Namandu hurried over to his dwelling place with Bekah in hand. She struggled against him, but she was no match for his size and brute strength. She knew God was with her and so she walked the rest of the way with calm assurance. As she walked, she observed the village around her. It was more than twice as large as Manu's village. It was neat and clean as Manu's village was, but there was no personality to it. There were no flowers, no area for the children to play. It was completely utilitarian. There was no happy laughter, no calling over to friends and family, nothing that triggered any warmth or comfort.

As Namandu walked, he talked to Bekah, but she was not listening. She was praying and talking to God. They approached what she assumed was his house. Like Manu's, his was larger than the others because of his status. Bekah heard what sounded like chanting coming from inside. A foul smell that almost made her gag emanated from it.

Suddenly a loud boom reverberated and the ground trembled as a child would if afraid. In a moment, all the birds in the area took flight. Large and small, they covered the sky, turning midday into dusk. The sound of their bird call and the flapping of their wings drown out the sound of the nearby waterfalls. Then an unearthly silence arose behind the noise. In unison, Bekah and Namandu both turned toward the falls and beheld a strange sight.

There were no falls. The high cliffs where the water had cascaded down were dry. Only small rivulets of water dripped from the rims. What they saw was a honeycomb of caves throughout the entire side of the cliffs. Then they heard several smaller booms and the ground shook again. Namandu was down on his knees, praying to his gods. Mbyja came out of the house but she stood her ground. She would bow to nothing; whether of this world or not.

She took one look at Bekah and declared to Namandu, "The gods are angry. You have robbed them of the sacrifice that had been dedicated to them. Old fool, so easily turned by the look of a pretty face and the lure of more power. The gods have declared your power to be taken from you and given to me. Get up. Give her to me. Go and order her people back to the hut. Then have the women gather the wood for the fire. We will see if her God is greater than mine."

Namandu hurried to obey. He had not had an open confrontation with Mbyja a long time. If he were honest with himself, he would admit that he feared her. It was true he had felt the strength of her power increasing, just as his appeared to be decreasing, but he always thought his gods would be faithful to him.

He wondered what kind of agreement Mbyja had made with them that they would show her a way to usurp his power. Fear began to grow in him; squeezing out the last of his power as a snake squeezes the life out of its victim. He ran to see that her orders were obeyed, the last vestiges of his self-esteem crumbling in the wake of her command.

He had to admit that he was afraid of her. There was no love lost between them. There had never been love, only an acknowledgement of each other's powers and a desire to use each other to grow stronger. Somehow, she had found a way to rob him of his strength.

Then he returned to his own hut. For the first time in his life, he felt alone. His voices were quiet. The power that he had worn for so long was gone and he felt naked. He hid in fear. Then he felt tremor after tremor. The ground shook and the people screamed. Was this a punishment from the gods? He got up and ran into jungle, fearful that the gods were going to destroy the village.

CHAPTER FORTY-TWO

JUNE 29
NORTHERN BLACK DEATH CAMP

After working over a year in these foul jungles of Paraguay, this contingent of the Black Death was ready to set the wheels in motion that would make it a force to be reckoned with. Since their rise to power, they had been searching the globe for an independent way to obtain uranium. They had hit the jackpot in the jungles of Paraguay. For three years, they had pumped money and manpower into this small country after discovering its rich sources of uranium. It had few large cities, and large areas that were uninhabited except for the local Guarani. These areas were perfect for setting up their training camps for their growing army of terrorists. The only other country they had to compete with was Brazil, and their interest was tied up in other natural resources. Government officials were easy to bribe, and everyone was happy.

They would ship the uranium to Iran, to be processed in their nuclear plants. There were several plants underground that could not be detected. They were planning to build small bombs that could be shipped all over the world to cause havoc. The world would be sorry it had not turned to the true faith.

Now their plan was coming to a culmination. Josef would observe from his place of safety, the results of the seven underground blasts they had planted. They were designed to divert the river away from the cliffs and feed into a natural ravine that went behind the village and fed back into the river about a mile south of the falls. Geologists had been employed and had mapped out the consequences of the blasts. This would allow them to mine for the uranium that was buried beneath the river. Now they would be mining on dry land.

The signal was given, and he heard the first blast, quickly followed by the other six. He watched as the ground started to shift, and waited for the bypass to open up and the river start to shift to its new route. Then something unexpected happened. An area of land about the size of a football field gave way. It dropped about fifty feet, causing the river to alter its course yet again. Except this time instead of avoiding the village; it was heading straight for it. It was close to two miles away, so it would take some time to work its way through the jungle before it reached them. At this point it was not traveling very fast, but minute by minute it was gaining speed and strength. It appeared as though the caverns of the deep had opened, and a wall of water began to build.

As minutes went by, other areas of land began to sink, first one and then another. The whole area on the top of the waterfalls must have been inundated with caves, cavities and fissures. Nowhere in the geologists' reports had it shown that the land was unstable. Looking around, Josef saw that nowhere was safe. Even the platform he was standing on began to sway. He looked out and saw all the workers scurrying about for safety, but none was found.

Instead of accomplishing their purpose, they had activated an earthquake of undetermined magnitude that was causing the unstable ground to crumble. Many men and millions of dollars of equipment were being buried in the rubble. He did not have much hope for himself, but decided he would try to get to more stable footing. As he descended the stairs carefully, there was another tremor and the platform crumbled. As he fell, he looked up. The last thing he saw was the platform he had been standing on falling on top of him.

As soon as the carnage started, a message was sent to the camp below on the other side of the river. They responded by sending up several rescue helicopters. They spotted dozens of men running from the area, trying to escape the fate of those who were already buried by the cave-ins and landslides. Unfortunately, they could not land where most of them sought refuge because the ground was so unstable. They had no equipment for aerial rescue. The men who escaped into the jungle would hopefully make it down to the lower camp. There was nowhere to land in the jungle to pick them up safely. After the first few shockwaves, the search and rescue teams determined that Josef, the head of the whole Paraguayan operation, was lost in the morass.

There was no fixing what they had broken. The beautiful waterfalls were now only a memory. The good news was that once the falls started to crumble, the river split. Part of it redirected itself back to its normal course. Unfortunately, it was going to go right through the village. It would take several minutes to get there. The second leg of the river would re-enter its banks about five miles south of the village. There was no telling what kind of effect all of this was going to have on the villages downstream. Maybe it will have lost most of its power by the time it reached them. The village at the base of the falls would be devastated.

CHAPTER FORTY-THREE

Mbyja grabbed Bekah by the arm and pulled her into what she had assumed was Namandu's home, but upon entering, she was sure that was not the case. There was a terrible odor coming from the small fire in the center of the room. Bekah stood still and observed Mbyja conversing, but not with her. The room was empty. "What is the matter? Do you not enjoy the aroma of my gods? I have asked them to come and live with me. That odor is a sign of their presence. Is it not pleasing to you?"

"No," Bekah replied. "It is a stench in my nostrils. My God has a sweet smell that calms, refreshes, and brings peace. I pray that His presence overpowers the foul smell of your gods."

At Bekah's words, the angelic beings cleared the room of foulness and in its place the Breath of God permeated the area. Bekah breathed deep and smiled. She turned to Mbyja and said, "My God is the only true God. You do not worship God, but devils. You have sold your soul to Satan in return for some of his power. You have fallen prey to his lies. Whatever he promised you is a lie. Everything he says is a lie. Has he ever followed through with a promise? We call him the devil, the father of lies."[254]

"We will see whose god is stronger, mine or yours. Right now you will be the sacrifice to my gods. I will laugh as I listen to

---

[254] John 8:44

297

your screams. I will watch your hair burn and your clothes smolder and burst into flame. I will watch your flesh incinerate." Mbyja grabbed Bekah and dragged her to the area of sacrifice. She commanded two men to hold her while she tied Bekah to the pole. "You can stand here until the time of sacrifice. I want you to think about the heat of the fire. I want you to smell the smoke. I want fear to invade you and fill you. Then you shall face my gods in the fire."

As Mbyja turned and walked away, Bekah looked past her and saw several women carrying wood and dragging branches toward her. She felt a shiver of fear run down her spine. She stood straight, and resolved not to give into it. Many people were milling about, fear written on their faces also. So many things were happening and they did not know what to think. The waterfall and river had disappeared. All that was left was a lake at the base of the cliffs where the falls had been. They felt as though this was a sign, but without the witch doctor, there was no one to interpret it and tell them what it meant. But they did not know where he was.

Namandu had been with Mbyja, but no one went to her hut unless summoned. Through the years, she had instilled fear in everyone who lived in the village. Lately, even Namandu appeared to be afraid of her.

Now word had been spread that the prisoners had a new and powerful God. Also, it was told that one of them had the sign of the great Chiefs on him. What a wonder that he would return at this time of need.

Bekah stood tall and called to the people. "Come and listen to me. I will tell you about my God. You will see, I will not die in the fire. My God will rescue me. He loved me so much He sent His Son as a sacrifice to pay for my sins; not just mine, but everyone's sins. He loves all of you and died for you so you could be reunited with the one and only true God.

"Mbyja's god is not a god, but a devil and demands evil sacrifices to satisfy his hunger for death and destruction. My God is a

God of love and peace, but He is also a God of power. After His Son Jesus was sacrificed, God raised Him from the dead. Can your god do that? He appears to be the god of death, not life."

While Bekah was speaking a crowd began to gather. "Call on the Name of Jesus and He will save you. If you are sorry, He will forgive you of your sins. Don't delay. Judgment is near."

Just then there was another shaking and the ground dropped down several feet. The totem Bekah was tied to begin to sway, and then fell over. It landed on a large rock and rolled off it, cutting the vines that tied Bekah's hands. As she sat up and looked around, she heard a loud roar approaching. A wall of churning water and broken trees was ripping its way through the jungle and across the village. As the water spread out over the village it lost some of its height and momentum and dropped many of the trees it had been carrying, but Bekah knew it would inundate her. She could hear the sound of it approaching. It got louder and louder. She took a breath and waited for the impact. In the natural way of things, it could kill her, or at least knock her out. There were large pieces of debris in the water that were traveling at a high velocity of speed. They could rip her apart. Her last thought before the water hit her was, "Well at least I'm not going to be burned in the fire." Abruptly there was silence.

Bekah opened her eyes. She was surrounded by a churning maelstrom. She had a clear view of everything around her. She was able to breathe; but try as she might, she could not remove the vines from her legs. Again God spoke to her. "Remember, My Word says that nothing can separate you from My love. Not even being swallowed by the water."[255]

After the Questers were released, they had walked to the top of a small rise near the witch doctor's hut. They wanted to keep their eye on Bekah, and also stay out of sight. They watched from behind the trees as Mbyja took Bekah and tied her to the totem.

---

[255] Romans 8:37-39

When the ground shook and the earth dropped, their small rise turned into a hill. They heard and saw a wall of water heading for the village. They were safe from the water, but they could see that Bekah was not.

They all rushed to try to save her but Manu stopped them. "Remember, this is what Bekah dreamed. I was meant to save her." Their weapons had been taken from them, but Manu crouched down and found a sharp stone. He looked at the swirling water, but the Voice of God spoke, "Fear not. Did I not say in My Word I would show you things to come?[256] I showed you this very circumstance in a dream. Go and save her in My power and might. You will not be alone."

As Manu dove into the brown, swirling water he felt a presence with him. It led the way and calmed the waters. Manu looked down, the water cleared, and he saw Bekah. She was struggling, trying to free herself. Manu swam down and quickly cut her loose. They rose to the surface together, making their way back to what now looked like a small island, the water dropping quickly. Everyone was cheering, and thanking God with all their might. Bekah told them of her experience, and again they thanked God for His supernatural intervention.

Everyone from the Quest was on the island except Axel. No one had seen him since he came in their hut earlier that morning. After giving Bekah a hug; they all began to look for survivors. They could see that there were pockets of them on other pieces of high ground. No one was sure why, but the water level was dropping quickly. Taking advantage of that fact, they split up in groups of two or three to look for the injured, and other survivors. They needed to get people to safety and salvage what they could of weapons and supplies.

Manu told Giancarlo, Philippe and Maitie to look for dry brush

---

[256] John 16:13

and start a big fire to act as a beacon for those swept away; and also to keep them warm. They would have to go a distance into an area of the jungle the water had not invaded. Night was falling and cooler weather was upon them. Manu called, "Pick up anything you see that is edible. If the flood killed it, it's fresh enough to butcher."

Manu, Josh, Renato Ted, Akeem, and Carlos all headed out in separate direction. By now the water had dissipated and it was draining into low areas. Manu asked Josh, "Did you see many survivors?"

"I saw about ten people just outside the waterline to the north. There were also several already up and trying to make their way to our hill. The water has gone down enough now we can probably call it a hill again."

Manu and Josh walked around for about an hour, but dusk was approaching and they needed to make their way back. They could see the light of a fire and headed that way. "I hope the others were more successful scavenging," Josh said. Food only stretches so far."

Once the water had gone down and people had started gathering, the first person to come was a woman carrying a large pot. Bekah and Giancarlo set out to the edge of the lake to see if they could find any clean water to cook with. It was a little murky, but she felt it was useable. She washed her hands and face, and tried to tie her hair in a knot. Bekah also realized she was still wearing the jeweled necklace Mbyja had put on her when she tied her to the totem. As she was heading back to the hill Bekah tripped over something. She looked down and saw a large, lovely, fat fish flapping on the ground. She looked around and saw several more. She and Giancarlo rigged up a way to carry them with several branches lying around. Looking about, she also found someone's bag of vegetables they had probably intended to eat tonight. She smiled and thanked God for his provision.

Everyone else had already returned and there was a small

pile of supplies. They counted fifteen other people on top of the hill. Thankfully, the young men had a substantial woodpile. At least they wouldn't be cold. Someone had found a cook pot, and Bekah started doing her magic on a small pile of meat. She was also attempting to cook the fish they had found on some hot rocks inside the fire pit. But, by far, the find of the night was a large bunch of bananas someone had carried in from the jungle. They were ripe, and they were enough for at least two for everyone.

There was not much conversation through the evening; everyone was enmeshed in his own thoughts. "Why did this happen? Who caused this? What are we going to do? Where will we go?"

Bekah's thoughts were tripping over each other, but she was aware that God had stepped in to bring hope out of disaster. Because of that she asked Renato to translate while she spoke to everyone standing around, the Questers, and the survivors who had come to their camp. "While our meal cooks I think we need to thank God, the one and only God, for our rescue. God tells us to come boldly before His throne of grace to obtain mercy and find grace to help in time of need.[257] God has shown His mercy by sparing us from death and destruction, and providing food and warmth to keep us safe and strong. Without Him we would have spent the night in the dark, cold and hungry."

Bekah looked at the villagers that were with them. "Have your gods ever provided for you in time of need?" she asked. "Do they love you as a father loves a child? Do they give you peace when you pray for it? Our God does. He brings hope to the hopeless, food to the hungry, health to those who are sick, and peace to those in turmoil. But most of all He loves us. Whether we are good or bad, He loves us. Some of you may have heard me this afternoon when I was tied to the totem. God tells us in His holy Book that He sent His Son Jesus to die as a sacrifice for the sins of the

---

[257] Hebrews 4:16

whole world so that we would not die in our sins, but have everlasting life with Him."[258]

Bekah paused to let them think on that. Then she stated, "God asks people to make a decision. He wants to know who you will choose, the gods your fathers served who only brought you fear and death, or my God, Who wants to adopt you as His children and bring you everlasting life. He said He sets before you the choice of life and death. He asks that you choose life, but it is your choice. What is your answer?"[259]

Everyone was quiet. Slowly they lifted up their heads and looked at one another. Bekah could see fear in their eyes, but she also saw hope. One by one all fifteen of them stepped forward and shook Renato's hand as a sign of acceptance, as the seal of a covenant. Bekah smiled at each one. Then she asked Renato if he would pray for them.

Bekah ended the night with another song. She felt such gratitude to God for all that He was doing. She mourned the loss of Mario and Axel. She was astounded to have found Axel here with this lost tribe. She prayed there would be time to talk with him. She wanted to know if he had repented and asked God's forgiveness for what he had done. Saying you're sorry to them was not the same as saying you're sorry to God.

---

[258] John 3:16
[259] Deuteronomy 30:19

CHAPTER FORTY-FOUR

JUNE 30
THE WASHOUT

A new day began in muted darkness. The sun could not be seen, and its warmth not felt because of the thick fog that permeated the area. The fire burned low and Bekah shivered. She stood up to add more wood to the fire and came face to face with someone she did not recognize. She was stunned when she took in his appearance, and assumed he was one of the angelic hosts that God had sent to guard them.

Startled, she backed up a step or two in surprise and put up her hands in amazement. "Don't be afraid," he said. "I come from the throne of God. He wants me to tell you that Satan has not given up. There is still more danger. It lurks on every side, but there is more to the battle than you can see with your eyes. A legion of angels has been dispatched to accompany you and respond to the Word of God spoken from your mouths. Be sure all of you keep your words full of faith. Do not give the enemy an opening into your camp. Don't be anxious, but keep your minds and hearts on Him for He cares for you.[260] Be continually renewing your mind to the Word of God, because that will be the weapon that defeats the enemy."[261]

The angel disappeared and Bekah looked at the people surrounding her. "Did you see?" she asked. "Did you hear what he said?" She looked at everyone and they all nodded their heads

---

[260] 1 Peter 5:7
[261] Romans 12:1-2

"yes" with a dazed expression.

"Was that your God?" one of them asked. "He was wonderful. Where did he come from? Where did he go? What kind of trouble did he say we are in? I am afraid." She looked around at the other villagers that were with them and they all nodded.

Bekah heard their questions and thought for a moment, "These people are new Christians. They don't even know about angels. They don't know about spiritual warfare. We are going to have to start from the beginning with everyone. Right now I will answer their questions the best I can. Then she was stunned to realize that they were speaking to each other and understanding each other. God was still breaking down barriers to allow them to communicate one with another.

"What you saw was a messenger from our God. God sent him to tell us not to be afraid, that He was sending help. But he also said to be alert, because Satan, the devil, God's enemy, wants to harm us. He is the one who destroyed your village. God saved you because He loves and cares for you. That messenger was what we call an angel. He came from Heaven, where God lives. Later we will tell you more about our God."

Bekah paused and Josh spoke up. "Right now it's important that we search the area again for any more survivors and anything that might be of use to us. Our first priority is survivors, the second is food. Go and search by twos and threes. Come back when the sun is high in the sky. Then we will eat whatever we have found, and make plans for where we will go and what we will do. We will build up our fire. Maybe the smoke will draw them."

The people dispersed and Bekah asked, "Josh, will you go look for some more wood, and anything else you can find? Please don't go far because I don't feel safe."

Josh took her hand. "Bekah, I don't think I should leave you. There is nothing here to steal. We will build the fire up and leave it. We won't go far. I know God will provide. He always has."

The fire was roaring and sending up lots of billowing smoke. "This should be visible for miles. Any able-bodied person should be able to make it here. Let's just pray that anyone injured, or unable to walk, will be found by someone, and be helped to our camp."

They set out towards the middle of the destroyed village, thinking that there might be something useable in the debris left behind by the deluge. They kept their eyes on the ground, not wanting to miss anything. Occasionally they looked up at the hill with the fire, observing whether any survivors were headed that way.

Bekah was the first to find a large knife, imbedded in the ground. She was so excited she called to Josh, who was about one hundred feet away. They had separated to cover a larger area. She stood up waving the knife, a big smile on her face. Josh waved, and gave her thumbs up, but continued his search.

"Who ever thought I would get so excited about finding a dirty, old knife," she thought? But Bekah realized some of her excitement was that she realized God was taking care of them, providing what they needed to survive. He had already saved all of them from death, brought them together, provided food and fire. He had all they needed at His disposal. We only have to trust Him, and know that in agreement with His Word, He will meet all our needs according to His riches and glory, by Christ Jesus.[262]

Josh called Bekah over. He was trying to get a basket out of a tree. It was hanging from a branch about ten feet up. That was an indication of how high the water got. Josh couldn't decide whether to try and get Bekah on his shoulders to cut it down, or to try to climb the tree. There were no low branches, so he would have to shimmy up it. They decided their best bet would be for Josh to lift Bekah to the lowest branch and see if she could pull herself up into the tree.

She kneeled on his shoulders and grabbed the branch. It was small, but helped her balance so she could stand. Then she

---

[262] Philippians 4:19

reached for a sturdier branch to pull herself up.

Bekah was strong, but had never been a body builder. She struggled, making no progress. Then she thought, "If I can make my way hand over hand to the trunk, I might be able to use the trunk and walk my way up, taking some of the weight off my arms. Then maybe I would have enough strength to pull myself up."

Josh saw what she was doing and encouraged her. "Come on Bekah, you can do it."

Bekah knew her muscles were giving out, but she used God's Word to give her strength. She repeated over and over, "I can do all things through Christ Who strengthens me,[263] for Your power is made perfect in my weakness."[264] As she continued her litany, Bekah refused to give up. She clung to the tree, gritted her teeth and kept trying. She took a deep breath and gave it all she had. It seemed like a miracle, but she made it up on the branch. Her arms and legs were shaking with fatigue, but she laughed and called down to Josh, "We did it, we did it."

Josh laughed with her. "We didn't do it, you did it."

"No," Bekah countered, "God and I did it."

Bekah managed to untangle the basket and drop it down to Josh; then he helped her get down from the tree, which was no easy feat. Then they looked in the basket together. They drew back in horror at what they saw. Inside the basket were several small skulls, likely from infants or small children. They dumped it on the ground, not wanting to even touch the things that were in it. There were several pieces of small bones, a braid of silver hair, what looked like a small ceremonial knife, and a piece of what looked like amber about the size of a fist with a large, black beetle in the center of it. Their horror turned to revulsion at the thought of handling any of the items to get them back in the basket. They knew they needed to destroy it and the only way they could think of was to burn it.

---

[263] Philippians 4:13
[264] 2 Corinthians 12:9

They knew Satan was still alive and well, and that he would not be happy about what they intended to do with his fetishes. They used sticks and leaves to handle the contents. Then, they turned to walk back to the fire at their camp. Unfortunately, Mbyja was standing there, looking like the princess of darkness, if there was such a thing.

"What are we going to do," Bekah asked?

Josh responded, "Remember, greater is He Who is in us than he who lives in her. Mbyja has given herself over to Satan. He controls her, but we have God's heavenly army fighting for us. I wish we could see them, but we will have to draw on faith. God already sent an angel and told us there would be a legion of angels fighting with us."

Then Josh turned back to Mbyja and called out, "Satan, Beelzebub, father of lies, accuser of the brethren, devil, and whatever other foul name you go by, you come out of her in the mighty Name of Jesus."

A piercing voice proceeded out of Mbyja's mouth, "I don't have to leave; she wants me to stay." A hideous laughter erupted from her. "Paul I know, and Jesus I know, but who are you? You should be afraid because we are many and you are few."[265]

Immediately, the sky was ablaze with a heavenly army. They were all about ten feet tall with huge white wings. They wore armor, and carried blazing swords. They were the most beautiful and fearful creatures ever to be seen on Earth. Nothing could stand against them when their swords were energized with the Word of God. They all landed, and stood around the huge clearing by the river, waiting for a command to be given.

Josh spoke to the one who appeared to be in charge. "What are they waiting for?"

---

[263] Philippians 4:13
[264] 2 Corinthians 12:9
[265] Acts 19:13-16

One of the angels replied with impatience. "We are waiting for the Word of God to be released. We are angels. We are all ministering spirits sent to serve those who will inherit salvation.[266] Speak His Word and we will go forth."

Josh stood, holding Bekah's hand and replied to the demons inhabiting Mbyja, "You do know me because I am a son of God,[267] a joint heir with Jesus.[268] I am a partaker of the New Covenant, I share in the inheritance of God's children,[269] and I'm your worst nightmare. Greater is He Who lives in me than he who is in the world.[270] The same Spirit that raised Jesus from the dead lives in me.[271] I speak to you in the mighty Name of Jesus.[272] Come out of her."

Mbyja immediately fell to the ground and began writhing like a snake. Her face contorted as she snarled and hissed. As Josh and Bekah ran toward her they could feel the sensation of movement all around them. The demons were coming out of Mbyja and the angels were sending them back to the pit from which they came.

As all this heavenly warfare was taking place, there was the sound of explosions in the area surrounding them. Across the river a contingent of men were firing grenade launchers in their direction. Mbyja got up and ran into the jungle before Josh and Bekah could catch her. They turned to run into the jungle, but saw that a large group of men were coming in their direction, herding thirty or forty captives before them.

From the south came another contingent. This one also had a small group of captives, and one of them was Mbyja. She snarled and spat at them and they kept their distance. Josh held Bekah's hand to try to stay together, but they were separating the men from the women. Bekah's faith waivered as she thought, "On no, these

---

[266] Hebrews 1:14
[267] Galatians 4:6
[268] Romans 8:17
[269] Colossians 1:12
[270] 1 John 4:4
[271] Romans 8:11
[272] John 14:13

310

are men from the other Black Death Camps. She questioned, "God is this part of Your plan?"

The captives were separated into three groups, men, women and children. Everyone from the Quest had been captured except Axel. There were about one hundred captives. There may still be some hiding in the jungle, but against the Black Death, there would be small chance of escape.

Then from the men, they separated Josh, Daniel, Carlos, Ted, Renato, Akeem and Manu. Out of all the prisoners, they were the only ones carrying weapons. Also Josh, Daniel and Ted certainly did not look Paraguayan. The rest of the men only had a few paltry knives and sharp rocks.

Then a group of men went over to talk to the man who looked to be the leader. They spoke excitedly for a short time and then came over and grabbed Akeem. "Oh no," Josh said. "Someone must have recognized him. Let's just stand quietly and pray. There's no need to draw attention to ourselves at the moment."

Akeem was brought before the man in command. "Who are you? What is your name? Why are you here among these people?"

"My name is Akeem Farsi. I am employed by the American C.I.A; but the C.I.A. did not direct me to come here. I am here to protect these people." Akeem felt that he had to tell the truth. He could not lie, and he was protecting these people from the works of the devil.

"Is that so? And do you also admit that you are a spy; that you went by the name of Jim and were left in charge of a camp about forty miles downriver? You were identified by two men who were part of that camp many weeks ago."

"I wasn't exactly a spy. I never gave the U.S. any information while I was in charge of the camp. I had heard some other things about Paraguay and wanted to find out if they were true."

"And what things could be so important that you risk your life to find out?"

311

Akeem thought for a moment before he answered. "I heard that the Spirit of God was moving down here and I wanted to witness it myself. I had a dream. In it God told me to go to the village just north of our camp. There I witnessed many things, not just things God did, but also things Satan did. He is God's adversary, and was battling for the people of the village. I would like to tell you that God won."

The commander looked impatient. Unfortunately, he was not interested in listening to Akeem's stories, and he certainly did not want to hear about Akeem's God. "Enough," he shouted. "I have other questions I need answered. What are those Americans doing with you? Do they work for the C.I.A. also?"

Akeem answered, "Why don't you ask them yourself?"

"I just may do that." He turned to one of the soldiers, "Tie him up and keep him separate. Something is going on here and I'm going to get to the bottom of it. Bring the other Americans over here, and the rest of the ones who had weapons," he commanded. Ted, Josh, Daniel, Renato, and Carlos were separated from the group. "Are there any other Americans in your group?" He glared at them. "You better answer honestly or it will go badly for your friend."

"No," Josh answered. "As far as we know, all the others are native Paraguayan. They speak Guarani, the language of the indigenous people. Some speak Spanish or English also, just because of trade in the area."

"And why are you here?" he questioned. You don't look like traders. In fact, you all look pretty worn and dirty. What are you doing in Paraguay, and more specifically, what are you doing in this village?"

"Well, if you want to know the truth, we all had a dream from God, and He directed us here. God told us to come to this village to bring them hope. They have been warring on other neighboring tribes, taking their babies, and burning them as a sacrifice to their gods. God wanted to put a stop to it. Looks like He used your explosions to do it."

Even though he was losing his patience, the commander was astounded. No one had ever told him a tale like this.

Josh spoke up again, "I might have been able to come up with a more believable lie, but you wanted the truth."

The commander actually laughed. "Do you think I believe in fairy tales?" Then with a sneer he ordered, "Bring his friend Akeem over here."

Two men grabbed Akeem and dragged him over to the commander. "Do you also believe the fairy tale this man told me?"

Akeem looked him straight in the eye and responded, "It is no fairy tale. God is doing something here. We don't know everything that will happen. God leads and guides us and we try to be faithful to do what He has asked us to do. We have seen the dead raised. We have seen angels. We have heard God's Voice. Many more things happened that only God could do."

"I have heard enough of your lies. If someone doesn't tell me the truth, we will test your God and see if He is watching." The commander spoke to one of the men holding Akeem. "Give me your machete."

Josh, Ted, Renato, Carlos and Daniel all joined hands and commanded the angels to stop the commander from following through with his threat. In the twinkling of an eye, God spoke to them and said, "Akeem already knows what is going to happen. As My Son said 'Not My will, but Thy will be done,'[273] so Akeem said to me. Now, be strong in Jesus and the power of His might."[274]

As the Words of God ended, the machete fell and Akeem's head rolled in the dirt, eyes still open and staring.

The commander gave back the machete. He looked down and observed a widening pool of blood. He barked an order to his subordinate, "Have some men get rid of the body. Throw it in the

---

[273] Matthew 26:39
[274] Ephesians 6:10

313

jungle for the wild beasts to feast on. He turned to the horrified group. "I will give you a day to think about what you saw and come up with the truth. It doesn't appear your God was paying attention."

CHAPTER FORTY-FIVE

JUNE 30
THE WASHOUT

They all clung to each other, not in fear, but in grief.

In the group of women, Bekah had no one to cling to. Her horror and grief were like a heavy pain in her chest, and her breath caught in her throat. She did the only thing she could think of, and fortunately, she made the right choice.

"Father,' she called to Him, "I feel so alone, and I don't know what to do. Please help me."

Suddenly, she felt a tug on her clothes. Mbyja whispered, "I am alone too. My gods have left me also," and she wept pitifully.

Bekah was startled by the words. This was something totally unexpected. "What do you want?" Bekah asked.

"I know who you are. I recognize your name, and that of Manu. I am Mbyja, my sister was Fuego. Her power was greater than mine, and so your father chose her for a wife. I was banished later for my sorcery. I was sent into the jungle to die. I wandered many days, but my gods protected me and brought me here. Now they have left me and I have no one. If my gods won't help me, maybe your God will. What kind of sacrifice does He want?"

Unbeknownst to Bekah, a very large angel was awaiting the Word of God to come forth from her mouth. Distracted as she was by Akeem's death, the attack of the Black Death, and now, Mbyja's account of her past, Bekah did not take the time to ask for God's

315

guidance. She took Mbyja at her word.

This was a mistake, because Mbyja's deliverance was not complete. There were still a multitude of demons inhabiting her. She craftily hid their presence and acted the part of a poor, lost woman who needed help. Bekah felt sorry for her. Satan played on her emotions, and she walked right into his trap.

Satan was smiling again. Things were not looking so good for God's camp. On the other hand, he had them all captured, one murdered, one an outcast, and one beheaded. He rubbed his hands together in anticipation. "A good days work, even if I do say so myself."

Again, Bekah began to pray and Mbyja distracted her. "What can you tell me of your God? Why should I believe in Him? Your father must not have believed in Him, he married a witch, and had the witch doctor perform the ceremony. Maybe your God is not as good as you think He is."

Hearing words that criticized God got Bekah's attention. It reminded her of the story of Adam and Eve, when the serpent questioned, "Did God really say?" She turned quickly to Mbyja and saw a sly smile on her face.

Realizing her omission, Bekah fervently prayed, "God forgive me for doubting you and forgetting to ask for your guidance. Please show me what I must do." Immediately, the angel appeared again. This time Bekah didn't hesitate. "Go forth in the mighty Name of Jesus. God has a plan. Help all of us involved in His plan do our part. Open a way where there seems to be no way. Jesus said He came to destroy the works of the devil. Now, we will go forth in His power and might to do the same."[275]

As Bekah continued to stand there and praise God, another tremor shook the ground. All the members of the Black Death were ordered to protect their stockpile of weapons. A stronger tremor hit,

---

[275] 1 John 3:8

316

and the ground surrounding the weapons opened up. The whole of the Black Death army except for four that were guarding the prisoners, were swallowed up along with their weapons. Their cries could still be heard as the ground closed over them. The four that were left deserted their posts and ran to go back across the river.

Everyone stood still, stunned by what had happened. Then, as a group, the believers shouted to God with a voice of triumph.[276] Bekah temporarily forgot about Mbyja and ran over to Josh and the rest of the Questers. Josh grabbed her in his arms and hugged her tight. She looked up at him with tears streaming down her face. "I'm so glad you are all safe, but my heart is breaking for Akeem. How hard it must be for you, Josh, having just been reunited with your childhood friend."

Back at the group of women Mbyja stood, uncertain what to do. She had burned her bridge with Bekah and must go on alone. She prayed that all her gods had not abandoned her. She invited those who had left to return. She could feel and hear the tumult inside her and knew some were still present. Whether they could win the fight against this God remained to be seen. This battle had been lost, but there would be more to come. She turned and ran down one of the paths into the jungle. Everyone was too focused on what had just occurred to even notice. Hopefully, that was not a mistake.

Josh said to Manu, "We need to gather all the people who are left so we can see how many we are. We also need to scout the area again and look for food, weapons, and anything else that might help sustain us. It might be wise to send several men across the riverbed to watch. The Black Death might send men back to punish us for our revolt. Manu, would you assign some men to take care of that?"

Josh did a rough count and estimated there were around seventy women and children and forty men left in the village, though

---

[276] Psalm 47:1-3

most of the men were older. He didn't know the number of people who usually lived in the village, or how many had been killed by the Black Death, but he understood that a large hunting party was due back tomorrow. These men must have been left to guard the women and children. There was no way of knowing what their reaction would be with all the death and destruction around them. One good thing is they had Renato, the rightful chief with them, and he spoke Guarani, although that didn't appear to be an issue anymore as all appeared to understand in their own language.

Another point of concern; it was discovered that Mbyja had escaped and Namandu was nowhere to be found. If they came in contact with the incoming hunting party, they could convince them to again take all the Questers captive again and sacrifice them to their gods. They prayed this would not be the case.

The group took time to pray again, asking for God's guidance. "Help us make the right decisions Lord. Remind us of anything we may have forgotten." Josh asked Renato, Manu and Daniel what they thought about sending the men from the village out into the jungle to search for the hunting party and tell them what had happened. They did not want another battle to occur.

Manu replied, "I think that's a good idea. I also think Bekah should go with the women to forage. Go in groups of four or five." He asked Giancarlo, Maitie and Philippe to get a few of the younger men and start hauling firewood, start a fire, and find something in which to carry water.

Daniel started to speak up, then saw a group of about twenty men approaching. He recognized them as the men who had prayed with them in the hut. They said they would walk along the riverbank in search of anything useful. They also wanted to talk with Renato more. One man stated, "Now that the village is in disarray, it is even more needful to have the proper Chief as the head of the village. There should not be much of a problem with the rest of the warriors, because they were very unhappy with the witch doctor and his wife.

318

They were also unhappy with their gods, but were afraid to speak about that. It only came out in hushed whispers when they were sure they were alone."

Daniel said to Renato, "If you feel comfortable with that, go with them. The more we can talk with them, the more they will see that we are for them and not against them. They will see that God is for them and not against them."

The small group walked across the dry riverbed. They could see about half a mile, before it took a bend. A few of the men had baskets and immediately started filling them with some type of crab. It would take a lot to feed so many, but there appeared to be an unending supply. They also saw several bunches of bananas, which they cut and left, to pick up on the way back to the village.

After a sparse but warming supper, the Word of God was again shared. Renato told the story of creation. He read from Genesis. The people listened with rapt attention, then, they began asking questions.

"Who is your God? Where does He come from? What does He look like?"

Renato spoke, "These are all good questions, and I will try to answer them. Our God is the One and only God. He was before all things. He has no beginning and no end. He created the heavens and the earth. He created the moon and the stars. He created all the fish in the waters and animals on land. He created everything that flies and everything that crawls. Then, after He did all that, He created people."

One man responded, "That must have taken Him a very long time. He must have been tired."

Renato replied, "The Bible, God's Book, says that He took six days to create the heavens and the earth, and when He was done with all His creating, He rested. He also encourages us to take a day of rest."

Continuing, Renato said, "Heaven is God's place. It is a

wondrous place inhabited by angels, and all God's people who have died. But God isn't just in Heaven, He is everywhere. He's here with us right now, but we can't see Him because He is a Spirit. But we can feel Him. When we pray we experience His peace, His comfort, His healing, and many other things. Our God is a good God. Can you say that about your god?"

The small crowd of people looked at one another, and began to shake their heads, "No". Someone spoke out, "Will you pray for your God to bring us peace tonight and protect us from any evil around us?"

Renato smiled. "God would like nothing better than to send His Spirit to comfort you, not just tonight, but every night. God wants to be your God, and He wants you to be His children. Would you like God to be your father?"

"I already have a father," someone said. "How can He also be my father?"

"That is the father of your flesh. God will be the Father of your spirit, the part of you that will live forever. What you all need to decide is who you want to spend forever with, your gods who are evil, and demand terrible sacrifices from you, or My God Who is good and wants you to love and serve Him. I will pray with you. If you agree with the prayer, at the end, say 'amen'. If you want to keep serving your god, say nothing."

Renato prayed. "Our Father, Who lives in Heaven, hear us tonight as we pray. We thank You that You sent Jesus, Your Son, to be the sacrifice for our sins. He died, was buried, and three days later You raised Him from the dead. Jesus died for the sins of the whole world." Renato looked around. "That includes you and me."

He smiled again and continued. "We are sorry for our sins and don't want to do them anymore. Please forgive us. Please send Your Spirit to protect us tonight and bring us peace." Lastly he added the "Amen".

"Now if you agree with this prayer, it represents your commitment to God and His commitment to you."

And they all said, "Amen."

Everyone sat and waited, not quite knowing what to expect. Suddenly the wind picked up. But on a cool night, it was a warm breeze. The fire had been roaring, but the night was cool and everyone was chilled. Renato said a thank you to God. It felt as though a fluffy, warm comforter had been placed around him. He felt his eyes get heavy. Looking at everyone else, they appeared to be experiencing the same thing. Rest came upon the group and they slept. A company of angels stood around them keeping watch.

CHAPTER FORTY-SIX

JULY 1
THE WASHOUT

As dawn broke and the sky lightened, men started pouring out of the jungle. There were approximately one hundred of them. They were tall and powerful men, the hunters and warriors of the village. Looking closely, they saw several of the new believers who had gone out yesterday to hunt. Unfortunately, Mbyja was also with them and she was pointing her finger at the mound, now covered with believers, new and old.

These men all stopped and surrounded the mound. One man stepped forward. He was older, but had a powerful build. "He must be the leader of the warriors," the Questers thought. He spoke to them in a loud voice. "I have heard a tale from this man, pointing to one of the new believers, and this woman, pointing to Mbyja. Now I will hear your tale."

Renato conferred with Josh, Daniel and Manu, and then stepped forward. "My name is Renato," he began. "Before you make any decisions, let me tell you something that I only learned two days ago. I knew I was born in Paraguay, and through a dream, my God revealed that this was my village. What I did not know was what I thought was a mole on my back, was in fact a tattoo; the mark of the High Chief. My father was Kauan. He was the old Chief's brother. He refused to sacrifice infants into the fire. The witch doctor told him since that he would not do the duties of a warrior, he would take me into training instead."

Hearing this news, Mbyja hissed. What could this mean to her? Would the leader of the group respond to Renato's information, or would he fall prey to her wiles, just like any other man she aimed them at.

"That night my father had a dream, directing us to leave. We went downriver and landed at the village by the big rock where I grew up. For some reason I didn't remember my childhood or this village until I had a dream about a week ago."

"I did not know I had the sign of the High Chief. I don't even know if I want to be High Chief. From what I understand, the last High Chief was poisoned by this woman," and he pointed his finger at Mbyja.

Mbyja looked up at the leader, and he glared down at her. She cowered back. Evidently, her spell was not successful. The leader motioned Renato forward. "I will see this mark," he stated. When he had seen it he grabbed Renato in an embrace. For a moment he was speechless. Then he spoke out. "Everyone listen to me. This must be a sign from his God. This man is my cousin. His father and my father were brothers. I was named after my uncle, his father. My name is Kauan. By rights, I am High Chief, but given the death my father had, I refused. I did not want to be poisoned by this witch also. She should be a sacrifice to your God as she was about to make one of you a sacrifice to her gods."

When Bekah heard that, she went running to Renato. "Please Renato. Don't let him do that. She may not appreciate the gift of her life, but we cannot let him do that to her."

Renato explained what Bekah had said, and how God doesn't want dead sacrifices, but a person who would love and serve Him with all their heart. He spoke loudly so everyone could hear of Jesus and His sacrifice, of not being servants of God, but sons and daughters.

Kauan said, "I would like to hear more of this God. Loose the woman and let her go."

"Noooo," Mbyja wailed! "Where will I go? I have no one."

"That is not my problem. For years you have manipulated those in power here to do your bidding. What normally happened was that those who opposed you suddenly had an accident or became sick and died. No more will that happen. A new God rules here and He is more powerful than any of your gods."

Kauan turned to Renato and said, "I have made a decision. Later we will talk more of your God, but now I choose Him over the old gods. From what I have heard and you have told me, He is the kind of God I want to serve."

He turned around and looked at all the men standing there. "What about you? Do you want to go back to the old ways? Do you want to burn another baby? I know I do not. If you agree, come and stand behind me."

There was a shuffling as the men looked around them, then they all began to move and stood behind the leader. "Good," he said. "Now pray to your God and ask if we can be His children also."

Renato prayed, and again asked if they were in agreement to say, Amen."

The area resounded with over a hundred Amen's. Then, spontaneously, everyone cheered.

The men brought forward the kills they had made. It had been a very successful hunting trip. In retrospect, maybe this new God was the author of the successful hunt. They certainly needed the extra food for all the additional mouths there were.

Suddenly, Mbyja came and threw herself at Kauan's feet. "Please don't cast me out. Let me stay. I promise not to practice any of the dark arts."

The people looked upon her with horror and she recoiled from them. "What is the matter? Why do you look at me like that?" she questioned.

Kauan responded, "The people are alarmed by your appearance. Your beauty has left you. Now you are horribly scarred."

325

Mbyja screamed as one in torment. "No! No! It can't be happening. I was terribly scarred when I was a child by the white man's disease. I came close to dying. Many died. When I was older I asked the gods to make me beautiful and I would serve them. They answered my prayer and I served them faithfully. Now they have left and taken my beauty with them."

Kauan spoke sternly, "I cannot help you. It was your choice to serve your gods. We here are serving the One, true God. If you want to stay here you must reject your old gods and their evil ways."

"I will not. They know me and my faithfulness. They will not leave me. They will come back, and then you will be sorry you cast me out. We will see whose god is really God." Mbyja began to mutter under her breath. She began to utter curses upon the village and the people living in it. She turned to Bekah and screamed at her, pronouncing a curse upon her. "You will die a horrible death, and the dogs will eat your flesh. Your God will abandon you and so will your friends. You will die alone and in misery."

As she turned away she spat on the ground seven times and made some signs in the air. Then she pushed through the crowd, hissing and spitting as she went. She rushed into the dry riverbed and started running erratically down it. Everyone watched in fascinated horror until she was out of sight. Then they turned back to Kauan and Renato for reassurance.

Renato did reassure them. He took Kauan's arm and began to speak. "We all stand here in the presence of Almighty God, Who is always with us. Satan, who is the god Mbyja has been serving, has already been defeated by Jesus, God's Son, when God raised Jesus from the dead. Then Jesus told us we have authority over the devil, who is Satan. He gave us the authority and the power to defeat Satan. He told us we have heavenly weapons, the most powerful being the Word of God. He calls it the Sword of the Spirit. We can also commission God's mighty angels, His warriors, to defend us against the attacks of the enemy."

326

Renato explained, "Angels are God's warriors. He sends them to help us in response to our prayers, and His Word that we speak. Some of you have already seen them at work."

The people again cheered, but Bekah felt a tremor of fear run through her. In her mind, she heard the words of Mbyja, and even saw her changed appearance, down to the spittle dripping off her chin.

Josh came over and stood beside her. He recognized the fear inside her for what it was; an attack of the enemy. He called Manu over and he prayed over Bekah with him. "Father, we come to you today standing with our sister. We come against the spirit of fear attacking her, and the words and curses spoken against her. Your Word says that we are protected from an undeserved curse."[277]

Manu prayed, "Father, I pray You send Your Holy Spirit to bring Bekah peace, and not just her, but all of us. We are fighting the enemy and he likes to cause fear and confusion, but we know You give peace and we thank You for it."

Everyone said, "Amen," and the mood lightened. People went about their chores encouraged by the changes made in the village. There was still devastation, but now there was hope. They now had food and a meal would be prepared. Afterward, they would sit and decide what they would do and whether they should go or stay.

Manu asked, "How many of you are there? There may have been some killed in the earthquakes or the attack. We know one is gone, Mbyja, and we have not seen Namandu since before the earthquake. We don't know if he is alive or dead. There is also another, a young hunter who had been traveling with us. We have not seen him since the earthquake."

Kauan responded, "We will all take a look around. I am asking everyone to tell us if they realize someone is missing. Right now we need to prepare the meat for cooking and smoking. We have a lot of hungry mouths to feed."

---

[277] Proverbs 26:2

327

It had already been a long day, and the sun was only partly past midday. But everyone was hungry. There had been no food since last night and though that soup had been warm, it did not satisfy everyone's hunger.

Some of the women, wanting to feel useful, took it upon themselves to scour the nearby jungle for any fruit, roots or vegetables they could add to the meal. They were not concerned with predators, the flood had driven them away or killed them, and it would be some time before they ventured back into the area. In addition, there were many dead carcasses that were easy pickings for them and required no stealth or effort to acquire.

CHAPTER FORTY-SEVEN

JULY 1
THE VILLAGE

It had been almost four days since they had heard anything from the Questers. It was late in the day, and Sherry was sitting with Noemi, Manu's wife, Ciba, Leonardo's wife, and the old woman, who was Miguel's grandmother. Sherry did not know her name, people just called her old grandmother. Noemi had just finished nursing her son, Juan, when someone came running up from the river. "Come quickly!" he yelled. "The river is sending down much debris. It is being propelled by a large amount of water. Several of the boats have broken loose and are heading downriver."

"Go and find Leonardo, Jose, and Isaac. Let them know what is happening if they don't already know. Is the flow of water over the jetty?" Sherry asked.

"Yes, you can't see the jetty, and the end of the dock has been taken away."

"Take down some rope and hooks with you. If our boats were taken, maybe somebody upriver lost boats and we can snag them as they go by. Even some of the debris may be useful, if for nothing else than firewood. I'll be right down, as soon as I get my medical kit. Someone may have been injured."

By the time Sherry got down to the river, the water had already started to drop and the current to slow down. She saw Leonardo, Jose, and Isaac standing and watching the turbulent water. She walked over to them and asked, "Was anyone injured or killed in the flood? What did we lose? Did we salvage anything?"

Leonardo responded, "As far as we can tell, none of our people were injured. Unfortunately, we did witness several bodies floating by, but were unable to retrieve them because of the swift current. We lost all the motorized boats, including Jose's and Isaac's. We also lost five of our large canoes and most of the small ones. Fortunately, all the weapons had been removed from the boats and are safely stored in one of our storehouses. Several other boats came down the river. We are sending out a search party of ten men to scout the shoreline for anything of value that makes its way to shore. Now that the water is slowing down, someone may be able to enter the river and swim to anything hung up by it."

Isaac questioned Leonardo with concern, "Is it safe yet for these waters to be entered? They are still flowing swiftly. Boats and equipment can be replaced, but people can't."

"You must remember, Isaac, that we are river dwelling people. The river is our life blood and we know how to navigate it. We will be careful. Also, in a situation such as this, we use life lines when we enter the water. We also know that God has sent His angels to protect us and keep us from harm."

"You're right, Leonardo, I forget we are not alone in this battle. Maybe I can take a few of my men upriver and see if we can find anything. Will you send a few men with us to help?"

"Good idea. I will send Ernesto and Juan. They are both strong, and good hunters. They recently helped Manu kill a wild boar that had been harassing the village. They will also carry ropes, and weapons to prevent attack by wild animals, or possibly bring down some for food for the rest of us."

As evening approached, both search parties returned. The river had returned to its normal flow, and both groups had been successful in salvaging useful items. The southern group had the biggest and best. They came back in one of the larger motorized boats, pulling two large canoes behind them. The canoes were also full of a variety of things they had found, not the least of which was a bag with fishing equipment in it.

The northern group also salvaged a canoe, but it had to be carried; it had a leak in the bottom. They pulled it ashore and would go back for it tomorrow. They also brought back two deer and three small wild boars. Both said they had only gone about a mile, and suggested that they get an early start tomorrow and see what else they could find.

Isaac went over and inspected the carcasses. He whistled. "Wow! You call these small. They must be about two hundred pounds apiece."

Leonardo laughed and answered, "The one they helped kill last month had probably been over five hundred pounds. It fed us for many meals. These were small in comparison and less dangerous to deal with. They will butcher these tonight and we will have fresh meat tomorrow."

CHAPTER FORTY-EIGHT

JULY 2
OGUNQUIT, MAINE

Joe had the prayer team gather that morning. He was going to place a call and see if he could talk with Connie and get some answers. They were in the dark about what was happening down there. They needed some quality time talking and praying with their southern arm. He did not want there to be any confusion, because confusion brought discord.

The Lobster Pot didn't usually open for lunch until eleven. Jean, the owner, had been giving them free use of the back room for their prayer every night and the making of the telephone calls. Prayer went on twenty-four seven at The Eye of the Needle, but they were smaller groups. With everyone together, Joe estimated they were surpassing seventy-five on a regular basis, and today there were many new faces in the crowd that he didn't recognize. Because of the increase in numbers, Jean was now allowing them to use the main dining room, and best of all, she was participating in all of the prayer and the phone calls.

After their prayer, Joe urged everyone to settle down so they could make the phone call. As Joe dialed the number, it became so quiet you could hear yourself breathe. Joe had put the phone on speaker and everyone was listening to it ring. No one was answering. Joe said, "They don't have an answering machine to pick it up, so I'm just going to hang on for a little while longer. Maybe they are having a meeting."

Suddenly someone picked up the phone and said "Hello."

"Hello. Who is this speaking? This is Joe Abernathy from Maine."

"This is Isaac Klein. I'm a friend of Josh's from Washington. How's it going up there? With Haydon Carlton down here you shouldn't have too much to worry about."

"You're right," Joe answered. "But we have all been feeling a persistent urge to pray. It looks like there's close to one hundred people here this morning. Some are here for curiosity, but most are in God's army. We have not heard from or been able to get in touch with the Questers. We are all concerned. Do you have any news? Also, things have been happening worldwide that may affect all of you. Have you heard that there was an earthquake about forty miles north of you?"

Isaac didn't want to admit that he was concerned, but he could no longer deny it. He believed that God was doing something down here. So much was happening it had to be God. But he didn't know how God worked. To him it appeared that even if you served God and did all He asked you to do, things didn't always come out the way you'd expect them to. God seemed to have His own agenda. Isaac knew that in the end, God wins, but there always seemed to be some casualties along the way. He trusted God, and knew God's way was the best way; he just didn't want to be a casualty. He was impressed by the number of people praying up there. Suddenly Joe's voice came over the phone, "Isaac, are you still there?"

Isaac realized he had been distracted. "Sorry Joe, my thoughts got sidetracked. In answer to your first question, we have not heard from them. They haven't called us, and our calls are unanswered.

Joe responded, "God tells us not to worry. I know that's difficult, but it's His plan and He's in control. This is another thing we just have to trust God on."

"You mentioned an earthquake. We did not feel anything

here, but yesterday the river rose violently for about an hour. I don't know if the debris we saw was a consequence of the earthquake or not," Isaac stated.

"Did it occur up near the northern village that the Questers are attempting to reach? I don't know whether Kent Knox has read you into the loop or not, but I think you should know, there is a large waterfall by the village. There are also two Black Death Camps in the area, one on top of the waterfall and one across the river. I spoke with Kent yesterday. He told me the Black Death has been mining on top of the falls for uranium. Maybe they detonated some charges yesterday and they are what triggered the earthquake. The explosion could have made a change in the course of the river, depending on their strength. Did Josh even know the camps were there? Will they leave the village alone?" Joe asked.

"Josh had the information on the two Black Death Camps. It's hard to say how safe the village is, they're so unpredictable. We don't know if their leadership is still intact, or how much damage they may have sustained. We do know they were mining for uranium at the top of the falls. The earthquake may have had something to do with the rise in the river. Another thing you can bet, if we knew about those camps, you can bet the Russians knew about them also. If the Russians had tried to take them out when they bombed their other strongholds in the Middle East, the damage would have been much more catastrophic."

There was dead silence in the room as this conversation was taking place. The magnitude of the situation was painting a bleak picture, and everyone was imagining the consequences of the situation. Since the Russian bombings a few days ago, and now this situation, the group had pulled together in a greater way. There were still periods of light heartedness and cheerful banter, but the specter of the end was becoming darker.

Joe sat with his head in his hands, not quite knowing how to proceed. He prayed for God's guidance and then launched out.

"Isaac, I don't know how much Bible study you have done since you came to believe that Jesus is the Messiah, and more importantly, your Messiah. You have certainly seen for yourself down in Paraguay, that God is moving, and strange and unusual things seem to be happening. We believe that many of the things that have been happening recently are harbingers of things to come. We believe there are Scriptures that tell us we are coming up to two very important events that will change the world as we know it forever. The first we believe is very close. We believe Jesus is coming back for His Church, which are those who believe He is their Lord and Savior.

"There are people who attend church, not to have an experience with God, but out of obligation. Jesus is coming back for His Church. Not the buildings, or the denominations, but the people who know, love, and serve Him with their whole being.

"The Bible says in Matthew 24:14 that the Gospel of the Kingdom will be preached throughout the world as a testimony, and then the end shall come.[278] We all believe that time is fast approaching. There are signs of His coming. It says there will be wars and rumors of wars, the sun will darken and the moon will turn red, and we will be persecuted by the unbelieving world. It says that people will have dreams and visions. Isn't that what has been happening? Aren't we a product of a dream? Hasn't God continued to speak to us and given us more dreams and visions?"[279]

Not hearing any response, Joe continued. "The Bible also says in 1 Thessalonians that if we are still alive when He comes that He will come down from Heaven with a shout, the voice of the archangel, and the trumpet call of God. Can you imagine seeing and hearing all of that? Then it says those dead in Christ will rise first. I wonder if we will get to see any of them. I get excited just thinking about it. Then it says that we who are still alive will come up with them into the clouds, meet Jesus in the air, and live with

---

[278] Wycliffe Bible, 2001, Terance P. Noble
[279] Joel 2:28-32

336

Him always. Has anyone ever taught you any of this? It's supposed to bring comfort and encouragement. I don't know about you, but it brings encouragement to me. In the darkness surrounding us, it brings light."[280] Jesus said He was the light of the world, and whoever believes in Him will not walk in darkness, but have the light of life.[281] That's a powerful promise, and one I cling to during these dark times."

Isaac finally replied, "I don't know whether or not you know, but my ex-wife was a devout Christian. I went to church with her a few times when we were first married, but I was not interested. But there was one thing that did interest me; it was when she talked about the End Times, when she talked about the Rapture of the Church. It was very compelling to listen to, then just as it is now. She read me the Scriptures from Joel, 1 Thessalonians and 1 Corinthians. Back then it sounded more like scenes from a science fiction movie. Right now, I feel like one of the characters in that movie.

"I remember that it said that in the twinkling of an eye, the dead in Christ will rise. Then we who are alive will be changed from mortality into immortality, and we will be caught up with Him in the clouds. We will meet Jesus in the air and be with Him forever.[282] I am so glad I am alive for such a time as this. It's amazing seeing Scriptures fulfilled before our eyes. But there is also concern for our friends who are out on the front lines fighting against the enemy. I wish I knew what was happening to them. This is where faith comes in, and I fear I am sadly lacking in that department."

Joe reassured him, "Jesus prayed for a young boy who was constantly having fits, falling down, and foaming at the mouth. He was terribly oppressed by the devil. The boy's father asked Jesus' disciples to heal him and they could not. Then the man brought him to Jesus. Jesus asked the man if he believed Jesus could do this.

---

[280] 1 Thessalonians 4:13-18
[281] John 8:12
[282] 1 Corinthians 15:50-58

337

The man replied, "Lord, I believe, help me overcome my unbelief."[283]

Isaac responded, "Isn't it amazing that God even takes our unbelief into consideration? I guess I'm not the only one who has doubts."

Joe laughed, "Not by a long shot. Do you think you and this man are the only ones who struggle? We all go through times of doubt, where our faith seems to falter. That's when we need to remind ourselves of all God has done for us; remember all the wonderful things we have seen and experienced. A living, breathing body is a miracle in itself. If we can't find anything else to thank Him for, we can thank Him for that."

"You're right Joe. Thanks for taking the time to share the Bible with me. It reinforced in me some things I had forgotten. It also made me think of my ex-wife. She planted some good things in me, and I still care for her very much.

"Here comes Connie. Do you want to talk with her?"

"Yes, I do. Thanks for sharing your heart with me Isaac. I will keep you and all the people down there in my thoughts and prayers."

---

[283] Mark 9:17-26

338

CHAPTER FORTY-NINE

JULY 2
THE WASHOUT

The hunters had gone out at sunrise and returned empty-handed. There was no game in the area. Not that they had expected any. The area around the village had been hunted extensively for hundreds of years. The hunters had to go further and further to bring back bigger game. Now, with approximately two hundred people to hunt for, unless they left on a major, multi-day hunting trip, there would be no food in the days to come. Thankfully, they had just returned from a long hunting trip and had great success. Even though the morning hunt was a failure, no one would go hungry today. But after everything that had happened, many people felt a change needed to be made. They needed to make a move.

Kauan had a horn blown to gather the people together. He looked over the group and saw that in spite of the adversity that had befallen them, very few were injured. Given the devastation of the village, that fact was remarkable. A thought came to mind that maybe the new God had protected them. That was unusual, because their old gods had never protected them, and demanded constant sacrifices from them just to survive. He hoped this new God would treat them better. He needed to learn more of Him, but first, he needed to take care of his people.

He called Manu and Renato over and told them of the failure of the hunt. He said he felt that the village needed to move to somewhere where the game was plentiful. He told them, "The village has hordes of dried meat, fruit and vegetables stored in the caves behind the waterfalls." Then his voice faltered as he looked to the pock-marked cliff that was full of caves and caverns, but devoid of water. Instead of the beauty of the falls, it looked barren and deprived of life.

He sighed, and continued his conversation. "We will send people into the caves to bring out the storehouse of food. We will bring what we can carry. Everyone will have to shoulder a load. This is what will keep us fed until we find a new place to establish our village. I do not expect any help from the surrounding villages. In fact, we must send out guards, to be sure none are following to attack us. We are a stench in their nostrils. They would sooner see us dead than alive."

"Where will you go?" Manu asked.

"I don't know," Kauan answered softly. "I just don't know."

"It is good you have the food," Manu replied. "Bring it out and we will eat what we can of the dried food, but we will cook for a big meal tonight to sustain us on our journey tomorrow. I don't know if we will all be going together. If you will let us, we feel the need to return home. We have fulfilled our mission; we have brought you the Gospel. We will speak tonight of our God and pray with any who would want to reject their old gods, who have done nothing for you, and accept this new God, who wants to adopt you as His sons and daughters."

Renato had sat there listening to what was being said, but also listening to the Voice of the Holy Spirit, speaking to him. He smiled a sad smile and then spoke up. "I'm sure the Questers will be allowed to leave. Is that not right Kauan?"

Kauan responded, "Yes, you may all go, and we will provide you with some of the food. There will be more than enough."

Renato continued, "As I was sitting here I felt that God spoke to me. He asked me to stay with your village, not as a Chief, but as a spiritual Teacher and Shepherd of the people. They will need to learn more about God and His ways, Kauan, we could help guide these people together if you would agree."

Kauan took his time to answer. He was surprised at the offer. He recognized what a sacrifice this would be for Renato, leaving his friends and family and staying with a group of people who were once his enemy. Also, there was a real danger in his staying with them. They were anathema to the surrounding villages, and once those villages saw their weakness, they would most likely join forces and attack. Their village was destroyed, and then they would be also.

"It must have been your God suggesting this, because from my standpoint, it seems like a bad choice for you. Anyone who stays with us is at risk. You must all leave tomorrow after the first meal is finished."

Renato countered, "With your own words Kauan you said it was a choice. I choose to stay. Maybe God will show us a place of safety. Maybe He will send angels to guard our borders and keep us safe. This is one of the things you need to learn about God. With Him, all things are possible.[284] This is what faith is, learning to trust Him. His Word says that faith is the confidence in what we hope for even though we don't see it.[285] His Book, which contains His words to us, also says that without faith it is impossible to please God. Anyone who wants to come to Him must believe He is the One true God, and that He rewards those who search for Him with their whole heart.[286] God wants to reward you, not punish you. I am staying to teach you these lessons."

Renato turned to the other members of the Quest. Philippe, Maitie, Giancarlo, Daniel and Manu already knew what was happening, but Carlos, Ted, Josh, and especially Bekah did not. He would explain it to them all, but he knew it would be very hard for Bekah to let him go. It would also be very hard for him to let her go.

---

[284] Matthew 19:26
[285] Hebrews 11:1
[286] Hebrews 11:6

341

She was the daughter of his heart and he had vowed to protect her with his life. He needed to ask her to release him from that vow so that he would be able to be obedient to the Voice of God speaking to him to stay with these people.

Renato walked over to the group that was sitting on the ground and resting. They were all hungry and tired, but food would be available soon. Renato shared with them what he had shared with Kauan. He told them God had placed a hunger inside of him to be a spiritual guide for them. He believed now that it was his purpose for coming on this Quest. No one argued with him. Not even Bekah. She had tears running down her cheeks, but she offered no objection, and released him from his vow.

Bekah came up and stood before Renato. "I knew you would not be coming back with us. I was afraid it would be because you were killed. This is still very hard. My heart wants to stay with you, but I know I must return to our village. You have always been there for me. Your leaving will be a tremendous heartbreak to me. I know that God sometimes asks us to do hard things, but thankfully, He always gives us the strength and the courage to do them."[287]

Bekah put her arms around Renato and they quietly hugged each other. Then the group of Questers went aside and sat quietly in each other's company.

In a short while, people started to bring out container after container of dried food. They were laying it on the ground because they had no other containers to put it in. Men and women were making large baskets out of river reeds. They had dried out after baking in the sun for a day and were easy to work with. Some women had started boiling water and making a savory stew out of the dried meat and vegetables. Several fires had been started across the clearing and pots of various sizes were turning up. What was good about dried food is it was easy to transport, it did not take up much room, and could be eaten either dried, or rehydrated.

---

[287] Philippians 4:13

While Josh was sitting and observing the business of the people, he asked for everyone's attention. "When everything was happening this morning, I developed a compelling sensation telling me we need to leave for the village today. We need to travel lightly and as quickly as possible. Does anyone else feel the same way, or am I the only one?"

"Strange you should mention that," replied Daniel. "I feel the same way. I thought maybe it was just because I wanted to get home to Sherry."

Manu, Carlos and Ted began to nod their heads in agreement. "As soon as we eat, and pack some supplies, let's get going. We can still make several miles today."

The three young hunters also nodded in agreement; their excitement showing in their faces. Only Bekah was slow to respond. Her heart was still grieving for the upcoming separation from Renato. Everyone was looking at her and she finally nodded her agreement. Tears kept slipping from her eyes. She was not able to control them. The one saving grace was that he was alive and not dead, and that he would be fulfilling the purpose God had called him for.

Manu rose and went over to where Kauan was organizing the people. He stood, and waited respectfully to be acknowledged. Though he was a Chief, Kauan was in charge of this camp and he waited patiently.

After talking to a small group of hunters, Kauan turned to Manu and nodded for him to speak. "We are grateful to have met you and acknowledge that you are the true leader of this village. We are glad you are letting Renato join you. Though we will miss him, this seems right to us also. We cannot travel with you. The rest of us must return to our village. We have been gone a long time and they are worried. If you agree, we will go after the meal. Also, we ask for a supply of dried food to help sustain us on our way. We should be able to travel quite a distance before dark, if we go soon."

"Yes, gather what you need and be on your way. I thank you

for helping the village during the time of attack." Kauan called over a few of his warriors. "Give these men the weapons they need to travel back to their village."

The men brought out spears, machetes, knives, and bows and arrows. Everyone took what they were comfortable with. Bekah even took a machete and a knife. Kauan called for food to be packaged for them, and a small pot provided. There were not many pots left in the village. He made sure their meal was served at once. He also felt a sense of urgency; but their village would stay for a while and make some hard decisions as to where they should go. Also, he wanted to hear more about the new God. He wondered how much of a change He would make in not just his life, but in those in the village.

All the Questers walked over to where Renato was visiting with a large group of people. He was telling them the story of creation. They all went up one by one to say their good-byes and moved aside, leaving only Josh and Bekah.

Renato spoke in a strong voice. "Bekah, remember, you are not alone without me. Manu is there. Also, I give Josh to you to love and care for, be joined to him. Josh, I give Bekah to you to love and care for, to be joined to her. God, in His wisdom has made you one flesh. I cannot be with you as you both go forth in life, but by the grace of God, I can see you married. Are you in agreement?"

As Renato was speaking, a look of surprise came on everyone's face, not the least of whom was Josh and Bekah. But the Holy Spirit spoke to them and gave them peace concerning it. Josh and Bekah held hands and declared that it was so. Then Bekah and Josh gave Renato a hug, and they all turned to leave. The sun was just past midday.

They decided the quickest way to travel at first would be the dry riverbed. They didn't know how long it continued, but it was easy going for now. They followed it for about six miles, then the river found itself and flowed back in its normal path. The only problem with that was they were now on the other side of the river.

Staring at the riverbank from the opposite side, they all sat down for a well-earned rest, and talked about their options.

"Well, as I see it, we can't cross here unless God parts the river like He did the Red Sea," Ted observed. "Sorry, I am just a little frustrated and got sarcastic."

"No problem," answered Josh. "I think we are all a little frustrated and tired. Returning home from a trip is always more challenging than setting out. Hopefully, we have accomplished what God asked us to do. I did not feel any hesitation about heading back to the village. Anyone else have something to say?"

Giancarlo stepped forth. "May I speak?" he asked.

Manu answered, "Please feel free to comment. I hope you have not been holding back."

"No, we have all felt that we had freedom to speak. So far, we chose to observe, not feeling we had anything to contribute, but now we feel we have some expertise that can help our situation."

"Please share it with us. Any suggestion will be helpful. Then we will all pray and ask God for His direction."

Giancarlo continued, "Maitie, Philippe, and I have been talking since we left the village. We think it would be a good idea for all of you to stay here for the night, set some snares, make a meal and wait for us to return. We will travel downriver for the rest of the day, about three or four hours, looking for anything that might help us. Maybe even a boat that could take us downriver, or just across the river. We will head back at first light and arrive in time for breakfast. Hopefully, we will have found something to help. We can travel quicker and cover more ground than all of us together." He looked at Manu to see if he had overstepped his bounds, but Manu appeared to be pleased with the suggestion.

"Let's pray," he said. "If God has no objections, neither do I. I think it's a good idea."

Everyone sat and spent several minutes praying and waiting. Finally Josh stood up and asked, "Did anyone feel or hear anything? Do you have any uneasiness or worry about what was suggested? If not, let's proceed with the plan."

The three young hunters headed south. Bekah asked Manu if he would go into the jungle with her and see if they could find some fresh fruit and maybe some root vegetables. As they walked across the riverbed, Manu put his arm on Bekah's shoulder and asked, "How are you doing? I know how hard it must have been for you to leave Renato."

"It was, and yet it wasn't. I think God had been preparing me for it. In my heart and mind, I had already seen him leave. I've been in a kind of grieving mode since Mario was killed. It seems to me that sometimes God kind of warns you that something is going to happen to prepare you, to give you time to stretch your faith. That didn't appear to happen with Mario's death, although we all recognized that something was bothering Axel. I don't think any of us were prepared for the magnitude of the damage he would cause."

"I remember you teaching us that we would have tribulation in this world, but that Jesus said He had overcome the world.[288] I just assumed if that was the case, things would get easier. I guess I was mistaken."

"You didn't remember the whole verse," Bekah reminded him. "He told us to be of good cheer. We can have comfort knowing that through the trials and tribulation, we are not alone. He is always with us. The Holy Spirit is in us. We should not be afraid of the devil. He should be afraid of us.

"We need to constantly remind ourselves that everything turns out according to God's purpose. It's not our purpose that is important, but His purpose. We can't look at the small picture of us stranded on the wrong side of the river. We have to trust God that He has a plan, and as long as we are faithful, we will see His plan fulfilled. When we don't understand why something bad appears to

---

[288] John 16:33

happen, we still have to believe that God is working things out. That is when faith comes in. We have to trust God. The Bible says to trust in God with all your heart and don't depend on understanding everything. With all your heart, rely on him to show you what to do, and He will show you what to do, and how to do it."

---

[289] Proverbs 3:5-6

CHAPTER FIFTY

JULY 2
THE WRONG SIDE OF THE RIVER

Philippe, Giancarlo and Maitie set out along the east side of the river. This was virtually unexplored area, because as far as they knew, there were no other tribes in the area. The going was difficult at first, because when the river slammed back into its former course, it was still flowing swiftly, hitting the riverbank just as a tsunami slammed onto the shore of the ocean and demolished everything in its path.

They had to climb over and cut through mounds of debris. Sometimes they had to leave the riverbank and go around. They were upset with the slow progress and questioned whether this had been a good idea after all.

After receiving a large and painful scratch from a broken piece of wood, Maitie sat down with a huff. "We're getting nowhere here!" He picked up a piece of wood and threw it as an expletive. "We've been walking for some time and haven't gotten very far. Maybe we should just turn back."

Satan again stood and watched his demons carry out his assignment. Frustration and discord were some of his best workers.

"No!" said Giancarlo. "I feel certain about this. We are going to find something. I feel inside me that God is urging me to continue."

"Well I don't feel Him saying anything to me. You go on if

you want. I'm heading back."

Division was another weapon. Divide and conquer. Alone, they were helpless. He needed to capitalize on their argument.

"You can't do that. We all need to stay together. We'll walk till dark. That's what we said we would do."

Maitie stood up in anger, "Who made you Chief?" he asked with resentment. "You're as bad as Mario was."

At the mention of Mario's name everyone was quiet. Given the circumstances of the last few days, they had not had time to discuss what had happened, or had any time to grieve his loss.

Mario had been the oldest of the group of young hunters. Daniel had spent more time with him, teaching him the Word of God, praying with him, grooming him to be a man of God. In turn, Mario shared with the rest of them the truths Daniel had shared with him.

Giancarlo answered Maitie, "Mario would not have wanted us to argue. I don't think God likes it either. Let's do what we said we would do. We'll stop at dark and light a fire. Maybe we'll see something to eat along the way. I'm sorry if I was too forceful. I really feel strongly that we must go on."

"Nooooo." Satan thought. "Fight back. Demand to have your way. Don't give in."

But no matter how loud Satan yelled and how frustrated he became, at the thought of Mario, all fighting ceased. Maitie hung his head. "You're right. I was being sulky, just like Axel had been. I repent. Please forgive me. The enemy is still laying traps for us to fall in. After we stop for the night, let's have a time of prayer and ask again for God's help. I know He wants us to succeed. God, I repent to You also for my bad attitude. Please forgive me."

Philippe said in a quiet voice, "Remember Daniel told us if we confess our sins to one another that God will forgive us and cleanse us of anything that would be displeasing to Him."

"Come on," shouted Giancarlo with enthusiasm. "We can

still cover some more ground before we stop. It looks like the water slows down up ahead. Maybe the debris of the jungle will clear."

As they walked, the debris did indeed clear and they saw a sight that left them speechless. The force of the water had etched out a small cove in the river, and floating in it were four small canoes, and paddles also.

They immediately recognized the implications of this find. They would now be able to paddle downriver, with the current. If they got an early start and didn't have any problems, they might be back at the village by nightfall tomorrow night.

They had the same idea. Maitie shouted excitedly, "Let's turn around and get back to tell the others what we found so we will be able to get an early start tomorrow, instead of camping here tonight and wasting tomorrow morning."

The three turned back, jubilant in spirit, praising God for His provision, their faith bolstered by God's faithfulness. They still struggled through the debris field, but their faces were joyful instead of downcast.

Satan was again defeated. He was finally getting worried. If things didn't turn his way soon, he would be finished. He was running out of strategies.

In what felt like a much shorter travel time, they saw the light of a fire and quickened their pace, practically running by the time they arrived. At first, everyone was alarmed by their appearance, not expecting them until the following morning. They thought they may have been chased. But then they saw their smiles and exuberance and realized something good had taken place.

Philippe was the first one to catch his breath, and began to tell the others what they had found. Maitie and Giancarlo chimed in. They were all smiling and laughing excitedly. Bekah walked over and invited everyone to sit down for the meal, and then the aroma of something wonderful assailed their senses and they realized how hungry they were. Bekah had again managed to make a savory stew out of almost nothing but some dried meat and vegetables.

After eating, prayers were said and everyone lay down to rest, an early day planned for tomorrow. As was custom, Josh commissioned angels around them to keep them safe.

CHAPTER FIFTY-ONE

JULY 3
THE WRONG SIDE OF THE RIVER

Even before the crack of dawn, the Questers were up and preparing for the day. A breakfast of water, dried meat and bananas was being served. The fire was dying down and water was poured over it to complete the process. Everyone was ready to set out with a light step and a grateful heart. In lieu of a prayer, Bekah sang How Great Thou Art. Their bodies may have been chilled by the cool morning, but their hearts were warmed by the grace of God.

Traveling a short way along the side of the river, they came to the debris field the young hunters had talked about. With several more men capable of using a machete, they were able to cut through rather than have to climb over most of it. Bekah thanked God she was in good shape and kept up without any difficulty. As she was stepping over a tangle of branches she let out a yell.

Everyone stopped and came to see what the problem was. She turned her head aside and pointed. Tangled in a pile of debris to the side was a dead body. It appeared to have been impaled by a broken branch. There was no way to tell if that was what caused his death or if it happened postmortem. Whatever the case, it was a hideous sight, and reminded them of the constant danger they were exposed to. Animals and insects had already been at the corpse, and it was truly a gruesome sight.

They continued on with some restraint, but even that terrible sight could not dampen their spirits. They came around the last of the debris field and saw the cove with the canoes. Upon closer inspection, there were even two paddles in each canoe. There was no damage to them. They appeared to be waiting to be found. They broke up into four groups. Trying to decide who went with who was a little bit of a challenge. Two each would go in three of the canoes and three of them in the last one. Bekah would be the odd person because she was the lightest. Philippe and Carlos would be in canoe number one, Maitie and Ted in number two, Giancarlo and Daniel in number three, and Manu, Josh and Bekah in number four. Brawn sat in front and brains sat in back. It was important to know how to steer, and Manu had the most experience. Anyone could paddle.

They set out into the current and it took them. It was pretty brisk, but no white water was visible. No one was familiar with the river this far north, so it was important to keep a close watch. Besides white water, there was debris, rocks, and islands to watch out for. No one could afford to lose this concentration. There were also swirls and eddies that tended to rock the boat. Bekah's was the last boat. The other three were spread out across the river, looking for the best route.

After traveling several miles, Josh heard a voice from one of the boats telling them to go to the right; a tree was blocking half the river. They all managed to maneuver around the obstacle without any difficulties. They continued on for a while longer and at midday pulled again to the west side to take a rest and have something to eat. It felt good to be on the right side of the river.

Maitie, Philippe and Giancarlo stood up and asked to speak to the group. Manu nodded his head, and Giancarlo spoke. "The three of us have been watching the scenery. We believe we recognized a burned out tree a short distance back. It was hit by lightning six years ago. Also, you must remember things look different riding on the river than walking beside it. We also thought we recognized the spot where we stole some meat from the jaguar on the way

354

out. That was less than two days out. If we are right, we believe we should be home before dark."

A smile spread on everyone's face. After a long and difficult journey the word "Home" conjured up warm feelings of comfort, family, friends, and rest. They sat for a few moments bathed in that spirit; then realized they needed to get moving if they were going to achieve their goal.

After getting in their boats, they re-entered the current. It had slowed down considerably from earlier in the day. They had to do more than just steer. Even with the rest they had taken, their arms were heavy from fatigue. But there were no complaints from anyone. They dug deep into their reserves, doing whatever it took to make it home.

Maitie called out, "There's our hunting lookout that we used to shoot the wild boar. Can you see it?" He pointed with his finger.

Philippe and Giancarlo nodded and gave a shout. "Maybe another two hours, if we can keep up our momentum."

"We are almost there; just one or two more bends in the river," Maitie called to the rest of them. Excitement propelled them faster.

Manu called ahead, "Go around the jetty and pull onto the beach on the south side of the dock. Hopefully, it will not be damaged, but I'm sure even if the beach had debris on it, they would have it cleared by now."

As they rounded the last bend, they saw the whole village lined up to meet them, with Noemi, Sherry and Lara right in the front. Lookouts had alerted everyone of their approach. Cheers were going up. Leonardo, Isaac and Jose stood on some rocks on the jetty and waved. There was an air of jubilation surrounding the village. God had sent them out and they had completed the task and returned. A shadow crossed Manu's face and he looked at Josh. They were both thinking the same thing. With the success had come losses. There would be time for that later. Right now Manu wanted to hug his wife and son.

Bekah looked up and saw Sylvia standing on the sidelines watching her. She ran towards her and engulfed her in a giant hug. They both were laughing and crying at the same time. The strain of the last few weeks was washing away with their tears and laughter.

A young woman Bekah did not recognize hung back while the reunion took place. Sylvia saw her standing alone and motioned to her to come over. Bekah looked at her and wondered who she was and why she hadn't seen her before.

Sylvia took her hand and turned to Bekah. "I want to introduce you to your step sister Luna. Fuego was her mother."

Bekah was stunned and stood there and stared at her. Finally she recovered herself and apologized for her rudeness. "I'm sorry. This took me by surprise. Until a month ago I had never even heard of you. I never expected to meet you."

Sylvia told Bekah the events that led to her being here. She also told Bekah that Haydon Carlton was here under guard.

Luna spoke quietly and told of her part in working for Haydon Carlton by guarding Sylvia. "I couldn't help myself. She was so kind to me, even when I was rude to her. When we were left behind by Haydon Carlton, Sylvia told me of Jesus. She said He would forgive my sins, all of them. She said God wanted to be my Father and wanted me to be His child. It seemed too good to be true. But I prayed with her, thinking maybe she was telling the truth. After the prayer, I knew she was. He is my Father and I am His daughter."

Luna hesitated again and then continued, "If you would let me, I would like to be your sister. I have no natural family. I am all alone, but Sylvia said she would be a mother to me. Isn't that wonderful? I couldn't believe it. How could God be so good to me when I have been so bad?"

She stepped toward Bekah and hesitantly asked, "Will you let me give you a hug?"

The two stepped forward, put their arms around each other and dissolved into tears of joy. Bekah smiled, thinking how different

God's plan looked from what she had thought was going to take place. She looked up at Luna and smiled, "I would be happy to be your sister."

Josh turned and saw Isaac standing behind him. He put out his hand to shake and thought better of it. He grabbed Isaac in a strong hug. "We're brothers now; we don't have to stand on formality."

Isaac answered with excitement, "I'm learning more and more about God each day. It's amazing everything that has happened down here!"

Isaac pulled Josh aside and whispered, "I have a favor to ask you. Would you pray for me? I asked Kent Knox to do me a favor and get my wife's phone number for me. She has been on my mind and I want to call her. I know she has prayed for me all these years we've been divorced. I just want to let her know her prayers worked."

Josh smiled. It was wonderful to see his friend wanting to share his salvation experience with his ex-wife. Josh laid his hand on Isaac's shoulder and prayed. "Father in Heaven, You are the God Who made the universe. You listen to and answer prayers every day and none are too big or too small for You. You know my friend's heart. He still has love for his wife. Give him the words to say to express his heart to her. I pray she be receptive. In all things we pray Your will be done. In Jesus' Name we pray, Amen.

Isaac smiled. "I'm going in the kitchen and call her right now. It's not that late yet." He walked away whistling. Josh smiled also. As Josh went to find Bekah he began to whistle.

A feast had been called for tonight. Given the short notice none could be sent to hunt, so they would draw from the stores they had set aside. There was an abundance of dried fish, and meat was still hanging in the smoker from the hunt two days ago. It would be a great celebration and none would go hungry. Even the prisoners would feast because of the tribe's generosity.

357

Everyone rejoiced, but they were cautious also. Twelve had left, Edwardo already returned, but only eight came back. Mario, Axel, Renato and Akeem were missing, and that was on their minds. But as those thoughts troubled them a Scripture came to mind. O death, where is thy sting? O grave, where is thy victory? As the crowds quieted down, Manu suggested they move over to the meeting place where everyone could sit and hear what needed to be said.[290] He asked Josh to explain the Scriptures.

The people settled down and Josh stood up to speak. "In these Scriptures God wants to comfort you if you are a believer, that death is not the end. There is a time that is coming soon when the dead in Christ will rise. Then a trumpet from Heaven will sound and we who are alive and believe will be changed to an immortal body and be caught up in the air with Jesus. We are to take comfort in these words."

Then Josh and Manu told the group the tale of what had happened on their Quest. It took over two hours to tell the tale, and that was an abbreviated version. The rest of the story would be saved for another day. They all grieved over Mario, and were bewildered over Axel's behavior. They were angry when they heard what had befallen Akeem. Josh reminded them that though Mario and Akeem's bodies were dead physically, they were now up in Heaven and more alive than ever before. Renato's choice did not appear to surprise them. They would pray for a great harvest of souls for him.

Manu stood. "Everyone go home. Get your cups and spoons and knives. Get your mats to sit on and return quickly. I can already smell the aroma of the meat coming from the pits. We will celebrate tonight. We will celebrate our return, and the completion of the task God gave us."

Manu turned to Noemi and hugged her to himself. During their separation he had thought about her often. Theirs had been an

---

[290] 1 Corinthians 15:51-58

arranged marriage, but the seeds of love had blossomed, and their separation had truly made him see her in a new light. She was not now just the pretty, young girl who had born him a son. He wanted her by his side always. He smiled down at her as she held their son. He reached down and took him into his arms. He had grown during the time they had been gone. He remembered he had almost lost them both during the difficult birth, and Sherry had prayed and God answered her prayer. That planted the seed of faith inside him that grew. It bloomed, and he became a believer. Now, because of that, every villager was a believer. God was truly amazing.

Daniel and Sherry walked back to the compound and into their house. He turned to Sherry and looked into her smiling face." I'm sorry; we worried about all of you. We were prisoners and they took our phone. Then when the river flooded, it was gone. Are you alright?"

"I'm more than alright." Sherry took Daniel's hand and placed it on the growing mound of her belly." Say hello to him or her. I keep going back and forth. I don't know which, and that's fine with me. See if he'll move for you. He moves quite a lot."

Daniel stood there with a look of concentration, then his eyes sparkled and a huge grin spread across his face. I felt that." He hugged her again and kissed her cheek tenderly.

Let me take a quick shower, although I'd like to stand there for hours washing off all the accumulated grime. Would you get me a towel and some clean clothes?" Even though the nights were cool, the sun was out all day and the water was warm. He let it run and run and run.

Josh and Bekah walked into the compound also, but found their way to Bekah's room. Bekah observed, "I hear the water running, there's no chance of a shower right now. Let's just wash our hands and face in the kitchen. There's always hot water there." Then they went and sat under their favorite tree. They were content in each other's company.

As they walked back to the meeting area, they met up with Daniel and Sherry. "Daniel," Josh questioned, "are Bekah and I really married in the sight of God?"

"Renato seemed to be acting like a Pastor to those people, and to us also. Does God see that as a marriage? We don't want to act on it if it's not. Do you need to do anything to make it official?"

"Well there are forms to fill out and papers to sign."

Josh stopped him. "We don't care about that; we just want to be right in the eyes of God."

Daniel smiled, "As far as God is concerned, I think the knot is tied. May I be the first to congratulate you, Mr. and Mrs. Joshua Randall? You may kiss the bride."

Josh threw his arms around Bekah and gave her a strong hug and a resounding kiss. "Well Mrs. Randall, what do you think of that?"

Bekah said soberly, "I think we'll have lots to tell our grandchildren, if we live to have them. The clock is ticking, and by what we did, we just pushed it forward. Time is running out."

"We can't worry about that now. Tonight is a night of celebration. Let's go and join the party."

CHAPTER FIFTY-TWO

JULY 3
THE COMING

The celebration went on far into the night. No one was worried about the Black Death; they appeared to have little impact on the world at the moment. Their organization was defunct, their strongholds had been annihilated, and their sources of munitions destroyed.

The warring tribe was gone. In its place was a group of new believers, who were being pastored by Renato, one of their own. There were still some unanswered questions, but nothing anyone was going to lose sleep over tonight.

The advent of the dream, and the call from God had fueled a revival in this village. A large baptism had taken place and over one hundred people had been baptized.

Just then little Maria, followed by her faithful puppy Hombrecito, came running towards the gathered group, calling out, "Mama, Daddy, look who I found. Eyo has come back to see us." Enrico had been the first in the village to be baptized. All remembered his jubilation as he came up out of the water leaping and shouting praises to God. Enrico, but Eyo to little Maria, had been dead for a few weeks. He died saving Maria from being gored by a large, wild boar.

People turned and stared. Everyone became quiet as they watched him approach, questioning how he could be there. Was that really him?

Now, as he neared the group that had been celebrating their victory over the devil, he was still laughing and shouting, "Hallelujah, hallelujah! Praise the Lord! Glory to God!" Then he stopped and held a finger to his lips. Everyone was quiet. There was an eerie silence reverberating through the atmosphere. Even the insects were quiet.

Daniel got to his feet. As he started to speak he felt some kind of movement. He couldn't say whether it was in the air or in the ground, but all his senses were on alert. A loud sound roared through the atmosphere. Daniel had never been in a large earthquake, but he had heard that sometimes loud noises accompanied them as the ground grated against itself.

Daniel had a split second to grab Sherry's hand, and glance at those surrounding him, and then they were gone.

A soft wind blew through the empty village, rustling the leaves. Just like Enoch, all the believers were gone because God took them.[291]

A reunion was taking place in the heavenlies. Friends and families separated by death were reunited once more. Death could no longer separate them.[292]

While there was rejoicing up above, sorrow reigned on the earth below. The earth was now devoid of any Christian influence. Although this would be a day of revival and many conversions would be experienced by people who realized too late that God was real. Until the Sword of the Spirit was taken up again, Satan had a free ride to kill, steal, and destroy.[293]

Many of those who had heard the Gospel would believe. They would be the embryo of new believers coming to Christ almost immediately after the disappearance. Many were in confu-

---

[291] Genesis 5:23-24
[292] 1 Thessalonians 15:52-55
[293] John 10:10

sion as to what had happened to those who disappeared. But there was grief for those who knew what had happened. They had heard the message of God and turned from Him instead of toward Him. Those above were experiencing a new beginning in Heaven. Those below were experiencing the beginning of the end.

1 THESSALONIANS 4:13-18

¹³ And now, dear brothers and sisters, we want you to know what will happen to the believers who have died so you will not grieve like people who have no hope.

¹⁴ For since we believe that Jesus died and was raised to life again, we also believe that when Jesus returns, God will bring back with Him the believers who have died.

¹⁵ We tell you this directly from the Lord: We who are still living when the Lord returns will not meet Him ahead of those who have died.

¹⁶ For the Lord Himself will come down from Heaven with a commanding shout, with the voice of the archangel, and with the trumpet call of God. First, the believers who have died will rise from their graves.

¹⁷ Then, together with them, we who are still alive and remain on the earth will be caught up in the clouds to meet the Lord in the air. Then we will be with the Lord forever.

¹⁸ So encourage each other with these words.[294]

---

[294] 1 Thessalonians 4:13-18 New Living Bible Translation

EPILOGUE

Kent looked down from his office in Washington D.C. Pandemonium had broken loose during the night as people wandered around in a panic. There were plane wrecks, car wrecks, truck wrecks, even bicycle wrecks caused by the disappearance of a great many people. Another thing that was also noticeable was that there were no young children in sight. He would make a closer examination, but it appeared they were all gone.

Isaac had mentioned something like this happening, but he had laughed, and dismissed it as fantasy. He wasn't laughing now. He had called home to his wife, fear gripping him. He had two small children, a daughter six and a son four. He was afraid of what he would hear. No answer at home. He tried his wife's cell. After four rings, it went to voicemail.

He hung his head. Kent knew his wife went to church. She had stopped asking him to come. She said he was a lost cause. Kent thought, "I guess she was right."

Axel stood alone in the jungle. The wind moaned through the trees and the insects buzzed. Other than that everything was quiet. He had been following the group of people who had left with Renato. Renato had tried to talk with him once. He thought maybe he would listen to him now. But then they were gone.

He knew exactly what had happened. Jesus had come back for His people. If he had asked God's forgiveness for killing Mario,

367

God would have forgiven him and he would be with them. But his pride held him back. Now they were with Jesus and he was here, all alone.

He cast away pride and dropped to his knees. "Father," he cried out! "Forgive me of my many sins. Forgive me for my sin of pride. I always thought I was better than everyone else. Forgive me for jealousy, envy, bitterness, and any other evil thing that is in me that would offend you. Please send your Holy Spirit to me to lead and guide me, and to comfort me in my need. Let Him be my companion in my time of desolation. Show me where to go, what to do, and what to say when the need arises.

"Unless You tell me otherwise, I'm going back to my village. Probably it is empty, because everyone was a Christian. But there were strangers there. Maybe I can share Jesus with them."

Haydon Carlton sat in a corner, muttering to himself, and complaining to everyone who came by. Finally he looked around and realized no one had come by for quite some time. All the prisoners were in the room sleeping. Then Haydon noticed, where are the guards?

He got up cautiously and looked around. The guards were gone, but their weapons were still there. After cutting himself loose with one of the machetes lying on the floor, he picked up an AK-47 and an M-16. He released the safety and let go a volley. Surely that would wake someone up. All the men who had traveled down the river with him jumped up in surprise.

You lazy lot. Get up and get going. I don't know where everyone has gone, but we're getting out of here. I have a treasure to find. Then he thought of his nemesis.

"Bekah Ryan, you haven't heard the last from me!"

Eleven people and a daring mission into the jungles of
South America to share the Gospel
with the last unreached people group on Earth.
God has a plan—that will come to pass, but Satan and
his cohorts are doing their best to sabotage it.

The incredible first book in this end time saga, **"THE CALL"**
is a full-blown modern adventure filled with stirring
entertainment all laced with life-applicable
Bible revelation and prophetic insight.

Get your copy at
AMAZON.com
and start your journey today.

Through their dreams eleven people are called by God to a small tribal village in the interior of Paraguay. Their courageous obedience is rewarded and the *spirit of Revival* begins to burn in the jungles, but just outside of the firelight—evil lurks in the darkness.

"THE QUEST" is the second book in this prophetic saga. Follow Bekah, Josh, Ted, and the others in their divine Quest to complete an eternally important part of God's great end time plan.

**Get your copy at
AMAZON.com
and continue your journey today.**